Illumined Shadows

Books by G.R. Lyons

Shifting Isles Series
The Prisoner
S.P.I.R.I.T. Division
Return to Tanas
Broken
The Five-Hour Wife
Betrayal
Addiction
Blindsighted
Libertas
More to be announced...

Matchmakers (A Shifting Isles Trilogy)
Second Chances
Second Drafts
Second Place
Matchmakers (complete trilogy)
Second Act: A Matchmakers Novella

Treble and the Lost Boys (A Shifting Isles Trilogy)
Ice on Fire
Heavens Aground
Illumined Shadows
Surviving Death: A Treble and the Lost Boys Novella

Illumined Shadows
Treble and the Lost Boys, Book 3

G.R. Lyons

Cover design by
Designs by Dana

GRL lion logo by
Natalie Fawn Danelishen

Copyright © 2018 G.R. Lyons
All rights reserved.

ISBN-13: 978-1731484826

CONTENTS

Illumined Shadows   1

Appendix: Glossary   320

AUTHOR'S NOTE

This story takes place in a fictional world. It pulls events and characters from the *Shifting Isles* series, yet can be read as a standalone. In the story, you'll find references to multiple gods and different names for days of the week, amongst other things. A glossary has been provided at the end for those curious readers who enjoy a little background worldbuilding.

Also, within the context of this book's setting, there is no arbitrary delineation between 'adult' and 'minor', thus the presence of teenagers in a night club would be considered perfectly normal.

TRIGGER WARNING

This story deals with traumatic incidents that may be disturbing for some readers. Caution is advised.

Prologue

Two years ago…

VICTOR LUCIUS clutched the blood-stained bracelet in his pocket as he walked through the hospital toward the long-term care ward. It was a path he could travel in his sleep. Every week, and sometimes more often, for over twelve years, he'd made his way down those same stark hallways and through those same swinging doors into the same cool room just to stop beside the same white bed. Not much ever changed. A few different nurses and doctors over the years, but one visiting day usually looked just like any other.

Except today would be different. Today, he'd have to tell Cam that he wouldn't be back for a few weeks, the longest he'd ever gone without seeing Cam since the incident. Vic was going to Erostil with Ryley and Zac for some music gigs, then he and Ryley would be staying on for work, trying to find out what happened to a kid who'd gone missing there some thirteen years ago. He had no idea how long that was going to take.

Of course, that was his job: finding people. He'd stay there as long as it took to find answers for his client, even if they weren't the answers the client wanted, even if it meant a longer separation from Cam. But he'd be back. He had to be.

Cam was the whole reason Vic had developed a career in finding people in the first place.

Vic nodded at a few familiar faces, then stopped at the door to Cam's room. He took a deep, bracing breath, and opened the door to let himself in, shutting the door softly behind him and pausing there a moment to take in the sight of the figure on the bed.

It never changed, but he kept hoping. Vic let out a sigh. Twelve long years. He ought to be used to this by now, but he couldn't help hoping that each visit might be different. That it might be the one when he found Cam awake.

He knew better, of course, but he couldn't help hoping. He had to keep hoping. Otherwise, the guilt would make him go mad.

Finally, he crossed the room, grabbed a chair, and sat beside the bed, taking Cam's limp hand between both of his own.

"Hey, kiddo," Vic said, the term coming out automatically even though it really no longer applied. Cam was almost twenty-seven now, no longer the fourteen-year-old boy he'd been when he first came to the hospital. Vic swallowed hard and forced on a smile. "You're looking good today."

There was no response, but Vic hadn't been expecting one. Cam lay there as still as ever, the slight rise and fall of his chest—aided by a machine, since he couldn't breathe on his own—and the persistent beep of the heart rate monitor being the only signs that Cam was still alive.

"I talked to the doctors at the lab yesterday," Vic went on. "They're so close, Cam." He tightened his hold on Cam's hand. "So close. All the tests they've run are looking really promising. They're running a few more trials, but it looks like they'll be able to start the new procedure within a month or so." Vic had already told Cam all the details, but he rattled them off again anyway, more to encourage himself than anything else since Cam probably couldn't hear him: "They're gonna use this nanotechnology to repair the damage to your brain, and they're pretty confident it'll be enough to get you out of the coma and on your way back to a normal life. It'll be a long recovery period, but I know you'll get through it. You were always such a tough kid. More than I gave you credit for."

Vic paused, swallowing down emotion, the guilt of his own words from twelve years ago weighing heavily on his shoulders. Besides, he had to stay positive around Cam, no matter what.

"They're pretty sure all your memories are intact," he finally went on. "At least, that part of the brain seems healthy. But they think you'll be able to wake up and eat and walk and talk again after some therapy and practice, and if you do remember *everything...*" He paused again, leaning closer and clutching Cam's hand like it would somehow help his words penetrate the coma. "Swear to gods, Cam, I'll get you the best therapist there is. I won't let it haunt you for the rest of your life. I promise. Whatever it takes." Vic sighed and shook his head. "And if you hate me, so be it. I deserve it. But just know that I'll be there for you, no matter what, even if you never forgive me."

Vic went on to talk about other, random things, trying to keep his tone light, mostly talking nonsense just for the sake of lingering there as long as he could, especially since he wouldn't be back for a while. Eventually, though, he knew he was going to have to wrap things up and get home to start packing. He took a deep breath and forced on a smile.

"So you remember I told you I'm going to Erostil for a couple weeks?" he asked even though he wouldn't get an answer. "Zac and Ryley and I are gonna play some gigs. Treble might even get a recording contract out of it if all goes well. How cool would that be? But I'll come see you just as soon as I'm back in town, I promise. And the doctors here will take good care of you while I'm gone. Maybe I'll have a lot of new, interesting stories to tell, not just the same old, boring crap about processing contracts at work." He chuckled. "And I've got a case. A missing kid. A cold case, actually, so it probably won't amount to much, but if I can find some answers for his family, it would at least give them some closure." He paused again. "Hells, maybe, by the time I get back, the lab will have called with a surgery date for you." Vic smiled at the thought. "We could get you out of this hospital, over to them…"

He trailed off, unable to finish the thought aloud. They'd been waiting so long for any sort of hope that it seemed like jinxing it to even plan on it actually happening, but he couldn't resist at least considering the possibility. To have Cam open his eyes again? Speak again? Walk again? There wasn't anything in the world Vic wanted more than that.

Taking a deep breath to brace himself, Vic got to his feet, kissed Cam on the forehead, and forced on a smile as he gave that limp hand another squeeze. "I love you," he murmured. "And I'll see you soon."

Vic held his breath for a moment, then carefully rested Cam's hand back on the bed and tore himself away, not allowing himself to look back as he left the room. His hand went automatically to his pocket, his fingers brushing over the bracelet he always carried with him, the only thing Cam had been left wearing the night Vic found him, broken and bleeding and discarded in an alley like garbage.

And it was all Vic's fault.

His hands tightened into fists. It was just a few weeks. He could make it a few weeks without visiting, and then he'd be back. With any luck, he'd be returning home to some good news.

Chapter 1

VIC CLUTCHED the blood-stained bracelet in his pocket as he paced his living room. He checked the time again. Ryley and Asher were now twenty minutes late.

"Vic, relax," Zac said. "They'll be here."

Vic grunted a vague response and kept pacing, only half paying attention to the sound of Zac tuning his violin. Ryley was finally back from Jadu'n for good, having gotten his magic under control, and Treble were supposed to be having their first official rehearsal with a view to performing regularly again. They'd had occasional practices on the days when Ryley had come home to visit over the past year or so, but they really needed to be at their best if they were going to try for a steady gig.

"Since when is Ryley ever on time for anything?" Adrian joked.

That almost stopped Vic in his tracks. Zac's shy, straight-laced boyfriend, who rarely spoke as it was, had said something in jest. The surprise of it was enough to make Vic laugh.

"Good point," Vic conceded. It was one of the things about his ex-boyfriend that Vic had always found particularly irritating, though that was nothing when compared to Ryley's cheating. Still, he tightened his hold on the bracelet and checked the time again.

Finally, a knock sounded right before Ryley and Asher let themselves in, not even bothering to wait for Vic to go answer the door.

"We're here!" Ryley called, breezing into the living room with Asher strolling along casually behind him.

Vic closed his eyes for a moment and let out a sigh. "Thank gods." He looked up at Ryley, and couldn't help asking, "Where the hells were you?"

Ryley blushed as he dumped his violin case into a chair and scrambled out of his jacket, tossing it lazily aside. Vic winced, tempted to go hang it up properly.

"Sorry," Ryley answered, not looking the least bit apologetic. "We were...you know...catching up." He waggled his eyebrows. Behind him, Asher chuckled and shook his head.

"You're the one who scheduled this practice," Vic pointed out.

"I know, babe, and I'm sorry, but–"

"You know I don't like it when people aren't where they're supposed to be."

Ryley sobered, a look of understanding falling over his face. "Shit." He moved closer and grabbed Vic's wrist, right above where his hand was still stuffed into his pocket and clutching the bracelet. "Babe, I'm so sorry. I didn't even think–"

Vic sighed, pulled his hand out of his pocket, and gave Ryley's hand a quick squeeze before letting go. His heart wasn't racing so badly now that Ryley and Asher were there. "No, I'm sorry," he muttered, feeling like a fool. "I was worried, that's all." Ryley nodded with understanding. "And I'm on edge." He quickly looked at each face in turn, addressing them all. "Tomorrow will be two years since Cam died."

Ryley winced. "Shit, babe, I didn't even realize..."

"You sure you're up for this?" Zac asked.

Vic waved it off. "It's alright," he said, more to convince himself than the others. "I'll be fine. Besides, he's–"

Ryley yelped, his hair falling free of a loose tail as his hair tie got yanked away by an unseen force.

"–here, apparently," Vic muttered with a laugh.

"Are you..." Zac began, looking at Ryley, "doing magic?"

"I–" Ryley started to answer, then stumbled as something invisible gave him a playful shove. Ryley laughed. "No, I think that's Cam."

The hair tie zoomed about for a few seconds before it finally went still, and Ryley snatched it out of the air.

Vic chuckled. "Brat."

A notepad—one of several that Vic had stashed around the house for Cam to use—floated up off the end table, along with a pen, and Cam wrote, *You know you love me.*

"Yeah, I do," Vic said, smiling in Cam's general direction. He never quite knew if he was looking at Cam's face, but he tried his best.

"Oh my *gods*," Zac exclaimed. "Your lives are so *weird.*"

Ryley laughed. "Right? There we were, all normal and boring, and now we've got magic and ghosts and..." He shook his head. "Who knows what's next?"

Vic chuckled along with the others even as a chill ran through him. Ryley's question sounded just a little too ominous. He could use a little more normal-and-boring. His life hadn't been free of at least some degree of weirdness in almost fifteen years.

He reached for the bracelet again.

* * *

VIC ALMOST sagged with relief when they halted practice an hour later. His fingers ached from so much playing after neglecting his cello for so long, having lost any reason to play regularly while Ryley had been away on Jadu'n.

It used to be he'd play for an hour every single night just for the enjoyment of it, but he'd lost the habit after he and Ryley had broken up and their trip to Erostil had come to nothing. Vortex Records had sent Treble on a trial tour on the tropical Isle, but the trip hadn't shown sufficient returns to justify a recording contract, and it wasn't long after that when Ryley had run off to get his magic under control. It seemed, for a while there, that Treble were done for good.

And Vic hadn't minded that as much as he'd thought he might. The experience of playing wasn't the same with he and Ryley no longer together. Their intimacy had always spilled over into their stage presence, their passion for one another coming out through their instruments, with Zac's violin adding another layer to the whole thing, tying it all together and making it even better. Vic could count on one hand how many times, on a night when Treble performed, he and Ryley had *not* fallen into bed afterward, since their expression onstage followed them home and exploded out of them in one final, intimate crescendo. Unless Ryley ran off for one of his hookups, of course, but that was a whole other issue. One that no longer mattered.

Still, without that connection as a foundation, Vic just wasn't feeling drawn to his instrument anymore.

"So," Ryley began, pulling Vic aside, "I'm gonna totally let it slide since we're rusty and you're having a rough day…" He paused, giving Vic a frown of concern. "But it feels like you aren't even with us today."

Apparently, his lack of connection showed.

Vic grimaced. "Sorry."

"No, babe, don't apologize. Just…" Ryley blew out a breath. "We don't have to do this if you're not up for it."

Vic shrugged. "I'm up for it."

Ryley raised an eyebrow. "Now say it again, but with *feeling*."

Vic snorted a laugh. "I'll get it back," he promised. *Somehow.* "Besides, Zac really wants this."

"Yeah, he does," Ryley agreed. Poor Zac had been trying some solo projects over the past several months, but he'd been having trouble making any of them stick, not as passionate about any of them as he'd been about Treble. Zac was itching to get the three of them back up onstage. "Well, enough of that for now," Ryley said, letting Vic off the hook. "Show me this house I've been hearing so much about."

While the others chatted in the living room, Vic gave Ryley a tour. He'd bought the house several months back, part of a plan that he and Asher were working on, hoping to ultimately set up a therapy office and halfway house for rescued kids. Vic felt ridiculous, living in the house all by himself while he slowly worked toward putting that plan into action—Asher still had a few more years until he had his therapy degree, after all—but Vic hadn't yet had a rescue case with which to test the arrangement. So he continued to live alone in the sprawling place.

Alone, except for Cam, of course. Despite being invisible, the ghost's presence helped the house feel not quite so empty.

Vic showed Ryley the main living spaces, followed by the bedrooms—one of which he used as his home office—and their attached washrooms, then took him down to the basement. The space was unfinished, but since the plan for the halfway house was still years off, Vic was leaving that for last. He was still furnishing and decorating the main floor as it was.

He outlined the plan he and Asher had come up with in terms of turning the unfinished space into a therapy office and extra bedrooms, then took Ryley outside to show him the secondary driveway and parking area with direct access to the walkout basement, which would ultimately allow him to keep the residential part of the house separate. From there, Vic showed Ryley the backyard.

Ryley came to a stop, gaping at everything he saw. "Wow," he breathed. "This could almost be Jadu'n."

Vic nodded slowly. "That was sort of what drew me to it," he admitted. The huge backyard was more a series of garden spaces, all walled off from the neighboring properties on either side and backing up to a wooded area that would never be developed. It was just the kind of tranquil retreat that his kids would need.

"Vic, this is totally cool," Ryley murmured, his voice

full of awe. He turned to look at Vic, shaking his head. "You're amazing, you know that?"

Vic shrugged under the praise.

"Come on," Ryley teased. "You know you are. I'm sure your boyfriend would agree with me."

Vic frowned. "What boyfriend?"

"Oh." Ryley blinked. "I thought…a few months ago…you said you were seeing someone?"

"Who– Oh." Vic nodded, then shrugged. "It didn't work out."

Ryley grimaced. "I'm sorry, babe."

Vic shrugged again. The quick breakup after the brief fling hadn't bothered him. And it was hardly the first time it had happened since he and Ryley had broken up two years ago. Vic had tried, off and on over the months, to start dating again, but no one ever really captured his interest enough to make an effort. He'd gone on a few dates with different guys, but nothing ever stuck, and when it came time for any sort of intimacy, Vic just couldn't get into it.

Not when Cam could show up at any moment.

Which meant the only action his cock had seen in the past two years was by his own hand.

And maybe that was for the best. Maybe that was what he deserved after his horrible failure with Cam.

* * *

THE BOY woke to pain, darkness, and motion. He groaned, then regretted it. The throbbing ache in his head grew to stabbing agony, but that was nothing compared to the rest of his body. His right side hurt from lying on it for so long, his neck bent at an uncomfortable angle. The carpet beneath him was rough, and the box that the carpet lined was so hard that it seemed to bite right into him.

If only he could have slept through this part, like he usually did. Then again, being trapped in the box was one of the few times he was truly safe, uncomfortable though it might be. The boy shifted over onto his back, stretching out as much as he could in the confined space, and felt around. His hands were cuffed—no surprise there—but he was able to stretch his arms out and study the box by touch. It was a different box than last time. He was pretty sure the box was actually called a *trunk*, from what the Sirs had said, but he didn't really know what a trunk was, exactly. He'd never been put inside one without a blindfold on, so he had no idea what it looked like compared to some of the other boxes he'd been stuffed into over the years.

He reached up and tugged at the blindfold, but it made no difference. The trunk was so dark, he couldn't see anything. He let the blindfold drop back into place with a sigh. Darkness was good. Darkness was safe. Despite the pain throughout his body from the party, the boy managed to relax by degrees. It was the only time he'd be able to do so.

His real torment would certainly start up again soon enough.

All too soon, the jolting, tumbling motion that rocked his body suddenly stopped. The boy winced, bracing himself. He heard a couple of *thud*s, the vibrations rolling right through him and making him shiver. He knew what came next. It was always the same.

Something clicked, and he felt the cool, fresh air on his hands and face as the trunk was opened. A moment later, rough hands were on him, twisting off the handcuffs and tossing them aside as he was hauled bodily from the trunk. The boy barely managed to get his feet under himself before they dragged him off.

A door opened and shut while three different voices surrounded him: two belonging to the men who carried him, and the third was the worst of all. *Oh gods*. He was back with Bad Man. He just knew it.

Like almost every other place he'd ever been taken, he was hauled down a flight of stairs, then forcibly stripped naked. It didn't matter how much he struggled. With two big men holding him and yanking off his clothes, he was powerless to fight back. Sometimes, he didn't even try. Why bother? This was his life. Had been as far back as he could remember.

Once he was naked, the men groped and fondled him for a few moments before they dumped him unceremoniously on the floor. A bare, concrete floor. The boy shivered. Yes, he was definitely back with Bad Man. Back with his most cruel tormentor. All the other men were bad, too, of course, but none of them were as violent or as humiliating as Bad Man was.

The blindfold was ripped from his head as the two men walked away, leaving him sprawled in the middle of the brightly lit basement while Bad Man looked down at him from the top of the stairs, wearing a vicious grin.

"Welcome home, boy," the man sneered.

The boy hugged his knees to his chest and ducked his head.

Bad Man let the other men out of the basement, then shut the door at the top of the stairs, trapping the boy in. He heard all their footsteps upstairs, heading away, then one set of footsteps returned.

Don't come down. Please don't come down. He was still sore from the last party, from all those men using him. *Please don't come down.*

The basement door opened. The boy whimpered, curling up tighter, but he knew it would do no good. Bad Man was bigger. Stronger. There was no escape. There never was. At least, not physically.

The moment Bad Man put a hand on him, the boy tried to disappear within his mind. A part of him was painfully aware of the abuse being done to his body, but he was able, from years of practice, to push it aside, pretend it wasn't happening. He hid away in the dark shadows of his mind, where it was safe.

He could *almost* ignore the hands forcing him into position. *Almost* believe yet another cock wasn't ripping him open and invading his body. *Almost* pretend he felt nothing when Bad Man punched him in the side, punishment for the sobs that escaped him.

The boy squeezed his eyes shut, surrounding himself

with his mental darkness, drifting off into a fantasy world where someone touched him nicely and held him gently, keeping him warm and safe.

It wasn't until he registered *actual* dark that he finally came back to reality. He was alone again, sprawled out on the concrete floor. Still naked, of course. And with several new aches in his body. One in particular that he had to force himself not to think about. He didn't even bother trying to sit up, knowing it would be too painful to do so. He was pretty sure he was bleeding, but was too afraid to reach back and check.

But it was over. For now. And it was dark. If the lights were off, it meant Bad Man truly had left. As long as he was in the dark, he was safe. The dark meant he was alone, no cruel hands touching him, no men fucking him, no tormentors beating him.

He tried to move, to get more comfortable, but choked when something cold and hard pulled against his throat. He whimpered, and slowly reached up to feel around his neck even though he knew exactly what he'd find: the metal collar, locked in place and attached to a chain. The boy felt along the chain, the links cold and rough under his fingers. Sure enough, it was looped around that pipe in the wall. Until Bad Man came back down and removed the collar, the boy would have only a few feet in any direction that he could move.

He lay back down right were he was and gave way to tears.

The sound of footsteps overhead made him wince, but he knew Bad Man probably wouldn't come back down again. Probably not until tomorrow. Maybe alone, maybe with another party. There was no knowing until it happened. The boy was determined to enjoy the reprieve as much as possible since he knew it wouldn't last. It never did.

A heavy *thud* sounded upstairs, followed by absolute silence.

Chapter 2

VIC SWITCHED off his alarm, considered getting out of bed to hit the gym and then go to work even though he'd requested the day off, and sank back into the pillows instead. He'd barely made it out of bed on this date last year, either. Maybe he could manage it next year. For now, he didn't want to move.

The edge of his bed dipped, and the nightstand drawer opened. Vic pushed himself up and turned on the lamp so he could see, then propped his pillows up against the headboard, leaning back and rubbing the sleep from his eyes while Cam pulled out his notepad and pen.

You alright? Cam wrote.

"Yeah, of course," Vic lied.

Vic, Cam scoffed, and Vic almost laughed. Funny how he was learning to tell his brother's tone just from the way the pen moved.

"Don't worry about me, kiddo," Vic said. "I just want to know how you're doing."

The pen wavered for a long moment, then finally wrote, *I'll be fine*.

"Are you sure?" Vic asked. He barely got the words out before something smacked him upside the head. "Hey. Brat."

That's what you get for using the 's' word.

Vic rubbed the back of his head, and nodded. "You're right." Once Vic had learned that Cam's mental essence still existed and that they could interact, he'd spent countless hours with the ghost, practicing different methods of communication while also giving Cam the much-delayed therapy he needed. Vic wasn't a psychologist, but he had some training as part of his job. The circumstances were hardly ideal since he couldn't see Cam's face or hear the inflections in Cam's voice, but at least he was able to help to some degree, and Cam had definitely been making progress, dealing with the horrors that he'd endured.

So much progress, in fact, that when Vic kept asking Cam if he was sure he was comfortable with some thing or another, Cam had declared the question off-limits.

You're making me feel like I don't know my own mind, Cam had angrily scribbled out one day, a few months ago. *Making me second-guess myself. I can make my own decisions, Vic.*

"You're right," Vic repeated. "I won't ask that again."

That's what you said the last time, Cam reminded him, though his tone seemed playful rather than scolding.

Vic chuckled. "I'll try harder, I promise."

Good. So I take it you're not going to work since you're still in bed?

Vic nodded.

So what are we doing today?

"What do you want to do?" Vic asked, wishing he could see Cam's face. "We can do a therapy session if you need. Or just hang out." He paused, bracing himself, then asked, "If you're ready, we can go face Da–"

NO, Cam scribbled, writing so hard that he nearly tore through the paper. *No, I'm not ready.*

Vic blew out the breath he was holding. *Thank gods.* He wasn't ready, either.

I've had almost fifteen years to deal with the attack, Cam wrote. *But as for–* The pen jerked to a stop, and Vic got the impression of Cam taking a deep breath before he went on: *It's only been two years since he killed me. I can't face him yet. It's too fresh.*

Vic nodded. It was the same for him. Hells, he wasn't sure if just seeing the man would make him break down into a complete emotional wreck or blind him with such rage that he tore the man apart with his bare hands.

Considering he was lying in bed instead of going about his normal routine, he feared it would likely be the former. *Coward*, he thought.

Well, since you suck and don't like playing video games with me–

"I told you I would if you really wanted to," Vic interrupted, and Cam playfully shoved him. "Brat."

I know. It's not your thing. So can we just like watch movies all day and not think about depressing stuff?

Vic sighed, then reached out, feeling around until he encountered Cam's form, and pulled the ghost in for a side-hug. "Whatever you want, kiddo."

Cam hugged him back, then started to set his notepad aside, only to snatch it back up again and write, *I love you, Vic. You know that, right?*

Vic pulled Cam close and kissed the top of his head, buying himself a moment to swallow down the lump in his throat. Cam could have so easily hated him for the rest of his life. Instead, he'd forgiven him and still loved him. "I love you, too."

They spent the rest of the day on the couch, watching comedy and action films just to pass the time, to help them both forget that it was officially two years that Cam had been dead. All they had to do was get through the day. One day to wallow or push reality aside.

But as soon as Vic's alarm went off the next morning, he was up and out of bed, determined to resume his routine. He hit the gym to clear his mind, then headed off to work, hoping to make a difference, hoping to find yet another way to make up for Cam.

All that greeted him once he reached his desk, though, was an inbox full of insurance policies to write up and contracts to review. Vic sighed. He needed another rescue case. Not that he'd wish for a kid to be abducted or disowned, but without having someone to track down and rescue, it was hard to feel like he'd ever manage to balance the scales and chip away at his failure.

Before he could even open his first file, someone breezed past his desk and dropped something on the floor.

Vic looked up and blinked. "Ryley?"

Ryley grinned at him as he yanked open his bag and pulled out a lanyard with what looked like his old company ID attached to it. "Hey, Vic." He threw himself into the chair at his old desk and switched on the computer.

"You're *here*," Vic said, still staring.

"Yeah." Ryley blew out a breath. "Almost late on my first day back. Typical me, huh?" He chuckled.

Vic slowly shook his head. "I didn't realize you'd gotten your job back."

"Oh, yeah. I came by yesterday to talk to the boss, and you weren't here…"

Vic nodded. "Took the day off."

"Ah." Ryley eyed him carefully. "You alright?"

"Yeah," Vic said, trying to brush it off. "You know–"

Another agent rushed over and stopped in front of Ryley's desk, interrupting him. "Oh, good. You're here. I've got a scene for you."

Ryley popped right back out of his chair and started grabbing for his phone and keys. "Where at?"

The agent handed Ryley a slip of paper. "That address. Body's inside the house."

"Has anyone been in?" Ryley asked, scooting around from behind his desk.

"No, the patrol officer just peeked in the windows and called it in," the other agent said, following Ryley as he hurried away.

"Got it, thanks," Ryley said, and turned to Vic. "Hey, if you need to talk later–"

Vic waved him off. "I'm fine. Go."

Ryley hesitated, then flashed him a grin and rushed off, disappearing through the bullpen on his way toward the front door.

Vic watched the man go, and let out a sigh. Ryley had barely been back for five minutes, and he already had a

ILLUMINED SHADOWS

proper case. Vic envied the man. He could use the distraction of a good rescue case right about then.

He glanced down at the scars across the knuckles of his left hand, then reached into his pocket, gave the bracelet a squeeze, and turned his attention to his work, hoping something in that inbox would give him even a shred of redemption.

* * *

THE BOY whimpered and curled in on himself as he listened to all the extra footsteps upstairs. It had been awfully quiet up there since Bad Man had left him two nights ago—too quiet, really—but now there was definitely something going on. If the multiple footsteps meant anything, Bad Man was probably having one of his parties again.

Which was weird, considering it was morning. At least, the boy assumed it was morning, squinting up at the tiny window over the shower in the corner, the only view to outside. Sometimes, if he looked out the window at just the right angle, he could see something blue instead of the empty, soothing blackness he saw out the window at night. He had no idea what the blue thing was, only that it signified day. But that was all he ever saw. And at that moment, chained as he was across the basement from the window, he couldn't see anything at all except just enough light to suggest it wasn't nighttime anymore.

Bad Man usually didn't have parties in the morning. Then again, Bad Man pretty much did whatever he wanted, and the boy couldn't stop him.

And the boy wasn't ready. His whole body hurt while his temples throbbed with the pressure of a growing headache, but those agonies paled in comparison to his simple need for both food and water. He'd already lost hold of his bladder and his bowels after trying with all his might to hold it all in, knowing Bad Man would be furious with him. But he couldn't help it. Chained as he was, he couldn't reach the toilet, so he'd made a mess, both of the floor and of himself, which meant he wouldn't be ready for Bad Man's party guests. It would mean a beating, for sure.

It didn't matter that Bad Man hadn't bothered to come down and free him so he had a chance to get ready before the guests arrived. The boy would be blamed anyway.

He tested the chain hooked to his collar, listening to it clang against the pipe it was attached to. There wasn't far he could move. He felt along the chain with both hands, trying to find any way to get loose, but the links were thick, the collar around his throat too tight to even fathom slipping free of it. He was stuck.

The footsteps overhead continued, and the boy curled up again on his side, the concrete floor cold and rough on his naked body. He pulled his knees up to his chest, hugged them, and tucked his hands up under his chin. This was going to be awful, he just knew it.

And he was still sore from when Bad Man had last used him. If there was a whole party now, he'd wind up bloody for sure. More than he already was.

The boy choked out another sob and tucked himself closer to the wall, barely noticing the cold, rough surface pressed up against his back as he continued to listen to all the activity upstairs. What was taking them so long? Why hadn't they come down yet? If he had to endure the coming torture, why couldn't they just get it over with?

Then all the footsteps moved away, and everything went silent again. The boy held his breath, waiting, straining to hear any little sound from upstairs, but there was nothing. He slowly let the breath back out, trying not to make a sound, and listened again. He kept waiting, fully expecting the door at the top of the stairs to fly open, the awful lights to blare on, the group of men to file down, but nothing happened.

The boy trembled, his whole body aching as he stayed curled up against the wall, but even when he was sure that a couple hours must have gone by, there was still no sound. Just like there had been ever since Bad Man last left him. Until all those footsteps, of course.

The silence was so strange. What was going on?

He waited and waited, trembling and crying. Surely, Bad Man would be coming down any moment.

Still, nothing happened. The silence stretched until the boy felt himself on the verge of panic. This had never happened before. The parties never came just to leave again without touching him. It didn't make any sense.

Hours passed. His headache grew to a stabbing throb, his hunger gnawed at him, his thirst was beyond desperate, and his entire body ached as he lay on the cold, hard floor.

And still, nothing but silence.

He tried to lick his cracked lips, but his whole mouth was so dry that it didn't help. His body felt wrung out, desperate for even just a drop of fluid. If he could just get over to the sink! But the chain was too short. He'd never make it.

The boy went limp, sinking into the cold, concrete floor, the whole room feeling like it was spinning even though he wasn't moving and couldn't see anything. His breaths turned erratic, and for a little while, he actually wished Bad Man would come down. It would mean punishment, and then being used, but he was so desperate for so many things that he was sure he'd pay any price that Bad Man demanded.

Then he wondered if he could die like this. Just go away forever, and never have to endure Bad Man's touch again. Or any of the others'. The thought brought a hint of peace to his dizzy brain. He could be free.

If Bad Man would stay away just a little bit longer…

* * *

BETWEEN FILES, Vic glanced at Ryley. The man had been smiling almost nonstop since he'd gone to examine that body yesterday. How Ryley could be so damned chipper about a corpse, Vic would never understand.

Ryley caught him staring, and flashed him a cheeky grin. "You have *no* idea how much I've missed this."

Vic scowled. "Smelly corpses?"

Ryley shrugged. "Being home, doing my job, something I'm good at. It's like life finally makes sense again, you know?"

Vic grunted. Ryley had a point. He couldn't imagine being dragged away from his life and his purpose for months on end. He'd go out of his mind.

"The only thing that *doesn't* make sense," Ryley went on, shooting him a look, his tone a little too teasing, "is the fact that *you* are still single."

Vic rolled his eyes. "I thought we went over this."

"Yeah, but, babe…" Ryley typed a few more words into his report, then spun his chair to face Vic. "I gotta be honest: I figured you'd be practically married by now."

Vic raised an eyebrow. "We dated for six years and never talked about getting married."

"Yeah, well…" Ryley floundered for a moment, then shrugged. "We knew we weren't gonna work."

Vic nodded. That much was true. It had just taken them both way too long to concede the point.

"I just can't believe you haven't found the right guy yet," Ryley said.

Vic shrugged, but before he could come up with a response, his computer pinged a notification, the sound somehow ominous, tearing his attention away from the conversation. He glanced at his screen, intending to set the notification aside for later, but the date on the case alert caught his eye. *12 Soldis 3578?* That was almost nineteen years ago.

Vic clicked on the alert to open the case file: a two-year-old boy who'd gone missing from the local hospital when his mother had gone into the emergency room, where she died from a gunshot wound. The boy had also been mildly injured, leaving his blood on the mother's clothes. That little DNA sample was the only identification they had for the boy. His mother had been identified from past hospital records, but her file showed no living relatives, and neither her DNA nor the boy's showed up in any other insurance database available at the time, which wasn't exactly unheard-of: Some people just liked living as anonymously as possible. The agent who'd originally been in charge of the case noted that he'd searched multiple times, but never found any other records. The missing boy had never been identified beyond an anonymous birth record and his DNA making him his mother's son, and no trace of him had ever been found since.

Vic clicked the alert again. Their computer system had automatically brought up the old case when a DNA match flagged in a new case. Vic checked the new case and sat back, stunned. It was the medical examiner's report for the body Ryley had recovered yesterday.

According to the report, the deceased man—one Dr. Bryce Ahriman—had skin under his fingernails and traces of blood and fecal matter in his pubic hair. When those samples had been run through the company's database, they linked to the only match the system could find.

A boy missing for nineteen years.

"Ryley–" Vic called, not even tearing his eyes away from his screen.

His voice must have been less steady than he thought because Ryley darted to his side rather than just answering back. "What's wrong?"

Vic gave Ryley a quick glance, then stared at the case notes again, old and new side-by-side on his screen. "Was there anyone else living in that house you went to yesterday?"

"No." Ryley shook his head. "No, the guy lived alone. Haven't even found a next of kin yet to notify. I'm gonna have a hell of a time working out his inheritance clause with no heirs to track down."

Vic pointed at his screen. "He had someone else's DNA on him."

"Whose?" Ryley asked, bending closer and scanning the screen. "Holy shit," he breathed. "A missing kid? And what's–" Ryley scrolled through the DNA profile generated from the samples collected during the autopsy. "You don't think…No, it couldn't be."

"Couldn't be what?" Vic asked.

Ryley frowned, thinking, then shook his head. "I was gonna say...blood in his pubic hair...Maybe the doctor raped him, and the kid fought back? Killed him? Except the scene was clearly an accident, and the M.E.'s report—" He nodded with his chin at the screen. "No indication that it was murder. The guy just choked on his dinner and died of asphyxiation."

"Wait..." Vic turned to the deceased's file and clicked on the client history attached to it. He scanned Dr. Ahriman's personal details: name, home address, place of work. "Holy shit." He switched to the cold case and pointed at the screen. "Your dead doctor worked at the hospital where this kid was taken from."

Ryley stared back at him. "You don't think...All this time..."

Vic nodded. He was sure Ryley was thinking what Vic himself was thinking.

"We have to go back to that house."

Chapter 3

VIC GOT into Ryley's car and immediately switched on his tablet. Ryley had already been to the scene, so he knew where they were going, leaving Vic free to study the case file along the way.

"You're sure there was no one else living in the house?" Vic asked again.

Ryley nodded, focusing on the road as he made a turn. "Granted, we only gave the house a cursory glance. Mostly focused on the body. But there weren't any obvious signs of anyone else living there."

"Hmmm." Vic scanned the case notes and medical examiner's report again, then went over the deceased client's insurance policy. There was nothing in it to indicate Dr. Ahriman had any dependents or cohabitants, but that didn't mean there weren't any in existence. It would hardly be the first time Vic had come across a client who had a policy that only covered the policyholder, leaving his or her cohabitants to purchase their own insurance or security policies, even though they occupied the same residence.

On that thought, Vic ran an inter-agency search on the address they were going to see. No results came up to indicate that anyone else held a policy tied to that house, but it could very well be that there was a policy out there belonging to a company that didn't participate in the sharing of information.

They'd just have to wait and see for themselves.

Ryley pulled his car to a stop and switched it off. "We're here."

Vic switched off his tablet screen, removed his restraint, and got out of the car, scanning the front of the house. "Gods." The place was huge. "Guy did well for himself."

Ryley snorted. "Wait 'til you see inside." He paused, then said, "Fair warning: It'll probably still smell like death in there."

Vic grimaced, and gave a tight nod.

Ryley waved his agency passkey at the electronic lock, and the front door opened. Vic went in first, checking all around the entryway, before Ryley followed and shut the door behind them.

"Clear," Vic said.

Ryley nodded, activated the door lock so no one could come in after them, and went on to the next room. "Clear," he called over his shoulder.

They checked the whole main floor, clearing every room, then stopped to listen. There was no sound from upstairs, but they went to check anyway, just to be sure, giving each room enough of a glance to determine there was no person to be found.

Ryley trudged back downstairs, and Vic followed, frowning at his tablet. The blood on the doctor's body tested fresh enough that it had to have gotten there shortly before his death, and there was no indication that anyone had left the house in the days the medical examiner had determined the man had been dead before he'd been found. So the boy *had* to still be there.

But there was no sign of him.

"Maybe we should look again," Vic said, glancing around. "Under a bed, or in a closet, or…"

Ryley shook his head. "If there's someone else here, you'd think there'd be a sign. You know…something moved, or…Hells…" He darted into the kitchen, and Vic followed, but Ryley just stopped and shook his head. "Food out, dirty dishes, *something*. But there's nothing here."

Vic clenched his jaw. *Damn it*. He wanted to find this kid, assuming the boy had ever actually been in the house. Maybe the doctor had gotten the blood somewhere else, then come home and died? He checked the house's alarm logs again, and muttered a curse. That was most likely the case. The last time the front door had been opened was just a few hours prior to the estimated time of death. The kid must be somewhere else.

But Vic had a gut feeling that the kid *had* to be there.

"There's gotta be something we're missing," Vic muttered, looking around. He gave Ryley a sideways glance. "There's not some sort of…spell or something you can use, is there?"

Ryley started to laugh, then tilted his head, thinking about it. "Huh. Maybe, but…if there is…I don't know of it." He paused. "I could jump over to Jadu'n. Find Master Ross and ask him and come right back."

Vic blinked. "You can do that?"

"Sure." Ryley grinned. "After learning to transport objects, it didn't take much to learn how to transport myself."

Vic slowly shook his head. He wasn't sure he actually wanted to see Ryley simply vanish before his eyes.

"Well?" Ryley asked.

"Well what?"

Ryley gestured at the room. "Do your thing."

Vic blinked, then slowly scanned the room. Ryley was right. Vic's gut was telling him the boy was in the house somewhere. He just had to go with his instincts. There had to be something they'd missed.

Closing his eyes, Vic took a deep breath, then looked around again. He crept upstairs, Ryley keeping several paces behind so as to stay out of his way, and checked each room one more time, looking under the beds, in the closets and cupboards, checking the ceiling for any sort of attic access, and finally knocking on walls and even checking the floorboards, just in case. The trail felt cold, somehow, so he went back downstairs and checked over the main level the same way.

The boy wasn't hiding behind any furniture, and there wasn't a single locked room in the house. He wasn't in a closet or cupboard. Vic was about to give up and check the backyard for any outbuildings when he walked past a bookcase and jerked to a stop.

"Vic?"

Vic held up a hand, asking Ryley for silence as he scanned the wall. Something about it didn't feel right. He paced slowly to the end of the bookcases, then around the corner, where a short hallway led into the kitchen. A doorway at the other end of the kitchen led to a small breakfast nook, which opened up into the other end of the living room, allowing him to loop around to where he'd started.

He stopped and stared at the bookcases again.

"What is it?" Ryley asked.

Vic tilted his head. "This wall," he said, holding out both arms with his hands spread as wide as the bookcase right before him. On the other side, that section of wall stuck out too far in the kitchen with nothing to account for it doing so.

He took a step forward and felt all around, shoving books aside, tugging on shelves, rising and ducking to see above and below eye-level.

Ryley chuckled. "Babe, what are you doing?"

Vic reached under a shelf, sliding his hands all around, and felt a small, metal handle.

He breathed a laugh. "A bookcase."

"What?" Ryley asked.

Vic looked over at him. "Do you remember that story Zac told us when he was studying Will Knightley in Music Appreciation?"

Ryley snorted a laugh. "When was he *not* studying Will Knightley? I swear, Zac was obsessed. Fanboying all over a dead guy."

Vic raised an eyebrow. "I seem to recall you being a rather big fan of that dead guy."

"Yeah, his music," Ryley scoffed, then rolled his eyes and sighed. "Fine. So he was hot. But his music was incredible. Come on, you love it, too—"

Vic shot Ryley a look.

"Sorry," Ryley muttered, chuckling. "Focus. Got it."

"*Anyway*," Vic said, "Zac said Knightley's family owned some land with an old Ceynesian estate that got torn apart in the Breaking of the World. When they explored the ruins, his brother seemed to just vanish, until he realized there was a hidden passage. Apparently, the Ceynesians were big on those, especially the nobility."

Ryley nodded slowly. "And…"

"And all of Morbran City is modeled after the Ceynesian architecture that originally stood here just prior to the Breaking."

Ryley frowned. "I don't get it."

In answer, Vic tugged on the handle, and one side of the bookcase popped forward about an inch.

Ryley gasped. "Holy shit."

They shared a look, then both pulled out their guns, turning aside to bracket the hidden doorway. Ryley gave a nod and pulled the door the rest of the way open while Vic whirled toward the opening, aiming into darkness.

"Vic," Ryley whispered. He nodded at the side panel of the bookcase, now exposed with the door open.

Vic found a light switch there, and flicked it on, flooding the hidden basement with light, though he still couldn't see anything from that angle. He started to creep down the stairs, then stopped when the stench hit him.

"Gods," he gagged, backing into the living room.

"What—" Ryley began to ask, then jerked back, wrinkling his nose. "Oh." He peeked in again, then pulled back. "Doesn't smell like death, but…I'll go look first."

Vic gave him a grateful nod. If there was a body down there, Vic didn't want to have any part of it. That was Ryley's area of expertise.

Ryley held his gun ready, just in case, and crept down the stairs while Vic waited, grimacing as the stench continued to spread.

"*Shit*," Ryley muttered. Vic peeked down, but he couldn't see much more than Ryley's legs. "*There's a body*," he called. "*Male. Young. Probably...fourteen? Fifteen?*"

Vic closed his eyes and sighed. *Gods damn it all*. He did not want to see another dead kid.

Then he heard Ryley gasp. "*V-Vic!*" Ryley called, his voice a strangled cry. "*He's alive!*"

Vic holstered his gun and flew down the stairs. He breezed past Ryley, who was backing away, his eyes wide and his face pale. Vic might not be able to handle death, but Ryley couldn't handle suffering, especially when it came to kids.

And as Vic approached the body, he was sure it was a kid. Slim and short, the boy couldn't have been more than fifteen or sixteen at the absolute most, if he had to guess. Which meant this couldn't be the boy they were looking for. Of course, that wasn't going to stop him. Vic had a chance to rescue someone, and he was damned well going to do it.

Ryley whimpered. "Vic–" He jabbed a finger, and Vic looked at where he was pointing. The boy was collared and chained to a pipe in the wall.

"Shit." Vic crouched down and carefully rested a hand on the boy's shoulder, afraid to move him in case he was injured. He lay facing away from Vic, his knees drawn up, arms curled in against his chest, though his whole body was limp. The kid was breathing, but it was shallow, and when Vic checked the boy's pulse, he found it weak and erratic. If the boy had been trapped down in that basement for at least three days—ever since the doctor had died—he had to be severely dehydrated. "Ryley, give me your lock picks and go get him some water."

"Water, right, water," Ryley muttered, pulling his lock pick set from his pocket and tossing it over before he bolted back up the stairs.

Vic made quick work of the lock, getting the collar off the boy and gently rubbing his chaffed skin.

"Hey there, champ," Vic murmured, brushing the

boy's hair out of his eyes. The hair was greasy from a few days without washing, his skin was dry, his lips were chapped, and his backside and legs were streaked with excrement—Vic had spotted the boy's waste over in the corner, about as far as the boy could probably go with the limitations of the chain—but the boy was alive, and that was all that mattered.

Even if he was so painfully reminiscent of Cam.

Shit. Vic needed to pull himself together before Ryley came back down.

The boy let out a low whine.

"Easy," Vic whispered. "It's alright, champ. We're gonna get you out of here."

The boy whimpered, his eyes slowly opening halfway before drooping shut again.

Ryley's footsteps were loud as he clambered back down the stairs. "Here," he panted, thrusting a cup of water into Vic's hand.

"Thanks." Vic bent over the boy. "Hey, kiddo," he murmured. "Have some water."

Another weak whimper sounded, but the boy didn't move.

Vic set the cup on the floor, dipped his fingers into the water, and touched the boy's chapped lips. He dipped his fingers again, then gently pressed into the boy's mouth, hoping the touch of water on his tongue would rouse him sufficiently so he could sit up and take a proper drink.

But still the boy didn't move.

"We need to get him to the hospital *now*," Vic said.

"Right." Ryley nodded rapidly. "One sec." He darted away, hurrying up the stairs. Vic heard him race for the front of the house, his footsteps thundering overhead. Maybe the poor man needed a second to breathe before they faced getting the kid to the hospital.

Vic dipped his fingers in the water again and touched the drops to the boy's tongue. It was hardly the most efficient way to go about it, but he had to do something.

Maybe it would be safe to move the boy. Without a

scanner, there'd be no way to know if the boy had any internal injuries, but with memories of Cam fresh in his mind, Vic was afraid to shift the boy at all, worried that he might suffer worse because of it.

He dripped more water into the boy's mouth, then heard Ryley's footsteps thunder overhead again before the man raced back down the stairs.

"Here," Ryley gasped, shoving a blanket into Vic's hands while also nudging Vic out of the way. Vic stumbled and caught his balance, then saw Ryley waving a scanner wand over the kid's body.

"Good thinking," Vic said, then asked, "You couldn't just...*magic* that here from the car?"

"I'm kinda freaking out here."

Shit. Vic grabbed Ryley's shoulder. "I'm sorry, Ry. Just breathe, yeah? It's gonna be alright."

Ryley gave him a grim look, clearly unsettled by being so near a suffering kid, but he took a deep breath and got through it, finishing the scan. The scanner wand beeped, and Ryley checked the readout. "No broken bones, no obvious signs of internal bleeding." He looked at Vic. "He *should* be safe to move."

Vic nodded. The scanner wand wasn't as precise as the holoscanners at the hospital, but it worked in a pinch. Ryley shoved the wand into his pocket while Vic unfurled the blanket and draped it over the boy, wrapping it around the slight form and then lifting the poor kid into his arms.

The boy's head lolled toward him while Vic headed straight for the stairs. He felt little hands weakly clinging to his jacket. Vic cradled the boy close to his body and raced out of the house, right behind Ryley, who helped Vic slide into the back seat without letting go of the boy.

Ryley dove into the driver's seat, and they tore off down the road.

"Ry?" Vic asked, eyeing the dashboard over Ryley's shoulder, looking for any signs of a flicker. He knew all too well how Ryley's emotions could let out uncontrolled bursts of magic, affecting nearby electronics. "How are you doing?"

"I'm alright," Ryley muttered. He glanced in the mirror at Vic, then blew out a breath. "I'll be better once I know he's gonna be fine." He shook his head and focused on the road. "Don't worry, Vic. I've got this."

"I know you do." Vic reached forward, gave Ryley's shoulder a squeeze, then sat back with a sigh.

He looked down at the boy to check on him. The little guy was shaking, his lips pale and cracked, his breath rapid and shallow. Vic held him closer.

"We're almost there," he murmured, just as much to himself as to the boy, checking the street to see how far they still had to go. "Almost there."

Vic looked down again, studying the boy's face while the little guy had his eyes closed. There was something almost fae about him, something pure and sweet in the fan of his eyelashes and the curve of his jaw. Despite the horrors the poor kid had most likely endured, he was the picture of youthful beauty and innocence.

From the front of the car, Ryley placed a call through the navigation system, dragging Vic out of his thoughts.

The hospital's emergency room coordinator answered, the woman's voice unfortunately familiar. Vic long ago lost count of how many times he'd spoken to her, bringing in his various rescues for emergency treatment.

"This is Ryley Skye with Sturmwyn Insurance," Ryley told her. "We're inbound with a teenage male, apparent severe dehydration—"

Vic looked down at the boy again. They should have brought some water along and spent the drive forcing more drops into the boy's mouth. He checked the streets again. At least they'd be at the hospital soon.

The boy stopped shaking. Frowning, Vic held his breath as he studied the boy's face.

The kid wasn't moving.

"Ryley!" Vic yelled, interrupting the man's conversation. "He's not breathing!"

"What? Shit!" Ryley checked his mirrors and accelerated as he told the coordinator, "He's in respiratory arrest—"

"What's your ETA?"

"Five minutes," Ryley said, then groaned. "Fuck, too long." He looked around rapidly and yanked the car over to the curb. "Scratch that. We'll be outside the ER in ten seconds. Send out a gurney."

Before Vic could ask, Ryley switched off the car and threw open his door. "Get out!" he ordered.

Vic rushed to comply, opening the door and maneuvering himself and the boy out of the back seat.

"Hang on," Ryley ordered. He slammed the back door shut, grabbed Vic, and closed his eyes.

Vic's body tingled and gave a slight lurch. Between one breath and the next, he found himself—still holding the boy and Ryley still wrapped around him—standing just outside the hospital.

Just in time for the emergency entrance to fly open, three nurses and a gurney spilling out to meet them.

Vic dropped the boy onto the gurney and stepped out of the way as one of the nurses climbed up and straddled the boy, pressing an oxygen mask to his face and inserting an IV in his arm while the other two nurses wheeled them inside. Vic and Ryley followed, watching as the fluids and oxygen did their work.

The boy started breathing again.

"Oh thank gods," Ryley gasped, grabbing Vic's arm and bending forward as though he might be sick.

Vic closed his eyes and sent up a silent prayer. Thank gods, indeed. And Ryley, too, for that matter. He pulled the smaller man to his side.

"You're amazing, you know that?"

Ryley took a calming breath. "It was just a transportation spell."

"And it saved his life." He gave Ryley a squeeze. "Thank you."

"Don't thank me until we know he's gonna live," Ryley muttered, fidgeting uncomfortably as he stared at the little figure on the gurney.

Vic squeezed Ryley again, then also turned his attention to the gurney as Dr. Garrison, one of the hospital's lead physicians, raced over and quickly checked the boy's vitals.

The doctor looked grim. "Give me a full scan."

The nurses maneuvered the boy into place at one of the scanning stations, then they all stepped back as the doctor pressed a button on the wall. The holoscanner turned on, a bar of blue light tracking down the boy's form from head to toe. Vic held his breath, waiting. The light winked out in time with a *beep*, and a hologram of the boy's body rendered in midair.

Dr. Garrison studied the rendering, then ordered more fluids, a blood sample, and a rape kit, amongst other things. Then he turned, spotted Vic, and walked over, offering his hand.

"Vic," the doctor said, eyeing him carefully. "Good to see you again."

Vic swallowed hard and nodded in response as he returned the handshake. He didn't want to be thinking about Cam just then, though it was difficult not to, considering the similarities.

Dr. Garrison shook Ryley's hand, his look still assessing but with a different quality. "Mr. Skye." He tilted his head. "Dr. Edrich told me you had an…*interesting* situation the last time you were here."

Ryley held his hands up. "I'm in control, I swear."

The doctor gave the lights and machines all around them a cursory glance, then chuckled and shook his head. "I can see that." He blew out a breath, and looked from Vic to Ryley and back. "So, what do we know about him?"

Ryley looked away, so Vic answered, "Not much. We found him held captive in a deceased client's basement. He wasn't coherent, so we have no idea how long he was down there."

"Any idea who he is?"

Vic shook his head, gesturing at the doctor's tablet. "I was hoping you could tell us."

Dr. Garrison frowned. "Hmmm." He clicked through a few menus, and shook his head "I'm sorry, no. His blood work does show a match to a sample already in our database, but there's no name attached to it."

Ryley whirled back toward them. "How come?"

The doctor shrugged, then clicked to another screen. "Huh. Two samples, actually. One, tied to a birth record. No name listed, though. And another, dated two years later...Looks like a sample the attending surgeon collected off another patient's clothes...nineteen years ago."

Vic blinked. "Nineteen–"

He shared a look with Ryley, who darted away a few steps to get as far from the hospital equipment as he could, scanned the room, and waved his hand. A tablet appeared out of nowhere—Vic's tablet, from the look of it, the one he'd left in the back seat of Ryley's car—and hurried back over to them as he tapped through the screens. "Any chance it's a match to this?" Ryley turned the tablet around so Dr. Garrison could see.

The tablet displayed the DNA file for the cold case that had prompted their search of Dr. Ahriman's house.

The doctor looked over the profiling markers and compared them to what showed on his own screen. "Yep. They're identical."

Vic glanced at the boy. "But...he's just a kid..."

Dr. Garrison shook his head and gestured at the hologram. "According to his birth record, his skeletal and brain development, as well as his blood work," he said, pointing at the vial that had just been processed, "he's twenty-one."

Ryley gasped. "We found him?"

Vic stared, slowly shaking his head. Missing for nineteen years, and—if Vic had to guess—held captive that long. It would explain how pale the boy was, like he'd never seen sunlight before, how unnaturally low his testosterone and vitamin D levels were, amongst other things, how short and frail he was. Captivity and trauma wreaked havoc on the body, but Vic had never seen such a bad case up close.

But they'd found him. A missing kid, a cold case, someone who had been given up on.

Vic wasn't done, though. Finding the boy was one thing.

Bringing him back to a normal life was going to be a whole different story.

Chapter 4

VIC SANK into his chair with a sigh, closing his eyes and tuning out the noise of the bullpen. He and Ryley had just gotten back to the office from the hospital. The boy was still unconscious, aided by a sedative, which allowed the doctors to continue getting much-needed fluids and nutrients into his system.

The kid was going to live, but his mental state was yet to be seen.

"Vic?"

Vic opened his eyes and straightened in his chair. His boss, Mace Parker, stood before his desk, looking at him with concern.

"Could you come to my office, please?" Mace asked.

Vic rose and followed him.

Mace closed the door, shutting out the noise of multiple conversations, and they sat across from one another, a heavy silence settling between them. Vic slipped his hand into his jacket pocket and clutched the blood-stained bracelet.

"You wanna tell me about this case?" Mace asked gently.

Vic took a deep breath and gave the man a rundown of everything from the DNA match that had flagged from Ryley's death case to getting the boy to the hospital. Mace nodded along silently, fingers steepled in front of his mouth and a frown on his face.

"I'm not sure where to go from here," Vic finished. "If he's been held captive almost his entire life, foster care won't work, and despite his age, I seriously doubt he lacks the skills to live on his own."

Mace's frown deepened. "Convalescent home?" he suggested, though even he didn't sound convinced by the idea.

Vic shrugged. "Yeah, maybe." It was probably the best choice, all things considered. His department had a budget for arrangements like that—though they'd never had such an extreme case before, requiring such extensive care—and the boy could get the therapy he was desperately going to need, and in a tranquil setting.

Mace narrowed his eyes, scrutinizing Vic's face for a long moment. "Why don't you take him?"

Vic flinched back. "*Me*?"

"Why not?" Mace asked, his eyes lighting up like he was warming to the idea. "It would suit your halfway house project, and your department's funds could pay you just as easily as a convalescent home."

"But…" Vic shook his head. "He's going to need intensive care. More than I'm trained for. I can't do that and be here and–"

"So work from home," Mace suggested.

Vic blinked, and couldn't come up with a response.

"Vic, look." Mace sighed, sat forward, and planted his elbows on his desk. "You're bored here. I've seen it coming on for a couple years now. And it's gotten especially bad since you haven't had a proper case in months." Mace paused, and Vic was about to argue the point until he realized Mace was right: Vic no longer felt challenged and purposeful in his work unless he had a rescue case. "Besides, you know you can work on contracts remotely just as easily as you can from that desk."

Vic nodded along. Gods knew he spent any number of nights working on contracts and insurance policies from his computer at home just for the sake of keeping himself busy. That all depended on Cam, though. If Cam needed therapy or just wanted to hang out, that was one thing. But if the kid needed space and didn't make an appearance, Vic had to kill time with paperwork. Otherwise, he'd go out of his mind, feeling like he wasn't doing enough to make up for his failures.

"What do you think?" Mace asked, cutting into Vic's thoughts.

Vic considered it. He *could* take the boy home to live with him. He certainly had the space. But did he have the skills necessary to get the boy the help he really needed? Or would a quiet, safe place be enough to get him started?

Or would it make things worse for Cam?

"I'll need to ask–" Vic began, then stopped himself. Mace didn't know Cam's ghost followed Vic around. Not that Vic was embarrassed by the notion, but not everyone believed in ghosts, and he didn't want to make Cam into a puppet in order to prove it. "The kid," he corrected himself after an awkward pause.

"Yeah, no, of course," Mace agreed, giving Vic an apologetic look. "Shit, I hadn't even thought of that. Yeah, of course he'd have to agree to it." Mace sighed through his nose. "Whatever you decide, we'll make it work. The poor kid deserves some good in his life."

Vic nodded. "Yeah. Yeah, he does."

That night, when Vic got home, he put his briefcase in his office, then went straight to the living room and perched on the couch, setting out Cam's notepad and pen.

"Cam?" he called, looking around.

The pen floated up and waved at him.

Vic breathed a laugh, then quickly sobered. "How are you? We haven't talked about–" He broke off, hating to even say it out loud. *The anniversary of your death.* Just thinking the words gave him a chill.

The pen hesitated, then wrote, *Wait, if we're doing therapy, shouldn't I be the one on the couch?*

Vic read the words twice while he struggled between wanting to laugh and wanting to scowl at the kid. "I can't believe you just made a joke like that."

I have to joke about it, Vic. If I don't, I might lose my mind. The pen paused, then looked a little too chipper in its movement as it added, *Which would suck, because that's all I've got left.*

Vic barked a laugh, though the humor felt bittersweet. "Cam!"

You love me, Cam wrote, adding a grinning smiley face at the end.

Vic sighed. "Yeah," he murmured. "Yeah, I do."

So...

Vic waited, raising his eyebrows, and could tell, as the pen started to move again, that Cam was changing the subject.

We're bringing the kid to live with us, right?

"I–" Vic blinked, and stared at the words again. "How do you know about the kid?"

The pen hesitated, then wrote, *I was there.*

"You were?" Vic gasped. Cam never came on rescue missions. *Never.* They'd always been too painful a reminder of what had happened to him.

You were thinking of me hard, Cam told him. *Kinda couldn't help but show up.*

Vic grimaced. "I'm so sorry." He still didn't quite understand how it worked, but just thinking of a ghost was often enough to create a sort of energy to which the ghost was attracted. The harder one thought about a ghost, the more the ghost was drawn in, especially when there was already any sort of strong, emotional connection that had developed during life.

Was he really trapped in there for nineteen years?!?

"I think so."

Shit.

Vic nodded. He didn't even bother scolding the kid for using profanity. The word was a gross understatement.

So we're gonna bring him home?

"Do–" Vic frowned, looking back over their conversation. That was twice now that Cam had asked if *'we'* were bringing the boy home, not to mention making it sound more like a statement than a question.

You told your boss you had to ask me, after all. So consider me asked. And my answer is yes.

"Cam..." Vic slowly shook his head. "I'm not equipped for this. The therapy he's going to need...And, besides, I can't risk his presence setting back your progress. Have you even thought about how hard it's gonna be, always having him around? Fragile as he is? After what he's probably been through?" Vic paused, then added, "After what you went through?"

Vic... The pen hesitated, then Cam wrote, *Your entire life has been about me for the past fourteen years. Hells, it's almost fifteen years now. And I'm better. Really. You've helped me so much. Maybe it's time for you to turn that attention on someone else instead.* Cam paused. *And besides that, I want him with us.* He underlined the *I* for emphasis.

Vic stared at the words, then looked up. Gods, he wished he could see Cam. It just didn't feel as effective, trying to have a serious conversation like this, when he couldn't look into Cam's eyes and judge how Cam felt about all this. Vic reached out, found Cam's shoulder, then rubbed his back. "I'm sorry, but I have to ask: Are you *sure*? And I mean really, really sure, Cam. Won't having him around upset you? The potential to bring up bad memories—"

Cam took a deep breath, and sighed. Rather, that was what Vic felt under his hand. He knew Cam wasn't actually breathing, but Cam said that mimicking behaviors like that helped settle him and keep him tethered to his humanity.

I'm not saying it'll be easy, Cam conceded. *But he needs this, Vic. He's just a kid. Yeah, I know you guys said he was twenty-one, but he's really just a kid. He's all alone in the world, and scared. You can help him.* Cam paused, then added, *I want you to help him. I* need *you to help him.*

"Cam—"

Before you find another excuse, Cam interrupted him. Vic shut his mouth, and the pen continued: *I know you feel guilty about what happened to me. But I'm dead.*

Vic winced.

I know you regret that, but it's true. But this boy isn't, Vic. He's ALIVE. And now he's safe because YOU found him. Just imagine how amazing it would be to see him eventually have a normal life? The life I couldn't have?

Vic swallowed hard. "Cam–"

It's not too late for him. You can help him. Please.

Vic started to shake his head.

Do for him what The Asshole didn't give you a chance to do for me.

Vic opened his mouth to say something, then felt his shoulders drop as Cam's words struck home. He hadn't been able to save Cam, but Cam was right. That *was*, as Cam put it, The Asshole's fault—though Vic would have gladly used a much stronger word to describe the man who had cut off Cam's life-support while Vic was out of town and unable to intervene. If the bastard hadn't pulled the plug, Cam could have gotten his experimental surgery and had another chance to live. That shot at redemption had been taken away from him.

It was too late to save Cam, but maybe he could save this boy instead.

Please? Cam wrote again, underlining the word. *Maybe we both need this.*

That did it. If Cam needed anything, he had to make it happen.

"Alright," he agreed. "I'll do it."

Now he just had to convince the boy to trust him.

Chapter 5

THE BOY couldn't quite open his eyes when he woke. His eyelids felt too heavy, his mind too hazy. He let out a groan. There was some vague sensation of Bad Man starving him again, but he couldn't quite remember, his thoughts too sluggish to make any sense. The boy sighed and waited for his head to clear.

If he'd been starved, then it must have been punishment for behaving badly, which meant he'd probably been abused as well. He shifted, and winced. Sure enough, his hole ached. Not as much as it usually did, but he could still feel it. There must have been a party, or maybe it was just Bad Man being especially rough with him.

The boy frowned, his eyes still closed. He didn't remember Bad Man coming for him before he went to sleep, and he always remembered. Even though his mental darkness made certain details hazy, he always at least remembered that much.

But, no, something else had happened between Bad Man coming for him and falling asleep, but he couldn't quite picture it.

He shifted again, then froze. He wasn't on the rough, concrete floor. He wasn't exposed. In fact, he couldn't remember ever being so comfortable and warm in his life.

Except…

There was something. Some vague, hazy memory. Some brief moment in which the fantasy within his mental darkness had seemed so incredibly *real*. He'd been wrapped up, safe and warm, in someone's arms, carried away from his torment, freed from the confines of his basement. It had felt so *good*. Even better than he felt now.

So it couldn't have been real.

The boy gasped, forcing his eyes open. He blinked hard, trying to clear his vision, and found himself in a strange, white room. Not the basement. *Oh gods*. Where was he? How had he gotten there? Why had Bad Man moved him again so soon? Was this some new punishment? What had he done wrong?

He tried to sit up, to get away, but his arms were weak. The boy looked down, trying to push the blankets away, then spotted the chain on his wrist. It didn't look like any chain Bad Mad had ever used before, but it ran from his wrist all the way up to a pipe sticking out from the wall.

He was still trapped.

The boy gasped for air, feeling dizzy, his heart racing. Then something loud beeped beside him, the noise repeating over and over until a door flew open and a stranger rushed into the room.

The boy screamed and threw his arms up, ducking his head. He should have known. All the lights were on. That only ever meant one thing.

"Easy there, easy," the stranger said. "It's alright."

"No!" the boy screamed, flailing. He tried to pull free of the chain on his wrist, tried to kick away the blankets weighing down his body, but he was still so weak, his head still so hazy.

The stranger touched his arm, and the boy screamed again.

"No! No, please!" he begged, bursting into tears. He didn't want this. Not again. Not ever again.

But there was never any escape. His fantasy was just that. It wasn't real.

Another stranger came in and helped the first try to hold him down.

"No!" he cried, fighting back. "Please!" *Oh gods.* What were they going to do to him? Would they use his body first? His mouth? Beat him? Maybe something new and scary? Bad Man did that sometimes. Said it kept things *'interesting'*.

The strangers shouted things at one another, more strangers coming in and surrounding him, all of them shouting more things while still trying to hold him down. The boy kept screaming, trying to break free. Gods, why couldn't he just ever be free?

"Easy there," one stranger said, grabbing his arm. "Easy. We're not gonna hurt you."

"Maybe we should sedate him again," another said.

They shouted more words, talking nonsense over his screams. The boy squeezed his eyes shut, still pulling and kicking and trying to get free while the strangers tried to hold him down.

Oh gods. They were all going to take turns with him, he just knew it. And he was already sore, which meant it was going to hurt like hell, especially when they punished him for fighting.

But he couldn't help it. He couldn't stop fighting. He didn't want them touching him.

"Oh, thank gods," one of the strangers said. "Vic."

Vic. A strange sense of ease washed through the boy. He wasn't sure how, but he knew that word. Just the sound of it was enough to send him slipping into the safety of his mental darkness, where he could disappear and feel safe, wrapped up warm and secure.

Suddenly, the strangers were all gone, no longer touching him, the sudden change pulling him back from the brink of disappearing entirely within his mind, enough that he could hear that they hadn't left the room.

"Hey, champ," a voice murmured. "Hey, it's alright."

The boy knew that voice. It was the nice voice. The nice man. The hazy memory came slowly flooding back to him. The nice man who touched him gently and gave him water, who wrapped him up all warm in a blanket and took him away from the basement.

But it hadn't been real. Had it? Maybe he'd finally just lost his mind.

"It's alright," the nice voice went on. "You're safe here, buddy."

The boy whimpered and ducked his head, still holding his arms up where they were when the strangers finally let go. He slowly cracked open his eyes and peeked between his arms. Sure enough, the nice man was there, crouched beside him, not looming over him like all the strangers had been. The boy stared at him. The nice man was actually *real*?

"Hey, champ," the nice man said again, a smile on his face. "I'm so sorry. I meant to be here when you woke up, but the sedative wore off early."

The boy slowly lowered his arms, tucking both hands up under his chin as he looked around. The strangers were all quietly leaving the room.

"You alright?" the nice man asked.

The boy choked back a sob, looking at the door. "I thought…they were…" He looked at the man again.

The nice man shook his head. "They won't hurt you. They're just here to help."

The boy frowned. It didn't feel like helping when they were trying to hold him down. Besides, he was already chained. His eyes went to the strange cuff on his wrist.

He looked at the nice man again, then all around the room. There was no sign of Bad Man. It didn't make any sense. Bad Man was almost always there. Sometimes to use him, sometimes to host his parties, sometimes to bring him food or taunt him with the lack of it. No matter who came to use the boy, Bad Man was always present, but now there were strangers everywhere, but no Bad Man to be found.

Oh gods. Did the nice man own him now?

"Is this my new basement?" he whispered, holding up his wrist.

"What?" the nice man asked. "No. No, of course not."

The boy blinked. "But...I'm chained."

"Wh– Oh. No, kiddo. That's not a chain. You see this?" The nice man pointed at the thing on his wrist, then traced the chain all the way up to the pipe on the wall. The pipe held some sort of clear bag with what looked like water in it, and it was that the chain was apparently attached to, not the pipe itself. "This is medicine. It's gonna help you get healthy."

The boy frowned.

"How are you feeling?" the nice man asked.

The boy tilted his head.

"Alright, how about this," the nice man went on. "How do you feel compared to yesterday? When I found you?"

"Oh." The boy tried to think. He was terrified, but he wasn't actually starving or thirsty anymore, despite how he'd felt when he first woke, and he wasn't cold. His head felt more clear, especially now that the fog of sleep had worn off. And he was warm. So comfortable and warm. "Better," he realized aloud, then shrank back. He wasn't allowed to feel better. It meant he'd have to pay.

The nice man smiled. "Good. That's good. That means this is helping," he said, gently tapping the thing on the boy's wrist.

The boy whimpered and grabbed at the chain, trying to pull it free.

"Hey, hey, easy," the nice man murmured, gently taking his hand and pushing it aside. "You need that, kiddo. You were severely dehydrated."

"Don't wanna pay," the boy cried softly.

"You don't have to pay for it, champ–" The nice man cut off suddenly, and a strange look crossed his face. "Oh." He grimaced, then put on a smile. "No, you don't have to pay for it. Not like that. Not at all, actually. I'm taking care of it."

The boy frowned. He had no idea what that meant.

"Hey, you know what?" the nice man asked, turning

his voice more cheerful. "We didn't get a chance to properly meet yesterday. My name is Victor Lucius. But you can call me Vic."

Vic. The nice man was Vic. The boy felt his mouth twitch like he might actually smile. "Vic," he whispered. He wasn't sure why, but that word felt good. Safe. Just like the man felt safe.

At least, he had when it was all part of a fantasy, the security of those arms holding him within the safety of his mental darkness. In the light of reality, it might be a different story.

Vic beamed at him. "And what's your name, champ?"

The boy frowned and tilted his head.

"What are you called?" Vic asked.

"Boy," he answered. Wasn't it obvious?

Vic's smile wavered. "That's it?"

The boy nodded. "Bad Man always calls me *boy*."

Vic frowned. "You don't have a name?"

The boy shook his head. "Isn't that my name?"

"No, that's what you are–" Vic broke off, then said, "Actually, you're a man, but…" He waved his hands. "Maybe that's a discussion for another time. You don't remember having a name?"

The boy shook his head again.

"Not even from before?" Vic asked. When the boy looked at him with a puzzled frown, Vic added, "From before the Bad Man had you."

The boy scowled. "Bad Man always had me."

Vic blinked. "You don't remember anything from before the basement?"

"No," the boy answered, shaking his head, but there was something there. Something vague and hazy, but no matter how many times he tried to make the picture more clear in his mind, it only got worse. He cringed and curled both hands into fists, rubbing them against his temples.

"Alright," Vic soothed, gently touching the boy's hands until he lowered them. "It's alright, champ. Don't worry about it." He reached into his jacket. "Here, tell you what." He pulled a mobile phone out of his pocket.

"No," the boy whimpered, tucking his hands up under his chin as he tried to scoot back. "Please..."

Vic went still, eyeing him over the phone. "What's wrong, kiddo?"

The boy looked at the phone, whimpered again, and shook his head as he begged, "Please, don't make me—"

Vic slowly lowered the phone. "Don't make you *what*?" he asked gently. "Talk to me. What's going on?"

The boy hesitated, watching Vic carefully, but when Vic didn't make a move to grab him, he said, "Bad Man had one of those. He'd shove his cock in my mouth until I choked, then he'd take a picture and show me..."

Vic cringed. "Gods," he breathed. "I'm so sorry." He shook his head, looked down at the phone as he quickly tapped on a bunch of things, then slowly turned the phone around so the boy could see the screen. "No pictures, I promise. I just thought we should pick a name for you."

The boy glanced at the screen, but didn't see anything that looked like a picture. All he could make out were a bunch of colors and tiny lines that made strange shapes.

"Since you don't remember your name, and there's no record of a name your parents picked for you..." Vic went on. He held the phone out toward the boy, giving a nod of encouragement. "Why don't you choose one?"

The boy eyed Vic before he carefully took the phone and held it in both hands, looking down at it. Closer up, the colors, shapes, and lines were more clear, but he didn't know what any of it meant.

"Scroll through those and see if there's anything you like," Vic said.

The boy frowned, staring down at the thing. He had no idea what Vic meant. What was *'scroll'*? And what was he supposed to be liking? He glanced up at Vic and saw the man's encouraging smile fade.

"Ah, you can't read, can you?" Vic asked.

"Read?"

Vic took a deep breath and smiled again. "That's alright." He held out his hand, and the boy slowly handed him the phone back, bracing himself just in case Vic changed his mind about the pictures. "We can teach you to read later, after you get settled in." The boy had no idea what that meant, but before he could ask, Vic went on: "Tell me if any of these sound good to you." He looked down at the colorful lines and touched the tip of his finger to them, making them slowly move across the screen. "Let's see. Aaric, which means *to rule with mercy*." He glanced up at the boy, then back down at the phone. "Parle. It means *little rock*. Weston. *From the west*."

The boy listened as Vic ran through several more names. None of them really stood out to him, but he supposed one was just as good as another. He didn't want Vic calling him *boy* like Bad Man had.

"Hurst, which is *lives in the forest*," Vic went on. "Tomlin. *Little twin*. Nyle. *Champion*. Colby, which means *dark*. La–"

The boy perked up.

Vic paused, looking up at the boy. "Colby?"

The boy nodded shyly.

"You like that one?" Vic asked.

The boy nodded again. "I like the dark," he whispered. "Dark is safe." Vic gave him a curious look, so the boy said, "When it's dark, I'm alone. Bad Man only comes for me when he turns on the lights–" He cut off and held his breath, looking around. All the lights were still on.

Vic went very still, then he slowly got up and crossed the room, tapping something on the wall by the door. The lights went off. The boy gasped, and watched as Vic went over to the window—bigger than the boy ever imagined a window could be—and pulled some cloth over it, dimming the light in the room even more.

It wasn't dark, but it was certainly better.

"How's that?" Vic asked, returning to the boy's side.

The boy looked at him. "Does that mean no one's gonna come fuck me right now?"

A look of pain crossed Vic's face before he put on a smile and shook his head. "No one's ever gonna touch you like that again."

"You promise?" the boy whispered.

"I promise."

The boy looked all around the room again, wishing it could be darker so he could be sure, but Vic looked like he was telling the truth.

And Vic seemed nice. Maybe he meant it when he said no one would come for him.

"So," Vic said, "Colby?"

The boy looked at Vic, studying his face, then felt the corner of his mouth twitch.

Vic nodded. "Look at that, champ. You've got a name."

The boy—Colby—felt a hint of a smile on his face for the first time in his life, and the answering smile on Vic's face somehow made the moment even better.

Chapter 6

VIC COULDN'T help grinning. Colby was smiling. Not much, but the change was noticeable. The slight tilt of his lips, the brightness of his eyes. Tiny changes in his face, but those changes made all the difference in the world. With just one five-letter word, the boy had gone from a terrified, trapped little boy to taking his first step toward freedom. He had a name now. A piece of his identity that he had chosen rather than having his entire being defined by others.

All in all, it was a great start. Vic couldn't wait to find another way to make the boy smile.

But Colby's smile faded, and he tucked his hands under his chin as he ducked his head, looking around.

"V-Vic?" he whispered.

"Yeah, buddy?"

"What if Bad Man comes back for me? Will I have to go back in the basement?"

Vic moved closer and just stopped himself from touching the boy. "No. Bad Man's gone. He's never coming back."

Colby frowned. "But–"

"He's dead, champ. He can't hurt you anymore."

Colby looked up at him from under his eyelashes. "Dead…like…"

Vic hesitated. Did Colby even know what death meant?

"Like..." Colby said, then he whispered a word that Vic couldn't make out.

Vic tilted his head. "Did you know someone who died?"

Colby swallowed hard and nodded.

Vic waited, watching him. Maybe Colby was finally remembering his mother. Maybe he'd actually seen her die, right there in the hospital, before the doctor had grabbed little Colby and taken him away. The combined trauma of watching his mother die and then being kidnapped and locked up could easily explain why he'd repressed the memory and thought he'd been in the basement forever.

"Do you want to see his body?" Vic asked gently. "It's still in the morgue. You can see for yourself that he's dead. It might help give you some closure."

Colby perked up slightly at that, big eyes looking up at Vic from under his eyelashes.

"Yeah?" Vic asked.

Colby nodded, then looked down at his wrist. "Will they let me go?" he asked.

"Yeah, of course." Vic slowly stood, not wanting to frighten the boy with his size. At six-foot-six, Vic towered over just about everyone. "Here, look." He grabbed the IV stand and pulled it away from the wall, then showed again how it was connected to Colby's wrist. Of course, Vic wasn't sure Colby realized he actually had a needle under his skin, hidden away behind the tape. Vic figured he'd save that little fact for later. "See, you're only attached to this. We'll just bring it with us." He paused. "Think you're strong enough to stand?"

Colby looked down at himself, then gave a slight nod and kept an eye on Vic as he pushed the blankets back. Thank gods, they'd put Colby in pants as well as the standard hospital gown after getting him cleaned up while he was unconscious. Vic went over to a cupboard where a patient's personal effects were normally stored, along with other basic toiletries and supplies, and grabbed a pair of generic slippers.

When he turned back around, he found Colby staring down at himself.

"Colby? You alright, champ?"

Colby turned his wide eyes on Vic, his gaze full of wonder. "I'm allowed to wear clothes?"

Vic felt something in his chest—something like heartbreak and relief all at once—seeing Colby's reaction. He put on a smile and crossed the room. "Yeah, of course." He uncovered Colby's feet, and moved slowly as he helped the boy into the slippers, making sure Colby could see everything he did.

"Bad Man never lets me wear clothes," Colby murmured, his awed tone making Vic want to hug the boy and punch someone in equal measure. "Unless they put me in the trunk," he added. "Or sometimes for the parties, when the guests want to tear them off themselves."

Vic cringed at the mental image. And that was probably barely scratching the surface of what Colby had endured. Forcing a smile back on, he said, "Well, now you can wear whatever you want. All the time," he quickly added. "Alright. Ready?"

Colby glanced at the door, his awe rapidly vanishing behind renewed nerves as he gave a tight nod. Vic watched while Colby eased himself off the bed, staying close in case the boy wasn't steady enough yet to stand on his own.

Once Colby was on his feet, the boy hugged himself, his little fists twisting into the fabric of the hospital gown as though he were afraid someone might rip it away from him.

"Here," Vic said, going back to the cupboard. He grabbed a robe and returned to the boy. "Let's put this on, yeah?"

Colby eyed him curiously, but uncurled himself just enough for Vic to disconnect the IV line and maneuver the robe over the boy's arms. Vic slowly overlapped the front panels of the robe and belted it in place.

He reconnected the IV line, took a step back, and watched as the boy just stood there, slowly lifting his arms until he was hugging himself again, but it wasn't as desperate a thing as it had been a few moments before. Colby fingered the soft terry, and looked up at Vic with something like a smile.

Fighting the urge to grin, Vic rolled the IV stand closer. "Hold on to that, alright?"

Colby looked up at Vic, then slowly reached out and grasped the cold, metal stand, tilting his head as he studied the thing from top to bottom and then traced the line from the bag to his wrist. He looked up at Vic again.

Vic put on a smile and held out a hand toward the door. Colby followed him, and Vic opened the door, standing aside to let Colby out first.

Colby froze, then jumped back when someone passed by the doorway, heading down the hall.

"It's alright, champ–"

Another nurse went by, and Colby let out a whimper, darting over to Vic and scrambling up his body until he had his legs wrapped around Vic's ribs and his head tucked against Vic's shoulder, his little arms wrapped around Vic's neck and his hands covering his own head.

Vic put one arm around Colby's back to steady him. "Hey, kiddo. Easy. It's alright. They won't hurt you."

Colby whimpered again, his whole body trembling.

Vic breathed a laugh. Probably inappropriate, but he couldn't help himself. The poor little guy was scared, but the fact that he'd gone to Vic for security felt better than it probably should have. Vic tightened his hold around Colby's back and used his free hand to grab the IV stand.

"You wanna go like this?" Vic asked.

He felt Colby nod against his neck.

"Alright," Vic murmured. "I've got you, buddy."

He carried Colby out of the room, getting curious and adoring looks from staff and other patients alike as he stopped by the nurses' station on his way to the elevator.

One of the nurses, Kristi, looked up from her computer and gave him a smile. "*Awww.* How's he doing?"

"Better," Vic said. "I'm gonna take him down to the morgue real quick."

Kristi's smile faded, and she gave a knowing nod. "To see Dr. Ahriman's body?" She shook her head. "Still can't believe one of our own would do such a thing. Guess you just never really know people, do you?" She gave Colby a sympathetic smile, but the boy didn't see it with his face tucked against Vic's neck as it was. "I'll let Dr. Garrison know if he happens to come by on rounds before you get back."

Vic gave her a nod of thanks, then continued on to the elevator. He stepped inside the car, thankful that it was empty, and selected the basement floor.

The car began to move, and Colby yelped, raising his head and looking around.

"Shhh, it's alright," Vic murmured.

"Where are we?" Colby whispered.

"In the elevator. It's an alternative to stairs."

Colby hunched his shoulders. "It's so small." He paused, frowning in thought. "Bigger than the trunk, though…"

Vic winced. He was going to have to ask Colby what that meant, exactly—the boy had mentioned a trunk twice now—but that could wait. In the meantime, he needed to reassure the boy that Ahriman was never coming for him again.

"We'll be out in a sec–" The car stopped, and a *ding* sounded as the doors opened. "See?"

Someone passed by as Vic carried him out of the elevator car, so Colby whimpered and ducked his head, hiding again. Vic made his way past storerooms and utility closets, far too familiar with the various wings of the hospital, thanks to years at his job. He found the morgue and stepped inside.

The doctor who worked the morgue's day shift looked up from her desk. "Hey, Vic. Been a while."

Vic gave her a friendly smile. "How are you?"

"Good. How are you? And who's this little guy?"

"This is Colby," Vic said, nodding toward the tiny

figure still huddled around him. Colby had yet to look up. "I wanted him to see Dr. Ahriman's body."

The doctor's eyes went wide as she rose from her desk. "Is this the boy he– Gods, poor kid. It's all over the hospital. It's all anyone's been talking about. We *worked* with this guy, you know?" She shook her head.

Vic grimaced in commiseration. He couldn't imagine finding out something so heinous about a trusted coworker. Sure, he'd found out about Ryley's trauma, but that was different. Ryley had been a victim. Dr. Ahriman was most definitely a villain.

"You're just in time," the doctor said, waving at Vic to follow her. "The funeral home is due to collect him in an hour."

Vic carried Colby into the next room, the air temperature dropping considerably. He felt Colby shiver, and tightened his hold.

The doctor walked up to the bank of cabinets that stored the bodies and used both hands to maneuver a heavy latch. She opened the thick door, grabbed the tray, and hauled it out. The body was still fully covered with a sheet, and the doctor paused before lifting it back.

"Hey, champ," Vic murmured. "Can I put you down for a minute?"

Colby whimpered, but slowly loosened his hold and slid down. Once the boy was on his feet, his little hands clutched at Vic's jacket as he stuck close to Vic's side.

"You wanna take a look?" Vic asked, then added in a murmur, "I'm right here."

Colby looked up at him, then slowly turned. Vic gave the doctor a nod, and she pulled the sheet back, exposing Dr. Ahriman's face. Colby cried out and hid behind Vic.

"Hey, champ," Vic murmured, twisting to try to see Colby as the little guy huddled behind him. "It's alright. He's dead. He can't hurt you anymore."

Colby whimpered, trembling, but slowly peeked around Vic's side. He gasped and hid, then tried again. By degrees, he slowly managed to creep around Vic's body, sticking close the whole time, until he finally took a step away from Vic and toward the remains of the man who had tormented Colby for almost his entire life.

The boy took another tiny step. Then another. Vic and the doctor waited in silence, occasionally sharing looks as they watched Colby's progress.

Vic's heart broke all over again, seeing the pain on the boy's face. "It's alright, kiddo."

Colby looked up at him, then back over at Ahriman's body before resuming his slow progress toward it.

Finally, Colby stopped right beside the body, hugging himself as he studied the motionless corpse. Trembling, Colby sucked in a breath and extended a hand.

He lightly poked at Dr. Ahriman's shoulder with the tip of one finger, then quickly yanked his hand back, braced for some sort of response. After nothing happened, he did it again.

Vic opened his mouth to say something, an encouraging smile ready on his face, but before he could, Colby let out a cry and bent over the body, beating his little fists on the corpse's chest while he sobbed and screamed. Vic looked at the morgue doctor, fully expecting her to stop the boy, but she looked like all she wanted to do was hug him. Or join him.

"Colby," Vic murmured after Colby had raged and cried for a full minute.

Colby broke away and turned right into Vic, sobbing as he hid his face against Vic's chest and clutched Vic's jacket in both hands.

"Shhh," Vic murmured, slowly bringing his arms around until he was hugging Colby, keeping his hold loose enough that Colby could break free if he wanted to. "It's alright, champ. He's gone. You're safe now." He looked down at the little guy in his arms, letting go of a lifetime of pain. "You're safe."

* * *

VIC CARRIED Colby back to his darkened room and got him tucked into bed. Colby had finally stopped crying, and he looked exhausted. His eyes were red, his cheeks pale. Vic had him blow his nose and wipe his face, then brought the blankets up a bit more, trying to help Colby feel as protected and contained as possible.

"Vic?" Colby whispered, blinking slowly.

"Yeah, champ?"

Colby looked down at his hands. "Do I belong to one of the others now?"

Vic frowned. "Others?"

Colby nodded. "Bad Man's gone, so I belong to one of the other Sirs now, right?"

Vic opened his mouth to ask what Colby meant, then it dawned on him. First the trunk, and now a mention of other men? Dr. Ahriman hadn't been the only one who had violated Colby, probably not by a long shot. "No," he insisted, pulling up a chair to sit near the boy while keeping himself at a slightly lower level, making him less intimidating. "No, no, no, kiddo. You don't belong to anyone."

Colby frowned. "Then this *is* my new basement," he whispered, gesturing at the room.

"No. This is the hospital. You're just here for a day or two to make sure you're healthy, and then you can leave."

Colby's eyes got big and his lip trembled. "But…" He looked away and whimpered, then glanced at the door. "Are you sure they're not gonna fuck me?" he asked.

"What? No. No, of course not. No one's ever gonna hurt you again, champ. I promise."

"But…they gave me clothes, and–" He gestured at the IV line, a puzzled frown on his face. "I have to pay."

Fuck, Vic thought. He shook his head. "No, kiddo. You don't have to pay for this."

"But Bad Man says I always have to pay."

"Not anymore," Vic said, forcing himself to keep his tone light even though he wanted to rage against the bastard that had done what he had to this poor kid. "Bad Man's gone. He can't control you anymore. You can go wherever you want when you leave here."

Colby looked up at him with those big, beautiful eyes of his, and tucked his hands under his chin.

"There are lots of places we could take you," Vic said. "Convalescent homes, which are kinda like this, but not so sterile. Or we could find you a foster family." Colby's puzzled frown deepened. He probably had no idea what Vic was talking about. Vic took a deep breath, then said, "Or…you could come stay with me for a while."

Colby's eyes went wide, and though Vic thought he saw relief there, he didn't want to count on it, just in case.

Before the boy could say anything, Vic rushed on: "I've got a spare bedroom. You can have it all to yourself. Sleep in a real bed instead of on the floor. And we'll get you some clothes. Maybe teach you to read, if you want."

Colby stared at him, then burst into tears.

"Colby? Hey, champ, what's wrong?"

Colby sucked in a breath and covered his face. "I don't want you to fuck me," he sobbed.

Vic blinked, his whole body going tense at the visual those words put into his head. *Good gods*. The poor kid. Colby could probably imagine it easily: someone of Vic's size overpowering him and using him without a care in the world. Vic would never do that—could never do that, especially to someone like this boy—but Colby didn't know that. Probably wouldn't even know any better. "Why would you think–"

Colby dropped his hands. "You're nice. I don't want you to be like Bad Man," he cried.

Vic felt that thing again, heartbreak combined with relief. "Hey, Colby, listen." He waited until Colby's eyes focused on his. "I promise I will never touch you like that. *Never*. But it's up to you. You're free now, champ. You can go wherever you want."

Colby frowned and looked around the room. "I've only been in the basements. And here…"

Vic hesitated a moment before he asked, "Do you want to stay here?"

"*No*," Colby answered immediately. He shrank back, eyeing the door as he did so, tucking his hands up under his chin. "Too many people." He paused, and glanced cautiously at Vic. "But…"

Vic sat forward slightly. "Look. I know you're scared. This is all new. It's going to take time to adjust. But if you come home with me, it'll be just us." *And Cam*, he thought, though he wasn't sure it was time to explain that quite yet. "Nice and quiet. And, like I said, you can have your own room, so if you need to be alone…"

Colby nodded slowly, a thoughtful look on his face. "But I have to pay–"

"No," Vic insisted, interrupting him. He paused, then said, "Tell you what. How about we make a deal?"

Colby took in a stuttering breath, then tilted his head in question.

"If you really insist on needing to pay for food and clothes and everything," Vic said, "how about I teach you to help me out around the house?"

Colby's head tilted the other way.

"I can teach you how to cook," Vic said. At the sight of Colby's puzzled frown, he clarified, "Make food. And I can teach you to clean, which you'll need to learn anyway for one day when you're on your own. Then you can do those things for me in exchange for taking care of you. How does that sound?"

Colby shrank back a little, whispering, "You're really not gonna fuck me?"

Vic shook his head. "No one is. Not ever again."

"Or use my mouth?"

"No."

"Or…beat me?"

"Gods, no." Vic cringed at the very thought of it.

Colby swallowed hard. "You p-promise?" he whispered just loud enough for Vic to hear.

"I promise." Vic paused, then asked, "Is that alright with you? Coming to live with me for a while? You can leave whenever you want. I won't own you, kiddo. You own yourself now."

Colby nodded slowly. "You're nice to me. No one's ever been nice to me before."

Vic managed a smile around the heartbreak and relief still playing havoc in his chest.

"Yes," Colby finally whispered, answering Vic's question.

Vic's smile grew. "Alright. Good. In that case, I'm gonna go get you some clothes and get the house ready for you to come home tomorrow."

He slowly stood, and Colby's eyes went wide. "You're leaving?"

"Yeah, just for a little bit."

Colby trembled, looking around at the room before turning his eyes back on Vic. "You'll be back?" he whispered.

"Of course, champ. I'll come back later today to check on you. And then, probably tomorrow, I can take you home."

Colby whimpered, then slowly nodded, looking down at his hands.

Vic hesitated, then tore himself away. He hated leaving the boy like that—alone and scared—but there wasn't much he could do. He'd just have to come back, like he'd promised, and prove to Colby that he could be trusted to keep his word. Taking care of that poor kid was probably going to be exhausting, mentally and emotionally.

But so completely worth it if he succeeded.

Chapter 7

WITH BLACKOUT shades added to the windows, clothes in the closet, and toiletries in the washroom, the guest room was ready. Vic checked everything twice to make sure he hadn't forgotten anything. The room was the farthest from Vic's own bedroom, which Vic hoped would give the boy a stronger sense of privacy and security.

Once he was satisfied everything was ready, he went straight back to the hospital, only to discover that Dr. Garrison had already rechecked the boy and was willing to discharge him early. It was sooner than Vic had planned on, but when he peeked in at the boy and saw how shattered Colby's nerves looked, he decided that getting the boy home and settled in sooner rather than later might not be such a bad thing.

Vic knocked on the door to get Colby's attention. "Hey, champ."

Colby brightened just noticeably. "Vic," he whispered.

Vic smiled and stepped fully into the room. "Dr. Garrison said you're healthy enough to leave," he said, and Colby drew back shyly. "It's up to you, kiddo. You can stay here another night, or we can get you home now."

Colby fidgeted, his little hands tucked up under his chin, then he reached out and pushed the blankets back.

Moving slowly, Vic set a duffel bag on the end of the bed and showed Colby the clothes he'd gotten for him.

"I wasn't sure what you'd want to wear," Vic said, "so I brought a bunch of different things."

Colby eyed the clothes, tucking his hands under his chin again.

Vic waved his hand. "You want to try any of this on?"

Colby looked down at himself, then back at the clothes before looking up at Vic. He gave a tiny nod.

"Alright," Vic said, giving him a smile. "I'll step out so you can get dressed, yeah?"

Colby nodded again, then watched Vic intently as he covered the window in the door and stepped out, pulling the door shut behind him.

Vic waited a full ten minutes before he checked on Colby's progress, just in case the boy needed extra time to work up the nerve to change. "Hey, champ?" Vic knocked on the door. He got no response, so he asked, "Are you all set?"

He thought he heard a shy affirmative, so Vic started to turn the door handle.

"May I come in?"

Colby was still silent, so Vic inched the door open and cautiously peeked inside. He found the boy sitting on the bed, wearing only sweatpants and a t-shirt, his knees drawn up to his chest and his hands tucked under his chin, giving Vic a wary look.

Vic gave him an encouraging smile in return. "Everything fit?"

Colby gave a tiny nod, then noticeably shivered.

"Here." Vic reached into the duffel bag and pulled out a long-sleeved shirt. "Why don't you put that on, too?"

Colby eyed the shirt, then slowly took it, watching Vic the whole time as he slipped it on. Once it settled into place, he looked slightly less haunted.

"If you're still cold," Vic went on casually, pulling out a hooded sweatshirt, "you can also wear this."

Again, Colby hesitated, but he slowly put it on, and

Vic showed him how to zip it up before he gently reached past the boy to grab the hood and tug it up over the boy's head. Colby rolled his eyes up, looking at the hood, then looked back at Vic's face.

"That alright?" Vic asked.

Colby looked himself over and almost smiled. Vic helped him put on socks and shoes, then grabbed the duffel bag and zipped it shut.

"Ready to go?"

Colby looked at the door, then up at Vic, then at the door again. Vic could practically see his mind working, weighing his options, deciding what was safer. Finally, Colby slipped off the bed and huddled near Vic, his legs tight together, his head down, and his hands hidden away in his sleeves and tucked up under his chin.

Vic headed for the door, but Colby didn't follow. The boy's eyes were wide, staring at the doorway, probably imagining all the people on the other side. Vic crouched down and held out the arm not holding the bag.

Colby whimpered, then shuffled over to Vic's side and extended his arms just enough to wrap around Vic's neck while Vic slowly hooked his arm around the boy's waist, lifting Colby to perch on his hip, just like they'd done that morning. The boy clung to Vic and ducked his head, hiding his face.

"I've got you, kiddo," Vic murmured, then turned and headed out the door.

Doctors and nurses gave him happy smiles as he made his way out of the hospital. Vic couldn't help smiling back. This was a good day. A boy rescued, a life saved. Even if the hospital staff would have to deal with the fact that one of their own had tormented the boy for nearly two decades, at least the story had a happy ending.

Vic got Colby out to his car and helped the boy into a seat, buckling the restraint for him while Colby huddled there, looking around uncertainly. Every time someone passed by, Colby flinched. Vic could almost hear the boy whimper each time it happened in the few seconds it took him to walk around to the other side of the car.

By the time Vic slid into the driver's seat, Colby was curled up in a ball, hunched down so he couldn't see anything.

"It's alright, kiddo," Vic murmured, just stopping himself from reaching out to touch the boy. "You're safe."

Colby whimpered, the sound muffled by his arms crossed over his head.

Poor kid. Vic switched on the car, selected his home address on the nav screen, and let the autopilot take over, wanting to have his attention on the boy just in case Colby needed anything.

The boy stayed curled up tight in his seat. Halfway home, he finally loosened his arms a little and started to peek out, then inched his head up until he could see out the front windscreen, his eyes going wide as he took in the passing scenery.

"There's so much," he whispered. He looked up at Vic. "How is there so much?"

Vic hesitated. How could he explain that the world was so big and full when all the boy had ever known were a few bland rooms? How could Colby even begin to reconcile such an idea? His entire life had been confined to trunks and basements, not even much of a window to look out of to give him a hint that there was something more. He may have gotten peeks of Dr. Ahriman's living room whenever the hidden door was opened, but that was probably it. As far as Colby knew, that featureless basement was almost the extent of everything that existed.

Before Vic could answer, Colby whimpered and hid his face again, sparing Vic the need to answer right away. He'd have to think of something for later.

They reached the house, and the car pulled automatically into the garage. It felt almost like stepping out of the world as a heavy silence settled over them.

"Colby?" Vic murmured. "We're home, kiddo."

The boy slowly peeked up at him, and Vic coaxed him out of the car. They went through the laundry room and into the kitchen, and as the main living areas of the house spread out before them, Colby hung back again.

It was only then that Vic realized just how intense a moment this was for both of them. This boy would be living in Vic's space, so Vic would have to adjust his routine. As for Colby, he had an entirely new environment to get used to, one that involved a lot more freedom than he'd ever known.

And it would be just the two of them. All alone. With Vic big enough to hold Colby down with almost no effort. No wonder the poor kid looked scared.

Vic faced the boy and crouched down. "I'll show you the house first, and then maybe we can get you something to eat, if you want?"

Colby looked up at him from under his eyelashes and gave a tiny shrug.

"Come on," Vic said, putting on a gentle smile, hoping to encourage the boy even though he had a feeling it was going to be a very long process to get the boy to open up and trust him.

He led Colby on a tour, the boy tiptoeing along shyly behind him as he named the different rooms and pointed out different things. Colby stared at everything in awe, as though he'd never seen paintings and windows and appliances before.

Then again, he might not have.

The whole time, Colby kept his arms tight to his sides, his hands tucked under his chin. Halfway through the tour, Vic started intentionally touching various things rather than just pointing them out, hoping the boy might get the idea that he was allowed to touch them, too, but Colby stayed firmly contained.

They got through the whole house—only peeking out at the backyard since Colby seemed overwhelmed by its size—then finally came to the basement door. Vic hesitated there. Would it be worse to be honest and admit to Colby that it was there? Or avoid it altogether and have it be a lie of omission? Which would Colby trust more?

Vic blew out a breath, and decided on honesty.

"This is gonna be the therapy office one day," he said, starting down the stairs.

Colby's eyes went wide and he gave a small whimper, then put his head down and followed. Once they reached the bottom, Vic went directly over to the doors that led outside, hoping to show Colby that he couldn't get trapped down there, that there was another way out.

But as Colby took in the unfinished space, all he did was shiver and reach for the zipper on his hoodie, his hands fumbling the pull as he tried to tug it down.

"Colby?" Vic strode over to him as the boy got the zipper undone and his hood pushed back.

"You want me naked down here, right?" he asked, his voice a low monotone.

"What? No." *Shit.* "No." Vic grabbed the bottom of Colby's hoodie and zipped it all the way up, then pulled the hood up over the boy's head. He crouched down so they were eye-to-eye, and tugged on the drawstrings for the hood, then pulled Colby's sleeves down over his hands and pushed his hands up toward his chin. "You don't ever have to come down here if you don't want to."

Colby frowned. "But this is where I belong."

"Not anymore." Vic firmly shook his head. "You're allowed to come down here if you want, but you certainly don't have to. Not ever."

Colby eyed him suspiciously. "You're not gonna lock me up down here?" he whispered.

"Never," Vic swore. "Besides, I couldn't, anyway." He gestured at the doorway that led out to the backyard, pointing it out again in case Colby had missed it the first time.

Colby tilted his head, glancing at the door from the corner of his eye, then looked back at Vic.

"I know this is a lot to get used to," Vic murmured, "but you're safe here."

Colby hesitated, studying his eyes. "You promise?" he whispered.

"I promise." Vic nodded toward the stairs. "Let's go get some dinner, yeah?"

Colby didn't respond, but he followed along when Vic headed up to the living room and shut the basement door. Vic made them dinner, and watched as Colby shyly picked at his food. The boy glanced at Vic between each bite, and Vic couldn't help but think the kid was either looking for permission to keep eating or waiting for punishment if he ate too much.

Poor boy. It would definitely take some time for Colby to get used to being free for a change.

Once they were done, Vic showed Colby how to wash the dishes and where to put them away, figuring he'd demonstrate it a few times before he let the boy try it on his own, then he steered Colby to his room.

"Why don't you take a shower and get some sleep?" Vic suggested.

Colby blinked sleepily at him even though he still looked on-edge.

"Go on," Vic said, giving him an encouraging smile. He gently nudged Colby into his bedroom, then slowly pulled the door shut between them, hoping the boy would understand that Vic was giving him space.

A long while later, Vic finally heard the shower come on, only to shut off a few seconds later. After a minute, the same thing happened, followed by the shuffling sounds of Colby drying off.

Vic's heart clenched. He had a sneaking suspicion the boy had rarely enjoyed a long, hot shower. Something else for them to work toward.

For now, though, Vic was exhausted, so he went to get ready for bed. He switched off all the lights along the way to his room, then set his alarm. Vic settled back against the pillows with a sigh, wondering if he was really cut out for this.

* * *

COLBY CURLED up on the floor in the dark, listening as silence settled over the house. He'd showered, just like Vic told him to do, but he couldn't bring himself to climb up into the bed, even though Vic had suggested it. Even though it looked so soft and warm.

Instead, he sat on the floor, naked, knees drawn up to his chest and his hands tucked under his chin. He stared at the doorway, just able to see the outline of it in the darkened room. Tired as he was, he couldn't go to sleep. Not yet. Not when Bad Man might still come.

Not when Vic might change his mind and come to use him in payment for everything he'd given him.

Colby whimpered. Vic was so nice, but until he'd come along and carried Colby out of the basement, Colby had never met a single man who didn't want to abuse his body in some way. It just didn't seem possible that there would be any exceptions to that rule.

Even if Vic had held him so gently. Colby trembled at the memory, missing the warmth and security of Vic's arms even though the thought of being too close to a man ever again was terrifying.

Colby looked at the door again, heart thudding in his chest. He wanted so badly to trust Vic, but it was way too soon to do so.

Uncurling himself, Colby stood and tiptoed across the room, then stopped to listen. The house felt eerily silent. He tried the door handle, and it gave easily under his touch, so he wasn't locked in. Sucking in a breath, Colby slipped out of the room, felt his way in the dark, and found the basement door.

He choked on a sob, then went down the stairs, down to where he belonged.

Chapter 8

VIC WOKE with his alarm and got up to get dressed for the gym, simply as a matter of routine. He was pulling on his shoes when he suddenly stopped, remembering the boy sleeping down the hall.

Could he leave Colby home alone for an hour? Would the boy feel afraid? Abandoned? Would he even notice? Maybe he'd sleep right through it and never know Vic was gone.

Vic chuckled as he inwardly chastised himself. He really hadn't thought this arrangement through, failing to consider just how many things might change.

At least Cam was comfortable with it. Rather, he'd been comfortable with the idea of it. It remained to be seen if Cam was actually onboard with the reality of things.

For that matter, Vic had yet to consider the idea of Colby being introduced to Cam's presence. He had no idea how the boy might react to the sight of a pen floating about, seemingly of its own accord.

Vic pushed the thoughts aside. He couldn't deal with any of that at the moment. For now, he needed to get to the gym. Even if it left Colby a little unsettled, Vic needed it for his own sanity, his own self-care.

He crept down the hallway, turning on a few lights as

he went, only to stop short at the sight of Colby's bedroom door standing wide open.

Vic peeked into the room, and froze. The bed hadn't been touched, and Colby wasn't there.

"Colby?" he called. He darted into the room and looked all around, but there was no sign of the boy. "Colby?"

No response came. Vic checked the room one more time, then raced down the hallway, checking the other rooms as he went, looking into closets and under furniture. He checked the alarm panel, but everything looked fine there. No indication of an exterior door being opened or the alarm being deactivated or faulty.

Colby wasn't where he was supposed to be, but where the hells had he gone?

Vic's heart started to race with panic until realization dawned on him. He moved across the living room, eyeing the door to the basement. Sure enough, it was only pushed to, not fully shut. Vic's heart clenched. Pulling the door open, Vic peeked down the stairs.

"Colby?" he called softly, then slowly walked down, scanning the dim, unfinished space.

He came to a stop, his heart breaking all over again at the sight of the boy. Colby was naked, curled up on the bare floor, sleeping fitfully.

Moving carefully, not wanting to frighten the boy in case he woke, Vic gathered that little body up in his arms and carried him back upstairs. He tucked Colby into bed, pulling the covers up to his chin. He wished he could get the boy into some clothes, but he was sure that would jostle him too much, and didn't want Colby to wake up to Vic touching him like that. He was probably lucky he'd managed to get the boy upstairs without incident. Having Colby wake to Vic moving his limbs about, pulling and tugging and touching him all over, would have been too much.

Vic stood back and looked down at Colby, bundled up in what could very well be the first real bed of his life. His heart ached, and Vic had to tear himself away.

His need for the gym became urgent. There was no way he was going to get through this project without having some kind of outlet for himself.

* * *

COLBY MOANED softly as he woke, floating in a warm, fluffy embrace. He kept his eyes shut, wanting the sensation to last just in case it wasn't real, in case it was just the fantasy within his mental darkness.

He lingered there, cushioned and comfortably surrounded. He didn't feel quite as secure and contained as he did when the nice man in his fantasies scooped him up and carried him away, safe and warm, but it was close. If only he could hide away in that feeling forever.

Colby slowly opened his eyes, checking his surroundings. He was in bed again. In Vic's house. Not the basement. His breath came out in a shudder.

That made eight days three times plus one more that he'd woken up that way. Colby started counting them from the second morning he'd awoken to find himself tucked into bed after taking himself down to the basement, where he thought he belonged. He never knew how he got back to the bedroom. He could only assume Vic put him there, but they never talked about it. And, still, Vic never touched him, never did anything scary, every day taking him away from the basement, over and over. In seven days, it would be eight days four times, assuming it kept happening.

There was probably a number that came after eight, but Colby didn't know it. He'd only learned to count up to eight by hearing Bad Man say how many men were going to use him on any given night. After eight, the only other number Colby knew was eleven—that was the biggest party Bad Man had ever had—but he didn't know what came between the two. Vic had said something about teaching him numbers after he learned the basics of reading, but Colby wasn't really sure he wanted to know. It would just make him think of more and more men.

Then again, eight days three times plus one day was also the longest, by far, that he'd gone without being abused. It used to be, the longest had been just four days. *Four.* And now it was so many more than that. Colby frowned. He almost wished he knew the name of the number for that many days.

Then wondered what one more than that would be. And one more than that. And so on.

But that was all assuming he got to go another day without being used. So far, Vic seemed to be keeping his promise that no one would ever touch Colby like that again. But was he just tricking Colby? Trying to get Colby to let his guard down? Or did he genuinely intend to keep his promise?

Were more days of freedom really possible?

Colby burrowed down under the covers and clutched the pillow, staring at the door, wondering if Vic might come in. He never did without knocking first and asking Colby's permission. His permission! As if Colby were allowed to choose.

Though Vic sure made it sound like he was.

Colby groaned and pulled the sheets over his head. It was all too much.

Then he gasped and threw the covers back, staring at the door, holding his breath. The more comfortable he was, the more he'd have to pay. And after so many days of so many wonderful things, he was going to owe a lot. So much more than he thought either his body or his mind could take.

Footsteps approached, steady and firm—never hard and angry like Bad Man's had been—and a knock sounded at the door.

"*Colby?*"

Colby froze, clutching the covers.

"*You awake, kiddo?*"

Colby held his breath. It was just like every other morning, but what if this one turned out different?

"*Hey, champ, I'm just gonna peek in and check on you. Is that alright?*"

Colby didn't answer, and after a long moment, the handle slowly turned and the door inched open.

Vic peeked in, but didn't step inside the room. "Hey, kiddo," he said gently.

Colby tightened his hands in the sheets.

"How are you feeling this morning?" Vic asked.

Colby was never sure how to answer that. If he said *good*, Vic smiled, but feeling good had always meant he had to pay. At least, until Vic came along.

Vic didn't press him for an answer, and instead asked, "You wanna try coming out here to eat today?"

Colby shivered. The only time he'd been out of that room since Vic had brought him home was when he snuck down to the basement each night. And every day, Vic tried to get him to come out and eat or just sit and talk, but the house felt too big. Too open. Colby had only ever been allowed to stay in the rooms where he was put, so the thought of venturing out and being able to move through different spaces sounded both exhilarating and terrifying.

"Alright, that's fine," Vic said, a gentle smile on his face. "Why don't you get dressed, and I'll bring breakfast in here?"

Colby stared at him, not really giving any sort of answer, but Vic smiled again, shut the door, and walked away. As soon as Colby was sure Vic wasn't going to come right back that moment, he jumped out of bed, scrambled into his clothes, layering one thing on top of another until only his face and hands showed, then rushed to make the bed, fussing over every little tuck and wrinkle until it looked like it had never been slept in.

He was done just in time for Vic to knock at the door again. "*Colby? I've got breakfast.*"

Colby hesitated, then shuffled over and opened the door, knowing Vic would have his hands full. He quickly stepped aside and watched as Vic came into the room and set a tray on the dresser, just like he'd done for every other meal since the day after he'd brought Colby home.

"Mind if I join you?" Vic asked.

Colby gave a tiny shrug, then waited while Vic

picked up the tray again and set it on the floor. Vic sat beside it and picked up a plate.

"Mmmm, smells good," Vic said.

Colby's stomach growled, but he couldn't quite make himself sit down and touch the food. Not yet.

"I sure am hungry," Vic continued, making it sound like an off-hand comment, but after hearing Vic say that at every other meal, Colby was starting to pick up on the pattern.

The very first morning, Vic had brought in breakfast while Colby cowered in the corner, waiting to see what he'd have to pay for it. When Colby had refused to touch the food, Vic had pushed his own plate aside, saying they didn't have to eat if Colby didn't want to.

It hadn't made any sense. There was no reason Vic couldn't eat just because Colby wasn't doing so. Bad Man had always done whatever he wanted, and Colby could only do things by permission. But Vic was doing things differently.

Then Vic had said that he was really hungry, and that Colby could decide how much Vic got to eat. Vic told him that he would only take a bite after Colby did, so however much Colby felt like eating would determine how much Vic got to eat as well.

That first bite had been nerve-wracking. Colby had snatched up a piece of toast, taken a bite, and quickly swallowed, then waited. Vic took a single bite of his own food, and set down his fork again. He made no move to eat any more until Colby took another bite. Then another. Eventually, Colby lost track and wound up eating all his food without paying attention to whether Vic was matching his bites like he'd promised.

And Vic had looked so happy that Colby had finished his plate.

So the pattern continued, every meal, every day. Vic wouldn't eat until Colby began, matching his bites until Colby gave in to hunger and ate without paying attention.

Colby kept waiting for Vic to just take over or make Colby pay for food with his body, but it never happened.

Now Vic sat, patiently waiting, not making a move to touch his food. Finally, Colby knelt down across the tray from Vic, and slowly reached out, picking up a piece of toast and taking a quick bite before setting it down again.

Vic took a bite of his own, then waited.

Colby reached for a slice of bacon next, and as soon as the flavor hit his tongue, he let out an involuntary moan and started eating in earnest, already forgetting that he was supposed to be watching Vic to make sure the man followed his promise. The food was just too good. He'd never known what bacon was before Vic had introduced him to it.

So many wonderful things he'd been missing out on.

Before he knew it, his plate was empty, and Vic sat back with a sigh, looking at him with a smile. "Thanks, kiddo. I needed that."

Colby felt his lips twitch. That was also part of the pattern. Vic always thanked him when they were done. Colby had never been thanked for anything before. It was…strange. And nice.

"You wanna come help me do the dishes?" Vic asked.

Feeling full and relaxed, Colby considered it for half a second, then glanced at the open doorway and shrank back. All those rooms out there. It was just too big.

"Alright, that's fine," Vic said, just like always. He paused, then added, "Although…"

Colby froze. That was different. He braced himself.

Vic sighed and gave him a smile, shaking his head. "When you're ready, champ. I know it's gonna take some time to get used to things."

Colby let out the breath he was holding.

Vic frowned in thought for a moment, then asked, "Maybe tomorrow?" He got that careful look on his face, the one that always came right before he said something that was going to make Colby nervous. "I've got some friends coming over for rehearsal." Colby's eyes went wide and he felt his heart start racing. Vic was having a party? Vic held up a hand and rushed on: "They won't hurt you, kiddo. I promise. We just have some work to get done—we haven't been able to practice since I brought you home—and I thought it might be nice for you to meet some other people. People not like the Bad Man."

Colby stared at him, unable to speak. There were going to be other men in the house? He knew Vic was nice, and so far Vic was nothing like Bad Man, but everyone else he'd ever known *was*, so he wasn't ready to believe there were other nice people in the world, the people at the hospital notwithstanding.

"Think you can try to come out and visit when they're here?" Vic asked.

Colby tightly shook his head. He didn't want a party. Not again. Not ever.

"Alright," Vic rushed to assure him. "That's fine. You can hide out in here if you need."

Colby relaxed just slightly, grateful for Vic's permission, but that didn't mean things couldn't change. What if Vic was just trying to get him comfortable now, only to drag him out and let his friends use him when they came over? Could he trust that Vic meant what he said?

Then again, Vic had kept every promise he'd made so far.

So that night, as darkness fell and the house turned quiet, Colby hesitated at the bedroom door on his way down to the basement. Vic said he could sleep in the bed. Kept putting him there every morning after he'd snuck down to the basement. Colby glanced over his shoulder, eyeing the bed.

He wanted to sleep there so bad. It felt so good, unlike anything he'd ever known in his life.

If Vic found him there in the morning, would he be mad? Would he finally snap and punish Colby? Or would he have that proud smile on his face like he got sometimes?

Holding his breath, Colby pushed the door shut again as quietly as he could, and tiptoed back to the bed. He carefully pulled the sheets back, glanced at the door, listening for any sounds of approach, and dove under the covers, pulling them up to his chin. The bed felt so warm and soft against his naked body, but he couldn't relax. Not yet.

He stared at the door, waiting and listening.

Finally, comfort and exhaustion took over, and despite his worries for what the morning might bring, he drifted off into the best sleep he'd ever known in his life.

Chapter 9

VIC HELD his breath as he tiptoed down the hall on his way out to the gym. Colby's door was closed for a change. Vic crept forward, gently pressed the door handle, and inched the door open just enough to peek into the room.

He squinted into the dark, and smiled at the sight of a lump under the blankets. Vic opened the door a little wider, letting in the hall light, and looked again. Sure enough, Colby was sleeping in his bed.

The boy looked tense, like he was bracing himself for punishment even in his sleep, but at least he was there. Once Colby saw that Vic praised him rather than punished him for it, maybe the boy would finally allow himself to enjoy something he'd always been denied.

Vic quietly pulled the door shut and went off to the gym with a smile on his face.

An hour later, Vic got home, checked on Colby—the boy was still asleep, thank gods—then went to shower and change. It was probably ridiculous to still be wearing his suits every day, considering he had nowhere to be, but he couldn't let go of the routine of it all.

He was knotting his tie when he heard a crash.

Vic raced down the hall and knocked on Colby's door. "Colby?"

The boy whimpered.

"Colby, I'm coming in to check on you, alright?" he asked, then eased the door open.

He found Colby on the floor beside the bed, the sheets twisted out of place as though he'd gotten tangled in them and fallen. Vic flicked on the light to get a better look. A water glass lay broken beside the boy, and Colby's little feet were bloody.

The poor kid was also naked. Vic sighed. At least they'd made progress, getting Colby to sleep in his bed, but they still had a long way to go.

"Hey, kiddo–"

"I'm so sorry," Colby cried, his eyes wide with alarm. "I'll clean it up. I'm so sorry."

"Hey, shhh." Vic crouched down and kept his voice gentle. "Things happen, champ. But we need to take a look at those cuts." Vic pointed at Colby's feet. "Is it alright if I carry you to the sink so I can clean those up?"

Colby shrank back, whimpering, then slowly nodded.

Vic grabbed a throw blanket from the end of the bed and wrapped it around the boy, keeping his hands from contacting Colby's skin. He lifted the boy up, stepping carefully away from the glass, and carried Colby into the washroom. Setting the boy on the counter, he tucked the blanket more securely in place, then gently took hold of Colby's feet, holding them up over the sink so he could rinse away the blood and get a better look.

He plucked out one shard of glass, then narrowed his eyes, trying to see if there were any more.

"Don't move," Vic told him. "I'll be right back."

Colby went utterly still, and Vic hurried out of the room. He retrieved his scanner wand from his briefcase, then raced back to Colby's washroom and waved the scanner from heel to toe on each of Colby's feet. The readout indicated no other presence of glass, and no damage to muscles or tendons. Just small cuts through the skin.

Vic set the scanner aside, applied a medical adhesive that worked in place of stitches, and got Colby's feet bandaged up, telling Colby everything he was doing as he went along, hoping to set the boy at ease.

Once that was done, Vic carried Colby back into the bedroom and set him on the bed, then pulled out some clothes and set them within easy reach so Colby wouldn't have to walk across the room.

"I think we'll need to stay off those feet for a day or two, just in case," Vic suggested.

Colby ducked his head and tightened the blanket around him.

"Hey, kiddo, what's wrong?"

"I'm sorry," Colby whispered, glancing at the mess on the floor.

"No. Hey. Colby, you're not in trouble." Vic crouched down at the foot of the bed, putting himself slightly lower than the boy. "Accidents happen." He started to reach for the boy, then stopped himself and pulled his arm back. "Did you fall out of bed?"

Colby gave one slow nod. "Had a bad dream. Woke up and forgot where I was, and..." He glanced at the mess again. "I'm sorry." He flinched back as though expecting to be punished.

"Colby," Vic said, then waited until the boy looked at him. "It's just an accident. Alright? We make mistakes, or make messes, and that's how we learn. It's just a glass. We'll clean it up, no problem. I'm not mad, kiddo. You're not in trouble."

Colby whimpered as he fidgeted and ducked his head again, watching Vic out of the corner of his eye as Vic left to grab a broom and dustpan, sweeping up the mess and taking it away.

"See?" Vic said. "All better."

The boy curled in on himself even more.

"Talk to me," Vic murmured. "What's going on?"

Colby fidgeted again, then said, "You're not gonna beat me like the puppy?"

"What puppy?"

Colby looked down, and mumbled, "Bad Man had a puppy, and it got into the basement, but it wasn't supposed to, and it had an accident, but before I could clean it up, Bad Man stepped in it, and he got real mad. He–" Colby whined, a brief, high-pitched sound so full of anguish that Vic felt his heart break again. "He got a stick and...and hit the puppy until it stopped moving." Colby's voice trailed off into a barely audible whisper at the end, like he couldn't bear to even say the words aloud.

Oh gods. Vic cringed at the image that those words conjured up, the poor boy having to stand by helplessly and watch as Ahriman beat a puppy to death. Was there no end to the doctor's cruelty?

He was just about to say something to comfort the boy when the doorbell rang.

Colby gasped, his eyes going wide.

"That'll be the guys," Vic realized aloud, checking his watch. "You wanna get dressed and come meet everyone?"

Colby whimpered and tightly shook his head.

"They won't hurt you, kiddo."

Colby shook his head again.

"Alright. That's fine. You can stay in here. Just try to stay off those feet as much as possible, yeah?"

Colby clutched the blanket but didn't say anything, watching in silence as Vic got up and left the room.

Vic shut the door, blew out a breath, and went to let in his visitors.

Zac, Adrian, Ryley, and Asher had all arrived at once, the lot of them spilling into the house and sharing hugs and handshakes all around.

"Where's the little guy?" Ryley asked.

Zac pointed right at Ryley, a goofy smirk on his face. Everyone laughed.

"Wha–" Ryley started to ask, then looked at each person in turn. "Oh." He rolled his eyes. Ryley himself was, by far, the shortest of the bunch, the only one of them under six feet. "Hey, at least I'm taller than him," Ryley said, gesturing vaguely to indicate Colby.

Zac patted Ryley on the head with his left hand, the movement striking Vic as forced, though he couldn't quite say why he got that impression. "Sure thing, pipsqueak."

"Fuck off," Ryley joked, playfully slapping Zac's

hand away, then looked at Vic. "How's it going with him, by the way?"

Vic glanced at Colby's door, then huffed out a breath. "Starting to get better, I think. It's gonna be a long process."

"Well, if anyone can handle it, it's you," Ryley assured him.

Vic nodded his thanks, though he still wasn't totally convinced he was equipped to give Colby everything the boy needed.

"Drinks?" he asked, changing the subject. He got everyone settled in, and while Adrian and Asher looked on, Vic, Zac, and Ryley discussed their plan for rehearsal while tuning their instruments and taking their places in the living room.

Vic started off the first piece, the notes sounding rusty and jarring until the violins joined in. He looked up at Ryley and Zac, trying to focus. The piece was an old favorite of theirs, one he should have been able to play in his sleep, but it just wasn't coming out right.

Halfway through, Ryley swung his bow out to the side and called, "Stop. Stop." A screeching halt sounded as Vic and Zac both stopped their own bows. Ryley sighed. "Vic, this piece is supposed to be *romantic*, not...I don't know...stalker-ish."

Zac snorted a laugh.

"I know, I'm sorry," Vic said. He blew out a breath, and tried to find the right headspace. *Romantic*. The best he could do with that was try to recall how it felt to play with Ryley when they'd been together. Probably not an ideal thought with Asher sitting right there, but it was all he had to work with. He looked at Ryley and gave a nod.

"From the top," Ryley said, and he and Zac both lifted their bows, waiting for Vic to start them off again.

Vic took a deep breath, set his bow to the strings, and started to play, drawing out that first soulful note. It still didn't sound quite right, but he ran with it, and moved on to the next note, then looked across the room, trying to ignore all the sets of eyes on him.

Straight ahead, right in his line of sight, he saw Colby's door open. Just a few inches, just enough for the boy to peek out, but enough for Vic to see Colby staring at him.

Vic frowned, and kept playing, watching the boy. After a few seconds, Colby inched the door open even more, then again until the gap was wide enough for him to crawl through. The boy shuffled forward on his hands and knees, keeping close to the wall.

His eyes never left Vic's hands.

Vic stared, playing purely by muscle memory as he watched Colby inch closer and closer. He couldn't even begin to guess what the boy was thinking or feeling, but if it got him out of his room—and with strangers in the house—it had to be good.

Colby stopped where the hallway opened up into the living room, and shrank back slightly. Vic kept playing, and waited. After a moment, Colby darted forward and hid behind the chair in which Adrian sat, then slowly leaned to one side to peek around it, his eyes still focused on Vic's hands.

Somehow, Vic kept playing without any conscious effort. A small part of his brain wondered if he was even doing it right, except that Ryley hadn't called another stop to things, but all he could really focus on was Colby.

The little guy was absolutely *riveted*.

And the sight of it was doing all sorts of horribly delicious things to Vic's body.

The piece came to an end, the final notes fading off into silence until Vic heard Ryley say, "Wow."

Vic blinked, tore his eyes away from Colby, and looked up at the man. "What?"

Ryley was staring at him. So was Zac, for that matter.

"I–" Ryley began, then blinked and shook his head like he was trying to get his thoughts in order. "I don't think I've ever heard you play with so much…"

"Feeling?" Zac supplied, looking just as dumbfounded as Ryley.

"I was going to say *passion*," Ryley said.

Vic frowned, not quite following what they were getting at.

"What the hells got into you just now?" Ryley asked.

Vic's eyes darted back to Colby's face. The little guy was still there, huddled behind Adrian's chair, staring intently at Vic and looking like he was both ready to bolt and hungry for more of whatever Vic could play.

Hoping Colby couldn't see it past the chair, Vic held out his bow arm and pressed down as he looked at all the other men, silently telling them to stay still and quiet. Ryley frowned, then glanced in the direction Vic had been looking. The man leaned slightly, trying to peek around Adrian's chair, then his eyebrows went up and he mouthed, "Oh."

"What?" Zac whispered, leaning close to him.

Ryley tucked his arm close to his chest and pointed. Zac started to look, then turned to Vic instead and raised his eyebrows in question. Vic nodded.

Zac cleared his throat. "So, how about we try *Celestial Light* next?" he asked pointedly.

Vic gave him a grateful smile when he saw everyone else catch on. They were going to pretend Colby wasn't there, not wanting to spook the boy.

The three musicians raised their bows and started to play. Vic only got through the first few notes before he looked at Colby, and once again, the boy's complete attention was on Vic's hands.

Vic's hands, playing a piece that Vic had composed, and it was enough to rouse the boy from his room despite his fears. The thought sent a bolt of desire right to Vic's core.

Oh gods. He was in so much trouble.

Chapter 10

VIC LET out a heavy sigh when Ryley called for a break about an hour later. He was in such a state that he didn't dare set his cello aside quite yet, but he needed the music to stop. Even for just a few minutes. The sheer awe on Colby's face hadn't diminished one bit throughout the rehearsal, keeping Vic's heart racing the whole time.

To say nothing of the uncomfortable crowding in his pants.

It had to be a fluke. It *had* to be. He just hadn't been touched by another person in too long, and music had always been closely associated with arousal. That was all it was. Just a habitual reaction. He wasn't attracted to the boy. He *couldn't* be.

But—*Fuck!*—now that he thought about it, Colby was *exactly* his type.

Small, slender, almost fragile. Beautiful, with a touch of the fae to his features. Innocent in so many ways. And he needed Vic. That was the part that always got him. If someone needed Vic, it was impossible to resist.

The others got up and stretched and moved around, and Vic glanced at Colby. The awe on the boy's face was slowly giving way to fear as he crouched behind the chair, listening to all the activity and waiting to be discovered.

Shit. Colby needed Vic right now.

Shoving arousal to the back of his mind, Vic set his cello aside, stood from the couch, and took the rocking chair right beside it instead, Colby's big, beautiful eyes fixed on him the whole time.

Vic took a deep breath, wondering if this was a monstrously bad idea—for both of them—and held out a hand. "Come here, champ."

Colby let out a tiny whimper, then scrambled forward and crawled up into Vic's lap, his little hands clutching the lapels of Vic's jacket as he sat there, shaking.

The room slowly fell quiet, and Vic risked a glance at his friends, certain they'd see on his face just how much he was struggling. Instead, all he found were looks of concern, their attentions all focused on the boy.

After a brief hesitation, Ryley took a step forward and crouched down. "H-Hey, kiddo."

Colby ducked his head, clinging to Vic as he peeked out at Ryley from the corner of his eye.

Vic took another deep breath. He needed to focus. Clearing his throat, he asked, "Do you remember Ryley?"

Colby gave a tight shake of his head.

"He was there when we found you," Vic explained. "He got us to the hospital when you stopped breathing."

Colby's shaking stopped for a split second. "Oh," he whispered, then took up trembling again, though it wasn't quite as severe as before.

Ryley fidgeted nervously, then his eyes lit up. "Hey, you wanna see something cool?" He waved his hand, and a column of smoke swirled up from his palm, dancing and changing colors for a few seconds until it melted away.

Colby lifted his head slightly, and Ryley grinned, all the tension fading out of him. Vic caught his eye, and Ryley gave him a subtle nod, telling him that he was alright.

Then Asher came over and crouched down beside Ryley, slipping an arm around Ryley's waist. "Hey, kiddo," Asher murmured. "I'm Asher. I'm Ryley's boyfriend."

Colby tensed again, eyeing him warily.

Ryley nudged Asher with his elbow, and told Colby,

"I know he probably looks big and scary, but he's a total softy. Just like Vic."

"Oh," Colby whispered, still curled up tight but now looking at Asher with more curiosity than alarm.

Vic bent down, just stopped himself from kissing the top of Colby's head, and murmured, "They won't hurt you, champ. I promise."

Ryley shifted aside and pointed up at Zac and Adrian, standing just across the room. "That's Adrian," he introduced. "He's really shy and quiet, too, but he's super nice." Adrian gave Colby a shy nod. "And that's Zac, Adrian's boyfriend."

Zac gave Colby a silly grin. "Hey, kid. Nice to meet you."

Adrian mumbled the same, and reached up to rest a hand on the back of Zac's neck, clearly needing to be grounded. He was doing so much better than he had in the past, but his social anxiety still popped up now and then, and Vic could only imagine that having to face a boy who had endured as much torment as Colby had was bringing up memories of the verbal abuse Adrian had suffered from his own father.

Unfortunately, Colby's eyes followed Adrian's hand, drawing his attention to Zac's collar.

Colby shrieked and threw his arms up over his head.

"Colby?" Vic asked, seeing all his friends look on with concern as he tried to comfort the boy. "Hey, champ, it's alright."

Colby shook his head tightly from under his arms, and whispered, "Bad man?"

"No, kiddo. No, Adrian is really good."

Colby shivered, peeked out at Zac again, then looked up at Vic from under his eyelashes. "But he has a collar."

Vic nodded slowly. How was he going to explain this? "Because he wants to," he began, and Colby's eyes went wide. "Sometimes, people *like* wearing collars. It's...a sign of commitment. Zac loves Adrian, so he wants to show the world that he belongs to him." He paused, then added, "And Adrian belongs to Zac, too, though he doesn't necessarily have to wear anything to show it."

"Um, about that..." Zac said.

Vic looked up and saw a blush creep over Zac's cheeks as a giddy smile took over his face.

"Since none of you noticed earlier," Zac continued, then he cleared his throat and looked at Adrian before grabbing Adrian's left hand with his own and thrusting both out for everyone to see.

Vic stared for a long moment, taking in the sight of them wearing matching rings.

Ryley gasped. "You got *married*?" He let out a shout of surprise and darted across the room to hug the couple.

Vic blinked. Zac and Adrian were *married*?

"When did this happen?" Asher asked, voicing Vic's own thoughts.

Zac took both of Adrian's hands, looking up at his boyfriend—*No, husband, apparently*—and shrugged, still wearing a big grin. "Yesterday," he said, turning to look at the others. "It was kind of on a whim. We ran into a little paperwork snag trying to combine our banks accounts last week–"

Adrian actually spoke up, adding, "Which I'd been trying to get him to do for months." He shot Zac a fond yet exasperated look. "I mean, we bought a house together, and we're committed to each other. It only made sense that our money should be *our* money."

"Even though it's mostly *your* money," Zac pointed out.

"Ours," Adrian insisted, using a firm tone that Vic had never heard come out of the man.

Zac shuddered just noticeably, blushing again, then said, "*Anyway.*" He cleared his throat. "The bank told us it would all be easier if we had a marriage contract on file, so…" He shrugged. "We just did it."

Ryley squawked. "And you didn't invite us?" he asked, gesturing at everyone in the room.

Adrian ducked his head, so Zac answered, "We didn't want it to be a big deal. The thought of a big wedding was kinda overwhelming for both of us, and—hells—we were already living together, so…"

"It was just a formality at that point," Adrian mumbled.

At that, Ryley seemed to finally remember that Adrian was nowhere near outgoing as him and probably couldn't have handled a big celebration, anyway. He took a step forward and gently hugged the couple again.

"Sorry, you're right. Congratulations, though. I'm so happy for you guys."

Zac and Adrian hugged him back, the former more exuberantly than the latter, then Ryley whirled around and looked at Asher.

"Maybe we should just do that someday," Ryley joked. "Elope. Just run off somewhere and get hitched."

Asher closed his eyes and sighed, then looked all around the room before focusing on Ryley again. "I had this whole thing planned for after dinner tonight, but…" He pulled a ring out of his pocket and dropped to one knee.

Ryley gasped and covered his face with both hands, then quickly lowered them. "Oh my gods, Ash! Are you serious?"

Asher nodded shyly.

Ryley let out an unmanly squeal and threw himself at Asher. "Yes! Oh my gods, yes!"

Zac barked a laugh, and even Adrian grinned as Asher slipped the ring onto Ryley's finger and pulled his new fiancé in for a kiss.

Vic held Colby a little tighter in his lap, his heart racing in his chest. Zac and Adrian were married, and now Ryley and Asher were engaged? A pang of longing shot through him. He wanted that. *Gods*, how he wanted that.

"Vic?" Colby whispered, cutting into his thoughts.

Vic blinked and tore his eyes away from the two happy couples before him, and looked down at the boy in his lap. He cleared his throat. "What's up, kiddo?"

Colby eyed Ryley and Asher, then looked up at Vic again. "What are they doing?" he whispered.

Vic glanced at the couple, then looked down at Colby. "They're kissing." His eyes darted to Colby's lips, and he had to force his gaze away. "It's something people do when they love each other." *Or attracted to each other...*

"Why?" Colby asked.

"Because...it feels good?" Vic answered, his tone making it almost sound like a question. How else could he explain the nuances of love and romance to someone who had never been exposed to either?

"Oh," Colby whispered, yet he still frowned, looking totally confused. "It looks...strange," he said, but rather than showing more confusion, his face only registered a faint distaste.

And no wonder, Vic thought, when he considered how Colby's mouth had been forcibly used all his life.

Which instantly put an image in Vic's mind of using Colby's mouth the same way, those full lips stretched around his cock while those big, beautiful eyes looked up at him.

Fuck. Vic squeezed his eyes shut and shook his head. He shouldn't be thinking like that. Not now. Not *ever*.

"Right, Vic?"

Vic blinked and looked up. "What?"

Ryley nodded at Colby. "He said kissing looked strange, so I told him it was perfectly normal. Right?"

"Oh." Vic cleared his throat, trying to focus. How the hells had he missed Ryley speaking? "Right." He shoved the thoughts aside and looked down at Colby again. "Yeah, perfectly normal." He scrambled for an explanation, and his brief fantasy, awful as it was, handed him the perfect idea. "What the Bad Man did? That wasn't normal. Not at all. But this?" He waved a hand at the two couples being all sweet and sappy in the middle of his living room. "This is what normal people do. Meet someone you like, fall in love, kiss, make a commitment to each other..." Vic trailed off before he could add *make love* to that list. Colby had a lot to learn about the real world, and Vic wasn't sure the boy was ready to handle the concept of sex that was not only pleasurable but consensual.

And didn't *that* just put all sorts of delicious images in his head.

Vic struggled to push the thoughts aside, trying to come up with anything that would keep his cock from going rock-hard right below where Colby was perched on his lap. That was the last thing the poor kid needed.

To say nothing of himself.

* * *

COLBY CRAWLED up into the rocking chair after Vic's friends left. He nudged the chair into motion and drew his knees up, hugging them to his chest as he watched Vic lock the front door and walk back into the living room.

"How are you feeling?" Vic asked, grabbing the big thing that made the pretty sounds and carrying it across the room.

Colby eyed the thing, wishing he could hear it again even though he'd been listening to it almost all morning. He'd never heard anything like it before.

"Colby?"

Colby tore his eyes away from the thing and looked up at Vic's face. The man was just standing there, holding the thing and watching him.

"Oh." What had Vic asked? "Um…" Colby thought about it for a moment, and found himself almost smiling. Being out of the bedroom and around all those people had been nerve-wracking, but the pretty sounds had made it all worthwhile. More than worthwhile. He wondered just what he'd give to hear those sounds again. "Good," he whispered.

A smile slowly appeared on Vic's face. "Good." He tucked the thing into a box, then sat on the couch a few feet away, watching Colby again. "I'm so proud of you, kiddo. You did so good today."

Colby found himself almost smiling again, and glanced across the room at the box.

Vic glanced over his shoulder, then looked at Colby again. "You really liked that, didn't you?"

Colby nodded.

Vic frowned for a moment, then asked, "Had you never heard music before?"

Music. So that's what the sound was called. Colby shook his head.

"Hmmm." Vic reached into his jacket and pulled out his phone. He tapped through a few things, then set it on the table just as more music started playing.

Colby gasped, staring at the phone. "It can do music, too?" he asked, blurting out the question without thinking.

Vic nodded. "It's a recording." He gestured at the room. "Zac, Ryley, and I recorded some of our music a while back for– Gods, I'm not even sure how to explain a recording contract," he mumbled, then shook his head. "Anyway, this is one of my favorites. Just the cello."

Colby tilted his head.

Vic pointed at the box. "That's a cello. What Zac and Ryley were playing is called a violin."

"Oh." Colby looked from the phone to the box and back. He'd really liked it when they all played together, but he decided he *loved* the cello. It was so beautiful.

"You know," Vic said, getting that tone of voice that indicated he was going to suggest something he wanted Colby to do, "if you come out of your room again tomorrow, I can play some more for you."

Colby brightened at that. He could hear more music? And watch Vic play it?

Definitely worth braving the expanse of the house and leaving the dark confines of the room.

He gave a tiny nod, and Vic grinned.

"And how was it having the guys here?" Vic asked.

Colby froze, then nudged the rocking chair into motion again. It had felt so nice when Vic had held him in that chair and made it rock back and forth. He wasn't sure why it felt good, exactly, only that it did. He drew his hands into his sleeves and tucked them up under his chin.

"They're good guys," Vic said when Colby didn't answer. "I know new people must be scary for you, but I hope you'll give them a chance."

Colby gave a shy nod. It *had* been scary, but not one of them had made a move to touch him. Every other man Colby had ever known had gone straight to hurting him in some way. But not Vic. And not Vic's friends. They all talked to him nicely and kept their distance.

Except with each other. All the men touched each other, but all in nice ways. It was so strange to see Asher put an arm around Ryley or Zac hold hands with Adrian. All those touches were so nice and gentle. Just like how Vic touched him.

"Vic?"

"Yeah, buddy?"

Colby thought for a moment, then asked, "You said your friends weren't like Bad Man, right?"

"Right."

Colby thought again. "So then they don't have sex?"

Vic spluttered for a moment, then said, "No, they do. Just...with each other." His eyes widened, and he rushed to add, "I mean Zac and Adrian only have sex with each other, and the same with Ryley and Asher. They don't share with other people, and definitely don't force anyone."

"Oh." Colby frowned again, then looked up at Vic, studying him, trying to reason through it all. "Is that where you go every morning? To have sex with someone?"

Vic looked taken aback, then shook his head. "No. I go to the gym." He paused, and when Colby gave him a confused look, he added, "It's a place for exercise. To get strong and healthy."

"Oh." Colby drew back a bit more. "Then when do you have sex?" he asked in a whisper.

Vic shrugged. "I don't. Not lately."

Colby's eyes went wide.

"I haven't in a long time," Vic added. "Just...haven't found the right person." Colby thought Vic's gaze flicked down to his mouth, but he couldn't be sure, it happened so fast.

And if Vic didn't have his own person for having sex

with like his friends had, did that mean it was only a matter of time before Vic used Colby, despite his promises?

Vic straightened, searching Colby's face like he could read his thoughts. "Not everyone has sex regularly. And some people don't want it at all. Like I said, Bad Man was an extreme." He paused, then held up his hands. "There's lots of people in the world. Some are good." He moved one hand out to the side, then did the same with the other hand, leaving a wide space between them. "Some are bad. Bad Man was way over here," he continued, shaking his left hand, "but there are lots of people over on this side." Vic waved his right hand, then lowered both to his lap and tilted his head in thought. "How did you figure out he was bad, anyway?"

Colby frowned. "I don't understand."

"Well, it's just…people learn good from bad through experience, and considering how young you were when he took you and how that life was all you knew…I'm just wondering how you managed to come to that conclusion if you had no basis for comparison."

"Oh." Colby's chest ached. The answer to that was easy, and it made him hurt all over.

VIC WAITED, watching the boy, wondering what was going through his head. A long moment of silence passed, and Vic wasn't sure the boy was going to answer.

"Colby?"

Colby fidgeted, then scrambled out of the rocking chair and crawled over to Vic, climbing up into his lap. The move surprised him—Colby had endured a lot more human interaction that day than he had in weeks—but it looked as though the need for comfort outweighed his fear of being too close to people.

Vic drew him up close, keeping him contained and warm, and felt Colby relax slightly. *Thank gods*. Maybe the boy was making progress, after all.

"It was the puppy," Colby whispered. He glanced up at Vic's face, and went on: "I'd never seen anything like it before. It was so cute and soft and warm. It looked so happy, and it wanted to play with me. And it curled up in my lap and fell asleep, and it felt so good." Colby paused, and Vic saw tears shimmer in his eyes. "But then Bad Man got mad because puppy had its accident..."

Vic sighed and pulled him close. "I'm so sorry, kiddo."

Colby sobbed, hugging his arms to his chest as he burrowed into Vic's embrace. "Why did he do it, Vic? Why did he have to hurt the puppy? It was so scared, and hurting, but Bad Man didn't stop."

Vic squeezed his eyes shut and tried to rock the boy as he held him. The poor, sweet kid. Having to stand by and watch, helpless, as Ahriman took out his fury on a small, defenseless creature.

Colby ducked his head and cried, so Vic held him in silence, rubbing his back and murmuring soft, soothing sounds to him. It was too bad Ahriman was already dead. Vic would have loved to have a chance to rip the man apart for all the things he'd done.

He looked down at the boy, and got an idea.

"Hey, champ?"

Colby sniffed and slowly looked up at him as tears kept running down his cheeks.

"What if we got a puppy?" Vic asked. "Would you like that?"

Colby's tears stopped and his eyes brightened for a split second—just long enough for Vic to catch it—before his face crumpled again and he shrank in on himself. "No," Colby sobbed.

"No?"

Colby shook his head. "I don't want you to hurt it if it has an accident."

"Oh, kiddo." Vic hugged him tight. "I wouldn't do that. Hey, look at me." He waited until Colby slowly looked up from under his eyelashes. "I'd be firm with it, yeah, if it ever misbehaved, but I'd never hurt it. Not like that."

Colby sniffed. "You wouldn't beat it with a stick?"

"No. Never."

"You promise?"

"I promise. Besides..." Vic trailed off, thinking. "You know, my brother and I always wanted a dog when we were kids, but our dad didn't allow it." He paused, then added, "And once I started working, I was at the office so much that it seemed cruel to leave a dog home alone all the time." To say nothing of the fact that Vic rarely had a steady place of his own, anyway, spending most of his adulthood, until recently, bouncing from friend's couch to hotel room to boyfriend's bed. "But now..." Vic looked around. He had a house, and a yard, and was home all the time. And even if he weren't home, Colby would be. At least, until the boy decided he wanted to leave. "What would you think of that?"

Colby stared intently at Vic, a combination of hope and fear warring in his eyes before he gave an unsure nod.

Vic smiled, warming to the idea the more he thought about it. Having a dog in the house would liven things up a bit, not to mention giving Colby another source of comfort. And that didn't even touch on the fact that dogs made great therapy aids, giving someone something to focus on outside of himself, something to take care of. Maybe, one day, the simple need to walk the dog would even get Colby outside.

"Hmmm." That got him thinking. He looked at Colby again. "Now, having a dog is a responsibility. We'll have to give it food and water every day, and make sure it gets exercise, and train it so it behaves. You think you can help me with that? If we get a dog, do you think you can come out of your room every day and help me take care of it?"

Colby nodded, his eyes wide with hope.

Vic smiled. "Good." Maybe Cam would like it, too. Then again, would the dog be able to handle an invisible, tangible presence? Vic would have to take the ghost along with him when he picked out a dog, just to see what happened.

Colby shrieked, scrambling to curl up tighter in Vic's lap.

Vic froze, then held the boy closer. *What the hells?* "Colby? Hey, kiddo, what's wrong?"

Colby whimpered.

"Colby?"

"There's someone here," the boy whispered.

Vic frowned. "What?" He looked all around, but the room was empty.

Colby whimpered again. "There's someone here," he repeated.

Vic opened his mouth to say something, then looked up when he saw one of Cam's notepads fly across the room while a pen hurriedly scribbled out a note.

Can he see me?!

Vic stared at the words, then looked down at the trembling boy in his arms.

"Colby?" he asked, heart thudding in his chest. Was it possible? "Hey, kiddo? What did you see?"

Colby trembled and slowly peeked out, staring at the spot where the notepad hovered. "It's a boy," he whispered.

Vic stared at Colby, then up at Cam's notepad. He slowly shook his head in awe.

"Yeah," he answered Cam. "Yeah, I think he can."

Chapter 11

VIC GOT Colby tucked into bed and shut the bedroom door, leaving the boy to rest in the dark. The poor kid had endured one hell of an overwhelming day as it was, only to have yet another stranger's presence thrown at him.

And just the fact that he could *see* Cam…

Vic sank onto the couch with a sigh.

Is he alright? Cam wrote, the notepad hovering at Vic's side as though Cam sat right next to him.

Vic blew out a breath. "I think so?" He shook his head. "I'd been putting off telling him about you, but I never would have guessed he could actually see you."

Seriously. Cam paused, then the pen wrote, *I peeked in on him when he was sleeping a couple times, but I tried to stay away other than that. I didn't want him freaking out if he saw me accidentally move something.*

Vic nodded slowly.

Shit. Is that gonna set him back if you tell him I've been here all along? It looked like he was finally starting to open up to you, and if I've ruined that–

"Hey." Vic reached out until he encountered resistance, then slipped an arm around Cam's shoulders. "Don't worry about it, kiddo. Besides, you know you're my priority."

Cam nudged him with his elbow. *He's important, too.*

Vic nodded. There was no arguing that point.

So I guess that means he's Tanasian, right? Like Summer?

Vic nodded. Summer Vas-kelen was one of Vic's clients—she'd technically been a rescue case—and was married to Athan, the man with whom Ryley had been cheating on Vic back when Vic and Ryley had been together. Now, oddly enough, Athan was a friend.

Summer was a bit odd—she had a tendency to see the world in her own, unique way thanks to the mental deficiencies with which she'd been born—but she was also a genius in addition to having the telepathic abilities that ran in Tanasian bloodlines. It was Summer who first saw Cam, and pointed out to Vic that the ghost was following him around. She got them started on the way toward developing a means of communication so that Vic could get Cam the therapy he needed.

It all came far too late, and was nowhere as efficient as being able to speak to one another face-to-face like the living could, but at least they had anything at all.

But Colby could see Cam? And both boys had suffered similar traumas. Maybe they would bond over it, or heal together. Hells, maybe Cam could finally have a *friend* as well as someone in his life other than just Vic. It seemed too good to be true.

Vic read Cam's words again, thinking them over. "Hmmm, yeah…" He pulled out his phone and called the hospital.

"*Denmer General*," the receptionist answered. "*How may I help you?*"

"Hi, this is Victor Lucius with Sturmwyn Insurance. Is Nurse Kristi there by chance?"

"*Let me check. Just one moment…Yes, she is. I'll transfer you.*"

"Thank you."

Vic heard a *beep*, and glanced at Cam's notepad as he waited. He probably could have gotten the information straight from the receptionist, but it would have required a lot more convincing on his part since Colby didn't have an insurance policy that listed Vic as his agent. Kristi, however, could skirt hospital policy. She'd been there when he'd brought Colby in, so she'd know exactly why Vic needed her to make an exception.

"*Thank you for holding. This is Kristi.*"

"Hey, Kristi, it's Vic Lucius."

"*Vic! Hey, how are you? Haven't seen you around here in a few weeks.*" She paused for a split second, then added, "*Though, of course, that's a good thing.*"

"Yeah," Vic said with a nod. Rescuing a kidnapped or disowned kid was one thing. Having to take that kid in for treatment of burns, scars, sexual assault, or other abuse always made a case so much worse. "Listen, I need a favor."

"*Sure thing. What's up?*"

"You remember Colby?"

Kristi sucked in an audible breath. "*Yeah. How could I forg– Wait, is he alright? Did something happen?*"

"No, he's fine," Vic rushed to assure her. "Still has a long way to go, but he's getting a little better every day."

Kristi sighed. "*Good. Thank gods. That poor kid.*"

"Yeah. Anyway, we had an interesting situation, and I was wondering if your lab could run a genetic analysis on his blood work."

"*Yeah, of course.*" Vic heard the rapid clicking of keys. "*Anything particular they should be looking for?*"

"See if he has any genetic markers for Tanasian ancestry," Vic said, then paused, thinking it over, before he added, "Actually, if you could run his mother's DNA for the same thing, that would be great."

"*Do we have– Oh, that's right. That was the only other record tied to his.*" Kristi kept typing rapidly for a few seconds, then said, "*Done. I'll send you the results as soon as I get them.*"

"Thanks, Kristi."

"*Anytime, Vic.*"

Vic pocketed his phone, and looked over when he saw Cam writing again.

And are we really getting a dog?!

* * *

COLBY WOKE from his nap and heard Vic's voice coming from the living room. There were weird pauses between everything Vic said. He must have been talking on the phone.

Colby rubbed his eyes and looked around, though he couldn't see much in the dark room. He wasn't sure how Vic had done it, but he'd made almost all the light go away even during daytime. It made the room feel so safe. Made it hard to leave.

But Vic had promised him more music if he came out of the room. Granted, that wouldn't happen again until tomorrow. That was what Vic had said. So Colby had until then to work up the nerve to actually open the door and crawl out.

Especially since there was someone else in the house. Someone Vic hadn't warned him about. It *almost* seemed like Vic hadn't even known the boy was there.

Footsteps approached, and a knock sounded. "*Colby? You awake, kiddo?*"

Colby hesitated. He was still tense from all the activity of the morning, and just wanted to stay hiding out in the dark. Alone. But he knew Vic would look in on him anyway, and he didn't want Vic to be mad, not after Vic had promised him more music.

He was just about to respond when Vic said, "*Hey, champ, if you're up, I'm just gonna check on you. Is that alright?*"

Colby still didn't respond, but the door handle slowly turned, and the door inched open.

Vic looked in and gave him a smile. "Hey, kiddo. How are you feeling? Did you get any sleep?"

Colby nodded shyly, his hands tightening around the edge of the pillow.

Vic opened the door a little wider, and nodded to one side. "You wanna come out and meet Cam?"

Colby shook his head, and drew his knees up to his chest.

"Hey, that's alright," Vic murmured. He slowly came

into the room and perched on the side of the bed. "Been kind of an overwhelming day, hasn't it?"

Colby nodded.

Vic smiled. "You did so great though, champ. I'm so proud of you."

Colby's hands loosened around the edge of the pillow.

"Maybe you can meet Cam tomorrow, huh? 'Cause he really wants to meet you." Vic paused, then added, "Officially."

Colby frowned. He wasn't quite sure what that meant, but he wasn't ready to ask.

"Anyway," Vic went on, "are you hungry? You passed out before we could have lunch, and I was just about to go make dinner."

Colby's stomach growled loud enough for them both to hear.

Vic chuckled. "Guess that answers that question. Tell you what: I'll go make something and bring it in here, and then maybe tomorrow we can try eating at the dining table instead. How does that sound?"

Colby nodded, grateful for a chance to hide out in the room before he had to face walking out that door again. It would be worth it tomorrow if Vic kept his promise about the music. For now, though, he needed to recover.

"Alright." Vic smiled, then reached out and ran a hand through Colby's hair.

Colby froze, heart thudding in his chest as his vision tunneled down to nothing.

Vic said something else, but Colby didn't hear it.

He disappeared within his mental darkness.

VIC RAN his fingers through Colby's hair, unable to resist touching the boy, and said, "I'll be right back, alright?"

Colby didn't answer. Vic waited, thinking maybe the boy was just being shy again, but then he realized that Colby was staring blankly at something, not blinking, barely breathing.

"Colby?" Vic pulled his hand back. "Kiddo? What's wrong?"

Colby didn't move. He lay there, frozen, staring into nothingness.

Vic waved a hand in front of the boy's face and got no response. He held his fingers near Colby's lips, and felt tiny panted breaths, then pressed his fingers to Colby's neck, and felt a rapid pulse.

Shit. Panic response. Vic had no idea what he'd done to set it off, but he had to ease the boy back out of it. A cold shock might do it, but the poor kid had endured enough stimulation for one day. He looked all around, then stood up and grabbed the blankets, pulling them up over Colby's head.

Colby always said the dark was safe. Maybe the dark would help him come back.

The boy was utterly still for several seconds, then Vic saw movement under the blankets. Colby poked his head out, blinking slowly as though he didn't know where he was.

Vic crouched down so he wouldn't be towering over the boy. "Hey, kiddo," he murmured.

Colby looked at him, then glanced all around before returning his focus to Vic's face. "This isn't the basement," he whispered.

"No, champ. It's your room. And you're safe here."

Colby frowned. "Bad Man..." he whispered, then trailed off, shaking his head in confusion before some sort of realization dawned on his face. "Oh," he mouthed, then looked warily at Vic.

"I'm so sorry, kiddo. I didn't mean to scare you."

Colby didn't say anything, but his expression did ease just noticeably.

Vic hesitated, then asked, "Can you tell me what I did wrong so that I won't do it again?"

Colby gave a tiny whimper and drew back, tucking his hands up under his chin while he clutched the edges of the blankets in his little fists. After a moment, he whispered, "My hair."

Vic started to nod. "You don't like your hair touched?"

Colby gave a single, slow shake of his head.

"Can you tell me why?" Vic asked.

Colby hunched a tiny bit more. "Bad Man."

Vic nodded. He'd figured as much, but that still didn't really explain it. "Can you tell me what he did?"

Colby's eyes flicked down to Vic's waist, then quickly away, barely opening his mouth as he spoke: "He'd hold my hair so I couldn't get away."

Vic cringed, an awful picture filling his imagination: Colby on his knees, his mouth being forcibly drawn onto Ahriman's cock until he choked. The poor kid probably thought Vic was going to do the same, now.

Which instantly brought back the fantasy of Colby going down on Vic, those perfect lips sucking him deep while his beautiful eyes looked up at him…

Vic inwardly cursed and tried to shut down that train of thought. He couldn't be letting his imagination run that way, wrong on more levels than he could possibly count. Vic cleared his throat and shook his head.

"How about…" Vic began. He started to reach out and touch Colby's hair again, then snatched his hand back. *Stupid. Focus*. He took a deep breath. "How about we cut your hair so it's too short to grab? Would that help?"

Colby's eyes widened, and his posture loosened slightly. "Really?"

"If you want," Vic said, nodding. "Absolutely."

Colby didn't answer, but his eyes were full of hope.

"Come on." Vic slowly rose and moved away from the bed, heading for Colby's washroom. Colby eased out from beneath the covers and stood, then winced and instantly dropped to his hands and knees. *Shit*. Vic had completely forgotten about the cuts all over his feet. He waited while Colby crawled across the room, and switched on the washroom light, looking around to find the best way to go about this.

Vic patted the bathtub. "Come sit right here, champ. I'll be right back."

Colby pulled himself up so he sat on the edge of the tub, his hands tucked up under his chin as he watched Vic leave the room. Vic hurried off to his own washroom and retrieved his grooming kit. Colby watched him curiously as he unpacked the pieces on the counter, debating just how short the boy's hair needed to go. It seemed a crime to cut off those beautiful curls, but if it made Colby feel safer, so be it.

Finally, he snapped on a guard and turned around.

"You know," he said, eyeing Colby, then crouched down and tapped a finger on the sleeve of Colby's sweatshirt, "it'll be easier if you take these off."

Colby drew back slightly, hunching his shoulders.

"You don't have to," Vic rushed to add. "But it'll be more comfortable afterward."

Colby studied his face for a moment, then slowly unzipped the hoodie and took it off, folding it carefully before he set it aside. He was even more hesitant with the two shirts he wore underneath, and sat there shivering once they were off.

Then Colby reached for the waistband of his pants.

"No, no, no." Vic gently grabbed Colby's wrists and pushed his hands away. "Not that, kiddo."

Colby let out a shuddering breath, and tucked his hands back up under his chin.

Vic moved closer, and reminded him, "I'm gonna have to touch your hair to do this. Is that alright?"

Colby shrank back a bit more, but managed a nod.

Vic gave him an encouraging smile, then switched on the clippers. Fear gave way to curiosity on Colby's face as the gentle buzzing sound filled the washroom. "Alright, here goes."

Colby went utterly still as Vic cradled his head with one hand and worked the clippers with the other.

Vic cringed as the first few silky strands fell into the tub, but he kept going. It would grow back eventually. Besides, this might actually be for the best. Now that the sheer desire for Colby was stuck in Vic's head, the less temptation he had, the better.

Because all he wanted in that moment was to throw the clippers down and run his fingers through those curls.

And that was just the beginning.

Fuck. Vic really needed to stop thinking that way. He sucked in a breath and kept working, tilting Colby's head to one side so he could trim carefully around his ears. The move exposed an old scar on Colby's neck, and once it caught Vic's attention, all the other scars suddenly jumped out at him.

So many scars all over that little body. Short ones. Long ones. Faint, silvery ones. Thick, ropy ones. Cut scars, whip scars, burn scars. They were everywhere, a painting of torment on the canvas that was Colby's skin.

And there was Vic, lusting after the boy, even after all Colby had been through. Gods, what kind of a monster did that make him?

Taking a deep breath, Vic mentally recited contract procedure while he kept working, shearing off Colby's hair until there was nothing on the boy's head longer than an inch, too short on which to get a grip. He switched off the clippers and stepped aside, gesturing at the mirror.

"What do you think?"

Colby looked up, his eyes wide as he took in his reflection. He slowly reached up and touched his hair, then tried to curl his fingers into it and pull. He tried again, and again, then reached out and grabbed Vic's hand, pulling it to his head.

Vic caught on and tried to grab Colby's hair, but he couldn't keep hold of the short strands between his fingers.

Colby almost smiled.

Vic cleared his throat. "That better?" he asked, and Colby nodded. "Good. Now…" Moving slowly, Vic reached out and brushed the stray bits of hair off Colby's neck, and felt how tense Colby's shoulders were. And no wonder. After the day he'd had, spending time around so many strangers, and then his panic attack, followed by sitting there half-naked while Vic touched his hair, of course the boy would be wound up. "Tell you what." He gathered the hair out of the tub and carried it over to the trash. "Why don't you take a hot bath, relax, and by the time you're done, dinner should be ready. How does that sound?"

Colby tilted his head, looking adorably puzzled.

"Have you ever taken a bath before?" Vic asked. "Or just showers?"

"Just showers," Colby whispered.

"Well, here." Vic reached past Colby, dropped the plug into the drain, and turned on the hot water, adjusting it so it wouldn't scald. "Let's get those bandages off. This'll be better than standing in the shower, anyway. Though the water might sting."

Colby nodded solemnly, and Vic couldn't help but glance at the boy's body again. Of course Colby knew all about cuts stinging in water. All those scars. *Good gods.* The poor kid. Vic shook his head and tried to push those awful visuals aside.

He got the bandages off Colby's feet, then gestured at the tub. "Why don't you see if that's warm enough for you?"

Colby gave him another puzzled frown, then twisted and reached down to touch the water. He snatched his hand back, and Vic started to dart forward to shove the boy's hand under cold water instead, assuming he'd been burned, then saw the look of awe on Colby's face. Colby dunked his hand right back under the water, and lifted it back up slowly, watching the drops roll down his forearm.

Vic froze, staring at him.

Colby whirled around and dropped to his knees beside the tub, thrusting both arms under the water and lifting them up, staring at his hands, then dunking them again. He turned to look up at Vic with those big, beautiful eyes of his.

"How did you make the water warm?" he asked in an awed whisper.

Vic blinked. The boy didn't know water could be warm? "You've never felt hot water before?"

Colby shook his head.

Holy shit. Vic glanced at the shower, thought of every night when he heard the water come on for mere seconds at a time, never long enough to really get hot.

"Have you always showered like that?" he asked Colby. "Turning the water on just long enough to get wet and then rinse off?"

Colby nodded as though it should be obvious. "It's how Bad Man said to do it."

Vic stared, then tightened his jaw. *Gods damn you, Ahriman*. He wanted to ring the bastard's neck. Blowing out a breath, he put a smile on his face and said, "From now on, I want you to turn the water on until it's comfortably warm, and leave it on while you shower, alright?"

Colby's eyes went wide. "I won't get in trouble?"

"No, kiddo. No, not at all. Besides, hot water is better for you."

"It is?"

Vic nodded. "It cleans better. And it's relaxing." He glanced at the tub and shut off the water before it could get too full. "Hop in there and just relax for a bit, alright? I'll go make dinner so you can have some privacy."

Colby's hands went to the waistband of his sweatpants, his little fingers twisting in the fabric as he hunched his shoulders, watching Vic step away. Vic paused at the doorway and dimmed the lights as low as they could go. Colby gasped and looked around, then let his shoulders relax slightly. Vic gave him a nod and walked out of the room, pulling the bedroom door shut as he left.

He stopped there, closed his eyes, and let out a sigh. That poor, sweet boy. Would there ever come a day when there was no new cruelty for him to learn about?

When he opened his eyes, he found one of Cam's notepads floating there, a question reflecting Vic's own thoughts.

He really didn't know that hot water was a thing?

Vic shook his head. "No."

The pen went at it again. *Gods, poor kid. Sorry, I was kinda eavesdropping but trying to stay out of sight.*

"That's alright." Vic headed for the kitchen, and Cam

followed, the notepad hovering along at Vic's side. "This is your house, too, you know."

I know. I just didn't want to freak him out again.

Vic gave Cam a nod of thanks and went about pulling things out for dinner.

That was a really nice thing you did. Cutting his hair, I mean. You have no idea how much I wanted something along those lines.

"What?" Vic asked. Cam had never mentioned anything like that. "And...how? You were in a coma—"

Yeah, but I was still very aware a lot of the time. I told you about all the things I heard you say to me when you visited.

Vic nodded slowly. That had been both thrilling and terrifying to learn, to find out—long after the fact—that Cam had been listening to all of Vic's ramblings every time Vic visited him at the hospital over the years. He couldn't remember half the things he'd ever said, though Cam had recited some of the more memorable ones, proving to Vic that he really had been aware despite not being able to respond.

And there were times I was very physically aware of my body even though I couldn't move, Cam went on. *I still don't think I can describe how fucking awful it was to be trapped like that while feeling like my skin was crawling at the memory of what happened. And I couldn't DO anything about it, you know? Couldn't scrub myself raw like I wanted to, or bundle myself up when I needed it.*

Vic cringed, trying to imagine himself in that situation. It was something he'd done several times over the years, initially as a matter of wishing he could take Cam's place, take Cam's suffering away and endure it himself. But this? Vic tried to picture being stuck in a hospital bed, conscious to some degree but otherwise paralyzed, unable to move or speak, unable to do anything for himself or ask for help, unable to express all his emotions, trapped within the nightmares of his own traumatic memories.

"I'm so sorry," he choked out.

An invisible arm wrapped around his waist and gave

him a squeeze, then pulled away again so Cam could write, *I know. And I'm sorry. I didn't mean to upset you.* Cam leaned against him, and Vic got the sensation of the kid letting out a heavy sigh before he went on: *I'm just saying…I get what he's going through. And I'm glad he's got you to help him. That's all.*

Vic nodded slowly. "Thanks, Cam," he murmured.

I'll bet that cutting his hair really makes things better for him. It'll be like a nice little reset, you know? Keeping the Bad Man from being able to grab him—even if it's all in his imagination now—and what grows back will be something that Bad Man never touched.

A hint of a smile pulled at Vic's mouth. "Yeah. I like that." He ruffled Cam's hair. "Thanks, kiddo," he said, then his stomach growled.

Cam shook beside him as though laughing, then wrote, *Alright, human. Go get started on dinner. And make it something good so I can enjoy it vicariously.* He added a winking smiley face.

Vic chuckled and shook his head. "Brat."

You love me.

"Yeah, I do." He bent to kiss the top of Cam's head. "Always."

* * *

COLBY WRIGGLED down under the covers and let out a sigh, rubbing his head against the pillow so he could feel the pull on the short strands of hair. He still couldn't believe Vic had cut it for him. That Vic had *allowed* it to happen. He reached up and ran his hands over his head, smiling to himself. Bad Man wouldn't be able to force him as easily now.

He knew Bad Man was dead, of course, but the other Sirs were still out there, somewhere. Any one of them could take Colby away if they found him.

Colby glanced at the door, the outline just visible in the otherwise dark room. He'd been so sure, when Vic touched his hair, that Vic was finally going to use him, punish him, make him pay for everything Vic had given him. Instead, the man had just given *more*. Comforted him. Cut his hair. Made him warm.

A moan escaped him as he thought of the bath. He'd had no idea water could feel so good. Between the music and the bath and the soft, fluffy blankets on the bed, Colby couldn't remember ever feeling so good in his life. Even with the fright of being around Vic's friends, he couldn't think of a better day.

And he'd get more music tomorrow.

Smiling to himself, Colby drifted off to sleep, and didn't wake until the next morning when he heard a soft knock on the door.

"*Colby?*" Vic called. "*You up, kiddo?*"

Colby huddled down under the blankets, ran a hand over his head, then said, "Yes."

A beat of silence passed, then the handle slowly moved and the door inched open. Vic looked in on him, and smiled. "Hey, champ. Good morning."

"Hi," Colby whispered.

"You stayed in bed again," Vic pointed out.

Colby gave a slow nod.

Vic smiled. "Good. I'm glad." He paused, then asked, "Are you hungry? I was just gonna go make breakfast."

Colby nodded again and was going to wait for Vic to leave, then remembered about the music. Vic promised him more music if he left the room. He hesitated just a moment, then pushed the covers back and sat up, drawing his legs free of the sheets.

Vic glanced at Colby's bandaged feet. "Hmmm, you want me to carry you out there?"

Colby considered for a moment, then nodded. His nerves were still a little frayed, and leaving the room again would be scary enough as it was. He still didn't trust Vic completely, but he usually felt safe when Vic held him, and it definitely beat venturing out on his own, especially if he had to face any more surprise visitors.

Vic slowly entered the room, then reached out and pulled Colby's hood up over his head. Colby almost smiled as he felt the hood drag over the short hairs, reminding him once again, and when Vic held out his arms, Colby easily leaned into him, holding on to Vic's shoulders as Vic lifted him off the bed.

Vic made a strange, soft sound—little more than a sigh—as he pulled Colby against his chest, but when Colby looked up, Vic only gave him a smile and carried him out of the room. He set Colby on a stool at the kitchen counter, then went about grabbing plates and other things Colby didn't recognize.

"Once you get used to being out here," Vic said as he worked, "I'll start teaching you how to cook and clean so you can help me. How does that sound?"

Colby slowly nodded. Vic had said something like that once before, and if it was a way he could pay for everything without Vic using his body, he'd take it.

"Think you're up for meeting Cam today?" Vic asked.

Colby tucked his hands under his chin. The idea of more strangers was scary, but Vic seemed eager for it. And, maybe, if Vic was happy, Colby might get more music. He made himself nod again.

Vic smiled. "Good. Cam's really looking forward to hanging out with you."

Behind Colby, someone gasped. "*Oooh*, is it time?"

Colby yelped and twisted around, clutching the counter when he started to fall off the stool. Vic darted over and caught him just as he spotted the boy from yesterday, standing there with a big smile on his face.

"Hey, what is it, kiddo?" Vic asked. "What's wrong?"

Colby huddled against Vic and pointed. Vic glanced over his shoulder, a confused look on his face for a moment before he said, "Oh. Is Cam here?"

Colby frowned. The boy was standing right there. How could Vic not see him?

"I'm dead," the boy said. Colby peeked up at him, and saw him shrug. "Just a ghost, so only certain people can see me. Vic can't."

Colby blinked, then looked up at Vic. "He's dead?" Colby whispered.

A look of pain flashed across Vic's face, then Vic recovered and nodded. "Yeah." He glanced over his shoulder again, then put on a bittersweet smile. "Cam, this is Colby."

Cam waved. "Hi."

"And, Colby," Vic continued, "this is Cam." He paused, his smile turning fond. "My little brother."

Chapter 12

"I'M NOT *that* little."

Colby looked from Cam to Vic and back. He had no idea what a brother was, but he got the impression that Cam and Vic knew each other really well, and the more he looked, the more he realized they had similar features.

"Remind him he's only two years older than me," Cam joked.

Colby tilted his head. "But he's so much bigger."

"What's that?" Vic asked, looking all around. "What did Cam say?"

"He said to remind you that you're only two years older than him," Colby told him, then frowned again. "You really can't hear him?"

Vic's smile fell, and he shook his head.

"Why?" Colby asked.

"Only some people can," Vic said. "I called the hospital so they could run some tests, though I think that's only a formality at this point. It's very likely you're part Tanasian."

"Like Summer!" Cam cut in, grinning.

"What's a summer?" Colby asked.

Vic looked surprised, then said, "Summer is a friend of ours. She's also Tanasian. She's the one who told me Cam's ghost was following me around after he died."

"Oh." Colby frowned, thinking. Something about that statement bothered him, but he couldn't quite work out what it was. Before he could make sense of it, Cam spoke up again.

"Did Vic tell you we're getting a dog?" Cam bounded over, a huge smile on his face, his eyes bright and happy. "I'm so excited! We've never had a dog before. Wait, who am I kidding? Of course you know that. You were there. He asked you." Cam laughed. "Sorry, I'm just super excited. I probably won't be able to play with it, but at least we'll have one, you know?"

Colby frowned. "Why can't you play with it?" he whispered. The very idea was awful. Colby missed the other puppy so much, and Cam looked so excited. It didn't seem fair that Cam wouldn't be able to enjoy it.

Cam shrugged. "Very few dogs can actually tell I'm there. I'll be able to touch it, of course, but it'll never come to me or anything." He shrugged again. "But that's alright. It'll be better than nothing. I'm glad you'll get to have one," he finished, a smile back on his face. "Dogs are great for healing."

"Healing?"

"Yeah, for helping you get over the scary stuff," Cam said. "I wish I'd had one, but I was stuck in a coma for a long time."

"What's a coma?"

"Cam," Vic cut in. He looked concerned and uncertain and upset all at once as he looked from Colby to Cam and back. "What are you guys talking about?"

Cam sighed and rolled his eyes. "Hang on." He walked over to a side table, grabbed a notepad and pen, and came back over. He marked down some small lines and shapes like Colby had seen on Vic's phone, then turned it around for Vic to see.

Vic chuckled and shook his head. "Brat." He reached out, feeling around until Cam moved in close enough for Vic to touch him. Vic ruffled his hair and stepped back. "Just stick to the positive stuff for now, alright?" Cam marked down something else, and Vic laughed, turning away. He paused beside Colby. "You alright with him while I finish breakfast?"

Colby slowly nodded. Cam was still very much a stranger, but he didn't seem all that scary. He couldn't explain why, exactly, but now that he'd gotten to really meet Cam, Colby didn't feel a desperate need to go hide.

"Alright," Vic said. "I'm right here if you need me." He paused, then looked around. "Either of you."

Cam laughed. "He's such a big softy," he said as Vic headed back to whatever it was he'd been doing in the kitchen.

"A what?" Colby asked.

"Never mind. Hey! You wanna see something cool?" Cam darted over to the big table, paused for a moment, then flashed Colby a grin as he walked right through it.

Colby gasped, staring with wide eyes.

"Pretty neat, huh?" Cam asked, then reached out and grabbed the table, nudging it just out of place. He paused, a guilty yet amused look on his face as he glanced at the kitchen.

Vic sighed. "Cam…"

Cam laughed as he tugged the table back to where it had been.

"Brat," Vic muttered, though he was smiling to himself as he shook his head.

Cam laughed again and floated right back through the table. "Vic likes things perfect," he teased. "Gods forbid something be out of place."

Colby tilted his head. He'd noticed as much, even with as little time as he'd spent outside the room. Everything was precisely placed, and if it was moved, it always wound up right back where it belonged. It was why Colby was so fastidious about making sure the bed was precisely made after Vic put him in it each night. He didn't want Vic to be upset that something had been left *wrong*.

"It's his way of maintaining a sense of control," Cam explained, almost seeming to talk to himself and waving his hand as though carelessly pushing the issue aside.

"Why?" Colby asked.

"Because–" Cam darted a look at Vic, then the smile fell off his face as he sighed. "Because what happened to me makes him feel *out* of control."

"Why?" Colby asked again.

Cam looked over at Vic, and sighed again. "Because he still thinks it's ultimately his fault that I'm dead."

VIC WHIRLED around at the sound of Colby's gasp. He found the boy cowering on the kitchen stool, his hands tucked up under his chin, staring at Vic with wide eyes.

Cam's notepad zoomed over, the pen scribbling furiously. *Shit, Vic. I'm so sorry. I think I screwed up.*

Vic looked from the notepad to Colby and back. "Why?"

Because I told him you felt responsible for my death, and–

Vic looked at Colby. "Kiddo…"

Cam grabbed Vic's wrist, and Vic watched in silence as Colby stared at the place where Cam was presumably standing, his fear slowly giving way to confusion.

"Oh," Colby whispered, then eyed Vic cautiously.

Cam wrote, *I just told him you didn't actually kill me.*

Vic sighed with relief.

But maybe we should tell him–

"No," Vic snapped, feeling his heart start to race.

But it might help him understand, Cam continued. After a pause, he wrote, *I could tell him if you–*

"No," Vic insisted.

But, Vic–

"No."

Why not?

"Because I can't say it!"

A heavy silence fell between them as the sound of Vic's words died away. Vic took a deep breath and sighed, then found Cam's arm and gave it a squeeze before he looked over at Colby.

"I'm sorry," Vic murmured. "It's just…"

Colby looked up at him from under his eyelashes,

fiddling with the drawstrings on his hood as a series of emotions crossed his face. "Are you sad?" he whispered.

Vic sighed again. "It is sad," Vic admitted. "But, no, I'm not sad now."

Liar, Cam wrote, adding a winking smiley face to show he was teasing.

"Brat," Vic muttered, but he found himself smiling all the same. He took a deep breath and straightened. "Let's keep it light for now, shall we?"

Sure thing, boss, Cam teased.

Vic chuckled and rolled his eyes.

They got through breakfast, then Vic gave Colby his first hands-on lesson in how to do dishes and clean the kitchen. He kept waiting for the boy to bolt, but Colby stayed right there the whole time, quickly and quietly doing whatever Vic said even when he grew more noticeably tense by the moment.

But once the kitchen was clean and they moved into the living room, he spotted Colby sending hopeful glances at the cello propped up in the corner. *Ah. Of course.* Vic had promised the boy more music if he willingly came out of his room. Vic grabbed the instrument and carried it to a place where he could comfortably sit and play.

Colby hesitated, then crawled up into the rocking chair and looked at him with eager eyes.

Vic shook out his hands, feeling his heart speed up again. He took a deep breath, carefully placed his fingers on the strings, grasped the bow, and started to play.

The first few notes seemed almost too loud in the room, but when Vic risked a glance at the boy, everything else fell away. Once again, Colby was absolutely riveted. He hardly blinked as his eyes followed the movements of Vic's hands, his lips parted in awe.

Vic closed his eyes and kept playing, losing himself in the music. It felt more profound, somehow. Deeper. Richer. More tangible. When the sensation faded, he opened his eyes and looked at Colby again, and the feeling surged anew.

It was so wrong, but he couldn't resist it.

In the middle of the next piece, Colby climbed down out of the chair and crawled closer, inching forward until he sat right at Vic's feet, his big eyes staring at the instrument as Vic continued to play.

Vic almost fumbled the bow, his heart racing and hands starting to sweat. Seeing the boy's reaction to his music was doing all sorts of delicious things to his body. He stared at Colby, playing simply on autopilot while his imagination showed him casting the instrument aside and pulling the boy to him, stripping Colby bare and playing that little body until it made its own beautiful sounds.

Fuck. He pushed through until that piece came to an end, then slowly lowered his bow. He didn't want that look off Colby's face, but he couldn't drag the moment out any longer without feeling utterly disgusted with himself. If he was going to have any chance of taming his sudden urge to pin that little body beneath his, he needed to kill the spark.

Colby slowly lifted his wide-eyed gaze to Vic's face, making his hood slip back off his head. "It's so beautiful," he whispered.

"Yeah," Vic answered, his voice huskier than he'd like.

Colby slowly lifted a hand, fingers outstretched toward the instrument, then snatched it back and looked down at the floor.

Fuck, I'm going to regret this. "You can touch it," Vic blurted out.

Colby's head snapped up, then he slowly lowered his gaze to the body of the cello. He stared at it for a long moment while Vic held his breath, watching, until the boy finally lifted his hand again and inched it forward. Colby stopped halfway and glanced up at Vic's face. Vic gave him an encouraging nod, and Colby slowly reached out farther, inching his way closer until his fingertips lightly brushed the polished wood.

Those big eyes of his went wide again. "It's so smooth," Colby whispered, slowly stroking up and down near the tailpiece.

Vic froze, his whole body tense as he sat there, fighting every urge to move, his jaw tight and his hands shaking. There was something so exquisitely erotic about watching Colby's little fingers caress his instrument, the slow, careful movements bordering on reverent. It didn't take any sort of mental leap for Vic's imagination to put those hands on his own body.

Fuck. This was going from bad to worse.

Colby moved his hand alongside the strings toward the bridge. The tip of his finger caught one of the tiny corners where the bridge was attached to the body, and Colby snatched his hand back.

"You alright?" Vic asked, frowning. "It's not sharp, is it?" He pried his left hand away from the fingerboard and touched the bridge.

Colby shook his head. "Startled me." Before Vic could say anything, Colby looked up at him and asked, "How does it work?"

"Ah, well–" Vic smiled as a wave of relief washed through him. This, he could do. Maybe getting technical about music would get his mind out of the very filthy gutter into which it had descended. He pointed out the various parts of the cello and tried to explain, in the simplest terms he could find, how each part contributed to the production of sound. Then he found himself veering off into music theory, coming to an abrupt stop when he saw the look of dazed confusion on Colby's face. "Here, why don't you try?" he suggested, holding out the bow.

Colby's eyes went wide. "M-Me?"

"Yeah. Go on. It's alright."

Colby slowly lifted a hand and grasped the bow. Vic showed him how to hold it, then had him draw it across the strings. The sound was jarring to Vic's ears, but when Colby's hand stopped moving, the boy's jaw dropped and his eyes widened right before he giggled.

Giggled.

It was a quick, tiny sound, but Vic recognized it for what it was. The boy actually giggled, the brief sound so full of joy and wonder that Vic couldn't wait to hear it again. Without looking, Vic brought his hand back up to the fingerboard.

"Do it again," he told the boy.

Colby drew the bow across the strings again, and he gasped. "It sounds different."

Vic nodded, moving his fingers. "And again."

Once more, Colby drew the bow and gasped at the sound. "How does it do that?"

Vic was hardly a music teacher, and he had a feeling the mathematics of shortening a string by pressing on it in different places to create different notes wasn't going to make any sense to Colby whatsoever, but he tried. The whole thing devolved into Vic demonstrating different fingerings and having Colby draw the bow to produce the sounds. It wasn't much of an explanation, but the utter delight never left Colby's face, especially when Colby handed the bow back and Vic went back to playing.

He didn't stop until he felt his stomach growling again. He checked his watch, stunned to see that he'd played all morning and that it was past lunchtime already. How he'd managed to play for that long without doing something completely stupid, he couldn't begin to guess. Thank gods for the excuse for a break. If he had to endure Colby's awed, adoring looks any longer, he might explode.

Vic put the cello away, promising Colby he'd play more tomorrow—assuming he could endure more of the boy's adoring looks—then waited, fully expecting Colby to disappear into his room now that the music was over for the day. Instead, Colby surprised him, staying out for lunch and then helping with the dishes again. His nerves grew more obvious by the moment, but the boy persisted.

It wasn't until after dinner, when it was time for showers and bed, that Colby finally looked like he was going to shatter if he didn't get to hide away soon. Vic ushered Colby into his room and wished him goodnight.

He was just pulling the door shut when Colby softly called, "Vic?"

Vic peeked back into the room. "Yeah, buddy?"

ILLUMINED SHADOWS

Colby hesitated, sitting on the end of his bed and eyeing the door to the washroom. "Can–"

Vic waited, but when Colby didn't speak, Vic asked, "Do you want a hot bath again?"

Colby nodded shyly.

"Hey, that's fine, kiddo. Besides, I told you: hot showers from now on, remember?"

Colby nodded again.

"Here, I'll show you," Vic said, heading for the washroom. Colby dropped to his hands and knees and crawled along after him, then huddled on the floor near the vanity, watching Vic as he explained how to make the hot water come on in both the shower and the tub, then went about filling the latter just like he had last night.

"Let's check those cuts real quick, yeah?"

Colby climbed up onto the edge of the tub and held out his feet without hesitation while Vic pulled off the bandages and checked everything over.

"Those are looking better." He prodded the cuts gently. "How do they feel?"

Colby flinched just slightly. "Stings a little."

Vic nodded and set the boy's feet down on the cold, tile floor. "Let's give it one more day and then we'll really try walking. How does that sound?"

Colby nodded. Standing carefully in the kitchen while doing the dishes hadn't been too bad, but it hadn't been totally comfortable, either.

"Alright." Vic stood and nodded at the tub. "You can pull the drain plug when you're done?" he asked, and once Colby nodded in answer, Vic took a step away. "Alright. Have a good night, kiddo. I'll see you tomorrow."

Colby gave him a shy smile, and started pulling off his clothes before Vic even left the room.

Vic hurried out the door before he could let himself see any exposed skin, and paused in the hallway with a sigh. He closed his eyes for a moment, only for his imagination to conjure up the look of pure bliss on Colby's face from his discovery of hot water yesterday. Vic groaned, bit off a curse, and took himself off to his room.

He rushed through a shower, trying with all his might to ignore the erection that had been plaguing him all day. There was no way he was going to be able to relieve himself without thinking of Colby, and the thought left him feeling vaguely ill. The longer he put it off, though, the worse it got. He wouldn't be able to sleep while that wound up.

And if he didn't do something about it now, and let the pressure build even more than it already had, how would he stop himself from doing something *really* stupid? Like…charging back into Colby's room and doing something that would destroy them both?

Vic squeezed his eyes shut, grabbed his cock, and jerked it as hard and fast as he could, just wanting it over with as quickly as possible.

A fresh wave of shame washed over him as he came, and Vic quickly rinsed the evidence away, hating himself even as the physical relief settled in. It wasn't perfect, but it took the edge off.

The next morning, after a good night's sleep and an extra-hard workout at the gym, he almost felt back to normal. He got home, peeked in on Colby—fast asleep in his bed, thank gods—and went to take another shower. Vic closed his eyes and let his head fall back, the hot water rushing over his skin and easing his strained, tired muscles.

He thought of Colby's delight at his first touch of warm water, the way the boy stared in awe as the drops ran down his arms, the way he eagerly dunked his hands under the surface over and over again. Such a simple thing. It was just hot water, something everyone enjoyed on a daily basis, but Colby had looked like he was experiencing magic.

Vic twisted around and turned the valve farther to the left. The extra heat struck the back of his neck, and Vic felt his entire body melting under the bliss of it. So simple, something he'd always taken for granted, something he never really stopped to think about.

But little Colby had reveled in it. Vic took a slow,

deep breath, and let himself just feel. Let himself experience every tiny sensation as the hot water beat down on the back of his neck and slowly spread, sending waves of comfort throughout his body, washing away stress and tension and darkness.

Why did he never take the time to enjoy this?

Vic sighed. He knew exactly why. There was far too much darkness in the world, and too big a weight on his shoulders for him to ever slow down and really indulge in things he loved, even the simple things. He needed to stay focused. He needed to keep working, and make up for his utter failure with Cam.

Still, Vic lingered another moment, then shut off the water, got out, and slipped into his usual businesslike demeanor, going about his routine of grooming and dressing even though, once again, he had nowhere to go.

Despite his dark thoughts, he found himself feeling much better, not tensing up quite as much when he sat down to play for Colby again. The looks on the boy's face were still tempting, but he endured it.

He felt just about settled and under control when his phone rang, interrupting the piece he was playing. The sound was jarring, especially with the way it cut into the music, and when he checked the screen to find Ryley calling—not from his own mobile but from his work line—a sense of dread washed over him.

Vic gave Colby a look of apology and set his bow aside to answer the call. "Hey, Ry."

"*Hey,*" Ryley said, his tone unusually serious. "*Have you logged in yet today?*"

Vic cringed. *Shit.* No, he hadn't. He'd barely checked his inbox yesterday, either. Mace was going to be furious if Vic didn't get some actual work done here pretty soon. "No," he answered.

"*Don't,*" Ryley insisted. "*Not yet. I'll be there in a few minutes, alright? Just…don't log in.*"

Vic's skin prickled. "What's going on, Ry?"

"*I'll tell you as soon as I get there. Just don't log in, alright? Promise me.*"

Vic pulled his phone away from his ear and checked the screen. Scrolling across the top were a series of notifications, some of which were clearly emails from work, contracts to process and case alerts to look into, all of them truncated or in code so they wouldn't be clear until Vic actually logged in to the company's database and pulled up the relevant case files.

Just how bad could it be?

He put the phone back to his ear, and heard Ryley say, "*I'm on my way, Vic. Just wait until I get there.*"

"Alright," Vic promised, then rang off, slowly and deliberately tucking his phone back into his inside jacket pocket, then reached for the other pocket instead, clutching the blood-stained bracelet.

"Vic?" Colby whispered.

Vic looked over at the boy. Colby was watching him with wide eyes, his hands tucked up under his chin. Clearing his throat, Vic forced on a smile. "Ryley's coming over for a minute. We have to talk about some work stuff. Why don't you go play with Cam for a bit, yeah?"

Colby eyed him curiously, then gave a shy nod and slipped down off the rocking chair, crawling away to his room. Vic watched him go, and waited for the door to close before he made himself get up and go through the motions of putting the cello away and fussily tidying up the room before Ryley got there, though there wasn't much to do in that regard.

Finally, the doorbell rang, and Vic hurried over to answer it, his imagination playing havoc. Just what was so serious that Ryley wanted to come tell him in person? The only thing he could think of was that one of his rescue kids had died. That was something that would have certainly come across Ryley's desk. The thought made Vic's heart ache. Gods, he did not want to lose one of his kids.

The look on Ryley's face when Vic opened the door just spiked his nerves even more.

"Hey, Vic," Ryley said, his expression more serious than Vic had ever seen.

"Hey." Vic stepped aside to let Ryley in.

ILLUMINED SHADOWS

Ryley looked all around. "Where's the kiddo?"

"In his room."

"Ah. Good." He paused. "You should probably sit down."

Shit. Vic headed for the living room and took a chair, bracing himself for the worst. Was it Zoey? Austin? Any of the dozens of other kids he'd rescued over the years?

"So," Ryley began, perching on the edge of a chair across from him. "You remember how we always used to swap alert requests?"

Vic gave a grim nod, his suspicions confirmed. This was definitely about a dead kid, but he couldn't begin to guess which one it might be.

Years ago, when Vic and Ryley had first started dating, they'd started swapping any alert requests they submitted to the company's database. The system allowed them to flag particular cases, contracts, or keywords for future reference, and the central computer would constantly scan any new information to see if it matched up with any of those requests, instantly sending an alert to the agent who'd made the request in the first place. Since Vic's and Ryley's cases often overlapped, any time one of them submitted a flag, he would tell the other, who would submit the exact same request. That way, if one of them was out of the office and an alert came in, the other would be able to address it.

So if one of Vic's rescued kids had died, and that information hit the Sturmwyn database, the computer would let both Vic and Ryley know.

"I got an alert this morning," Ryley said, stating the obvious. Vic nodded along, gesturing at him to continue. Ryley sat forward. "Vic…" He hesitated, fidgeting in his chair. "It's about Cam."

Vic froze, trying to process the sudden change in direction. "What?"

Ryley nodded slowly. "A DNA sample came in, and it flagged a match in the system." Ryley paused again, and Vic's heart raced as he braced himself, a chill rushing through him.

"What match?" Vic whispered.

Ryley looked up at him from under his eyelashes, watching him carefully, then took a deep breath and said, "We finally have a name for Cam's attacker."

Chapter 13

COLBY LOOKED up when Cam's laughter broke off.

"Cam?"

The ghost looked over at the door, frowning. "Vic's thinking of me really hard."

"What?"

Cam fidgeted. "It's…I'm not really sure how to explain it, but I can tell when he's thinking of me. It's how he can call me to him when I'm not around."

Colby frowned. He had no idea what Cam was talking about.

Cam hesitated, then said, "Hang on. I'll be right back." He went to the door and disappeared right through it, leaving a heavy silence in his wake.

Colby waited, watching the door. Several minutes passed before Colby gave in to curiosity and crawled over to the door. He held his breath, listening. There were voices coming from the living room—Vic's for sure, and he thought the other one must be Ryley's—but he couldn't make out what they were saying. He was just about to reach up and grab the door handle when Cam suddenly burst back in.

The ghost floated right through the door, panting heavily as he began to pace from one end of the room to the other. Cam looked on the verge of panic.

Colby's eyes went wide. "Cam?"

Cam shook his head, barely sparing Colby a glance as he kept pacing.

"What happened?" Colby asked, drawing in on himself. Should he hug Cam? Hold him, like Vic held Colby when he was scared? He had no idea what to do, and Cam wouldn't stop moving. "What's wrong?"

Cam turned and paced toward him, then went back the other way, still shaking his head.

"I can't–" Cam gasped.

"Cam?" Colby followed the ghost with his eyes, growing wider with worry at every passing moment.

Cam choked out a cry. "I have to go."

Before Colby could say anything, the ghost vanished. Colby blinked, then stared at the empty space where Cam had just been. Where had he gone? And why? Cam had been so cheerful just a few minutes ago. Laughing freely like nothing was wrong. And now this? It didn't make any sense. What had he seen? Or heard?

What was so bad that it could leave Cam looking as haunted as Colby felt at the memory of Bad Man?

* * *

FIFTEEN YEARS. Vic slowly shook his head. Fifteen years, he'd been waiting for exactly this moment, and now that it was here, he thought he might shatter into a million pieces.

Cam's attacker had been identified. They had *proof*. A DNA match. It didn't get any more concrete than that.

"Here," Ryley murmured, handing Vic a tablet.

The device was already logged in to the company's system, the case flag already on display on the screen. Vic looked at the DNA analysis, comparing the profiling markers between the new sample and the one that had been logged after Cam's body was recovered. The analysis linked the two with a calculated 99.9% certainty.

Fifteen years, and they finally had a name: Logan Jarvis.

Vic's hands shook, and Ryley caught the tablet before Vic could drop it. Ryley set the tablet aside and took Vic's hands instead.

"Babe?" Ryley asked. "What do you need? Tell me what you want me to do. We can go after this guy. We've got his name and address now—"

Vic shook his head.

"Are you sure?" Ryley asked. "We can go right now if you—"

"I have to tell Cam, first," Vic said, staring at the tablet even though the screen was off. "Fuck," he gasped. "How am I gonna tell him, Ry? After all this time? We'd given up hope that this guy would ever be found…"

"He's a tough kid, Vic. You're always saying how well he's done despite everything that happened to him."

"Yeah, but…this?" Vic pulled his hands free and gestured at the tablet, then sank back into the couch with a heavy sigh. "What if Cam isn't ready to hear it? What if Cam isn't ready to face him?"

Ryley eyed him for a moment, then asked gently, "Are *you* ready to face him?"

"Of course I am," Vic answered quickly. Too quickly, even to his ears.

Ryley reached out and gave his knee a squeeze. "Babe, it's alright if you're not. There's nothing wrong with that."

Vic shook his head. "Doesn't matter. If Cam's ready, I have to be. But how can I tell him? What if it sets him back? Or what if he thinks he's ready to face the guy, and we go, and all it does is crush him?"

Ryley grimaced. "I don't know, babe. Gods, I wish there was something I could do…"

Vic looked at Ryley and reached out to give the man's hand a squeeze. "Thank you for coming to tell me. Thank you for being here."

"Anytime, hon."

A few minutes later, Ryley left to go back to the office, and Vic sank into the rocking chair, idly pushing the thing into motion as he stared at the floor.

He lost track of time as he sat there, trying to sort through all his thoughts and feelings. Vic traced the scars across the knuckles of his left hand, the memory of that awful day coming back in full force and weighing heavily on his heart. Someone had attacked Cam, yes—and now that someone's name was known—but it didn't change the fact that it never would have happened if Vic hadn't done what he had.

If Vic hadn't said those awful words.

He was vaguely aware of the shuffling sounds of motion before Colby crawled up into his lap and snuggled up against him. Still staring at the floor, Vic wrapped his arms around the boy.

"Hey, kiddo," he mumbled distractedly.

Colby was silent, though Vic could feel the boy watching him. Vic blew out a breath. He needed to get his shit together and focus. There was so much to do, and just sitting there—dwelling on the past—wasn't getting any of it done.

But he just wanted a few more minutes. Just a little more time to bear himself up for facing the darkness and calling on Cam so he could tell his brother what he'd learned.

A feather-light touch trailed across his forehead, and Vic's eyes drifted shut. His lips parted as a subtle, pleasurable shiver ran through him. The touch moved down his cheeks, over his nose, along his jaw. Vic forced his eyes open, and saw Colby watching him curiously, the boy's little hands trailing all over Vic's face and somehow managing to make all the tension disappear.

Vic closed his eyes again and sighed, going boneless in the chair. "My sweet boy..." he whispered.

Colby's touch stuttered for a split second before continuing on just as it had, somehow easing every inch of Vic's body from just that little bit of contact.

He blew out a breath and looked down at the boy, feeling a slight smile on his face.

Colby tilted his head. "You don't look so sad now," the boy whispered.

Vic's smile grew. "How did you think to do that?"

"It helps me," Colby said, giving a slight shrug.

"Does it?"

Colby nodded.

"Hmmm." He'd have to remember that. Vic grabbed Colby's hand and kissed his knuckles. "Thank you for that."

Colby frowned, looking puzzled, and Vic realized what he'd done.

"I'm sorry, kiddo." Vic let go of Colby's hand. *Shit*. "Sorry. I shouldn't have done that."

Colby looked down at his hand, fingering the spot where Vic had kissed, then looked up and opened his mouth like he was about to say something.

Instead, something across the room caught his eye. Colby did a double-take, then shrieked, scrambling on Vic's lap as he tried to pull his body in as tight as it could possibly get while grasping for something to hold on to.

"Colby?" Vic froze for a moment, eyes wide, before wrapping the boy tight in his arms and pulling him close to his chest. "What is it? What's wrong?"

"Bad Man!" Colby gasped, ducking his head, his little hands clutching Vic's jacket so hard that his fingers turned white.

"Bad Man?" Vic looked all around, frowning. What the hells was the boy talking about? "Colby? Hey, champ, there's no one here."

Colby peeked up at him, then started to look out, only to shriek and curl up again.

Vic blinked. What in the gods' names was going on?

"Colby–"

Cam's notepad flew off the coffee table, the pen frantically writing before the note was shoved in Vic's face.

I think there's another ghost here.

Vic frowned at the words. "What?"

I can't see it, the pen hurriedly added, *but I can sort of sense it, I guess. There's another ghost here.*

Vic stared, then scanned the whole room before he looked down at the boy in his arms.

Oh gods. Colby could see ghosts. And Ahriman was dead. Long enough dead that he must have learned to take visible form.

The Bad Man had returned.

Chapter 14

VIC LAY Colby on the couch and covered him with a blanket, even pulling it over the boy's head so Colby would have the comfort of darkness if he woke.

The poor kid had shivered with fright in Vic's lap until he'd fallen asleep from sheer exhaustion. And Vic had no idea what to do. Colby had been finally free of Ahriman. Free of the basement. Free of his torment. Just starting to open up and live. And now this!

Vic should have realized it sooner. With Colby able to see Cam, and mere thought able to draw a ghost's presence, it should have been obvious that the ghost of Ahriman would ultimately make an appearance.

And all this after Vic had promised that the Bad Man would never hurt him again.

Now, they'd probably be starting all over. Of course, that was assuming that starting over was even possible. How in all seven hells would Colby ever heal properly if Bad Man could follow him anywhere he went?

Would he never be free?

Vic went to his office, looking for a distraction, only to find the notifications on his screen for messages from work, the one that Ryley had told him about seeming to glare at him amidst the others. It looked like Vic would never be free of his own torment, either.

He went through his inbox, trying to ignore the alert tied to Cam's case, but his attention kept getting drawn back to it. The only thing that successfully distracted him, if only for a moment, was an email from Denmer General, confirming that Colby was, in fact, half Tanasian.

Vic sat forward and read through the blood analysis for both Colby and his late mother. According to their genetic markers, Colby's mother was full-blooded Tanasian, and his father was presumed to be Agori, though they still had no identity for the man. Vic set the file aside and pulled up what information he had on Summer Vas-kelen, the only other Tanasian he personally knew. According to her file, she was only $1/32$ Tanasian, yet her telepathic abilities were highly developed. So with Colby being half Tanasian? There was no telling what his mind could do.

But that would have to wait. Maybe he could talk to Summer—assuming she could understand his request, and he could understand her answer—but first he needed to get a handle on more pressing matters.

He no sooner started to think of Cam than a notepad lifted from his desk.

He's still asleep out there. Is he gonna be alright?

Vic blew out a breath. "Gods, I hope so." He paused, his hand going to the bracelet in his pocket. "Cam, listen. We need to talk."

I know.

Vic hesitated, then said, "It's about–"

Cam interrupted him by double-underlining his last words. Vic read them over again, a sense of dread washing through him as he picked up on Cam's meaning.

"Cam–"

Sorry. I was there. You were thinking of me really hard, so I couldn't resist showing up. Cam paused, then added, *I heard everything Ryley said.*

"Shit," Vic breathed. "Cam, I'm so sorry."

The pen waggled in a way that Vic had learned was meant to represent Cam shaking his head, then wrote, *It freaked me out for a bit, but I'm alright.* After a moment, he added, *I think. How are you with it all?*

Vic shook his head. "Doesn't matter."

Sure it does. You had to deal with it, too.

"Not like you did."

Yeah, well...

Cam left it at that, and Vic cast about for something to say. He glanced at his computer screen.

"Do you want to see any of this?" he asked, closing out the files for Colby and Summer and pulling up the new DNA record that linked to Cam's case.

No, that's fine, Cam wrote, stopping him. *I'll take your word for it.*

Vic nodded slowly. "We know his name now."

I know. I heard that part.

Vic hesitated, then asked, "Do you want to go see him? We have his address. You can finally have a chance to face him."

Cam's pen wavered for a long while, then finally wrote, *No. I guess I'm not as ready as I thought I was.*

Vic slowly let out the breath he was holding. *Thank gods.* He really wasn't ready, either. Maybe it made him a coward, but so be it.

Which was odd, considering how long they'd waited for exactly this chance. So many years spent agonizing over the fact that Cam's attacker could never be identified, and now he had been. Of course, if Vic ever had to look the man in the eye, he wasn't sure anything could stop him from beating the man to death for what he'd done to Cam.

And, for Cam's honor or not, Vic didn't want Cam to see him like that. Hells, Vic didn't want to see *himself* like that, but it didn't change the fact that he'd dreamt of doing exactly such a thing ever since he'd found Cam's body.

So what are we going to do about our unwanted visitor? Cam asked.

Vic flinched, trying to catch up to the subject change. "Oh." Ahriman's ghost. Vic cringed. "I have no idea." He paused, then asked, "You said you can't see him?"

Not really, no. It's a weird thing. I mean, there's millions of ghosts out there, but not all of them make themselves visible, not even to each other. Not all of them know how. The pen stopped for a moment, then continued: *Of course, time and motion work differently in this state, too, which probably plays a part in it all.*

Vic frowned. "*Time* is different?"

Yeah. It's totally weird. It's like time feels normal while also feeling faster and slower, and all at once. It's really hard to describe.

"Try," Vic asked, sitting back in his chair. Gods knew he could use the distraction.

Well...say there's a problem you're trying to solve or a thought you're trying to reason out. It might take us both the same perceived *amount of time—let's say several minutes—but while the actual time it takes you might be several minutes, it might happen for me within what you would consider seconds.*

Vic's eyebrows went up.

Or I can sort of just...fade out for several hours, just kinda float along without any thought or intention, but not feel bored. Like all that passage of time isn't tedious like it was when I was alive. So hours pass, but they only feel like seconds. The pen moved as though Cam chuckled. *Some of the other ghosts could probably explain it better. Vorena, especially. She's the oldest ghost I know.*

Vic blinked. "So you do see other ghosts."

Yeah, a few. After I realized Summer could see me, I started tagging along with her sometimes while you were busy at work, just to have someone to talk to. Her family is close with this other big family that has a lot of Tanasians in it, so there were a ton of ghosts hanging around. Mostly their ancestors, but some others, too.

Vic straightened in his chair. "Do you think there's any chance they would know how to keep a ghost away?"

Huh. Maybe? It's not something I've ever wondered about. Cam added a smiley face with its tongue sticking out.

Vic snorted a laugh. "Brat."

But I could ask. Or Summer might know. Might be faster to call her.

"Really?"

Yeah. You know that whole thing about ghosts being tied to certain energies, so we can visit the living who we were close to in life? Cam paused, and Vic nodded. *Same thing applies between ghosts. We have to build up a bond before we can regularly sense one another strongly enough to track one down.*

"Ah," Vic said, though he still wasn't sure he entirely understood. Probably wouldn't understand until he was dead himself and could experience the phenomenon directly, something he really didn't want to consider at the moment. Pushing the thought aside, he grabbed his mobile and dialed a number.

Why are you calling Athan? Cam wrote.

"Because Summer still hasn't gotten the hang of using a phone," Vic quickly explained while the line rang.

Cam's notepad and pen tilted back and shook, giving Vic the impression of a huge belly laugh. The thought brought a smile to his face.

"*Hello?*" Athan answered.

"Athan, hi, it's Vic."

"*Vic!*" Athan's usual monotone took on the slightest hint of pleasant surprise. Difficult to tell when it came to the Falsiners, but Vic hoped he was reading it right. "*How are you? Haven't seen you in a while.*"

"Yeah, sorry about that. I've got a pretty involved case going on right now. How are you? How's the family?"

In the background, a baby cried, and Athan breathed a laugh. "*Never dull,*" the man answered, a hint of fondness in his voice.

"I'm sure," Vic laughed.

"*So what can I do for you?*"

"I was hoping your wife could help us with a ghost question."

Athan's voice took on a hint of alarm. "*Is something wrong with Cam?*"

"No, no, Cam's fine–"

"*Ax and fawn. Thank gods. Summer would have been upset otherwise.*"

"No, we're all good there," Vic said, not wanting to delve into his and Cam's personal demons. Summer didn't need to be subjected to all that. "It's another ghost, actually. This case I have right now, the kid I rescued...His abuser died, which is how we found the kid in the first place–"

Athan hissed. "*And now his ghost is present,*" he said, instantly catching on.

"Yeah. We need to know if there's any way to keep him out of the house or...something. I'm not sure. It's just...he's scaring the boy."

"*I can imagine.*" Athan paused, then covered the receiver while he presumably spoke to someone on his end, hints of garbled voices coming through until Athan returned. "*Summer says she doesn't think so, but she can ask around. And that you might try asking Ryley.*"

Vic blinked. "Ryley?"

"*Maybe he can use a spell or something.*"

"Oh." Vic nodded slowly. "Good point."

Now why didn't we think of that? Cam wrote.

Vic chuckled silently, then said, "Yeah, thanks, Athan."

"*No problem.*" The baby screamed again. "*I should be going.*"

"Yeah, of course. Hey, let me know if you guys ever have a night free. I'd love to have you over for dinner," Vic offered, thinking it would be nice both to see his friends and give Colby a chance to meet another Tanasian, although Athan himself might prove too intimidating for the boy. He'd have to ease him into the idea.

Athan sighed. "*I will ask Father to look after my boy as soon as he can,*" the man said, sounding grateful for the invitation.

Vic laughed. "Talk to you soon."

"*Thanks, Vic.*"

Athan rang off, and Vic dialed Ryley's number.

The line clicked open, followed by a thump and a curse before Ryley said, "*Vic? Are you alright? What do you need?*"

"Slow down, Ry, everything's fine."

Ryley blew out a breath. "*Sorry. I've just been worried about you guys all day. How's Cam doing? Does he know yet?*"

"Yeah, I told him," Vic said, eyeing Cam's notepad. "We're dealing with it." *Eventually*, Vic thought.

"*Good. Alright, good. I'm glad.*" He blew out another heavy breath. "*So what's up?*"

"Shit, I shouldn't be bothering you with this while you're at work—"

"*Hey, babe, it's fine. Besides…I'm going cross-eyed trying to make sense of this inheritance contract that just got dropped on my desk. You're saving my sanity with this interruption. Seriously.*"

Vic chuckled. "Alright. In that case…you wouldn't happen to know of a spell that can banish a ghost, would you?"

Ryley barked a laugh. "*Cam getting on your nerves?*"

Hey! Cam wrote, though he was clearly laughing since the pen stuttered as it moved.

Vic started to laugh, then quickly sobered. "No, actually…It's Ahriman."

"*What?*" Ryley gasped.

"Yeah."

"*Shit. Fucking bastard. He's a ghost now? Fuck, of course he is. And he's following the kid, isn't he?*"

"Yeah, I think so."

"*Poor little guy*," Ryley murmured. Vic heard him blow out a heavy breath before he went on: "*To answer your question, there's nothing that I know of, personally, but I could do some research. Ask around.*"

Vic sighed. "Thanks, Ry. I know it's probably a long shot, but if I can't keep this guy out of the house…"

"*Colby's never gonna get better. Yeah. Shit. Alright. Let me see what I can do.*"

"Thanks, Ry," he said again.

"*No problem, babe*," Ryley said, and rang off.

Do you think he'll find something? Cam asked.

Vic sighed. "I have no idea."

The pen wavered, then wrote, *Alright, scarier thought...*

"What's that?"

Do you think he's here now, listening? Do you think he knows we're trying to get rid of him?

"Shit," Vic swore. He set his phone aside, scanning his seemingly-empty office with narrowed eyes. "Ahriman, if you're here...I won't let you touch him," Vic growled. "Do you hear me? You're never touching that boy again."

Of course, unless Ryley, Summer, or one of Cam's ghost friends found something, Vic's words were nothing more than an empty threat.

Chapter 15

A PIERCING cry woke Vic in the middle of the night. He sucked in a breath and sat up, fumbling to find the switch to turn on the bedside lamp. Ahriman's ghost had been plaguing them for a few weeks now, showing up at odd intervals and sending poor Colby into fits, that panicked cry becoming a regular sound in the house. This was the first time it had happened during the night, though.

Rubbing the sleep from his eyes, Vic tossed back the blankets and started to get out of bed, only to stop at the sight of Colby scrambling down the hallway, heading straight for Vic's room.

The boy was wearing all his layers, as usual, as well as clutching the comforter from his bed, the thing haphazardly wrapped around him so that he kept tripping on a corner of it as he tried to navigate in the dark, constantly looking over his shoulder as he went.

"Colby?"

Colby reached Vic's room, dropped the comforter on the floor, tripped over it, and dove onto Vic's bed, clambering toward the pillows and then burrowing down under the sheets at Vic's side. Vic held utterly still, staring at the tiny, shivering lump in the middle of his bed.

"Colby?" Vic's heart broke for what felt like the hundredth time that week alone. The poor, sweet boy. And, so far, there was nothing they could do about it. Summer and the other ghosts had struck out in terms of finding a way to keep a ghost out of the house, and Ryley was still looking, but not having much luck. The only thing the mage had been able to find so far was a spell that would banish *all* ghosts from a particular location.

But that would mean banishing Cam as well, and that was one thing Vic was absolutely *not* willing to do.

Vic slowly reached out and rested a hand on the blankets, right over where he thought Colby's shoulder might be. "Hey, kiddo. I'm so sorry."

Colby whimpered in response, the sound loud enough to pierce the layers that covered him.

Vic sighed and lay back down, lifting the edge of the blankets just enough to peek under them. "Colby?"

Colby let out a whine, then shuffled over until he was curled up tight at Vic's side. Vic pulled him in close, rubbing his back and tucking the blankets around Colby as securely as he could.

"I'm sorry, champ," Vic murmured. "I didn't think you'd ever see him in the dark."

"I g-got up to u-use the washroom," Colby whispered, his voice shaking, "and h-he was there just as I turned the light back off."

Shit. "Did he touch you?"

Colby gave a tight shake of his head. "I don't think he can. Not like Cam."

Vic nodded slowly. Cam had said as much a few days ago. Ahriman was still a new ghost, so while he'd managed to make himself visible, he had yet to learn how to make himself tangible. With any luck, they could escape that altogether, but Vic wasn't holding his breath. If the ghost ever did manage to touch Colby, things would get so much worse for the boy.

Vic tightened his arms, then felt an invisible touch on his wrist just as he saw the bed dip on Colby's other side.

"Cam?"

Cam gave his wrist a squeeze, then lay his arm alongside Vic's where it wrapped around Colby.

Vic gave him a grateful smile, then looked down at Colby and murmured, "We've got you, kiddo. Cam's here, too. We won't let him get you."

Colby peeked out just long enough to look over his shoulder, then glanced at Vic before hiding his face again.

Poor thing. Vic tugged the boy's hood up, his fingers lingering just a little too long on Colby's forehead before Vic reached back to switch off the lamp, casting the room into darkness before he settled back down with a sigh.

"We've got you, kiddo," he said again. "You're safe."

* * *

VIC GROANED when his alarm went off in the morning. He'd barely slept all night, waking in fits and starts to make sure Colby was actually feeling safe enough to get some sleep.

Then again, if he were really being honest with himself, that was hardly the only reason.

He switched off the alarm, then slowly lay back down, holding his breath while he waited to see if he'd woken Colby. Peeking under the blanket, he found the boy still fast asleep. *Thank gods.* Vic let out a sigh and pulled Colby close, deciding he'd skip the gym just this once. He knew the guilt would be hitting him any moment, but he couldn't resist another few minutes of having Colby sleeping beside him.

Even if it took everything he had to ignore the fact that his cock was rock-hard and so painfully close to what it wanted.

Vic took a deep breath, and let it out slowly, then did it again, counting the breaths and then mentally reciting the names of his rescues. It didn't take long before all thoughts of arousal were gone. He probably could have just thought of all the cruel things Ahriman had done to Colby, but that would require thinking of Colby, thinking of how warm and soft and small the boy felt there in his bed.

Fuck. He went through the list again, just in case.

Something invisible brushed over his arm and pushed Colby harder up against him before drawing back again, Cam's notepad floating up off the nightstand and coming into view. Cam must still be there, helping shield Colby from the Bad Man.

You look like shit.

Vic snorted a laugh. "Thanks a lot, brat."

Did you sleep at all?

"Not really."

Hmmm. I kinda had a feeling.

"Why's that?"

Cam started out with the winking smiley face this time, then wrote, *I got the impression you were rather enjoying yourself.*

Vic froze. "What?"

Vic, come on. Seriously? You should see the way you look at him.

Vic's hand automatically went to his pocket as his heart started to race, only to remember that he was in bed and that Cam's bracelet was on the dresser, across the room. "Cam…"

Hey, look. It's not like you're ever gonna act on it, right? At least, not until he's ready–

"Cam–"

Actually, I think it's kinda cute.

"He'll never be ready," Vic hissed. "And there's nothing to act on."

The pen danced for a moment, and Vic got the impression of amusement in its motion as it wrote, *If you say so.*

Vic narrowed his eyes at the words. "You're the last person who should be making light of this," Vic growled, then held his breath for a moment before letting it out heavily. "Shit. Cam, I'm so sorry–"

I know. It's alright. But, seriously, Vic–

"Cam–"

No, just listen, the pen wrote insistently, and Vic shut his mouth. *I'm not upset. It doesn't bother me, though it's obvious you think it should.* Cam paused for a moment, then continued: *But just think about it. You might be just what he needs. And he might be just what you need. Someday, as he trusts you more, this might be something really beautiful.*

Vic shook his head. There was no way he'd ever be able to have what he wanted. He was stupid for even wanting it in the first place. Colby could never be his.

"Can we just focus on keeping him safe?" Vic asked. *From myself, included.*

The pen lifted and dropped, giving the impression of a sigh. *Yeah, fine.* Cam paused, then added, *You know, this would be a really great time to have a dog.*

Vic breathed a laugh and rolled his eyes. "One thing at a time, kiddo. Besides, with Ahriman in the house now, I can hardly leave him alone long enough to go out and find one."

You could take him with you.

"Did you see how long it took to get him just to leave the bedroom?"

You could ask him. He might be up for it, especially if it meant not being home alone when the Bad Man might show up.

"Hmmm." Vic gave a slow nod. Cam had a point. Still, he couldn't imagine Colby being ready to leave the house yet, even if it was to go pick out a puppy. Vic yawned. "We can talk about it later." He settled back down and tried to close his eyes.

A few minutes of silence passed, until he heard the scratching of Cam's pen again.

You know, this is officially the second gayest thing I've ever done.

Vic frowned. "What's that?"

Spending the night in bed with two guys. Wait, does that also count as incest since you're my brother?

Vic groaned. "Cam." The bed shook, and Vic imagined Cam laughing. "Brat," he muttered, then frowned again as he read back over Cam's words. "If this was the second, what was the f–" The answer hit him before he could even finish asking the question. "Cam!" Vic hissed.

He popped up onto his elbow, his eyes wide as he stared at the pen. "That is not funny!"

It's kinda funny.

"Not. Funny," Vic bit off, the old guilt and terror surging back up out of memory.

I'm sorry. You're right. But I have to laugh about it. Sometimes, that's the only way I can deal with it.

Vic's heart sank. "I'm so sorry, kiddo."

I know you are. I'm sorry, too.

Vic found Cam's arm and gave it a squeeze, then he yawned again.

The bed shook with silent laughter. *Go back to sleep, you dork.*

Vic knew he really ought to get up, but more sleep sounded way too tempting. He lay back down and felt Cam reach over him to put the notepad back on the nightstand, only to snatch it up again.

You've got a text from Ryley on your phone.

Vic grabbed his mobile and checked. Sure enough, the lock screen showed all the usual notifications for texts and emails that had come in throughout the night, all of which he'd ignored, then spotted the one from Ryley. He opened it up, and smiled.

"He thinks he found a spell."

Right on!

Vic nodded agreement, then set his phone aside. With that hopeful prospect, he could definitely spare another hour for sleep, so he settled back down and let himself drift off.

Exhaustion took hold, so when he finally woke again, he had just enough time to eat and get dressed before the guys would be there for band practice. Vic eased out of bed, got dressed, and slipped out of the room. He left his bedroom door open, like always, and headed for the kitchen. Vic gulped down a cup of coffee, and considered going to wake the boy so he could eat, then decided against it. Poor Colby needed his sleep. Vic could make him something later, after he woke.

He was just finishing the dishes from his own late

breakfast and wiping down the counters when the doorbell rang. Vic hurried to answer it, and stepped aside to let everyone in. Hugs and handshakes were shared all around as Ryley, Asher, Zac, and Adrian filed inside and gathered in the living room.

Ryley grabbed Vic's arm, and they hung back from the others.

"Hey," Ryley murmured, "can I talk to you for a second?"

"Yeah, sure."

Ryley gestured at the hallway, and Vic nodded. They told the others they'd be right back, then headed toward the spare bedroom that Vic used as an office.

"I can try that spell today if you want," Ryley began, and Vic gave him a grateful smile. Then Ryley lowered his voice. "But we can talk about that later. I just wanted to see how you were do–"

Ryley broke off and came to a stop. Vic followed his gaze, and remembered that his bedroom door stood wide open, and that Colby was still in his bed, plain to see. Vic darted over and pulled the door shut, but it was too late.

Clutching the door handle like a lifeline, Vic closed his eyes, took a deep breath, and turned to face his friend.

Ryley stared at him for a long moment, then asked, "You wanna explain to me what the *hells* the little guy is doing in your bed?"

* * *

COLBY STIRRED at the sound of approaching footsteps and whispered voices. Blinking the sleep from his eyes, he peeked out from under the covers and found himself alone in Vic's bed, the blankets tucked tight around him.

He looked up and saw Vic and Ryley coming near, only for them to suddenly stop for a moment before Vic rushed to shut the door. Colby frowned. Ryley was supposed to be nice, right? So why would Vic try to keep him away, especially when it was Ryley who was going to be making Bad Man's ghost leave?

Unless Ryley was going to demand Colby in payment? Colby frowned. No, Vic swore Ryley would never do such a thing. Colby looked all around, the room feeling suddenly too big. He needed Vic.

He slipped out of bed and hurried over to the door. He tried the handle, but it wouldn't budge.

Then he heard Ryley speak.

"*You wanna explain to me what the* hells *the little guy is doing in your bed?*"

"*Ryley–*" Vic pleaded.

"*Please tell me that's not what it looks like.*"

"*Nothing happened, Ry. I swear.*"

Colby frowned. Nothing happened? What did that mean?

"*It's just…*" Vic went on. "*Ahriman drove him out of bed last night, and he was scared, so Cam and I protected him. That's all.*"

"*Oh.*" Ryley paused, then blew out a heavy breath. "*Yeah, of course. Alright. That makes sense. Poor kid.*"

Vic made a noise of assent.

"*Gods, I'm so sorry, Vic. I don't know why I thought you would ever…*" Ryley trailed off, and Colby frowned, straining to listen. "*Vic?*"

"*What?*" Vic muttered.

"*Alright, so, you say nothing happened, but you look guilty as all hells.*" After a moment, Ryley added, "*Actually, you look fucking exhausted. Babe? What's going on?*"

A moment of silence passed, then the door handle twitched under Colby's hand. A dull thud sounded through the wall just beside the handle, and Colby pressed his ear to the door, holding his breath and listening.

Vic mumbled something that he couldn't make out.

"*Come again?*" Ryley asked.

Vic sighed heavily. "*I want him.*"

Colby frowned. What did that mean?

A tense pause followed, and when Ryley spoke again, all the upset in his voice was gone, replaced by concern. "*Babe…Oh my gods. Are you alright?*"

"*No, I'm not,*" Vic answered, his voice thick with some emotion Colby couldn't make out. "*It's torture, Ry. Having him near...unable to touch him.*" Colby's eyes went wide. "*I can't remember the last time I ever wanted someone this bad.*" He paused, then added in a whisper, "*Not even you.* Shit. *I'm sorry.*"

"*No, babe. Hey, don't be sorry. It's alright. I get it.*"

Vic scoffed. "*How can you? How could–*"

"*I went through the same thing with Ash, remember? Alright, granted, so the circumstances were different, but...I still had to force myself to resist him, to stay away from him, for his own good, to protect him, no matter how much it hurt me. So, yeah. I get it, Vic. I do.*"

Vic groaned. "*I just feel like such a fucking monster. How can I want him, Ry?* Him, *of all people. What kind of sick freak does that make me? I'm no better than Ahriman or any of the rest of them–*"

"*Alright, first of all,*" Ryley interrupted. "*You stop that shit right now, you hear me? You're a good man, Vic. One of the best men I've ever known. You are* way *better than Ahriman. You're in completely different leagues.*"

"*But–*"

"*No, listen. You are not a monster. Besides, you can't help who you're attracted to. You can't. It just happens. But you* can *help how you react to that attraction. And I know you. You would never hurt that poor kid.*"

"*What if I can't resist? What if the temptation becomes too much...and I snap?*"

"*You won't–*"

"*But I might–*"

"*But you* won't," Ryley insisted.

"*But I want him to be mine,*" Vic said, and another thud sounded through the wall. "*Sometimes, it's all I can think about. Kissing him. Touching him. Making him* mine *in every sense of the word.*" Vic sucked in a breath. "*And I'll never have that. Not with him. Because I could* never *do that to him without hating myself for the rest of my life.*" He barked a humorless laugh. "*And gods know I've got enough reason to hate myself already as it is.*"

"But Cam forgave you, right?"

"Yeah, he did. But he's still dead. And, ultimately, that's still my fault."

"Vic," Ryley breathed. *"Babe, one of these days you really need to forgive yourself for all that."*

"I can't. And now with this—" Vic gave a shaky exhale. *"Maybe I should just send him away, you know? Before I do something really stupid. That's what I should do. Send Colby away. Put him in foster care or a convalescent home or—"*

"Vic, hey, whoa. Calm down. Breathe. Hey, maybe you just need a break, yeah? I mean, this whole arrangement has disrupted your routine, and I know how you are about routines." Ryley breathed a laugh. *"What if you try coming back to the office—"* Vic started to protest, so Ryley rushed on: *"Even if it's just for a few hours a day. Just to give yourself some distance from the little guy, get your mind back in work mode, give yourself back some routine and perspective."*

Colby stifled a whimper.

"I can't do that now. I can't leave him home alone. Not with Ahriman in the house."

Colby let out a shuddering breath as relief washed through him.

"And if I can get him out of the house?" Ryley asked. *"What then?"*

A few seconds of silence passed. Colby tightened his grip on the door handle, his legs shaking beneath him.

"Even then, I—" Vic began. *"Gods, I still don't know if I can keep doing this. I can't have him think of me like he thinks of Ahriman. If I ever did anything to hurt him—"*

"You won't, Vic—"

"I'm not so sure anymore. Especially after last night. It was all I could do to keep my hands off him." Vic paused, and Colby heard some moving around. *"And when he watches me play, it's even worse."*

"Huh," Ryley said. *"I thought I saw something there that first day he came out, but...I just convinced myself I was imagining it."*

ILLUMINED SHADOWS 153

"I have to send him away, Ry. I don't think I have another choice. I'm not sure how much longer I can do this."

Colby scrambled across the room and dove back under the covers, shivering in his dark nest. He didn't want Vic to touch him like Bad Man had, but he didn't want Vic to send him away, either.

He had no idea what to do.

* * *

VIC LET out a heavy sigh when Ryley pulled him in for a hug.

"It'll be alright, babe," Ryley told him. "You're a good man. Somehow, this is all gonna work out."

"Gods, I hope so," Vic muttered, then pulled back and scrubbed a hand down his face before shoving his hand into his pocket, clutching Cam's bracelet in his fist.

"You still up for practice?" Ryley asked. "Or we can cancel and just do the ghost thing."

Vic glanced at the closed bedroom door, then looked down the hallway, just able to see the others laughing and chatting in the living room. He took a deep breath and straightened. "I'll be fine."

"Are you sure?"

"I–" Vic broke off and laughed.

"What's so funny?"

"Cam. He *hates* that question." Vic shook his head. "It's nothing. Never mind." Vic took a deep breath and blew it out hard. "Yeah, practice. I need to think about something else for a while."

"Alright," Ryley said, eyeing him carefully, but he turned and headed for the living room nonetheless.

Vic gave his bedroom door one last glance, then followed.

Turning his mind onto music—instead of Colby and Cam and ghosts and other matters—was a welcome distraction. His focus wasn't quite as complete as he normally expected of himself, but their rehearsal still came off well, their progress toward getting back to a regular gig more promising now than ever before. Several times, Vic caught himself wishing Colby could be sitting right there, watching Vic play with those adoring, riveted looks of his, but he was also glad for the break. The passion wasn't quite there without his little audience of one, but at least the monster of guilt gave him the slightest reprieve.

When it was all over, and Zac and Adrian had said their goodbyes, Ryley and Asher made no move to leave.

"You wanna try the spell now while I'm here?" Ryley asked.

"Yeah." Vic nodded. Maybe, if they could banish the ghost, Colby would be a little less clingy. The thought brought a bittersweet ache to Vic's chest. Still, it had to be done.

Ryley nodded at the hallway. "We might need him. Just in case."

"Ah." Vic frowned, but headed off to his bedroom anyway. He had no idea what Ryley could possibly need Colby for in order to perform the spell, but it wasn't his place to question it. Magic was Ryley's business. The man must know what he was doing.

Vic knocked on his bedroom door. "Colby? You awake yet, kiddo?"

It was past lunchtime, and Colby had yet to make an appearance. Vic wasn't sure if the boy was just that tired or if he was hiding out, avoiding the visitors. He hoped it was the former. The poor kid had finally been making progress with the latter, and Colby needed more of that.

Vic inched the door open, and found Colby still curled up in bed but peeking out at him. "Hey, champ."

"Hi," Colby whispered.

"Ryley's here," Vic said, and Colby gave a slow nod. "He wants to try the spell to make the Bad Man go away."

Colby's eyes brightened. "Really?"

"Yeah. You wanna come out here and help him?"

Colby hesitated, then slowly crawled out of bed. He took a step toward Vic, then whirled back and started fussing with the sheets, trying to make the bed in a hurry.

Vic almost told him to leave it, but he needed some

ILLUMINED SHADOWS 155

semblance of order. He went to the other side of the bed, helping Colby straighten and tuck in the sheets and return the pillows to where they belonged.

"Thanks, kiddo."

Colby almost smiled.

"Ready?"

Colby fidgeted, then darted over to Vic's side.

Vic caught him and lifted the boy up onto his hip. Having that little body in his arms again was exquisite torture, but when he heard Colby sigh with relief, he straightened up and pushed temptation aside. He had to.

They headed back to the living room, and just as Vic was bracing himself for Ryley's reaction, he found an unexpectedly fond smile on the man's face instead.

Ryley smirked at him, then tilted his head to look at Colby. "Hey, kiddo."

"Hi," Colby whispered.

"You ready to see some magic?" Ryley asked.

Colby fidgeted, looking like he wasn't sure how to answer.

Ryley gave the boy an indulgent smile, then turned serious as he looked at Vic again. "I can undo the spell if it goes wrong," he assured him.

Vic gave a tight nod. They couldn't banish Cam. It would be like failing his brother for a third time, and Vic would never survive that.

Ryley glanced at Colby, then added, "But that'll mean Ahriman stays, too."

Vic took a deep breath. "As long as you're sure you can undo it…"

"Yeah," Ryley said. "That'll be the easy part, if it comes to it. The hard part's gonna be banishing one ghost without the other."

Vic took another bracing breath. "Alright." He nodded. "Let's try it."

"Alright." Ryley looked at Colby. "Hey, kiddo, you think you can help me with the spell?"

Colby frowned, his hands tightening around the lapels of Vic's jacket. "Spell?"

Ryley smiled at him. "It's magic. But I need your help to do it so we can make the Bad Man go away."

Colby looked at Vic, who gave the boy an encouraging nod, then Colby looked back at Ryley and dipped his chin.

"Alright," Ryley said and headed out of the living room. "Follow me."

Asher filed out after him, and Vic followed, carrying Colby to the entryway.

They gathered at the front door, and Ryley turned to face them, pulling a vial out of his pocket.

"What's that?" Vic asked.

"Ahriman's blood," Ryley explained. "Not critical for the spell, but it's supposed to help focus the magic on the target." He clenched his hand around the vial, then blew out a breath and looked at Colby. "Right, so, this is gonna be the scary part," he said. "I need you to think of the Bad Man for me, so that he'll come here."

Colby whimpered and hid his face against Vic's neck.

Ryley gave Vic an apologetic look, then took a step closer and reached out, stopping just short of touching the boy. "I know it's scary, kiddo, but I need him to be here so that you can tell me if the spell works or not, since I can't see him."

Vic looked at the boy in his arms. "I'm right here," he murmured. "We all are. We won't let him hurt you."

Colby slowly peeked out at them.

"And Cam," Ryley said, giving Vic a significant look. "Cam should be here, too."

Vic felt a hand grab his arm, and realized Cam was already with them. "He's here."

Colby looked down at Vic's side, and almost smiled.

"See?" Ryley said. "We're all here, and we won't let Bad Man get you."

Vic tilted his head down and met Colby's eyes. "Think you can be my brave boy and let Bad Man come here one last time?"

Colby whimpered, then gave a slowly nod, stopping abruptly as he gasped and hid his face again.

Ryley grimaced. "I take it he's here?"

Vic felt Cam's head move against his side. "Cam just nodded, so…yeah."

"Right." Ryley blew out a breath, looked all around, then focused on Colby again. "Hey, kiddo, I need you to help Vic hold onto Cam for me. Can you do that? Otherwise he might go away with the Bad Man."

Colby whimpered and immediately shot out a hand, grabbing at what appeared to be nothing. Vic felt Cam move in closer, wrapping his arms around Vic's waist, and Vic put an arm around his brother's ghost while still holding Colby up on his hip. Asher stepped in behind where Cam stood, putting his arms around the lot of them. They all clung to one another, and Vic gave Ryley a grim nod.

"Alright." Ryley turned for the door. "Here goes nothing." He looked at Asher, who gave him an encouraging smile, then Ryley opened the door and walked out toward the street.

Vic watched as Ryley came to a stop just behind Vic's mailbox, still clutching the vial in one hand while he lifted the other hand in front of himself, his palm facing out. Ryley stood there for a moment, then turned to his left. He slowly traced the front of Vic's property and disappeared from view.

Colby started to peek out, then whimpered and ducked his head again. Vic shushed him, and tightened his hold on Cam. He wanted Colby more comfortable and safe, but he couldn't lose his brother. Not again.

Finally, after several agonizing minutes, Ryley reappeared from the right, completing his circuit of the property and coming to a stop at the same point where he'd started. Vic watched, seeing a look of extreme concentration on his face.

Ryley lowered his hand, and Colby gasped, his head jerking up off Vic's shoulder.

Vic tightened his hold on Cam. "Colby? What's wrong?"

Colby stared, his big eyes wide and surprised. "Bad Man just flew out the door."

Vic blinked. "What?"

Cam shook beside him, the motion reminiscent of laughter.

Colby pointed just as Ryley stepped up onto the front porch. "Bad Man's out there. He looks stuck."

Ryley grinned. "It worked?"

Colby tilted his head, staring at the street.

"Kiddo?" Vic asked. "What is it?"

"He looks mad," Colby whispered.

"But he's out there, right?" Ryley asked, glancing over his shoulder even though he couldn't see anything. "He can't get in?"

Colby slowly shook his head, then looked at Ryley. The boy studied the mage for a moment, and slowly relaxed, almost smiling at him.

Ryley smiled back, then looked at Vic. "Please tell me Cam's still here."

Before Vic could say anything, he felt Cam pull away, and something invisible almost shoved Ryley off his feet. Ryley caught his balance, then laughed.

"I take it that's a yes," Ryley chuckled.

Vic reached out, felt around for his brother, and hauled the kid in for a hug. "Brat," he chastised, but the word had no heat, his entire body sagging with relief that the spell had worked. One threat to Colby, gone.

Now to decide what to do about another.

Chapter 16

COLBY SAT down on the floor of the shower and hugged his knees to his chest while the hot water continued to beat down on him. He knew what he had to do, but the thought terrified him.

His emotions were all over the place, making his thoughts bounce from one thing to another and back again so fast that he couldn't seem to pin anything down. The morning had started out so wonderful, waking up all warm and safe in Vic's bed, then took a horrifying turn when he overheard Vic and Ryley talking about him. It had only gotten worse after that when he'd had to face Bad Man, but then everything became wonderful again when Ryley's spell had cast Bad Man out of the house.

The memory of that moment almost made Colby giggle: seeing the ghost just *whoosh* right out the door, like some invisible force had sucked him out, and then watching him beat his fists on an unseen barrier. The fury on Bad Man's face had been terrifying, but he couldn't get back in. Colby was safe.

Then again, Colby was only safe as long as he stayed inside the house. If he went outside, Bad Man would be able to get him. And Vic had talked about sending Colby away, which would mean having to endure Bad Man's presence all over again. Would Ryley do another spell wherever Colby went? What if he couldn't? What if he didn't want to?

But staying meant Vic wanted to touch him.

Colby didn't want Vic to be like Bad Man, but at least staying here meant he'd be free of the real Bad Man. Staying could be scary and awful, but leaving would be worse. He'd have to face his nightmares all over again. There was no way he'd survive that. He couldn't go back to that torture, not now that he knew the alternative.

Sucking in a deep breath, Colby got up on shaky legs and finished his shower, being extra thorough. Maybe, if he was prepared, it wouldn't be so bad, wouldn't be so painful. Maybe, if he got himself ready and started accepting it now, it wouldn't be so scary. And this was Vic, after all. Vic always touched him nicely. With any luck, this wouldn't be any different. Scarier, but no different.

Once he was as clean and stretched as he could get, Colby shut off the water, dried himself vigorously, and darted out to the bedroom. He snatched up his hoodie and slipped it on, zipping it all the way to his chin. The single layer wasn't nearly enough, but it would bolster him for the walk down the hallway. It would be the little bit of security he needed to get him to his goal.

Taking another deep breath, Colby walked out the door.

* * *

VIC SAT up in bed, going through his inbox on his phone so he'd know what contracts he had to work on tomorrow. He still had to decide what to do about Colby—whether to send him away or bear the torture of letting him stay—but he didn't want to think about that at the moment. It was too hard to decide. He didn't want Colby to leave, but he didn't see how the boy could safely stay, either.

A soft, shuffling sound reached his ears, and he looked up to see Colby coming down the hallway. Vic blinked. The boy was wearing only his hoodie, his little body practically swimming inside the oversized garment without all his other layers to fill it in. The thought of Colby being naked under that thing sent an unbearable bolt of arousal straight to Vic's cock. *Fuck*. He bunched the sheets in his lap with one hand and clutched his phone with the other as Colby stepped into the room.

"Hey, champ." Vic swallowed hard. "What's–"

Colby took the phone from him and set it aside, then stripped off his hoodie with shaky hands and climbed up on the bed, straddling Vic's lap.

"Don't send me away," the boy begged.

Vic blinked, trying to process the words. "What?"

"Don't send me away," Colby repeated. "I'll do anything you want. Just…please…let me stay."

Vic held up his hands, his fingers twitching with the need to touch all that exposed skin. "Colby–"

"You can fuck me," Colby pleaded. "Use me however you want. Just don't make me leave."

Vic was pretty sure his heart was going to jump out of his chest, it was beating so hard.

Fuck. He had a lap-full of very naked, beautiful boy, fresh from a shower if the clean scent of him meant anything. His skin was even still a bit rosy from the hot water. Then again, that was probably made worse by sheer nervousness. Vic never would have imagined that Colby had the courage necessary to make such a move.

Colby was offering him the very thing he'd been aching for ever since he was a teenager—and more so since he'd met this beautiful, sweet boy. Feeling the warmth of that little body pressed up against his, Vic's imagination raced with all sorts of filthy images, every possible way he could possess this boy and make him his.

But it was all just so wrong.

"Colby," Vic forced out, his voice breaking on the word. His cock throbbed with need, but Vic had to resist. He couldn't do this. Not to him.

"Please," Colby whispered, pressing closer. The little guy's body trembled as his knees tightened around Vic's hips, his hands desperately clutching Vic's shoulders. Colby shifted and let out a whimper, their foreheads touching and their noses pressed alongside one another, bringing their lips within a breath's space of contact.

Fuck. Those lips. It would take the barest effort for Vic to tilt his head and capture those lips with his. Gods knew he'd fantasized about it enough, and now it was on the verge of happening, assuming he lost all self-control.

No. He couldn't do it. The whole thing was just so wrong. Vic swallowed hard and tried to take a deep breath, but his chest ached while his heart continued hammering away, his whole body thrumming with need. It was so wrong, but he wanted it so badly.

"Please," Colby whispered again, the movement of his mouth making his lower lip brush against Vic's.

"Fuck." Vic grabbed Colby's head with both hands and crushed their mouths together. *Oh gods*. Colby's lips were perfect. Full and soft and warm. A voice in the back of Vic's head screamed at him that this was so many kinds of wrong, but he couldn't help himself. It just felt so damned good.

Except Colby was still. Not kissing back at all.

Vic blew out a shaky breath as he pulled back just enough to see Colby's face. He'd crossed a line. He knew it. Now that he'd actually taken something from the boy, Colby would be sure to panic.

Except he didn't see panic on Colby's face. All the determination and fear Colby had shown when he first came to Vic's room had melted away, replaced by confusion and curiosity.

Vic blinked, trying to catch his breath, and braced himself. Maybe the panic just hadn't hit yet.

Colby met Vic's eyes for the first time since coming into the room, then flicked his gaze down to Vic's mouth. Vic groaned at the sight. Colby tilted his head, a thoughtful look on his face, then slowly leaned in.

The boy touched his mouth to Vic's tentatively, curiously. He pulled back, then tried again. Vic let out a sigh as their lips connected once more, and he gently returned the kiss, letting Colby control the pace. The boy slowly caught on, watching and feeling the way Vic's mouth moved and trying to replicate it until Colby started to kiss back like he'd been doing it all his life.

Vic felt a moan rise up from somewhere deep inside him at the same moment Colby let out a whimper, but not like any whimper he'd made before. Instead of fear, the sound was full of longing.

"Fuck," Vic breathed, throwing his arms around Colby and holding him tight as he deepened the kiss, coaxing Colby's mouth open until their tongues were battling for contact and their breathing became so erratic that they finally had to pull back just to get some oxygen.

Colby's skin was reddened all over, his eyes wide, his pupils so large that they nearly swallowed all the color. He slowly caught his breath, then let one hand fall away from Vic's neck only to bring his fingers up to his own bottom lip, touching it experimentally. The boy lightly touched Vic's lips, then traced his own again.

"That was kissing?" Colby asked in a whisper.

Vic nodded, not even bothering to try using words.

Colby lightly stroked his bottom lip from one side to the other, then one corner of his mouth twitched, curling up into a hint of a smile. He looked up, meeting Vic's eyes.

Colby whispered, "Can we do it again?"

Vic moaned. "Oh gods." He just caught the growing smile on Colby's face as he swooped in to kiss the boy again. He couldn't resist. He was going to hate himself once this was over, but at the moment, he couldn't stop himself if his life depended on it.

He held Colby tighter, his hands moving all over that slim, naked back, barely even noticing all the scars under his fingers. Colby tilted his head, effectively deepening the kiss, and put his arms around Vic's shoulders, his little hands scrabbling for something to hold onto, his slender fingers clutching Vic's hair again as he pressed forward, their chests hard up against one another.

Colby gasped, pulled back just a bit, and looked down.

Vic blinked and sucked in a breath, trying to get his

head to clear. Had he done something wrong? Had he crossed another line without realizing it?

He followed Colby's gaze, and saw the boy's hard cock jutting straight up at him, now sandwiched between their bodies.

Colby tilted his head. "That's never happened without the candy before."

Vic blinked. "Candy?"

Colby gave a slight nod. "Bad Man's special candy. He'd make me take it when I wasn't behaving." His frown deepened. "It made it so I couldn't move, couldn't fight them. But then that would happen," he continued, gesturing down with his chin.

Vic stared at him. *Oh gods.* Ahriman had drugged the poor boy. Drugged him into submission. "And this *never* happened without the dr– The candy? *Ever?*"

Colby looked up at him and shook his head.

Fuck. Vic tightened his hands on Colby's sides, fighting the urge to touch the boy in ways he'd only dreamt about.

In ways that Colby had apparently never experienced.

He shouldn't touch the boy. He knew he shouldn't. But he *had* to. Otherwise, he might lose his mind.

And Colby didn't look scared. More confused than anything. It only made Vic want to touch him more, want to give the boy the kind of pleasure he'd probably never known.

Or was Vic just trying to justify touching Colby for the sake of his own pleasure? Gods knew Vic had been desperate to have his sweet boy in all sorts of filthy ways from the very first day Colby had crept out of his bedroom to watch Vic play, but following through on that desire would only make him as bad as Ahriman. As bad as all the other men who'd had Colby. As bad as the man who'd abducted Cam.

A sick feeling wormed its way through Vic's gut, but temptation was still there, his heart slamming in his chest as his fingers itched to move.

His hands inched down to Colby's hips, his thumbs

resting along the creases of the boy's thighs, that hard cock jutting up between them, right within Vic's reach. A shudder ran through Vic as he fought to keep his hands still.

"Vic?"

Vic blinked and jerked his head up, tearing his eyes away from Colby's cock.

Colby frowned. "You look…" He trailed off, then reached up and gently brushed his fingertips along Vic's eyebrow.

Vic melted into the touch, letting out a sigh. Such simple contact, yet the few times Colby had done so, it always sent the tension right out of him. Vic had no idea why it worked, only that it did, and that he loved it.

"Gods, that feels so good," he murmured.

Colby stilled.

Vic opened his eyes. *Shit*. He couldn't be letting Colby make him feel good, not even so innocently. The poor boy had been used for other men's pleasure all his life. Vic couldn't be just another name on that list of monsters. He didn't want to, but he had to stop this.

He opened his mouth to say something, only for Colby to swoop in and kiss him again. Vic groaned, unable to resist kissing him back. Those lips were so perfect. Vic wasn't sure he'd ever get enough.

Colby leaned closer, his cock nudging against Vic's belly, and let out a moan that sounded of half pleasure and half surprise. Had the boy ever experienced any sexual pleasure of his own? Trauma could do all sorts of unusual things to the body, and if he'd only ever been hard while under the influence of a drug, it was entirely possible that Colby had never felt an orgasm in his life.

The very idea was too tempting to resist.

"Colby," Vic whispered, leaning into Colby's touch as the boy resumed trailing his fingers all over Vic's face. "May I touch you?"

Colby paused, tilting his head. "You are touching me."

"No, I mean…" Vic inched his hands closer to one

another, his thumbs almost brushing the base of Colby's cock.

Colby looked down, then looked back up at Vic with a puzzled frown.

"Has anyone ever touched you there?" Vic whispered.

Colby shook his head, still looking confused.

Gods, forgive me. Vic slid one hand over, gently wrapped his fingers around the base of Colby's cock, and slowly stroked up toward the head.

Colby threw his head back and gasped, then gave an involuntary thrust into Vic's fist. "Vic..." he moaned.

Vic slid his other arm around Colby's waist and urged the boy closer, bringing their foreheads back together. "Does it feel good?"

Colby let out a shuddering breath and nodded.

Vic stroked again, and Colby slowly let go of Vic's shoulders, bringing his hands down Vic's body until his little fingers curled around the waistband of Vic's pants.

"No, sweetheart," Vic whispered, letting go of Colby just long enough to bring the little guy's hands back up to his shoulders. "Just hold on to me."

"But–"

Vic shook his head. He knew he shouldn't be touching the boy at all, but keeping it all about Colby rather than his own pleasure was the only way he thought he could justify it. The only way he could survive it. "This is for you."

Colby started to protest, but Vic took hold of his cock again, stroking faster and more firmly, tearing a cry out of the little guy's throat. "Vic..."

"That's it," Vic whispered. "Just feel. Enjoy it."

Colby whimpered and moaned again, squeezing his eyes shut and holding on to Vic so hard that his arms shook. Vic kept stroking, dividing his gaze between his hand and Colby's face, loving the view of Colby's cock sliding through the former and making sure there was no sign of fear on the latter. With another moan, Colby thrust into Vic's hand at the same moment he jerked forward, slamming their lips together. Vic sighed as he returned the kiss, clutching that little body in his arms while he kept stroking the boy faster.

"Vic," Colby whined between kisses. "Oh gods, Vic…What…What's happ– *Oh*." Colby let out a shout, and Vic felt the little guy's cock pulse in his hand, covering his t-shirt with cum. Colby held on to Vic's shoulders so tight through the release that Vic was pretty sure he was going to be bruised, but it was completely worth it. The boy let out one more moaning gasp and collapsed against him.

Vic pulled his hand from between their bodies and put both arms around the boy, holding him close as he came down. It took everything Vic had to keep still, his own cock—rock-hard and aching—pressed firmly between their bodies, but he couldn't do anything about it. *Wouldn't* do anything about it. This couldn't be about him. It had to be about Colby, and only Colby. It had to be about the boy's pleasure and nothing else. Otherwise, Vic couldn't live with himself.

The rise and fall of Colby's chest had just begun to slow when Colby suddenly sucked in a breath and burst into tears.

Shit. Vic loosened his hold just in case the boy wanted to get away, but Colby only clung tighter, clutching Vic's shoulders and twisting Vic's shirt in his little fists as he cried these great, screaming sobs that seemed far more intense than such a little body could manage.

Vic held him through it, stroking his back and murmuring to him, just letting him cry. Hells, the poor guy more than deserved it.

"I've got you," Vic told him, rocking slightly as he held the boy. "My poor, sweet boy. It's alright. I've got you."

Colby cried for almost an hour, the sobs letting up only to start afresh. Vic felt the tears soaking into his shirt, and held the boy tighter. Finally, the sobs gave way to shuddering gasps, then to occasional sniffles, then steady, shallow breathing. It was several more minutes before

Colby finally lifted his head from Vic's chest, blinking heavily as he sniffed.

"Hey, sweetheart," Vic murmured, reaching up to wipe away a few stray tears. The poor little guy looked exhausted, and his face was lined with pain. "Headache?"

Colby slowly nodded.

"Tell you what: Why don't you go stand in a hot shower for a few minutes, blow your nose real good," Vic said, gently rubbing Colby's back, "and I'll go get you something for that headache. How's that sound?"

Colby blinked, and started to nod again, then he gasped and reached for the waistband of Vic's pants. "I didn't—"

"Hush." Vic caught the boy's hands and brought them up to his mouth. He kissed Colby's knuckles, taking a deep breath as he fought the urge to let Colby touch him. "I'm just fine."

"But—"

"Let's just get rid of that headache so you can get some sleep," Vic murmured. He reached past Colby, grabbed a throw blanket lying across the foot of his bed, and wrapped it around the boy as he gently nudged him. "Come on."

Colby blinked again, then finally seemed to take Vic at his word and slowly got up off the bed, clutching the blanket around himself. He took one shaky step, and Vic caught him around the waist.

"I've got you, sweetheart," Vic murmured, lifting the boy to his hip, Colby's arms immediately going around Vic's shoulders.

Vic carried Colby down the hallway and into his own room, setting the boy on his feet and getting the shower started while Colby stood there, his eyelids drooping as he rubbed his temples. He left the boy to shower, took the blanket back to his room, restored his bed to rights, then went to get a glass of water and a bottle of pain meds, setting both on the washroom counter beside a pile of clean clothing, including all of Colby's usual layers. Vic was sure the boy would put on every single one of them.

He stopped at the bedroom doorway on his way out, listening to the shower run. His traitorous mind easily conjured up images of that beautiful, naked body, all soapy and wet, warm and slick. That body that had just been in his arms, that had finally gotten to experience real pleasure, and at Vic's hands. That body that was still so close, separated by a mere wall.

Vic clenched his hands into tight fists. The boy wasn't his. Colby deserved every ounce of pleasure Vic could give him, but it would all have to be on the boy's terms. Vic had no right to touch him otherwise, and gods knew he'd probably never get the chance again. That moment had been a beautiful fluke that would have to remain an exquisite memory.

Taking a deep breath, Vic firmly shut the bedroom door, and went back to his own room.

He changed his shirt, settled back into bed, and picked up his phone, but he couldn't focus on it. Instead, he kept glancing down the hallway at Colby's bedroom door, waiting for any sign of the boy. Maybe he'd come back for more. Maybe he'd want to try again.

Vic cursed himself and shook his head. Foolish, wishful thinking. Colby was probably freaking out right about now. If the boy did come back, it would only be in search of comfort.

An hour passed, and there was no sign of the boy. Vic got up and crept down the hallway, then eased Colby's door open. The light was off, and Colby was curled up in a tight ball near the edge of his bed, the sheets pulled up to his ear. In the washroom, the pills were gone and the water glass was empty. Vic sighed. With any luck, the boy would get a good night's sleep, and they could deal with any potential fallout in the morning.

He went back to his room, checked his phone one more time, and started to set it aside when he spotted Cam's notepad sitting out on the nightstand, words from that morning's conversation standing out to him.

You know, this would be a really great time to have a dog.

A grin took over Vic's face as he put the notepad away, snatched his phone back up, and opened his email. He shot off a message to Roz, an old friend who ran a dog shelter that specifically catered to finding homes for rescued or abandoned dogs as well as training dogs to be placed in therapy situations, such as companions for the elderly or service dogs for people with medical conditions. Vic had used Roz's service a few times to get companions for his own rescues, giving the kids a source of comfort as well as something on which to focus.

Cam was right. This was definitely the time for exactly that. And with Ahriman now banished from the house, Vic could safely leave Colby home alone to go out and choose a dog, assuming he couldn't convince the boy to go with him.

Vic finished his email and switched off his phone, then collapsed into bed, exhaustion taking over even as he wondered what the morning might bring.

* * *

VIC JOLTED awake in the middle of the night. He held his breath, listening, trying to figure out what had startled him out of sleep. It hadn't been a dream. At least, not one that he could remember.

He started to sit up and reach for the bedside lamp when he realized there was something draped across his leg, something heavier than the usual weight of the blankets. Vic switched on the lamp, and froze.

Colby was curled up at the foot of his bed, his little body wrapped around Vic's calf.

"Colby?" Vic whispered. He tried to pull his leg free, but Colby had the blankets pinned down too tight. "Sweetheart?" He pushed the boy's hood back and ran his fingers through Colby's hair.

Colby stirred, then sucked in a breath as he stiffened. Vic snatched his hand back. *Shit*. He'd completely forgotten about Colby's reaction to having his hair touched. Vic waited, bracing himself for panic, but Colby looked up, spotted Vic, and slowly exhaled, his body shuddering with relief.

"Hey, kiddo," Vic murmured. "You alright?"

Colby idly curled and uncurled his fingers, brushing them across the blanket right over Vic's knee. "I'm sorry. I got scared."

"Hey, that's alright. Don't apologize."

Colby gave a shy shrug. "I thought I wanted to be alone, but…" He trailed off and looked around timidly. "I woke up alone, and you were too far away…"

Vic felt heartbreak and relief shoot through him, and he found himself smiling. "I'm right here," he said.

"Vic?" Colby whispered.

"Yeah, kiddo?"

Somehow, Colby managed to curl himself up even tighter than he already was. "Would you hold me?"

That bittersweet feeling slammed into him again. Even though he knew the temptation would be unbearable, he couldn't resist having that little body in his arms, especially if Colby wanted it, too. Just the fact that Colby had *asked* for it was amazing. Vic couldn't say no to that.

Vic pushed the covers back. "Come here."

Colby scurried up toward the pillows on his hands and knees, burrowing under the blankets and curling up tight at Vic's side.

Vic switched off the light, settled down on his back, and wrapped the boy up in his arms.

Colby let out a sigh, his body melting against him.

Vic couldn't help but smile. "There's my sweet boy."

Colby rubbed his cheek on Vic's shoulder, and a moment later, he was fast asleep.

Vic lay awake for hours, reveling in the comfort of another body next to his, made even better by knowing it was Colby, all tucked up at his side, warm and safe.

If only it could last.

* * *

VIC SHOT his hand out and fumbled for his phone, trying

to switch off his alarm before it could wake Colby. The sudden movement jostled the boy, still tucked against his side, but before Vic could apologize, he saw the boy watching him, his eyes peeking over the edge of the blankets. He looked as though he'd already been awake.

"Hey, kiddo."

"Hi," Colby whispered. Under the covers, the boy moved his hands up to the edge of the blankets, clutched them in his little fists, and tucked his hands slowly under his chin, exposing the rest of his face.

He didn't look afraid. Vic couldn't believe it. The sight made him smile.

"There's my sweet boy," Vic whispered.

And Colby actually smiled back. It was a soft, little smile, but a smile nonetheless.

"Sleep alright?" Vic asked.

Colby slowly nodded. "Vic?"

"Yeah?"

Colby hesitated, then asked, "Why didn't you use me last night?"

Vic's heart clenched, and he swallowed hard. "What do you mean?"

"You're bigger than me. Stronger. And I said you could." Colby paused, then added, "And you told Ryley you wanted to."

Vic felt the blood drain out of his face. "What?" *Oh gods.* "You heard that?" *Shit.* "Colby, I am so sorry. I never meant for you to–" Vic broke off, his hand twitching with the need to reach for Cam's bracelet.

"So why didn't you?" Colby asked. Somehow, he looked more curious than afraid.

Vic studied the boy's eyes for a moment, then took a deep breath. "Because–"

The nightstand drawer opened, cutting him off. Vic saw Cam's notepad float out, and the pen wrote something quickly before it got set down again.

When nothing happened for several long seconds, Vic reached for the notepad. "Did he leave?" he asked Colby.

Colby nodded.

Frowning, Vic picked up the notepad.

Tell him. About me.

Vic's blood ran cold, and his hand shook as he set the notepad down again.

"What did he say?" Colby asked.

Vic looked at him. "He wants me to tell you what happened to him."

Colby tilted his head, his face bright with curiosity despite a flash of worry that crossed his eyes.

"He never told you?" Vic asked.

Colby shook his head.

Vic considered for a moment, then blew out a breath and sat up. If he was going to tell Colby everything, he couldn't do it lying down like that. He leaned back against the headboard, and Colby scooted up to snuggle into his side, saving Vic the added agony of having to look the boy in the face as he spoke.

It was going to be hard enough as it was.

Vic took a deep breath and looked across the room, Cam's bracelet just visible at that distance, resting in its usual spot on top of his dresser.

"It was fifteen years ago. I was sixteen years old…"

Chapter 17

Fifteen years ago…

SIXTEEN-YEAR-OLD VICTOR Lucius showered twice and changed his outfit three times before he made himself stop fussing and go downstairs. His parents were out of town for the week, the first time they'd ever left him and Cam home alone.

Which meant Vic could *finally* get away with going out to the club without his parents being there to ask where he was going. He was perfectly, painfully aware that his parents would never accept the fact that Vic was gay. He'd heard their homophobic comments over the years, so Vic had been struggling in silence, ever since he was twelve and realized he was gay, knowing he had to keep it a secret.

But now, with his parents not looking over his shoulder, he could finally have one night to just be himself. To have a taste of freedom. It would have to be enough. It would hold him over until he had enough money of his own so he could move out and have his own life, free to live and love the way he wanted.

He could be strong and keep his secret for another year or two, as long as he had this night of freedom.

Cam barely glanced up from his video game. "Where are you going?"

Vic froze, swallowed hard, and said, "I'm...gonna go hang out with the team. I'll be back in a couple hours."

Cam scoffed. "You're always hanging out with the team."

"Well, you're always sitting there playing video games," Vic shot back, then winced when he saw Cam's expression fall. It wasn't Cam's fault he was always sick. The kid had been born with a weak immune system, which meant he was in bed with a cold or a flu more often than not.

Which meant Vic was the one who got to play football and have perfect attendance and grades at school and help out at the family business in order to make Dad proud. To make up for Cam's shortcomings.

Then again, there was no *'got to'* about it. He *had* to. It was the only way to protect Cam from Dad's verbal abuse. The more he did to keep Dad proud, to keep Dad's focus on him, the less Dad would complain about all the things Cam couldn't do.

"Can I come with you?" Cam asked, sitting up and looking excited despite just recovering from a cold.

Vic felt the blood drain out of his face. He couldn't let Cam see where he was really going. Cam wouldn't understand it. Besides, this was *his* night. His one night to be himself for a change, no parents looming over him and no little brother tagging along.

"Dad wouldn't be happy if you got sick again," Vic said.

Cam's smile dropped right off his face, and he slumped back on the couch with defeat.

Vic tried to think of something to say to make him feel better, then gave up and turned for the door. Cam would be fine. And this was Vic's night. He wasn't going to let anything get in his way.

"I'll see you later," he threw over his shoulder as he let himself out the door.

Vic grabbed his bicycle, not even daring to borrow

the extra car. He sucked in a breath and pushed off, heading straight for downtown.

He'd memorized the directions for weeks, having traced the route on the map on his phone over and over as he counted down the days until he could finally have this night out. The dark city zoomed by, his legs pumping, taking him closer to his goal.

He found the club and slowed, coasting by the entrance and staring at the line of men waiting to get in. Vic found a bike rack about a block away, chained up his bike, wiped his sweaty palms on his jeans, and headed across the street.

Several men leered at him as he joined the line and made his way inside. He felt himself blushing, both aroused and unnerved by all the attention. He'd had plenty of girls look at him that way, flirting with him at school or at home games, but it felt nothing like this. This felt *good*. This was the first time he'd ever been allowed to look at other men, allowed to notice other men looking at him, and he never wanted it to end.

Someone tugged on the back of his shirt. Vic took a deep breath and turned, eager to see who he'd get to talk to—Maybe flirt with? Maybe more?—then jerked back, stunned, when he saw his little brother standing there.

"*Cam*?" he gasped. Vic clenched his hands into fists. "What the hells are you doing here? Did you follow me?"

Instead of answering him, Cam glanced around from under his eyelashes. "Vic, what is this place?"

Vic paled as he suddenly realized his secret was out. He didn't want Cam to know. He didn't want anyone in his family to know. This was going to ruin everything.

"Go home, Cam," Vic ordered, grabbing his arm and steering him back toward the door.

"Vic, wait." Cam struggled, then looked up at him and asked, "Are you *gay*?"

Vic felt the blood drain out of his face all over again. "What? No! I–"

"Because this is a gay club, Vic," Cam insisted.

"I know that!" Vic snapped.

Cam flinched. "I don't think we should be here."

"Then go home," Vic growled.

Cam looked around again. "Let's both go home, Vic."

No. No, he wasn't going home. Not even now that Cam knew. He'd been waiting for this experience for years, had been planning this particular night for weeks. He wasn't going to go home without having at least a taste of an encounter with another man.

"Go away, Cam," Vic insisted. "I'll be home later."

"Come with me," Cam insisted, still scanning the crowd with uncertainty.

Vic scoffed. "Chill out, Cam. It's not like they're gonna rape you." *Now just go away. Please go away so I can have this.*

"Vic—"

"Go home, Cam!" Vic yelled, catching the attention of a few men nearby. "You shouldn't be here."

"Vic, please, just come home with me—"

"Fuck!" Vic yelled, stepping back and glaring at his brother. "Why can't you leave me alone for just *one* night? One night, Cam! That's all I wanted. One night with no parents and no little brother breathing down my neck—" He turned away, hands on his hips, his wonderful night slowly unraveling all around him. He looked back at Cam. "Gods, I wish you'd just disappear for a few days so I can finally live my own life for a change."

Cam slumped with defeat. "Vic—"

"Go away, Cam. I don't ever wanna see you again!" Vic yelled, then spun away and disappeared in the crowd.

CAM STARED after his brother. He felt rooted to the spot, unable to follow Vic, unable to move. Vic had never talked to him like that before. Sure, his big brother had been irritated at times when Cam's health had gotten in the way of his plans, but *never* anything like this.

"Your brother's a dick," someone said.

Cam turned to see who had spoken, and saw a man eyeing him from the bar.

Cam scoffed. "You can say that again," he mumbled, idly fingering the bracelet he wore, the one Vic had given him for his birthday last month. So much for the sentiment of that gift. "He treats me like a little kid," Cam said, kicking petulantly at the floor.

"In that case," the stranger said, "how about we get you a man's drink? You look like you could use it."

Cam eyed the stranger. He looked nice enough, and the guy was offering him a grownup drink? Dad never let him do that, even when he was safe at home. Cam glanced around again. He wasn't sure he really liked this place, but if Vic was going to do something under Dad's nose, then Cam could damned well do the same.

He hurried over to the bar when the stranger patted the stool beside him. Cam climbed up onto it and let out a sigh. He really shouldn't have biked all that way after Vic, especially when he was still recovering from a cold. His lungs felt weak. Sitting down for a bit felt like a great idea. Besides, he could finally have a grownup drink without Dad knowing, and then he could go home and go to bed. Gods knew he'd feel rotten tomorrow, but for now, he was going to enjoy it.

Cam scanned the crowd one more time, looking for Vic, but there was no sign of him.

"There ya go," the stranger said. Cam turned to see the guy slide a glass toward him, the thing filled halfway with some golden brown liquid. "Drink up."

Cam took the glass and chugged back a huge swallow.

The stranger laughed as he choked, and pounded Cam on the back.

"Whoa there, big guy," the stranger said. "There's no rush. Take your time. Savor it."

There was something weird in the man's eyes as he said that, but Cam brushed it off. The guy was probably just teasing him for being a little too eager. What did Cam know? He'd never been to a bar before. He took the guy's advice and slowed down, sipping his way through the rest of the drink. The taste was weird, and it burned as it went down, but when he looked down the bar in either direction, he saw all those other men laughing as they sipped or tossed back their own drinks, and Cam started to feel like his own man for once in his life.

No constant sickness. No coddling mother. No father who constantly reminded him that he wasn't good enough. Just for this night, Cam was going to forget it all and pretend to be a normal, happy, healthy person.

Vic would be pissed if he found out Cam was drinking, but Cam didn't care. Besides, now they'd both have secrets to keep for one another. If Vic wouldn't tell Dad about Cam's drinking, Cam wouldn't tell Dad about Vic's outing. It was only fair.

Cam finished his drink, and spun around on the stool to look for Vic. He wanted to find his brother so they could go home and make a pact, promising never to tell Dad a thing.

He almost fell off the stool as he completed the turn, the room suddenly spinning.

"Whoa, there." The stranger caught him, chuckling in Cam's ear as he steady him.

Cam swayed and put a hand to his forehead. *Shit*. "I don't feel so good." Was there something about not drinking alcohol right after a cold? He knew the one about not mixing alcohol and medication, but he hadn't taken any meds that day, so he should be fine.

Still, something didn't feel right.

"Let's get you some fresh air," the stranger suggested.

Fresh air. Yeah, that sounded like a great idea. He could go outside and clear his head, then go find Vic and go home.

The stranger steadied Cam as he got to his feet, and Cam stumbled along, having to cling to the stranger as they squeezed through the crowd and made their way outside. The cool, night air slapped him in the face, but it didn't do a thing for his head. Everything was still spinning. The lights were all blurry. The shapes going hazy.

He stumbled against the stranger, who pulled him closer. "Easy, now. I've got you."

Cam frowned. Where was he again? And who was this guy?

The stranger stroked a hand down Cam's back and gave his ass a squeeze.

Cam flinched and tried to pull away, but his vision was tunneling down, and he wasn't quite sure he could even feel his legs anymore.

They rounded a corner, and the stranger slipped an arm around his waist, eager fingers groping at his crotch.

Then everything faded to black.

* * *

VIC FOLLOWED a guy who beckoned him across the dance floor. He pushed Cam out of his mind, determined to salvage some aspect of this night before his entire life went to shit. Cam would tell Dad, and then all seven hells would break loose. For now, though, he was damned well going to enjoy this experience.

He'd figure out how to start his life over later. After Dad inevitably kicked him out.

A small part of him hoped Cam wouldn't ever say a word to Dad, but he wasn't sure he could count on it. Not after the things he'd just said. Still, he was pissed. This night was supposed to be perfect, and it was already falling apart.

But with an attractive guy looking him over and inviting him into the backroom, maybe the night would get better. Maybe he could finally experience the bliss of being touched by another man, and hold on to that memory once his life exploded when his parents came home.

Vic stepped into the backroom, shivering as the door shut behind him, the flashing lights and booming music of the club giving way to shadows and the sounds of fucking all around him. He squinted into the dark corners, his cock going rock-hard at the sight of naked men at every turn. Men stroking cocks. Men on their knees. Men pressed up against the walls, their asses being fucked hard, moaning and grunting in time with every thrust.

Gods, it was everything Vic had dreamt about.

The handsome stranger grabbed Vic and pressed him back against the wall. Vic moaned, leaning into the touch. A hand slithered down inside his pants, and Vic gave a shout, his eyes rolling back. There was a hand on his cock. A hand that wasn't his own.

Oh gods. It was just so fucking *incredible*.

Vic thrust into the touch, then gasped as the hand was ripped free, only for Vic to be spun around and shoved against the wall again. He threw out his hands, bracing himself, and glanced over his shoulder.

The handsome stranger reached around and yanked Vic's pants open, shoving them down to his knees. Vic gulped, feeling his face go red. His ass was bare in a room full of strangers, and he was suddenly sure every pair of eyes in the room was on him. His heart raced, and he was tempted to pull up his pants and run, but then a hand was on his cock again, and his brain short-circuited. Nothing else mattered but that touch.

Something cold drizzled down his crack. Vic shivered, and tried to look over his shoulder. The stranger jabbed a couple of fingers between his cheeks, roughly spreading around something slick. *Lube*, Vic realized.

He tried to grab onto the wall, but there was nothing to hold on to. *Oh gods.* Was he really ready for this? He wanted an experience with a man, but did he want it this way? He'd always pictured himself as a top, but maybe this was normal? Maybe, being a kid, with an adult bigger than him standing behind him, maybe this was the way things had to be?

But he didn't want it this way. Not really. Even though it would be an experience, it wasn't shaping up to be the perfect first time he'd dreamt about.

Then, suddenly, it was too late, as a hard cock suddenly ripped him apart, shoving its way inside him all in one go.

Vic screamed, his entire body tensing up around that painful intrusion. *Fuck. Oh gods. Fuck.* It *hurt*. It hurt so much more than he'd ever imagined.

The stranger reached around again and grabbed Vic's cock, stroking it back to life. Despite the pain in his backside, Vic moaned.

Then the man began to move, pulling out until Vic almost felt relief, only to shove back in again as hard as he could, slamming Vic against the wall. Vic turned his head to one side, flatted his hands against the wall, and endured.

Grunts were heavy in Vic's ear as the man continued to fuck him, Vic's bare ass getting slapped hard with every thrust of that cock into his body. The pain eased a bit, and there was even a little pleasure when the man hit what must be his prostate in just the right way, but it still wasn't the beautiful experience of his fantasies.

What the hells had he been thinking?

The man's pace stuttered, and he shouted into Vic's ear, slamming hard and deep a few more times before slumping against Vic, squeezing him against the wall.

Vic hadn't come. Not even close. Hells, he wasn't even hard anymore.

He just wanted to go home.

Finally, the man pulled out, and Vic scrambled to pull up his pants as he watched the guy toss the condom aside. Vic cringed. He hadn't even thought of that. Thank gods, the stranger had.

How stupid could he be?

His hole ached and his ass was still slick and sticky with lube, but Vic didn't care. He had to get out of there. He just had to get home, and then he could shower and scrub away this gods-awful experience.

Vic fastened his jeans and ran out of the club.

He sprinted across the street, unchained his bike, and raced home, keeping himself pressed up on the pedals rather than riding the seat, his ass too sore to even consider it. He got home in record time, tossing his bike aside and rushing inside. He'd put the bike away properly later. After a shower.

After he talked to Cam.

Vic stripped off his clothes as he crossed his room,

and jumped into the shower even before the water was hot. He scrubbed himself down, feeling used and dirty and humiliated. His dream shattered as he watched the water swirl down the drain.

Taking a deep breath, Vic pressed his hands to the wall and hung his head. He closed his eyes and mentally braced himself. He needed to be calm when he talked to Cam. He'd have to apologize for what he said, and hope Cam would keep his secret.

Otherwise, if Dad found out about this night, his entire life would implode.

Vic drew himself up, got out of the shower, got dressed, gathered up his discarded clothes and tossed them in the laundry, then headed down the hall.

"Cam?" He checked Cam's room, but his brother wasn't there. Vic went downstairs, but Cam wasn't playing his video games, either. Frowning, Vic called, "Cam?"

There was no response. A chill ran through Vic, the house eerily silent.

He ran back upstairs and checked every room. Every closet. Under every bed. Then he went downstairs again and did the same. He looked in every cupboard, behind every piece of furniture, and dug through the basement and garage, but there was no sign of his brother.

Shit. Vic had told Cam to disappear for a few days. Maybe Cam had done just that.

Vic raced back up to his room, grabbed his phone, and dialed Cam's number. The call rang four times, then went to voicemail.

Cam was probably ignoring him. Understandably so.

"Cam, look, I'm sorry about what I said, alright?" Vic told him. "Just come home and we can talk about this."

He rang off and set his phone aside, then just stood there, staring at the thing, waiting for Cam to call back.

An hour passed, and Cam still hadn't returned his call. Vic dialed his number again, and once more Cam ignored it, letting it ring through to voicemail.

"Cam, it's late. Just come home, alright? I'll make it up to you, I promise."

Vic set his phone aside and slumped onto his bed, then stood right back up, the pressure on his ass a painful reminder of how the night had gone so far.

He wandered downstairs and turned on the wallscreen, idly flipping through channels while he kept one eye out the front window, waiting to spot Cam returning home.

Two more hours went by, and still no word from Cam.

Vic groaned and grabbed his phone again. He just wanted to go to bed. Get some sleep, forget about his shattered fantasies, and move on.

"Cam, where the hells are you?" he said to Cam's voicemail. "I'm getting worried." *Past worried*, he thought. "Please, come home."

An hour later, after Vic had nearly paced a hole in the carpet, he pocketed his phone and darted outside. The early hours were creepy, the city so dark and silent as he grabbed his discarded bicycle and headed back toward town, retracing his steps and scanning all around.

Maybe Cam had an accident. Maybe he fell off his bike, weak from his recent cold. Maybe he was hurt. Maybe he couldn't reach his phone. Maybe he'd gone to the hospital and they'd called Dad instead.

No, Vic would have gotten an angry call from Dad if that were the case.

Fighting exhaustion, Vic pushed on.

He checked every inch of the streets he traveled, but there was no sign of Cam.

The club was just shutting down for the night when Vic reached it. He jumped off his bike and ran up to the door, yanking his phone out of his pocket as he went.

He pulled up a picture of Cam and held it up to the first guy he reached. "Have you seen my brother? He was here earlier."

"Sorry, kid." The guy brushed him off and stumbled away.

Vic asked the next guy, and the next, and every other man he could catch as they filed out of the club, but not one of them had seen Cam. He hung around the doorway until the last person left, locking the front door, then slumped down on the sidewalk, watching the men all disappear into the night.

That was when he looked up and spotted the bicycle rack across the street, the same one where Vic had chained his own bike earlier. Vic got up and sprinted over to it. Cam's bike was there. Had probably been there when Vic raced out of the club earlier, and he'd been too frantic to notice.

So where the hells was Cam?

"Cam!" Vic shouted, looking all around. "Cam, where are you?"

The only response he got was a few people yelling at him to quiet down.

Vic called Cam again, the repetitive sound of the four monotone rings grating on his nerves. Once again, voicemail. "Cam, please. Please call me back. Or just come home, alright? We can talk about this. I'll make it up to you. Whatever it takes. Just call me back."

He lowered his arm with a sigh and looked around again. Where the hells was Cam?

Vic wandered the streets all around the club in every direction, trying to figure out where Cam might have gone. On foot, all alone. None of Cam's favorite places were anywhere near there, but maybe anger and determination had carried him far enough. Vic got on his bike and spread his search, going to Cam's favorite park, then the arcade—even though he knew perfectly well that it was closed at that hour—and even Cam's school, but there was still no sign of the kid.

He headed back toward the club, deciding to start over his search from where he'd last seen Cam. Vic pulled out his phone again as he went, dialing Cam's number as he coasted down the street just around the corner from the club.

The phone rang in his ear, and the sound seemed to echo.

Vic jerked his bike to a stop, frowning as he listened.

The phone kept ringing while the sound repeated somewhere nearby.

The hells? Vic climbed off his bike and let it fall to the ground as he trailed the noise. The ringing stopped as the voicemail picked up, so he rang off and dialed again. Sure enough, the sound started up in time with his phone.

Vic turned down the alleyway behind the club, the noise getting louder as he went. The sound stopped again, so he dialed once more, heading deeper into the shadows until he saw the light of a screen on the ground.

He froze on the spot, then slowly crept forward, eyes fixed on the cracked screen.

Vic calling...

"Cam," Vic choked out, darting forward and snatching up Cam's phone, the screen displaying all of the missed calls Vic had made.

Vic whirled around, looking in every direction, trying to see anything in the shadowy alleyway, but his brother wasn't there. Just the discarded phone. All those calls Cam had never seen.

Pocketing Cam's phone, Vic dug through every inch of the alley by the light of his own phone screen, then emerged back onto the street, filthy and dripping with sweat, all alone in the early morning silence. Cam's bike seemed to glare at him, all by itself in the rack just down the block.

Vic shuffled out into the middle of the empty street, slowly turning as he looked in every direction. Cam could be anywhere.

He had no idea what to do.

* * *

VIC STUMBLED his way down yet another street. He'd been searching for Cam for two days, showing his picture to anyone he came across, checking in at the hospital and every doctor's office he could find, but coming up with nothing. His brother had simply vanished without a trace.

With little food and no sleep, Vic kept searching. He

had to find his brother. Cam's immune system was weak, probably even more so after the last cold he'd had, which meant he could be violently ill somewhere and in need of help. But Vic had to find him, first. He had to find Cam and get his brother treated.

He no longer even cared if Dad found out. He'd take whatever punishment Dad gave him, as long as he knew Cam was going to be alright.

Vic pushed on and kept searching, his arms shaking as he tried to steer his bike, his eyes burning from lack of sleep. But he couldn't rest. He couldn't stop until he found Cam.

Night began to blanket the city once again. Vic hadn't seen his brother in forty-eight hours, and he felt like he'd been down every single street and alleyway in Morbran City without finding so much as a hint as to where his brother might be.

Cam was out there somewhere. All alone. Probably thirsty and starving. Maybe scared. Vic had long ago given up on the idea that Cam was probably just hiding out, being petulant and angry, though he'd been tempted to cling to that idea. No, something was very wrong. He had to find Cam *now*.

Vic brought his bike to a stop and rubbed his eyes. He was so desperate for sleep, but he couldn't let himself stop searching until he found Cam and got his brother home safe. He scanned the street he was on, then pushed on to the next. Vic had to keep going. That was all there was to it.

He reached another alleyway and stopped. A chill ran through him, one that he couldn't explain. He'd already searched this alleyway twice, but something about it called to him now. Staring into the shadows, Vic slid shakily off his bike and let it fall to the side as he took one unsteady step after another toward the garbage bin in front of him.

Vic stopped. Maybe he was just delirious from lack of food and sleep, but he got the most dreadful feeling that Cam was here.

He took another step forward and stopped again. Beside the garbage bin was a new heap of trash bags, all piled haphazardly and spilling out onto the pavement. Swallowing hard, Vic took one more step, and froze.

A hand. There was a hand poking out between two garbage bags. Below the hand, around a frail wrist, was a bracelet. The bracelet Vic had given Cam for his birthday.

"Cam!" Vic cried, darting forward and yanking garbage bags aside, slowly but surely unearthing his brother's body.

Vic froze again at the sight of Cam. His brother was naked, his body covered in blood and bruises.

He was still breathing, but barely.

Vic fumbled for his phone and dialed an emergency number.

The call was barely answered before tears streamed down his cheeks as he begged, "Please, help. My brother's hurt. He needs help…"

* * *

VIC STARED through the window in the door, his eyes riveted to Cam's fragile form lying in the hospital bed. Cam was utterly still except for the shallow rise and fall of his chest, aided by a machine. Cam couldn't breathe on his own, and that was the least of it.

Dr. Garrison's gentle words buzzed angrily through Vic's head on repeat.

Head trauma…brain swelling…broken and bruised ribs…internal bleeding…fractured wrist…semen in his rectum…no DNA match…torn anus…carpet fibers under his fingernails…

Coma.

Vic pressed his hands over his ears, but it didn't stop the horrible words dancing around inside his brain. His brother had been raped. Beaten to the point of unconsciousness. Tossed into a garbage pile and left for dead.

And all because Vic had shouted cruel words at him instead of taking him home.

Vic's phone rang again. He barely gave the screen a cursory glance, and shoved it back into his pocket. His father hadn't stopped calling since the hospital had called the man to give him the news on Cam's presence there. Vic's life would be over as soon as his parents returned home—he knew they were already on their way, cutting their trip short—but he didn't care. Nothing could be as earth-shattering as hearing his own words run through his head as he watched Cam hover on the edge of death.

He couldn't speak to his father yet. The anger and accusations would come soon enough. For the moment, all he could do was stare at Cam and beg all the gods to let Cam survive.

"Mr. Lucius?"

Vic blinked and tore his eyes away from the window. One of the nurses approached him, wearing a gentle smile as she held out a bag. Vic reached out mechanically and took it.

"We normally give a patient's personal effects to the parents," the nurse explained softly, "but considering what was on that, I thought you'd prefer to have it."

Vic blinked dumbly at her, then slowly looked down at the bag. Moving on autopilot, he opened the bag and reached in, pulling out the only thing it contained, the only thing Cam had been wearing when the ambulance had brought him in.

A woven bracelet, one that Vic had given Cam for his birthday just last month, the braided threads stitched through with words that were now stained with blood.

Clutching the bracelet in his right fist and choking out sobs, Vic turned and punched the wall with his left hand. Then he did it again. And again. Over and over, sobbing and screaming, Vic punched the wall until his own blood ran over his fist, the stitched words stained with his brother's blood now permanently visible to him, even when he closed his eyes.

Always brothers, forever friends.

Chapter 18

VIC FELT the silence like a heavy weight as he finished telling the story, idly rubbing the scars on the knuckles of his left hand, his eyes still fixed on the bracelet across the room, his own words—from all those years ago—haunting him.

I wish you'd just disappear for a few days...

Vic squeezed his eyes shut. He'd gotten exactly what he wanted.

A sniff broke the silence, and Vic blinked a few times, trying to get his bearings, then looked down. Colby was still curled up against him, his little hands clutching Vic's shirt, tears streaming silently down his cheeks.

"Oh, sweetheart." Vic pulled the boy into his arms.

"I'm so sorry," Colby whispered.

Vic shook his head and kissed Colby's hair. "I didn't mean to upset you." He gave the boy a squeeze. "But that's why," he said, answering Colby's question. "It's my fault that some monster got Cam, so now I have to make up for it. That's why I do what I do. I find and rescue kids so they don't have to suffer like Cam did."

Colby looked up at him. "Like you saved me?"

"Yeah." Vic gave him a smile. "Exactly." He paused, then added, "Sometimes, it never feels like enough. But using you would be unforgivable."

Colby frowned and looked away, his tears stopping as a thoughtful look crossed his face. After a few moments, he looked up at Vic again. "How is Cam always so happy if that happened?"

"Well..." Vic idly rubbed a hand along Colby's arm as he thought of an answer. "He's had a lot of time to deal with it. The whole time he was in a coma, I visited him at least once a week, talked to him, just sat with him. He was conscious far more often than I realized, since he couldn't move or speak. Couldn't open his eyes. He had all those years to think about what happened to him, to accept it and move on."

Colby's thoughtful frown deepened. "So I can be happy, too?" he whispered.

"Yeah." Vic held the boy close. "Of course you can. It might take some time, but you can get past it all. I know you can." Vic paused, then added, "And I'll do whatever I can to help you get there."

Colby looked up at him from under his eyelashes. "Does that mean I get to stay?" he whispered.

Vic's heart broke all over again, seeing the hope and worry in Colby's eyes. "Of course, sweetheart. Yeah, of course you get to stay."

Colby's eyes brightened and a hint of a smile showed on his face just before he burrowed in closer and hid his face against Vic's shirt. Vic rested his cheek on the boy's head, and let out a sigh. Still, he couldn't resist smiling. Even knowing how difficult it was going to be having Colby around, the thought of watching the boy open up and finally live was just the thing he needed. Maybe last night was just the beginning. He could channel that determination—that sheer need to give Colby anything and everything he might want or need—and finally have a chance at redemption.

"Vic?"

"Yeah?"

"If Cam was asleep all those years, how did he die?"

Vic's heart clenched with pain even as the old fury rose up again. His jaw tightened at the memory of that gods-awful phone call, the one he'd gotten while on Erostil two years ago. Vic was supposed to be focused on getting Asher back home after he and Ryley had rescued the man from his life of isolation on a deserted island, but that phone call had destroyed Vic's entire world.

He could still hear that cruel voice telling him, "*Your brother is dead...I found out last night that you were out of town, so I figured this was my chance to finally put Cam out of his misery. You've been letting him linger for far too long. It was time for him to go.*"

Vic's hands tightened into fists.

"Vic?" Colby asked.

Vic looked down and saw the boy's eyes widen with worry. Taking a deep breath, Vic closed his eyes and tried to push the rage aside. Poor Colby didn't need that right now.

He'd just about gotten himself calm enough to answer when his phone beeped a notification. Vic grabbed his phone, and smiled when he saw what was on the screen. A response from Roz. Keeping one arm around Colby, he thumbed open the message. It seemed Roz had just taken in a bunch of new dogs, so Colby would have several to choose from.

Assuming Vic could get the boy to actually leave the house.

He looked down at Colby. "What do you say we go pick out a dog?"

The little guy's eyes lit up, and Vic couldn't help but grin.

* * *

VIC SWITCHED off the car and turned to look at the boy curled up in the passenger seat. Colby had been nervous about leaving the house, bundling up in all his layers and huddling in a ball the whole way across town, but the prospect of seeing a puppy must have greatly outweighed his fear. After a long, serious talk about the responsibilities of owning a dog, Colby had gotten into the car with little coaxing on Vic's part, and peeked up at Vic with bright eyes as soon as they came to a stop again.

"We're here," Vic said, then leveled a look at him. "Now, there's gonna be a lot of dogs in there, and—trust me—it's really tempting to want to take them all home, but we can only pick one, alright?"

Colby nodded slowly, glancing at the building out of the corner of his eye. "What happens to the other ones?"

"They'll all get homes," Vic told him. "Someone else will come along and adopt them."

Colby hesitated. "You promise?"

Vic nodded. "I promise." He paused, then asked, "You ready to go?"

Colby gave the outside another nervous glance, then nodded. Vic went around to the other side of the car, picking the boy up right out of the seat and lifting him to his hip. Colby held on, ducking his head. Vic was tempted to make him walk, but Ahriman was still out and about in the world, and Colby was pushing his boundaries just by leaving the house, so at least they were making progress.

Vic walked up to the entrance and knocked on the door. The lights inside the entryway were off, but Vic knew Roz was in there. They had a long-standing arrangement that he could bring in rescues to pick out a therapy dog during off hours so that the experience wouldn't be as overwhelming. Sure enough, he spotted Roz through the window as she hurried across the entryway to open the door, a big smile on her face.

"Hey, Vic." She stepped aside. "Come on in."

Vic thanked her and carried Colby inside. The boy was hiding his face, but as soon as the front door was shut and locked again—and a series of excited barks reached their ears—Colby perked up.

The boy looked at Vic with wide, eager eyes.

"*Oooh*," Roz said, grinning at Colby. "I think they know you're here, kiddo. You wanna go meet them?"

Vic smiled at her enthusiasm. It was probably just what Colby needed to make the experience more comfortable. The boy looked shyly at Roz, but he gave a nod.

Roz beamed at them and hurried off, waving at them to follow.

The barks and yips grew louder as they reached the row of cages. Despite all the noise, Colby's gasp was easy to hear. The boy's eyes grew impossibly wide as he took in the sight of all those dogs dancing about excitedly in their separate spaces.

"What do you think?" Vic asked, watching Colby look from one dog to the other.

"There's so many," the boy whispered.

Vic gave a slow nod. There were probably only twenty dogs there—a mere handful compared to all the ones that existed in the world—but Colby had probably never imagined so many at once. Would the boy even understand that there were thousands upon thousands more out there?

"Do you see one you want to meet?" Vic asked.

Colby kept looking from one to another so fast, Vic wasn't sure he'd be able to pick.

"Hey, Roz? Do you think we could—"

"Way ahead of you," she said with a grin as she darted over to the wall and pressed a button, unlocking all the cages at once.

The dogs flooded out, some heading straight for Vic and Colby while others darted down the hallway to the large, indoor play area where toys were scattered about. Just beyond the play area was a door to a fenced yard. Vic considered taking them all outside to see if he could coax Colby out there, but that was probably pushing things. For now, he walked Colby over to the play area and set the boy down.

Colby went right to his hands and knees and started crawling about amidst all the dogs, a smile slowly growing on his face as one after another tumbled about, wagging their tails and showing off their toys.

It was like the boy hadn't even noticed Vic's absence. A bittersweet feeling shot through Vic, both glad for the boy's sake while also missing that clinging sense of being needed.

Roz came up to Vic's side, and they both watched the boy. "What a sweet kid."

Vic nodded.

"Looks like he's gonna have a hard time choosing," Roz teased.

"Yeah, I was afraid of that," Vic muttered, though the sight of Colby actually *smiling* was worth it. "Thank you again for this."

"Hey, like I told you before: anytime. Besides…" She nodded at Colby. "That little face just made my day. Hells, I wanna take *him* home."

Vic barked a laugh even as a stab of possessiveness shot through him. *Mine*. He shoved the thought aside. He couldn't be thinking that way. It wasn't right, and it certainly wasn't fair to either of them. Colby wasn't his. Would never be his. He couldn't keep him forever.

He shoved his hand into his pocket and clutched Cam's bracelet as he watched Colby play with the dogs. One of them curled up in Colby's lap and licked the boy's face.

Colby giggled—actually giggled—and Vic felt another piece of his shattered world settle back into place.

COLBY SANK his fingers into the puppy's fur, smiling at the sensation. He'd missed this so much. The soft touch. The sweet smell. The happy look on its face as it scampered about in play. His heart hurt, thinking of the poor, sweet puppy that Bad Man had killed, but seeing so many others running about, happy and free, gave him so much hope.

But he could only pick one? It seemed an impossible choice. He wanted them all. He wanted to keep them all and play with them, hold them and see them live. See them safe.

Eventually, the puppies all wandered off and played by themselves or with each other, except one that stuck close to Colby's side. It looked so much like the puppy that Bad Man had killed, except it was a little bigger. It nosed its way right into Colby's lap and curled up there, looking up at Colby with a happy, smiling pant. The puppy jumped up and licked Colby's face, then dropped back to his lap and just sat there, wagging his tail and looking around.

Colby smiled, hugging the puppy close. It felt like the puppy had chosen him, like it wanted to stay right there in Colby's lap forever. And Colby wanted that one, too. If he could only pick one, this would be it.

He was just about to turn around to find Vic, then spotted Cam on the other side of the room. The ghost was laughing, rolling around on the floor with a small dog that kept darting forward and back and jumping all over Cam, its tail wagging like crazy. Cam looked so happy.

And none of the other dogs seemed to notice him.

Colby glanced down at the puppy in his lap, hugging it close even as he got ready to let it go.

VIC WALKED over and crouched at Colby's side. It looked like he'd taken a liking to one of the dogs in particular, so Roz ran off to grab a leash while Vic had a talk with the boy.

"Hey, kiddo."

Colby looked up at him with such happiness in his eyes, Vic thought his heart might burst.

"Who's this?" Vic asked, reaching out to the puppy in Colby's lap and scratching behind its ears. He trailed his hand down to the dog's collar and read the tag dangling from it. "Sharma, huh? He seems like a good boy. What do you think?"

Colby nodded, his eyes full of longing.

"Is this the one?" Vic asked. "Or do you want to think about it some more?"

Colby curled his arms around the puppy, then slowly let go and looked across the room, pointing. "That one."

Vic frowned. The other dog was playing on its own and had barely spared Colby any attention. "Are you sure?"

Colby nodded, a solemn, determined look on his face.

"Colby." Vic waited until he had the boy's attention, then asked, "Can you tell me why that one and not this one?"

"Because that one can see Cam," Colby told him, "and Cam really wants a puppy, too."

Vic blinked, that bittersweet feeling rushing through him again, his heart both breaking and bursting with joy all at once. He looked across the room, watching the lone dog. He couldn't see Cam, but the longer he looked, the more he could imagine his brother there, playing with it.

It was all he could do to stop himself from yanking Colby into a hug, not wanting to frighten or overwhelm the boy, yet desperate to show him how grateful he was.

Roz skipped back over. "Alright, Vic, we've got–"

"Hey, Roz?" Vic interrupted her. "We're gonna need two."

Roz didn't even miss a beat. "Sure thing," she said, beaming at him, and darted off again.

Colby gave Vic a puzzled look.

"What do you say," Vic began, "we get that one for Cam, and this one for you?"

Colby's eyes lit up like he'd just been given the greatest gift in the world. "Really?" he whispered.

Vic nodded. Even though he had no idea how he was going to handle two dogs in the house after years of having none, he couldn't resist that face. "Really."

Colby let out a happy squeak and hugged Sharma close, then turned and called out, "Cam!" He waved excitedly, a big smile on his face.

The lone dog scampered over, seemingly following Cam.

"We get to take them home!" Colby said.

An invisible force tackled Vic, almost knocking him over. Vic laughed and hugged Cam back, then drew Colby in as well when the boy joined them. The pure joy on Colby's face was breathtaking. Vic wished he could see Cam's face as well, but just feeling his brother's happiness was better than nothing.

Roz came over with two leashes in her hands. "*Awww*, aren't you guys adorable." She crouched down and scratched both dogs behind the ears. "These little furballs going home with you?"

Vic nodded, and Colby wouldn't stop smiling.

"So, fair warning," Roz said, patting Cam's dog, "Patches is probably gonna be a handful. They're a loving breed, but they need firm discipline since they don't always behave and are easily distracted."

Vic grimaced, then saw Colby tilt his head as though listening.

Colby leaned close to Vic and whispered, "Cam promises to play with her a lot and take good care of her." He pulled back, his eyes wide with worry, as though Vic was going to change his mind.

Vic gave the boy a smile. "Alright." He glanced where he thought Cam must be sitting. "Thank you."

Colby sighed with relief.

"Now, Patches is fully grown," Roz continued, either not noticing or choosing to ignore the mention of someone she couldn't see, "but Sharma here is gonna get pretty big. Is that alright?"

Vic looked at Colby. "What do you think?"

Colby eyed the dog in his lap. "Puppies grow?"

"Yeah, just like people," Vic said. He looked Sharma over, considering the breed: a domesticated variant of the giant wolves of Falsin. "He'll probably be as big as you are by the time he's done."

Colby's eyes went wide, and he hugged Sharma closer.

"He might be a challenge to walk once he gets bigger," Roz told Colby, "but they're very protective." She nodded at the dog sitting in Colby's lap and looking around like he dared anyone else to get too close to his boy. "It's a good sign when they take to someone like this so easily."

Vic tilted his head. "What do you say, kiddo?"

In response, Colby just kept hugging the dog like he'd never let it go.

Vic smiled. "Let's get these guys home, yeah?"

Colby beamed at him.

Vic left the boys to play with the dogs for a few minutes while he filled out the paperwork and got Roz paid, then they got the dogs on their leashes and headed outside. Colby walked alongside Vic, eagerly clutching the end of Sharma's lead. He stuck close, but didn't even seem to notice that he stepped outside all on his own without a hint of fear.

Vic smiled.

They piled into the car, then stopped off at a pet store on the way home to get a few more supplies. Colby and Cam stayed with the dogs while Vic ran in to get what they needed, then they went home to get everything unpacked and set up while the pups explored their new territory.

The next several days were a chaotic mess. Vic ultimately got the dogs housebroken, but it was a stressful process, especially since Colby went into hysterics the first time one of the dogs had an accident. Vic should have expected it. After Ahriman had killed the only dog Colby had ever known—and for that very thing—it should have been no surprise that Colby would have expected the same result when it happened again.

It took some work, but Vic eventually got Colby calmed down, and they cleaned up the mess together, then showed the dogs where to go to get outside. Colby stopped at the doorway, too nervous to venture into the backyard himself quite yet, but he'd get there. The house was still a large space for him compared to what he'd always known. Someday, though, he'd be ready to push those boundaries a little more.

And having the dogs would certainly help with that.

In addition to that adjustment, Vic also had to balance getting his contract assignments done while starting to teach Colby about household chores as well as starting his lessons in reading and math. He downloaded some learning games onto a spare tablet, and when Colby wasn't playing with Sharma, the boy spent hours riveted to the screen, learning the alphabet and practicing basic math skills. He was oddly resistant to the latter at first, until his natural aptitude for the subject started becoming apparent. The more levels Colby passed in the games, the more he seemed to like it.

Slowly but surely, as the weeks and months passed, they developed a routine in which their afternoons were spent in companionable silence, both of them sitting on the couch, Vic working away on his laptop and Colby intent upon his lessons. As things began to settle, life started to feel really good. Vic could definitely get used to this.

Then he got a phone call from the boss.

Vic stared at his mobile, hesitating to answer it, then hating himself for hesitating. There were only two or three reasons Mace might be calling him, the most likely one being a new kidnapping or missing-person case. Of course Vic couldn't ignore that. Not a chance.

But the thought of leaving Colby, even for a few days, made his heart ache.

Vic set his laptop aside and stood as he answered the phone. "Lucius."

"*Hey, Vic. It's Mace.*"

"Yes, sir?"

"*I can't believe it took so long for this to happen, but I finally have a case for you.*"

Vic gave Colby a quick glance. The boy was still curled up on the couch, riveted to his math game, one hand tapping the buttons while the other absently stroked Sharma's ears. He was about to respond to Mace, then did a double-take. Colby wasn't wearing all his layers, and Vic hadn't even noticed until that moment. All the boy had on was a t-shirt and pants. No extra shirts. No hoodie. No hands tucked away in his sleeves.

When had *that* happened?

Even surprised as he was, Vic felt a smile on his face. His sweet, beautiful boy was clearly getting more comfortable. There were suddenly no words to describe how lovely it was to see Colby sitting there like that, not hidden away, a hint of a smile on his face as he focused on learning something while enjoying the comfort of Sharma's presence.

"*Vic?*"

Vic gave a start. "Yes, sorry." He headed for his office and shut the door. "So, the case. Where at?"

"*Down near Westfield, just like the last one.*" Mace paused, and Vic grimaced. His last case, before Colby, was a boy who had escaped the walled commune down near the southeastern tip of Agoran. Austin hadn't said much about what abuse he'd suffered in Westfield City, but at least he'd been brave enough to escape, and then Vic had been called in to help get him settled somewhere far away.

Scary, but not surprising, how many of Vic's cases came out of that area.

"Another kid?" Vic asked.

"*Yeah. Hunter. He got himself out of Westfield and started to seek help, then ran off, then came back. Real skittish, this one. They've tried all sorts of things, but can't get the kid to trust them. They're hoping you can get through to him.*"

Vic switched on his computer. If he knew Mace, all the preliminary case details as well as his travel arrangements would already be in his inbox. Sure enough, a new message popped up on his screen.

"Just got your email."

"*Good. But…are you gonna be able to do this? I've been reading you case notes on Colby as they come in…*"

Vic looked toward his closed office door, picturing the sweet boy just down the hall. "I'll just have to deal with it. The separation might set him back a bit, but he's made some really good progress." Vic paused, considering. "Might actually be a good test to see how he handles a disruption like that." Though the thought of having to walk away from the boy still stung. Would Colby be able to handle it?

Would Vic?

Chapter 19

COLBY WATCHED Vic out of the corner of his eye as they did the dishes that night after dinner. Vic had been preoccupied with something all day. Ever since that phone call.

As soon as the kitchen was clean, Colby grabbed Vic's hand and tugged him out toward the living room.

Vic chuckled. "Where are we going?"

Colby pulled him over to the rocking chair and looked up at Vic from under his eyelashes. Vic smiled at him and sat, holding the chair still while Colby crawled into his lap, fast becoming his favorite place in the world. Colby leaned against Vic's chest, and let out a sigh when Vic's arms came around him.

"You doing alright?" Vic murmured, touching his fingertips to the back of Colby's hand, which was clutching Vic's jacket.

The hold was so automatic, Colby hadn't even realized he'd done it. He slowly let go and tipped his head back so he could see Vic's face as he reached up to trail his own fingertips across Vic's forehead.

Colby had no idea what had possessed him to do that the first time he'd tried it, but it had felt right, somehow, and Vic seemed to love it. Vic's eyes slipped closed, and Colby smiled.

"You are such a sweet boy," Vic murmured, then his eyes flew open. "I'm sorry, I shouldn't call you that."

"I like when you call me that," Colby whispered, feeling suddenly shy even though he couldn't stop smiling. "I like being your sweet boy–" He ducked his head and went back to clutching Vic's jacket. The words were true, but saying them made him feel like he was missing something. For a moment, he thought it was because he ought to feel some sort of wrongness—since Bad Man had always called Colby *'boy'*—but it wasn't that. Before he could work it out, Vic spoke again.

"Yeah? I like it, too."

Vic hugged Colby tighter, and Colby's smile grew. He'd never thought it was possible to feel so happy, but he did. Vic had given him so much, and things just kept getting better. Bad Man was gone. He had Sharma. Cam had Patches. Colby was learning all sorts of new things. And Vic was always there, taking care of him.

Colby looked up again, eyeing Vic hopefully. Vic smiled, moved a hand up to Colby's jaw, and bent down to kiss him. Colby couldn't help but moan a little. Kissing had looked so weird the first time he'd seen Ryley and Asher do it, but now that he'd gotten to experience it, he loved it. Vic was right: It felt so good.

And though Vic kissed him whenever Colby wanted it, Vic had still never tried to do anything that made Colby uncomfortable. Nothing like that one night in Vic's bed had ever happened again, either. Colby had never asked, and Vic had never offered. It wasn't that Colby didn't want it, since there were plenty of times that his body had reacted to their kissing just like it had that night, but as the months had passed, and Vic had continued to be so careful with him—to say nothing of the haunting guilt Colby now recognized on Vic's face ever since Vic had told him what happened to Cam—Colby began to realize that Vic wasn't ready for more either.

Besides, there were still plenty of days when the nightmares haunted Colby enough to drive him back to the safety and darkness of his room. It was happening less and less, but it hadn't entirely stopped. Vic said it might never stop, not for the rest of his life, but that it would get better.

Colby kissed Vic again and smiled. He believed that. It already was so much better. Much more than he'd ever imagined. The fantasies of his mental darkness were nothing compared to the happiness and freedom he felt, thanks to this man.

Vic gently broke the kiss and stroked Colby's cheek with his thumb. "We need to talk, sweetheart."

Colby drew his hands up under his chin.

"That phone call I got earlier?" Vic began, and Colby nodded. "That was from work. There's a boy I need to go rescue."

Colby's eyes went wide. "Another boy like me?"

Vic nodded. "It's gonna mean I'll have to be gone for a few days," he explained, and Colby tensed. "Do you think you're up for staying here alone with Cam and the dogs? Or you can go stay with someone. Ryley and Asher, or Zac and Adrian."

Colby glanced at the front door, then back at Vic's face as he curled up tighter. "Bad Man..."

"Or they could come stay here with you," Vic hurried to add. "It's up to you, kiddo. You know they won't hurt you."

Colby slowly nodded. He didn't *know*, not exactly, but Vic trusted his friends, and Colby was slowly starting to trust them himself.

Sharma darted over and put his front paws across Colby's legs.

Vic laughed and scratched the dog behind the ears. "Besides, you'll have this big guy to take care of you."

Colby found himself smiling. *'Big guy'* was an understatement. Sharma had gotten huge over the past few months. And Colby loved him more than almost anything else in the world.

Then Patches started barking and ran over to join them, clearly not wanting to be left out. The smaller dog jumped about, wagging her tail and begging for attention.

Cam must have been taking a rare break because he almost never left his dog alone, spending endless hours playing with the little ball of energy while Vic worked and Colby learned.

"Yeah, you'll look out for him, too, won't you, girl?" Vic asked with a laugh, trying to pet Patches while the dog continued to bounce around.

Colby giggled at the sight, then sobered when Vic caught his eye. The man was looking at him with a combination of fondness and worry. Colby took a deep breath and put on a smile. He didn't want Vic to leave, but he couldn't make him stay, not when he knew why Vic did what he did. Vic would never be truly happy until he could make up for Cam.

So Colby would be brave and let Vic go. If it meant another boy could be as happy and free as he was—if it meant another life could be saved—it would be more than worth it.

* * *

VIC WENT downtown the next morning to run a few errands before he had to catch his flight the following day. He'd left Colby doing his lessons and playing with the dogs, curious to see how the boy handled the brief separation. Colby still slept through it every morning when Vic left for the gym, so this would be different: a last-minute test run to see how Colby handled being alone in the house. He'd offered again to see if Ryley or someone could come stay with him, but Colby had been insistent. He wanted to try it on his own.

His sweet boy was getting so brave.

Vic smiled to himself over the thought as he stepped into the electronics store. Part of his department budget included getting a prepaid phone for each of his rescues. Mace's idea, so that the kids would always have a way to reach Vic in case they needed it. Sometimes, a foster situation wasn't as stable as Vic had been led to believe, and the kid had to be pulled and placed somewhere else. Other times, the kids were too abused or jaded to trust even the best situations, and ran again, then needed the security of a familiar voice. Most of the time, though, the kids just wanted to stay in contact with Vic, looking for reassurance or wanting to thank him again for saving their lives.

He loved those calls.

But Vic was currently out of phones, so he had to grab a few before he went to find Hunter. The store owner knew him well, and quickly got him what he needed. Vic was back out the door in a few minutes, heading for his car so he could get back home and pack.

Vic rounded the corner and almost ran into someone in his hurry.

"Goodness, sorry–" He looked up and sucked in a breath.

The man and woman before him both stared at him in blank shock for a moment before they all stepped back away from one another.

Vic's hands curled into fists. He hadn't laid eyes on them in years, but his fury came back in full force. Clenching his jaw, Vic stormed around them.

"Victor–" the woman called.

"No," Vic barked, whirling around to face them. He tried to find the words through the fire of his rage, but couldn't seem to say anything else. "Just...no," he spat, then turned and strode away.

It wasn't until he was in his car that he realized he was gasping for breath, his heart racing with fury and fear.

* * *

VIC SAT in the garage for a long while before he felt calm enough to go inside. He didn't want to subject Colby to his anger. Or Cam, for that matter. Then again, his brother may have been witness to the whole thing. Vic had been thinking of him hard enough, that was for sure. *Shit.* He'd need to check on Cam. Make sure the kid was alright.

He took a deep breath and started to get out of the

car, then stopped when his mobile rang. Vic pulled it out and checked the screen.

Vic cleared his throat, blew out a calming breath, and answered, "Hey, Athan. How are you?"

"*Hi. Good. And you?*"

Vic reached for Cam's bracelet, trying hard to drive away thoughts of his encounter in town. "Good. What can I do for you?"

"*I hate to sound like we're inviting ourselves over, but Father offered to babysit tonight, and Summer is eager to finally meet your Tanasian rescue…*"

"Oh." Vic nodded to himself. They'd all been trying to get together for months, but between one thing and another—particularly after Summer gave birth to their second child—they hadn't been able to make it happen.

"*It's probably a bad time–*"

"No, actually…" Vic began. It was about time Colby got to meet another stranger, particularly one who shared his rare traits. Besides, Vic could certainly use the distraction, and he hadn't seen his friends in months. "Yeah, come on over. We'll have dinner."

"*Thanks, Vic. Summer will be thrilled.*"

Vic rang off, pocketed his phone, then took another deep breath and went inside.

Colby looked up from his tablet and smiled. "Vic!" His smile faded, and he quickly set his tablet aside, scooting out from under Sharma—the big dog was draped across Colby's lap again—and running to Vic's side.

Vic caught him and lifted the boy to his hip. Colby wrapped his arms around Vic's neck and gave him a tight hug, then pulled back and kissed him.

All the tension in Vic's shoulders started to melt away, and he hugged Colby again, closing his eyes and rocking side to side as he soaked in the warmth of the little guy in his arms.

Colby gave a start, then leaned back to look at Vic. "Cam looks scared," he whispered, nodding with his chin at something behind Vic.

Shit. Vic glanced over his shoulder even though he

knew he wouldn't be able to see Cam. He set Colby back on his feet. "I need to go talk to him for a minute. Is that alright?"

Colby nodded, and watched with those big, beautiful eyes as Vic reached out, squeezed Cam's hand when his brother grabbed him, and headed down the hall to his office.

He pulled Cam in for a hug. "Were you there?"

Cam nodded against his chest.

"I'm so sorry, kiddo."

Cam pulled away and snatched up one of his notepads. *I hate him. I know it's been almost three years, but I still hate him for what he did.*

Vic sighed and put an arm around his brother's shoulders. "I don't blame you, kiddo. And I'm so sorry. I guess I couldn't face him yet, either."

I don't think I'll ever be able to face him. What kind of father kills his own son?

Cam dropped the pen and burrowed into Vic's embrace again. Vic held him tight, swallowing down his own rage and grief.

"I'm so sorry, Cam. I'm so, so sorry."

Chapter 20

VIC SAT in the rocking chair with Colby in his lap, the pair of them watching Patches play with Cam. The dog had been hard-pressed to get Cam to throw her toy at first, but now it seemed like the ghost had managed to push his anger aside for the time being.

Vic wasn't sure he could say the same.

Colby reached up and trailed his fingers over Vic's face. The touch worked its magic, though Vic was still surprised at the sudden relief he felt. He'd started to think nothing would ever make him feel better again.

He looked down at Colby, and the boy stretched up to kiss him. Despite how unsettled the day had made him, Vic found himself smiling. It was so perfect. He couldn't explain it, but something about having that little guy in his arms made everything seem right in the world.

A bittersweet pang shot through him when he realized this wasn't just physical attraction anymore.

Before he could follow that thought, the doorbell rang. Colby tensed, then slid off Vic's lap and darted over to the couch, curling up with Sharma and sinking his hands into the dog's fur. Vic gave the boy a reassuring smile as he got up to answer the door.

Summer tackled him with a hug before he could say anything. "Hi, Vic!"

Vic chuckled and hugged her back. "Hey, Summer." He looked up and gave Athan a nod of greeting.

"Vic." Athan shook Vic's hand.

"Come in, come in," Vic said, standing aside.

Summer darted over the threshold, but Athan called after her. "*Sevgani–*"

"Oh, right." Summer stopped and clasped her hands in front of herself. "Sorry, I got excited and forgot."

Vic tilted his head in question.

"It's–" Athan started to explain.

"Athan said your friend looks like a grownup but is fragile like a baby," Summer cut in, "so I have to be calm around him like I am with *my* babies."

Vic glanced at Athan, who shrugged. "It was the best I could come up with at the last moment."

"Ah." Vic gave him a grateful nod. Summer could be overwhelmingly cheerful when something caught her interest, and Vic wasn't sure how Colby would handle that. "Come on. I'll introduce you."

They headed for the living room, and while Athan and Summer stopped several feet away—Summer almost vibrating with excitement as she stood there—Vic continued across the room to help ease the boy.

"Athan, Summer, this is Colby," Vic said, hugging Colby to his side when the little guy clung to him. "Colby, these are my friends."

Colby eyed them carefully, then looked up at Vic and whispered just loud enough for Vic to hear, "He's so big."

Across the room, Athan breathed a laugh. Besides being taller than Vic and having unusually pale skin, the man's keen senses could pick up just about anything.

"He's a Falsiner," Vic explained. "Falsiners are especially tall, and they have really sharp eyesight and hearing." He paused, then said, "You know, Sharma here comes from a kind of wolf that lives on Falsin."

"He does?"

Vic nodded. "You think Athan can meet him?"

Colby gave a shy nod, and Athan slowly walked over and crouched down, letting Sharma sniff his hand.

Athan murmured something to the dog in his native tongue, then looked up at Colby. "Your *kuryavsu* is beautiful."

Colby frowned, and glanced at Vic, who gave Colby an encouraging nod.

"It means *'wolf pup'*," Athan explained.

"*Kuryavsu*," Colby whispered.

Athan smiled. At least, to the extent the Falsiner could show a smile with his marble features. "Very good."

Colby relaxed slightly and smiled back.

"And Summer," Vic said, "is part Tanasian, like you are."

Colby looked over at Summer, who stood there silently for a moment, until Colby gasped. "She said something without moving her mouth," Colby whispered in awe.

Summer laughed and clapped her hands as she bounced in place. "It worked! I wasn't sure it would but I've been practicing and it did! His head is open like mine so it worked!"

Vic looked from Summer to Colby and back.

"Vic?" Colby asked, tightening his hold on Vic's jacket.

"It's alright. She's just talking to you with her thoughts. It's called telepathy. It's the same thing that lets you hear Cam."

"Oh." Colby frowned, looking confused, and Vic wasn't sure he had any better way to explain it.

Patches jumped up and ran for the back door, and after Sharma whined and fidgeted for a moment as though reluctant to leave Colby's side, he did the same.

"*Oooh!*" Summer gasped, darting after the dogs and almost pressing her nose to the glass as she looked out at the backyard. "It's so pretty!"

Athan chuckled and shook his head. "I'd better let her go explore, if that's alright."

"Yeah, of course," Vic said, then looked down at Colby. "You wanna try coming outside with us?"

Summer gasped again. "Oh, please?" She beamed at

Colby, then darted over and took his hand, tugging him toward the door. "Come on an adventure with me!"

Colby looked at Vic with wide eyes.

"It's alright, sweetheart. I'm right here. And Ryley spelled the backyard, too, remember? Bad Man can't get you back there."

Athan opened the door, and the dogs darted out while Summer kept looking at Colby expectantly. With one more glance at Vic, Colby ducked his head and followed Summer outside, checking over his shoulder every few steps to make sure Vic was right behind him.

"Oh!" Summer let go of Colby's hand and ran to the nearest garden bed, then stopped and gently trailed her hands over every plant within reach. Then something else caught her eye and she flitted off to investigate that instead.

Athan chuckled. "She did the same thing just after we met," he said, a hint of fondness in his voice.

Vic glanced at him. "Yeah?"

Athan nodded, never taking his eyes off his wife. "Her brother kept her so confined that she thought *my* backyard was a whole new world, even though it wasn't all that much different from her own." He paused, his lips quirking into a hint of a smile. "I love how she loves the simplest things. Reminds me not to be too serious."

Vic smiled and nodded along. Colby was the same way, now that he thought about it. Between his lessons and playing with Sharma, the boy had spent countless hours over the past few months just learning the various rooms and objects in Vic's house, studying the colors and shapes with his eyes and his hands, trailing his little fingers over every surface and exclaiming over the different textures. When Vic looked over to where Colby stood by Summer now, the pair huddled around a tree that dominated one corner of the yard, he found the boy gently fingering the leaves that hung down in front of him, his eyes bright and happy.

A quiet stillness washed over Vic even while that familiar, bittersweet sensation ran through him. He tried to see the yard from Colby's perspective, admiring it for the beautiful, miraculous wonder that it was, something created by the gods and then further shaped by human hands. The shades of brown, rough in texture, rising up out of the earth, branching off and exploding out in soft shades of green, shadowing gently over the springy grass and silky flower petals.

The sunlight danced over Colby's skin as the boy turned his face up toward a vine trailing along the fence just above his head. He reached out, brushing his fingers through the leaves, tracing the vine as it wound its way across the boards and then slithered down to the ground, bringing the boy's attention to a bed of wildflowers that grew there, his soft gasps carrying across the yard over the gentle sound of the breeze through the leaves.

Vic stared at Colby, utterly transfixed by the joy and wonder on the boy's face. Out there, amongst the soft sounds and colors of nature, Colby looked even more faetouched than Vic had thought when they first found him. His bright eyes were wide as they took everything in, his body unfurling from its usual stooped, shy posture while his fingers reached out to touch everything around him.

Colby suddenly turned to look at Vic and gave him a brilliant smile, then went back to discover more.

Vic felt that smile like a knife right through his heart, the ache somehow both painful and beautiful. Being able to watch his sweet boy experience the beauty of nature for the first time in his life was both so utterly lovely and such a devastating reminder of just how much Colby had been denied.

And the brilliance of Colby's eyes in that moment was doing horribly delicious things to Vic's body. He could so easily imagine it: stripping his sweet boy down to nothing, laying him down on the soft grass, and worshiping every inch of him in a way that Colby had never known.

"If you don't mind me saying," Athan said, cutting into Vic's thoughts, "you look unusually stressed."

Vic went still, then gave a slow nod while trying to

decide how to answer that. He wasn't ready to go into the complications of his attraction to Colby—talking about it all with Ryley had been difficult enough—so he grasped for the next thing on his mind and blurted out, "I ran into my parents today."

"Oh?" Athan asked, his eyebrows raised just a tiny bit, probably as far as they could go. "I take it, from your tone, that it wasn't a good encounter."

Vic shook his head. "I don't like to talk about it much, but..." He blew out a breath. "My father is the reason Cam died. He took Cam off life-support while I was out of town and couldn't stop him."

Athan hissed. "Ax and fawn," he muttered. "That man does not deserve to be called *father*." He shot Vic an apologetic look.

Vic waved a hand. "No, I'd agree with you. I haven't spoken to the bastard since." He forced his fist to relax, and reached for Cam's bracelet instead.

"I am so sorry," Athan murmured. "Where I come from, a man would be sent to the wolves for such a thing."

"Sent to the wolves?"

"Killed." Athan smirked at Vic, gesturing at Sharma. "Our beasts are much more vicious than this pup here."

Vic laughed. "I bet," he said, watching Colby and Sharma roll around playfully on the grass.

Despite wearing a sundress, Summer threw herself down in an unladylike heap and giggled as she watched Colby play.

Athan muttered something under his breath and shook his head, but he had a fond smile on his face nonetheless. "My child wife," he joked. "Twenty-eight years old, and she's still so innocent in so many ways."

Vic chuckled as he nodded. Regardless of her genius intellect, Summer's deficiencies gave her an almost childlike mentality, making much of her behavior immature in comparison to her adult body.

Colby was the same, in a way. Adult in form, but still having a lot of catching up to do in terms of experience, learning, and mental development. Then again, that was part of what Vic loved about the boy. Even considering the horrors Colby had endured, he still had such a strong sense of innocence about him.

Summer hissed and shot out a hand, pointing at Colby. "You have hurts!"

Colby looked down, and quickly tugged his t-shirt back into place, hiding one of the many scars on his body. His laughter faded, and he curled into Sharma as the dog wrapped himself around the boy, trying to give him comfort.

Summer sucked in a breath, squeezing her eyes shut. "Too much. Too much..."

Athan was across the yard before Vic could even think about moving. Not sure what was going on, Vic darted over, grabbed Colby under the arms, and lifted the boy to his hip. Colby instantly wrapped his arms and legs around Vic, and Vic rocked him, feeling all the tension inside that little body.

"Shhh," Athan whispered. Vic turned and saw Athan gently rubbing Summer's back.

Summer took a deep breath and blew it out slowly, her eyes still closed. "I'm alright," she whispered.

"I'm sorry–" Vic started to say, though he still had no idea what exactly had happened.

"No, it's fine," Athan insisted, then looked down at Summer. "He didn't hurt her."

Summer shook her head in agreement as she looked up at Vic. "He was showing me movies in my head. They were scary."

Vic blinked. "Movies?"

Athan looked vaguely puzzled for a moment, then breathed a laugh. "Telepathy." He nodded with his chin. "I think your boy there was projecting."

"Projecting?"

"Thinking about what happened to him," Athan said, "and projecting those images outward, so Summer was able to see them through the holes in her mind." He paused, his eyes tightening in the slightest hint of a frown.

"At least, that's how Uncle Beni explained it. Not really my uncle, just my stepmother's best friend, but he's Tanasian, as well. I'm not sure I fully understand all the aspects of telepathy myself, still."

Vic hugged Colby tighter. "But it's part of how they can see ghosts, right?"

Athan nodded, and Summer took another deep breath before she looked up at Vic, her face showing its usual cheer again. "He needs a happy. There's too many scary movies in his head."

Vic cringed. That was an understatement if there ever was one.

Summer gasped. "Maybe we can make his hurts go away?"

Vic and Athan shared a look, both of them clearly confused. "Go away?" Vic asked.

Summer nodded, an excited smile on her face. "I can talk to Deyn. She was really good at it. She can help Colby make the hurts go away."

"Are you following any of this?" Vic asked Athan.

Athan shook his head. "Summer?"

Summer rolled her eyes in exasperation, then launched into a speech that included all sorts of biology jargon that went right over Vic's head, but he thought he got the gist of it once he mentally translated Summer's unique way of speaking: Tanasian telepathy could be expanded into telekinesis, which could be fine-tuned down to a form of internal bioengineering, allowing the practitioner to physically alter his or her body by seeking out some physical defect and then ordering the requisite cells to either die off or regenerate, thus correcting any number of ailments from simple blemishes to cancerous tumors.

In other words, Colby might be able to make all his scars disappear. Permanently.

"Does that really work?" Vic asked, his eyes wide, imagining his sweet boy free of the marks that all the bad men had given him.

Summer nodded. "Deyn was really good at it. She regrew her arm after it got cut off."

Vic blinked, at a loss for words.

"Who are we talking about here?" Athan asked, his marble features pulled into a hint of a frown. "Who's Deyn?"

Summer brightened. "Oh! My great-great-great-grandmother's ex-husband's daughter's daughter-in-law." She paused for half a beat, then added, "Or your stepmother's foster father's best friend's mother-in-law."

Vic looked at Athan, who slowly shook his head and shrugged.

"So?" Summer asked, grinning with excitement.

Vic tilted his head, looking down at Colby. "What do you think?"

Colby frowned, clearly confused.

"Summer thinks she can find someone to help you make all the scars go away."

Colby's eyes went wide. "Really?" he breathed, then looked at Summer, a smile of pure joy slowly taking over his face.

And Vic fell in love with him even more.

Chapter 21

VIC FINISHED packing and peeked into Colby's room. The boy had gone to bed right after dinner, the intensity of the afternoon having done him in. Besides having to deal with Summer's exuberance, there had apparently been a whole bunch of ghosts who showed up along with the particular one that Summer had mentioned, all of them wandering about the backyard and looking on as the one ghost helped Colby learn how to embrace his Tanasian abilities.

The poor boy looked exhausted by the time they called it quits for the day, but at least there had been some success. Colby had managed to make part of one of his scars fade away.

The joy on his face, once he realized he could do it, had been breathtaking. Vic smiled, just thinking of it.

He couldn't wait to see how happy Colby would look if the boy ever managed to get rid of all of them.

Colby stirred, blinking the sleep from his eyes as he peeked out at Vic over the blankets. "Vic?"

"Hey, sweetheart. Sorry, I didn't mean to wake you."

Colby sat up, clutching the blankets, his eyes going wide. "Are you leaving?"

"No, not until tomorrow," Vic told him, and Colby noticeably relaxed. "You hungry at all? You didn't have much for dinner."

Colby nodded and slipped out of bed, then turned back and quickly put the sheets to rights even though he'd be diving right back into them in a couple hours. Vic smiled at the sight, and jumped in to help him.

Vic warmed up some leftovers from dinner and cleaned the kitchen while Colby ate. Afterwards, they curled up on the couch together, with the dogs nestled in close, and Vic showed Colby how to make and accept video calls on his tablet.

"So I'll call you from here," Vic said, starting a call on his mobile, "and then…"

Colby's tablet displayed a notification for an incoming call. The boy was still learning to read, but the green and red buttons were easy enough for him to understand. Vic had him tap the icon to accept the call, and Colby gasped when Vic's face showed on the screen.

Vic smiled. "Just like that."

Colby looked from Vic to the live video and back, then Vic showed him how he could see Colby on his phone.

"Now you try," Vic said, ending the call and then taking Colby through the steps to call Vic from his tablet. "So if you get really scared, you can call me. Anytime, sweetheart."

"Really?"

Vic nodded. "And I'll call you every day while I'm gone."

"You promise?"

"I promise."

Colby smiled, then tipped his mouth up for a kiss.

Vic blindly set his phone aside and gave him just that, keeping it soft and sweet, both of them smiling all the while.

Gods, he was going to miss his sweet boy.

Vic double-checked that he had everything packed for tomorrow and got ready for bed. He was just about to switch off the bedside lamp when he spotted Colby huddling in his doorway.

"Hey, sweetheart. Something wrong?"

Colby fidgeted. "I don't wanna be alone," he whispered.

Vic's heart clenched. "Come here."

Colby darted into the room and scrambled up onto the bed. Vic switched off the lamp and lay down, then felt Colby burrow in close, resting his head on Vic's shoulder and letting out a contented sigh.

Vic couldn't help but smile. "Goodnight, sweetheart."

"Goodnight, Vic," Colby whispered.

Vic closed his eyes, holding the boy close, committing to memory every little sensation of having Colby in his arms. He replayed that moment over and over in his head as he drove to the airport the next morning, then on the flight south, and again as he checked into his lonely hotel room and headed off to meet the agent in charge of Hunter's case.

Thank gods, he'd get to rescue another kid, but he couldn't wait to get back home.

* * *

COLBY OPENED the door to the backyard to let the dogs out, then hesitated. Everything out there was so beautiful, and he wanted to see it all again, but the thought of going outside without Vic made him nervous. It was all just so open and exposed.

Then again, Bad Man wasn't out there. At least, the ghost couldn't get into the yard. As long as Colby stayed away from the edges, he should be safe.

And he really wanted to see the pretty flowers and hear the birds and touch the leaves again.

Taking a deep breath, Colby stepped outside and pulled the door almost shut, afraid he might get locked out somehow. He tucked his hands up under his chin and wandered after the dogs, slowly losing himself in the beauty and tranquility that surrounded him.

He went to what he decided was his favorite spot in the whole garden, though picking a favorite was difficult. It was all so beautiful. So comforting. Still, the little pond near the back corner, with its stone bench and surrounded by so many plants and trees that one couldn't see the fence to the next yard, kept drawing him back.

Colby stepped around the pond and climbed up onto the bench, hugging his knees to his chest as he watched the water flow. He took another deep breath, smiling as he let it out on a sigh. This place was so wonderful, so exquisitely different from everything he'd ever known. The colors. The sounds. The smells. The simple freedom to move about and get fresh air when he wanted, to put on clothes and watch the dogs scamper about while he sat there, just enjoying.

To say nothing of sleeping in a bed, or learning new things, or any of the dozens of other simple, wonderful experiences he'd had ever since Vic had brought him home.

He'd been so scared at first, so sure that Vic was going to ultimately hurt him despite all his promises, but Vic had stayed true to his word. Vic had given him life when all he'd known was fear.

Colby wasn't perfectly free—not yet—but it seemed more possible now.

Patches scrambled across the yard, yipping excitedly, while Sharma lay down in the sun. Colby giggled and shook his head. Cam's dog was such a handful. She'd gotten better, but still didn't behave quite like Sharma did.

Then Colby looked up and saw what Patches was heading towards.

"Hello," Deyn murmured. The ghost peeked out at him from behind a tree.

Colby started to shrink back, startled by her sudden presence when he thought he was alone, then relaxed when he recognized her. She was the one Summer had called in, the one who'd sat with him yesterday, helping him learn how to do more special things with his mind.

He didn't understand any of it, but he knew it worked. One of his scars had started to slough away before the strain of effort became too much, and they'd stopped. But at least he knew it was possible.

He couldn't wait to try again.

"Hi," he whispered back.

"I was hoping you might come out today," Deyn said, wandering over to sit nearby. "I came back to see the garden again, and thought of going inside to see you, but...I didn't want to invade your space inside."

"Oh." Colby hesitated, then gave a tiny shrug.

"You see, my stepson–" the ghost began, then laughed. "Gods, that seems such a strange thing to call an eighty-three-year-old man..."

Colby tilted his head, not sure he understood what she meant.

Deyn waved a hand. "Anyway, he's always had some pretty intense social anxiety issues, so I understand not just popping in unannounced. Especially indoors."

"Oh." Colby nodded slowly. "Thank you."

Deyn nodded back. "Still, I hope I'm not disturbing you."

Colby shook his head. "I was just thinking..."

"Yes?"

Colby fidgeted. "I wanted to try some more..."

Deyn smiled at him. "Of course. I'd love to help."

Colby smiled back, and scooted closer. He slowly reached out and took the ghost's hands, and they closed their eyes. He felt the weird pressure in his head when Deyn slipped inside, some sort of advanced telepathy that allowed her to not only read his mind and hear his thoughts but actually travel deeper into his brain, into the parts that controlled his body. There was so much of it he didn't understand, but if he focused, it was easy enough to follow along with her mind as she led him down into the tiny parts that made up his skin and blood and other inside pieces, all the way down until they encountered one of his scars.

Deyn patiently showed him how to tell his body to kill off the cells he didn't want and make new ones in their place, slowly but surely recreating the skin so that the scarred tissue disappeared and new, healthy skin took over. It was exhausting work for someone like him with little practice—Deyn said she'd been able to do the same thing with her own body in a matter of seconds when she was alive—but when they finally stopped, and Colby looked down, one of the scars was completely gone.

He stared at the spot, running his fingers across the skin over and over. There wasn't a hint of discoloration or roughness. It was like the scar had never been there.

Colby looked at Deyn, tears springing to his eyes as he smiled gratefully at her. A little bit of Bad Man had been banished from his body. He couldn't wait to make the rest of it go away.

And he couldn't wait to show Vic.

* * *

VIC CREPT down the dark alley, eyes narrowed as he scanned the shadowy nooks. He came to a stop, listening. Feeling. Sensing out the boy's presence.

And trying with all his might *not* to think of Cam. The setting was too eerily familiar.

A moment later, he could tell exactly where the boy was hiding. There was neither movement nor sound, but somehow Vic was absolutely certain that Hunter had wedged himself into the tight space between a garbage bin and a stack of pallets.

Vic crouched down, making his height less intimidating. "Hunter? My name is Victor Lucius, but you can call me Vic. I'm here to help you."

There was no reply, but Vic hadn't expected one right away.

"I know you're scared, champ," Vic murmured. "But it's gonna be alright. You don't have to keep running. I can get you somewhere safe. Wherever you want to go. A convalescent home, or a foster family. Whatever you prefer." He paused, catching a hint of motion in the dark. "We'll get you some food and some clothes. You can have a real life. Start over."

A head tentatively poked out from behind the stack of pallets.

Vic offered the boy a soft smile. "Hey, there, kiddo. Here." Vic reached into his bag and pulled out a bottle of water. He held it out to the boy, who eyed it with obvious need.

Like so many other kids who got out of Westfield City, Hunter had escaped his abusive home and—by lucky chance—run into an insurance agent who promised to get Hunter the help he needed. The boy had started to open up and talk about the horrors he'd endured, about why he'd run away from the walled city, but then he'd spooked and run away again, not quite ready to trust anyone.

Vic had come south, expecting to find the boy sitting in the insurance office with the case agent who had called Vic in. Instead, he'd showed up to find the agent in a state of panic since Hunter had bolted, so Vic had immediately hit the streets, using his strange, sixth sense to find the boy.

Considering what the agent had told Vic about the boy's life, Vic couldn't blame him for running again. Even if he hadn't heard about Hunter's trauma in particular, Vic would have been able to guess. All his darkest cases seemed to come out of Westfield, so it didn't take much imagination to figure out what the boy had suffered, hunger and thirst being the least of those yet the quickest and easiest for Vic to solve.

And between having no money and shying away from people, Hunter probably hadn't been able to get a drop of water—to say nothing of food—in at least a couple days.

Vic waited, watching the boy. Finally, Hunter darted out from his hiding spot and snatched the bottle from his hand. He scurried back into the shadows, wrenched off the cap, and tipped the bottle back, chugging the entire contents in one go, leaving him panting as he shrank from Vic again.

"A-Are you gonna fuck me now?" the boy asked.

"What?" Vic gasped. He cringed, the very thought making him ill. The fact that the poor boy assumed he had to pay for water with his body was a tragedy in and of itself. Then again, Colby had been the same way. As had many of the other kids Vic had rescued over the years.

"No, champ," Vic murmured. "Never. No one's ever gonna touch you like that again."

Hunter whimpered, his hands clutching the corner of the pallets as he peeked out at Vic. "But–" He frowned, looking suddenly confused.

"I promise, kiddo," Vic went on. "I won't hurt you." He paused, his hand automatically going into his pocket, his fingers desperately clutching Cam's blood-stained bracelet. The familiar presence grounded him. "Tell you what: I saw a diner around the corner. How about you follow me, and I'll get you a burger or something? It's way past dinnertime, and you must be hungry."

Then Vic waited, maintaining eye contact. He saw the play of emotions cross Hunter's face, saw him considering whether to trust Vic, saw him weighing his fear against his need to simply survive.

Wrong though the thought might be, the sight made Vic so grateful for Colby's progress. His sweet boy was coming back to life. With any luck, the same would be possible for Hunter someday.

Keeping his eyes on Vic, Hunter slowly emerged from his hiding spot. His whole body trembled as he stood there, whether from fear, hunger, or exhaustion, Vic couldn't tell. Probably a combination of all three. Finally, Hunter gave a tentative nod.

Vic smiled with relief, and slowly rose, not wanting to frighten the boy. And, unlike Colby, this one actually was a boy. Hunter claimed to be sixteen, and he was small for his age, making Vic a giant beside him. Vic gestured at the end of the alley and turned away.

After a moment, he heard the sound of tentative footsteps following him.

They were seated in a quiet corner of the diner, and Vic watched Hunter look around warily as the waitress hurried off to fill their drink orders.

"You alright, champ?"

Hunter's gaze flicked up to Vic's face. Vic could almost see a dozen different questions get considered and discarded as the boy looked at him, until he finally asked, "Why are you helping me?"

Vic gave a slow nod. He'd expected the question. It usually always came at some point, the poor kids unable to conceive of a person who actually wanted to do good after experiencing so many people who were bad. For once, though, the question didn't carry quite the heavy weight that it normally did. His worst case ever was slowly but surely finding a happy conclusion, and Vic felt like he was on the verge of finally shaking off the mantle of guilt he'd carried ever since he'd found Cam. He wasn't quite there—and he wasn't sure what it would take to finally get him over the edge—but he was close.

Reaching for Cam's bracelet, Vic looked at Hunter and said, "I failed to protect my little brother, and someone hurt him. Abused him sexually for two days and then left him for dead. I found his body, and I've been finding abused kids ever since."

"Oh." Hunter blinked at him, then studied his eyes, seemingly looking for truth. The boy gave a nod, apparently satisfied that Vic was being honest. "I'm sorry," he whispered.

Vic gave the boy a smile. "Thanks, kiddo."

Hunter fiddled with the silverware as he stared down at the table, then he jumped up and ran for the door.

"Hunter!" Vic called. The boy didn't stop, so Vic threw down some money to cover the food they'd ordered and ran after him. "Hunter, wait!"

He caught up to Hunter on the sidewalk, but the boy kept running.

"Hunter–"

"I have to go."

"Hunter, wait. Just let me help–"

"No." Hunter stopped for just a second, then continued on at a fast walk, gasping for breath. Vic stuck close to his side, waiting, and Hunter finally continued, "I have to find him."

"Who?"

"You found your brother. I have to go find–"

Vic waited, but Hunter didn't continue. "Hunter? Did your brother escape, too? Is he out here, somewhere?"

Hunter shook his head tightly. "No, I don't have a brother. Just my–" He glanced up at Vic as he kept moving. "My best friend." He stopped and turned to Vic with a shadow of grief crossing his features. "They told me he was dead," the boy said, tears shimmering in the corners of his eyes. "But he's not. He can't be. He can't be dead. I don't believe it. He had to have gotten out like I did. He *had* to." He paused, then mumbled, "But why he ran away without me…"

"Alright, alright," Vic murmured, crouching down and rubbing the boy's arms while Hunter fought his tears. "When was the last time you saw him?"

"About a year ago," Hunter cried.

Vic thought back. He'd had three rescues in that area from around that time. "Can you tell me his name? Maybe he was one of my cases. I could tell you where he is."

Hunter opened his mouth like he was going to answer, then he choked out a sob and took off again.

"Hunter!"

"I'm going to find him and you can't stop me!" Hunter yelled.

"Hunter, wait, please!"

Hunter slowed and turned to face him, crossing his arms over his chest.

Vic reached into his bag and pulled out the prepaid phone he'd brought along. "Take this. Go find your friend, if that's what you have to do. But if you ever want help, call me. Please. Anytime. My number is in the contacts."

Hunter took the phone, gave Vic a hesitant look, then nodded gratefully. "Thanks, Vic."

"I can help you find him–"

Hunter shook his head and started walking backwards. "I have to do this on my own."

Vic nodded, about to let the boy go, then quickly dug out some coins and stuffed them into Hunter's hand.

Hunter looked at the coins curiously, and no wonder. Money wasn't used in Westfield, where everyone was poor and everything was shared. Including the bodies of children.

"Silver," Vic explained. "For food and shelter."

Hunter gave a slight nod as he eyed the coins with suspicion, but stuffed them into his pocket anyway. He looked up at Vic, smiling gratefully through his tears, and took off again, sprinting down an unfamiliar street in an unfamiliar city, in search of his lost friend.

Vic watched him go, forcing himself not to go after the boy. Kids did that sometimes. Usually, Vic could talk them around, but the steel in Hunter's eyes had been undeniable. There was no stopping the boy.

He only hoped that, someday, Hunter would call.

Vic reached for his phone, then headed back to the hotel first, wanting quiet and privacy before he made a call of his own. He barely had the door shut before he hit *Send.*

Colby's face showed on the screen, and the boy smiled as he gasped. "Vic!"

Vic sank onto the end of the bed and grinned. "Hey, sweetheart."

"I did it! I answered the call."

"Yeah, you did. We'll have you using all sorts of technology in no time."

Colby giggled, and Vic's heart swelled at the sound.

"How are you?" Vic asked. "Did you have a good day?"

Colby nodded. "Look!" He jumped up, the view going erratic for a moment while the boy got himself situated, then Colby held the tablet with one hand while he used the other to lift the hem of his t-shirt a few inches, showing his belly. The fact that Colby had voluntarily showed more skin had Vic so stunned that, for a moment, he wasn't sure what he was supposed to be seeing.

Then it hit him. One of Colby's scars was gone. A particularly nasty burn scar that he'd gotten when Ahriman had been angry and forced himself on Colby while still holding a lit cigarette in his hand, the burning end jabbed into Colby's belly while Ahriman kept a bruising hold on Colby's waist. Vic had nearly lost his lunch when Colby had explained that one to him.

But now there was no sign of it. Colby's skin was free of blemish where the scar had once been. It was like it had never existed.

Vic smiled. "Sweetheart, that's wonderful!"

Colby tilted the screen back up so Vic could see his face. His lovely, grinning face, those big, beautiful eyes bright and happy.

"It's gone, Vic! It took a long time, but it's gone. And I can do the others. I can make them all go away!"

Vic kept smiling so hard, his cheeks ached, and he had to swallow down emotion. "I'm so happy for you."

Colby giggled again.

"How are the dogs?" Vic asked. "Are they behaving for you?"

Colby nodded. "We went out to the backyard for a while."

"You did?" Vic's heart swelled again. His sweet boy was getting so brave. "Did you have fun?"

Colby nodded again.

"Good," Vic said, then saw Sharma nose his way into view, draping himself over Colby's lap. Then Vic finally noticed where Colby was. "Are you in my bed?" Vic asked, struggling not to laugh.

Colby ducked his head. "Yeah?"

"No, that's fine, sweetheart. If you feel safer there, that's fine."

Colby smiled again, then settled down on his side and lay the edge of his tablet against the pillow. Unable to resist, Vic scooted up the bed and did the same, lying down to face him even though they were hundreds of miles apart.

"I miss you," he murmured.

"I miss you, too," Colby whispered, then he gasped. "Did you save Hunter?"

Vic sighed. "Not quite."

Colby whimpered, his eyes going wide with worry.

"No, he's alive," Vic rushed to assure him. "But he said his friend was missing, too, so he wanted to go find him."

"Oh." Colby frowned. "Poor Hunter."

"Yeah."

"I'm sorry, Vic."

"Thanks, sweetheart." Vic checked his watch. "But that means I can probably come home tomorrow if I can get my flight changed."

Colby's eyes brightened. "Yeah?"

"Yeah. Why don't you go get some sleep, and I'll call you in the morning and let you know."

"Alright," Colby said around a yawn.

Vic chuckled. "Sweet dreams, my sweet boy."

"Goodnight, Vic," Colby whispered.

"Goodnight." Vic ended the call, then switched apps on his phone and looked into getting his flight changed. He couldn't wait to get home and see his boy.

Chapter 22

COLBY LOOKED at the clock. He was still learning how to understand the numbers, but he knew Vic said his flight would arrive at half one in the afternoon, and that was what the clock showed right then. At least, Colby was pretty sure. If he was right, it meant Vic would be home soon. The man just had to drive from the airport.

Of course, Colby had no idea what *flight* and *airport* and all that meant, but he knew it took time to drive to places, so he still had to wait for Vic to arrive home. He looked all around. The bed was made, and the kitchen was clean, but he wanted to do something more. Something to cheer up Vic after his rescue mission hadn't gone quite the way he'd wanted.

Colby glanced out the front window, spotting the mail man. He shrank back, sinking his fingers into Sharma's fur when the dog sat beside him, wagging his tail. Vic hadn't said anything about bringing in the mail—that was always Vic's job since Colby couldn't find the nerve to go out there, not when Bad Man could show up just beyond the mailbox—so Colby had seen the mail arrive yesterday and let it sit out there overnight. Now there was more mail to bring inside.

Maybe he could be brave, just this once. It was only a short walk. Just down to the curb and back. Colby could go out there, grab the mail, and run right back into the house. Bad Man might not even be there. Maybe he was off somewhere else. And even if he was there, Colby could get away before Bad Man had much of a chance to say anything.

He could face that, right?

Besides, even if Bad Man had practiced enough to be tangible, he couldn't be strong enough to drag Colby away. Colby could get free if the ghost touched him.

But first, he had to be brave enough to walk out that front door.

Colby clung to Sharma and looked around. Patches was bouncing around wildly, missing Cam. The ghost had left to greet Vic at the airport, wanting some alone time with his brother. Apparently, it was what they did after most of Vic's rescue missions. Cam wouldn't actually go on the mission himself, the sight of another abused or neglected child being too upsetting for him, but he'd meet Vic on the way back and they'd recover together.

Knowing their history, Colby could hardly blame them.

Though it meant, for the time being, he was truly home alone with the dogs, not even Cam's presence to make the house not seem quite so empty.

Colby could just wait and let Vic get the mail when he got home, but he wanted to do something for Vic. Something to cheer him up, to make him proud.

And facing his fears might be just the thing.

Colby darted into his room and dressed in all his extra layers, zipping his hoodie all the way up and then pulling on his socks and shoes. Feeling better armed, he got out the dogs' leashes and headed for the front door.

Patches jumped around so much that it was all Colby could do to pin the dog down long enough to get the leash clipped to her collar. Sharma was much easier, sitting there quietly and wagging his tail. The short walk hardly justified the extra effort, and the dogs would probably be confused to just be turning right back around again once they reached the curb, but Colby needed that extra layer of protection. Maybe, someday, he could go out there alone. For now, he wasn't sure he could get through it without the dogs at his side.

Colby flipped the lock, closed his eyes, took a deep breath, and opened the door. He turned to grab the leads, but Patches bolted before he could get a secure hold.

"Patches!" Colby yelled. He watched in horror as the dog took off down the walk, stopping here and there as various smells distracted it but still hurrying away.

Colby didn't think. He ran out after her, yelling over his shoulder, "Sharma, stay!"

The big dog whined, but sat down right in the middle of the doorway, wagging his tail and watching as Colby took off toward the street, hoping to catch Patches in time.

They reached the sidewalk, and Colby almost caught up when Patches caught sight of something and sprinted off to the next yard. Colby went after her, gasping for breath before they were halfway to the intersection. The little dog sprang from yard to yard, stopping to smell one thing only to jump up and dart off again. Colby had to catch her.

If anything happened to Patches, Cam would be devastated.

* * *

VIC FELT Cam's presence the moment he got into his car.

"Hey, kiddo." Vic pulled his brother in for a hug when the ghost leaned against him. "Missed you."

Cam dug a notepad out of the console. *Missed you, too. Almost came with you on this one, actually.*

Vic's eyebrows went up. "Yeah?"

Couldn't quite do it at the last minute, but…maybe someday?

"Hey." Vic gave his brother a squeeze. "You have nothing to prove to me, alright?"

I know. But…maybe…to myself? I'm tired of being scared all the time, Vic. Not being able to face it all. Cam paused, then went on: *I know I'm not ready to face Dad any time soon, but the rest of it? Maybe it would be good for me to finally go on a case with you.*

Vic smiled, then kissed the top of Cam's head. "You are such a tough kid, you know that?"

Thanks. Cam moved the pen about indecisively for a moment, then wrote, *I think I wanna go face Jarvis.*

Vic froze. He'd been trying so hard to forget that Logan Jarvis even existed in the world, that Cam's attacker was out there somewhere, walking around freely, as though nothing had happened.

"If that's what you want," Vic finally said.

You don't have to come with me if you're not ready.

"I didn't say I wasn't–" Vic hurried to protest, but Cam cut him off.

It's all over your face, Vic. And that's fine. I can find him and face him on my own, I think.

Vic shook his head, but he didn't say anything. Was he really that much of a coward that he couldn't bring himself to face his brother's attacker?

Gods. Maybe he was. He'd put it off long enough.

I'm sorry, Cam wrote. *Let's not talk about this now. I'm sure you're dying to get home, and I know Colby misses you.*

Vic blew out a breath, and smiled. "Yeah." He gave Cam another squeeze, and reached over to switch on the car. "And gods know what Patches is up to with you not there to keep her occupied."

He felt Cam laugh, then his brother shifted aside so Vic could select their destination from the nav screen and get the car on the road.

Vic switched on the autopilot in case Cam wanted to talk, but his brother continued silent, leaning casually against him. Despite his disappointment over not really being able to help Hunter and his worries about Cam wanting to face Logan Jarvis, Vic found himself smiling at the sensation of having his brother near. He took a deep breath, and let it out on a sigh, so glad to be going home.

Cam tapped him on the arm to get his attention. *I've always loved that tree. I can't believe how big it's gotten.*

Vic looked out as the car crossed a stone bridge over a river that ran through part of Morbran City. Along the banks, the row of lamp posts gave way to an enormous weeping willow tree, the pendulous branches trailing down to the water's surface. When they were kids, Vic and Cam used to play at hiding out under that tree even though the branches hadn't hung low enough at the time to properly conceal them. Now, though, it looked like they could have crawled under there and gone entirely unnoticed by anyone passing by.

It was so beautiful. And it was right there, easy to see, probably passed by all the time, yet Vic had stopped noticing.

He straightened in his seat and looked all around, taking in the idyllic beauty of his hometown. How long had it been since he'd truly appreciated such things? He imagined Colby going about and gaping in quiet awe of the trees and the stonework that made up this storybook village, just as the boy had taken in Vic's backyard. Such a simple thing, yet it had given Colby hours of pleasure. Vic grinned as he imagined some future day when he could take the boy on a tour of the town, picturing that lovely face and those big eyes taking in all the lush intricacies around them, almost hearing Colby's every soft gasp when he discovered some new, wonderful thing. Vic could show him that very tree. Or take him through one of the parks. Or walk him through the stunning, ancient buildings of Denmer University, the heart of Morbran City.

He could tell Colby about the city's founders, Gabriel Morbran and Evan Sturmwyn, and how they opened a home for disowned children, the home ultimately developing into a school which later expanded into Denmer University, the city itself spreading out all around it, the various developers replicating the original architecture and preserving the area's charm, creating—in Vic's opinion—one of the most beautiful cities in the world.

How had he lost sight of that? How had he ever come to take it all for granted?

With Colby in his life now, he doubted he ever would again.

"So beautiful," he murmured.

Cam nodded against him.

The more they passed, the more things Vic found that he wanted to show Colby someday. He'd have to be patient. The poor boy was barely able to make it out to the backyard, and their one trip to Roz's store had taken a lot of coaxing, neither of which involved too many strangers. Still, it was possible. One day, they might be able to walk through downtown, hand in hand, just enjoying the sights and the fresh air.

What are you thinking about?

Vic blinked and read the words again. "What do you mean?"

You've got this sappy smile on your face.

Vic felt himself blush and looked away, clearing his throat.

You can say it, you know. It won't bother me.

"Say what?"

You love him.

Vic stared at the words. "Cam…"

What? You do. It's obvious. And I'm happy for you. Honestly. I mean it.

"Cam–"

I think, given time, he might be able to love you, too.

Vic looked away, shaking his head and cursing himself. Stupid to let his mind wander to such beautiful dreams, because that was all they could ever be.

Hey, don't be like that. You can be happy, Vic. I want you to be happy. And I want him to be happy.

Vic frowned. Could he have that? Could he really, truly have such a thing?

"I–"

He broke off, staring out the front windscreen as the car neared the house and pulled into the driveway. The front door was ajar, and Sharma sat in the opening, staring out and wagging his tail.

The hells? Cam scribbled out.

"I have no idea," Vic said, slamming down the brake before the car could even reach the garage. He switched off the car and got out, running to the front door. "Colby?"

Sharma was up on his feet and jumped aside as Vic barreled into the house.

"Colby?" Vic called.

Vic raced through the house, yelling Colby's name over and over. His blood roared in his ears as he checked and rechecked every room, not wanting to believe that the boy wasn't there.

"Colby!" He checked all through the backyard, then ran back into the house and stopped in the middle of the living room, panting. "Cam?"

A notepad flew off the end table. *I don't see him anywhere.*

"Can you feel him?"

Hang on.

Vic kept trying to catch his breath, his heart racing as he stared at the idle pen for several long, tense seconds.

Finally, Cam wrote, *I'm so sorry. It's too faint. I don't have a strong enough connection to him yet to go straight to him.*

"Shit," Vic breathed.

I'm so sorry–

"No, it's not your fault," Vic rushed to assure him. He looked all around again, then grabbed his phone.

Ryley answered on the first ring. "*Hey, babe. How–*"

"I need your help," Vic gasped.

"*Where are you?*" Ryley asked, his tone all business.

"At home. I–"

"*Hang on.*" Static came over the line right before the call clicked off, and Vic just started to lower his phone to dial again when Ryley appeared right before him. "Babe? What's wrong?"

"Colby's gone."

"What?" Ryley gasped. "Shit. Why? Where?"

"I don't know." Vic's heart started to race again, his hands shaking so much that he almost dropped his phone, images of finding Cam's body bombarding his mind. If anything like that had happened to Colby…

"Vic," Ryley snapped, then grabbed him by the arms. "Breathe. Alright? I know you're worried, but we'll find him."

"But he never leaves the house," Vic said, pulling away and pacing the living room. "He wouldn't–"

Ryley looked at the door. "Hang on."

"What?"

Vic followed him to the entryway, and blinked dumbly as he watched Ryley bend down and grab the end of Sharma's leash. The dog was still standing there, never moving away from the open door.

"Why…" Ryley started to ask.

Vic looked all around. "Patches is gone."

"What?"

"Cam's dog."

Sharma whined and fidgeted by the door.

"Where's Colby, boy?" Ryley asked.

Sharma barked and took a step toward the door, then looked back at them.

Ryley looked up at Vic. "Worth a shot."

Vic sucked in a breath, gave a sharp nod, and followed Ryley out the door, taking over Sharma's leash as soon as they were on the sidewalk.

Sharma tugged them down the street, straining against the leash with all his might, veering off and sniffing the ground only to charge forward again.

"We'll find him, Vic," Ryley assured him. "It's gonna be alright."

Vic gave him a tight nod, but never took his eyes off the dog. They *had* to find Colby. He wasn't sure he would survive it if they didn't.

Chapter 23

COLBY GASPED for breath, but kept running. He kept almost reaching Patches, only for the dog to sprint off again, her attention caught by some new thing.

Heart racing, lungs burning, muscles aching, Colby kept going. He wasn't going to let anything happen to Patches. Not if he could help it. Cam had wanted that dog so badly, and always looked so happy whenever he played with it. Colby couldn't bear to see the devastation on the ghost's face if the dog got lost or hurt, especially after everything else Cam had suffered in his life.

Patches stopped and sniffed around in a garden bed. Colby felt a moment of relief and sprang forward, only for the dog to get distracted by something else and take off again.

Colby let out a cry and followed. He wasn't sure how much longer he could go on—he'd never run like that before, not *ever*—and his strength was quickly giving out. But he couldn't stop. He couldn't let Cam down. And Vic would be hurt if Cam was hurt.

There was no way Colby could let that happen.

He pushed on, his feet screaming with pain and his heart feeling like it might burst out of his chest. They raced down one street, then another. Then another still.

Patches turned and darted through an intersection,

just barely missing a passing car, the first Colby had seen. Colby lurched to a stop and threw his arms up, cringing back, then peeked out and gasped with relief when he saw Patches just sneak by and hurry down the sidewalk. The car only veered slightly and continued on, paying them no mind.

Colby kept running. Even as tears of despair started flowing down his cheeks, he kept going. He wasn't going to stop until Patches was safely within his grasp.

The dog started to veer into the street again, then darted the other way at the last moment, diving into a hedge. A moment later, it popped back out and continued on down the sidewalk, slowing a bit to sniff around and then speeding up again, then sniffing around once more. Five times, Colby almost reached her, only for the dog to pull ahead.

"Patches!" Colby cried, the name coming out as little better than a desperate gasp.

Finally, the dog veered off, sniffed around for a moment, and stopped, squatting down to relieve itself.

Colby sucked in a breath, put on a burst of speed, and stumbled to a stop with his foot planted on the end of the leash just as Patches was about to take off again.

Gasping for air, Colby dropped to his knees and clutched the leash in both hands, reeling the dog in and then gathering it up in his arms, his whole body shaking as he held it tight. He wrapped the end of the leash around his wrist, and held the dog tighter. It wasn't getting away again. Not if he could help it.

Once his heart wasn't racing quite so badly and his breath began to slow, Colby stood up, his tired legs and sore feet protesting the movement. But he had to get home.

And as he turned around to find the way, he realized he was horribly, hopelessly lost.

* * *

VIC CURSED under his breath. Sharma kept running in

odd directions, following Colby's trail, when all Vic wanted to do was run straight to his boy. But Colby could be anywhere. He tried not to panic, but the uncertainty was killing him.

"What if we don't find him?" Vic asked, glancing at Ryley, who jogged along at his side. "What if–"

"Don't think like that," Ryley said, reaching over and giving Vic's arm a squeeze. "I'm sure he's fine."

Vic opened his mouth to argue, then decided against it. All sorts of horrible images ran through his mind. What if Colby was lost? What if he'd been hit by a car? What if he'd fallen somewhere and couldn't call out for help?

What if he'd been taken?

It was that same panic from fifteen years ago, that same desperation that had fueled him for two days straight as he tried to find Cam. How could it all be happening again? How could he once more be wildly searching for someone he loved?

And his sixth sense was failing him. He almost always managed to find whomever he was looking for with little effort, but even following Sharma, he couldn't seem to tap into whatever inexplicable gift he had for tracking someone down, right when he needed it most.

Maybe he was just too panicked. Too frantic to be rational. But he couldn't calm his mind long enough to think straight. He had to get his sweet boy back. He *had* to.

He looked at Ryley. "Is there any kind of…spell, or…"

Ryley frowned in thought, then shook his head. "Maybe? I know there are tracking spells, but they only work when you place a tracker on something so you can find it later."

Shit. So much for that idea.

"I can jump over to Jadu'n real quick and ask–" Ryley started to offer.

"No, not yet," Vic panted, and nodded at Sharma. "Let's keep looking."

Ryley nodded. "We'll find him, Vic. I know we will."

Vic pressed his mouth into a grim line. He was too

worried to be hopeful. Not yet. Colby was out there, somewhere, probably scared out of his mind and all alone. Vic had to find him.

Sharma darted across the street, and Vic followed.

* * *

COLBY HELD Patches to his chest as he walked down the street. His chest heaved and his heart raced, his eyes wide as he looked around, trying to find his way, but he didn't recognize a single thing.

And why would he? He'd only left the house once, and hadn't looked out to see where they were going. The world was so big and scary. And now he was somewhere in it, with no idea how to get back to the safety of home.

Of Vic.

Maybe Vic would find him. Colby tried to hold on to that thought. If he couldn't find his own way home, maybe Vic would get back to see Colby wasn't there, and would come out looking for him. But how would Vic find him? Everything was so big, and went in so many directions. Where would he start? How could they ever possibly find one another?

"No," he cried, shaking his head and feeling more tears on his cheeks. He had to get home. Somehow, he had to make it there. He couldn't bear the thought of never seeing Vic again.

Especially since it meant being out in the world where Bad Man could find him.

As though his thoughts had conjured him up, the ghost suddenly appeared right in front of him.

Colby cried out and jumped back, clinging to Patches and ducking his head.

"Boy..."

Colby whimpered, backing away.

Bad Man came after him, a cruel sneer on his face.

"No!" Colby cried, stumbling over something and almost falling down. He caught himself and backed up again. "Stay away!"

"Boy…"

"Leave me alone!" Colby shouted. He looked all around frantically, then took off running, struggling to hold Patches in his arms as he went. His whole body hurt, and running with the dog was so much harder, but he had to get away. He couldn't let Bad Man get him.

"Boy! Don't you run away from me! You're mine, you hear me? And you have to help me. No one else can see me!"

"No!"

Bad Man surged forward and tried to grab him, but his hands passed right through Colby's body.

"Boy!"

"No!" Colby screamed, then choked out a sob. "Go away!"

He kept running, gasping for air and stumbling along, his legs aching and his feet screaming in pain, his vision blurry from the tears that just wouldn't stop. Somehow, he had to get home. If he could just get home, he'd be safe. Safe from Bad Man.

Safe with Vic.

But he still had no idea where he was, or how far he had to go.

He kept running. He couldn't stop. He wouldn't.

Bad Man wasn't going to have him again.

* * *

VIC WAS just about to give up all hope. Sharma had led them on a wild chase through the neighborhoods, down one street, then another, the dog sniffing along the zigzag trail until they were over a mile from home. And were they even on the right path? Had Colby really gone this way?

Where in the gods' names was his sweet boy?

"Did you hear that?" Ryley asked.

"What?" Vic gasped, looking around wildly as he strained to listen.

"There!" Ryley said. "Someone's shouting–"

Another scream sounded, and Vic and Ryley looked at each other.

"Is that—"

"It's Colby," Vic gasped, and they took off running in the direction of the sound. "Colby!" Vic shouted.

Sharma barked, then they heard, "*Vic?*"

"Colby!"

Vic pushed Sharma's lead into Ryley's hands and sprinted forward, heading for that voice. He rounded a corner and jerked to a stop, gasping with relief when he saw Colby just ahead, then took off running again.

"Colby!"

Colby's eyes went wide. "Vic!" The boy put on a burst of speed and met him halfway, barreling into Vic's arms and sobbing as they collided, both of them dropping to their knees right there on the sidewalk.

"Vic!"

"I've got you, sweetheart," Vic gasped. "I've got you."

"Vic!" Colby cried.

"You're safe." Vic held the boy so close, he was afraid he might squeeze the air right out of him, but he couldn't help it. He had to feel Colby. He didn't ever want to let go. "You're safe. I've got you." He pulled back just enough to see Colby's face, brushing the tears off his cheeks, then yanked him into a tight hug again. "What in the gods' names are you doing way out here?"

Colby choked out a sob, then sniffed. "Patches got out. I had to save her."

"What?"

Colby leaned back slightly and rubbed his sleeve across his nose, the movement awkward as he still had Cam's dog in his arms. "I wanted to go out to get the mail. I wanted to be brave and make you proud since your rescue didn't work, but Patches ran outside before I could grab her leash." Colby sniffed again. "I couldn't let her get hurt. Cam would have been so sad."

Vic stared at the boy, then pulled him into his arms again.

"And then I was lost and Bad Man was there and I was so scared I'd never see you again!"

Vic's heart clenched, and he squeezed his eyes shut, holding Colby as tight as he could. "My sweet boy. Oh gods. It's alright. You're safe. I've got you, sweetheart. It's alright." He pulled back again and wiped away more tears. "Come on. Let's get you home." Vic stood, and Colby struggled to do the same, wincing as he got to his feet.

"Here." Ryley stepped in. "Let's do it the fast way." He flashed them a smirk, then wrapped his arms around both Vic and Colby before transporting them all right back into the house.

Colby yelped and burrowed into Vic, then slowly peeked out, relaxing slightly when he realized where they were.

"Sorry, kiddo," Ryley said, standing back. "Didn't meant to startle you."

Colby looked around again. "Are we home?"

"Yeah. Just a magic trick. Got us back here in an instant."

"Oh." Colby looked all around, glancing from Ryley to Vic and back, then to each of the dogs. He did it again, as though mentally cataloging everyone to make sure they were all there, then looked to Vic's side. "Cam, I'm so sorry. I didn't mean for her to get out!"

Vic blinked, then saw Colby step aside and hug what appeared to be nothing but air.

"I'm so sorry," Colby cried.

Vic held his breath, waiting, then saw Colby pull back and nod.

"What did he say?" Vic asked.

Colby tucked his hands up under his chin. "He said he can't believe I risked seeing Bad Man to go after Patches," he answered. "But I couldn't let Patches get hurt!" the boy insisted. "Not when Cam loves her so much. I didn't want Cam to be sad. He's already lost enough as it is."

Vic stared at Colby, utterly speechless.

Here was a boy who had endured innumerable horrors—probably more than Vic would ever know—a boy who could have so easily turned out bitter and angry and hating everything about the world because of what was done to him. Instead, Colby had such an incredible capacity for caring. For the enjoyment of beauty and goodness. For friendship. For joy.

For love.

Colby had run out that door without a second thought, braving the presence of his worst tormentor, all for the sake of not letting Cam have another reason to suffer. He'd faced his greatest fear just to protect Cam's happiness.

Vic's heart broke even as he fell utterly, hopelessly in love.

And if Colby—sweet, tortured Colby—could face his nightmares, it was damned well time that Vic stopped being a coward and did the same.

Chapter 24

VIC PULLED Colby into his arms and settled back on the pillows with a sigh.

"I'm so glad you're safe," he murmured, though he'd already said it a dozen times that afternoon. "I was so worried…"

Colby snuggled in closer, nuzzling his neck.

Vic smiled, kissed the top of Colby's head, and sighed again. He couldn't seem to let the boy out of his sight, not after thinking he'd lost him. And Colby seemed to need it as well. They'd both headed for Vic's bedroom after showering, some unspoken agreement settling between them, both of them needing to be close to one another.

"I need to go do something tomorrow," Vic said. Colby tensed, and tipped his head back to look up at him. "Probably just for a few hours. But I need to do it. It's a long time in coming." He paused, staring across the room at Cam's bracelet, resting in its usual nightly spot on top of his dresser. "I've put it off way too long."

"Vic?"

Vic put on a smile and looked down at the boy. "Nothing for you to worry about, sweetheart. It's just time for me to face my demons."

"Oh," Colby said, an adorably puzzled frown on his face.

Vic slowly reached up and rested a hand along Colby's jaw. "Come here."

Colby brightened, and moved right in for a kiss.

Vic smiled, turning to his side so he could face the boy and draw him in closer, their bodies pressed together everywhere they could manage as they kissed and held one another. Time disappeared as they got lost in the moment, the warmth and sweetness carrying them away from the real world.

Colby gave a soft whimper, pressing harder into Vic, then his whole body tensed. Vic sucked in a breath between kisses, feeling Colby's hard length against his own, separated by layers of fabric. It took everything he had to keep still, planting his hands firmly on Colby's back, determined not to let them move, determined to keep his hips still when all he wanted was to rock into Colby and share that exquisite feeling.

But it had to be up to Colby. If the boy wanted more, Vic would give it, but there would be no taking pleasure from the boy. Not yet. Not until Vic had earned it.

* * *

COLBY WOKE alone the next morning and checked the time. Vic must have gone to the gym. The big man had been oddly preoccupied last night, even as he'd held Colby, even as they'd kissed. Colby hugged Vic's pillow and pulled the blankets up to his chin. He'd felt Vic get hard last night while they were kissing, but Vic hadn't moved to do a thing about it. He just kept kissing Colby back and holding him close for as long as Colby wanted, never so much as hinting at trying to make something more happen between them.

And Colby had felt so grateful. Not that he didn't want it. There was a moment, last night, when he'd almost opened his mouth and begged Vic to touch him again, begged him to make him feel all those amazing things, but he realized he wasn't ready yet. He needed something else before anything like that could happen again.

Somehow, he got the feeling Vic wasn't ready yet, either. Vic said he needed to go face his demons, and maybe that meant that something would change if he succeeded.

And Colby had a few more demons to conquer, himself.

He got up and made the bed so the room looked nice when Vic got home from the gym, and after Vic showered, they had breakfast together, after which Vic left again, a look of grim determination on his face. Colby waited until Vic's car headed down the street, then he went to his room.

Colby shut the door and pulled the shades down, casting the room into total darkness. He considered going out to the garden again to do this, but he wanted to see if he could manage it without Deyn's help. And the darkness would keep him safe.

Bundled up in all his layers, Colby gathered up his comforter and made a nest for himself in the middle of the bed. He lay down, wrapped up safe and warm, and closed his eyes, taking slow, deep breaths as he turned his thoughts inward and concentrated on his goal.

Slowly but surely, one scar disappeared, followed by another, then another. He focused on the smaller ones first, building up practice and endurance. By the time he wore himself out and had to stop, he still had several more to go, but when he tugged his clothes aside and looked at his skin, he couldn't help smiling.

He was banishing Bad Man from his body, one tiny bit at a time.

* * *

VIC PULLED up to the address he'd programmed into the nav screen and eyed the building. It looked like any other in Morbran City. Inviting. Beautiful. Intricate stonework covered over in trailing ivy.

But inside, somewhere, was a monster.

Vic blew out a breath and glanced at the passenger seat. "You ready for this?"

Cam's pen floated up. *I think so.* He paused. *What if I see him and get scared?*

"Hey." Vic reached out, found Cam's shoulder, and gave it a squeeze. "You have *nothing* to be ashamed about if you're not ready to face him. Nothing at all, alright? This is the first time you'll be seeing him since it happened." *And the first time I'll ever set eyes on him.* "I'd be surprised if it *didn't* trigger something." Vic gave him another squeeze. "You don't have to go in there if you don't want to."

No, I want to. It's just… Cam's shoulders lifted and dropped as though he'd sighed. *I've imagined this moment for so long, and I don't know if it's going to go like I think it is or if I'm just gonna freak out and run away.*

"Whatever you do," Vic said, "will be right. For you. Whatever you need. And I'll be right there with you the whole time."

Cam rested his head on Vic's shoulder and nodded, then sat up again and wrote, *And I'll be there for you.*

Vic smiled. "Thanks, kiddo." He looked at the building again and blew out another heavy breath. "Alright. Here goes."

Cam set his notepad down, gave Vic's hand a squeeze, and they got out of the car.

Vic walked into the office building and looked around. He had absolutely no plan for how to go about this, but he couldn't stop now that he'd started. They were going to face the man, and that was all there was to it. Drawing himself up to his full height, he strode up to the receptionist and cleared his throat.

"Yes, sir?" the woman greeted him. "What can I do for you?"

"I'm here to see Logan Jarvis," Vic told her.

"Did you have an appointment?" she asked, turning to a computer screen sitting on the counter.

"No."

She turned back to him and clasped her hands before herself. "I'm very sorry, sir, but no one can see Mr. Jarvis without an appointment."

Vic clenched his jaw, fighting for patience, then pulled out a business card and handed it over. "Tell him it's urgent."

The woman frowned as she took the card from him and read it over. "Sturmwyn Insurance…" She looked back up at Vic. "Is there a problem with one of his contracts or policies? I can run it by his personal assistant–"

"It's a private matter."

"Mr…" The woman looked back down at the card again. "Lucius. I–" She did a double-take and read the card again, then looked at Vic with wide eyes. "Missing persons? But–"

"Like I said," Vic told her, "it's a private matter. And I need to speak with him immediately."

The woman hesitated, then stepped aside to grab her phone. "Let me see what I can do, sir."

She turned away and called someone, speaking in hushed tones so Vic couldn't quite make out what she was saying. Vic strolled about the reception area, keeping his footsteps slow and even, trying to maintain a semblance of control while his heart was galloping away.

Fifteen years, and he was finally going to face Cam's attacker. He didn't care what he had to do to make it happen, but he wasn't leaving that office until he saw the man.

"Mr. Lucius?"

Vic turned and strode back over to the counter.

"Mr. Jarvis is in a meeting at the moment," the receptionist told him, "but he should be back in his office in about ten minutes."

Vic gave a sharp nod even while his nerves spiked. Having to wait to face the man was only going to make it more difficult. Then again, he'd already waited fifteen years. He'd just have to bear a few more minutes.

"Thank you."

"If you'd like to wait over there," the woman said, pointing at a seating area, "his personal assistant will be down to get you."

Vic nodded again, then walked over to a chair. He

didn't want to sit—he was far too restless to sit—but he needed to at least try to appear calm.

An invisible touch tapped him on the arm. Vic looked around, then pulled out his phone and opened a texting app.

I'm scared, Vic.

Vic's heart clenched. *Poor Cam.* He found Cam's arm and gave it a squeeze. "You don't have to do this if you don't want to," he whispered.

No, I want to. Cam paused, then typed out, *It's just scary to think I haven't seen his face since he–*

Vic waited, watching the cursor just sit there.

"Say it, Cam," Vic urged him.

I don't know if I can.

"It's time, kiddo." Vic kept a hold on Cam's arm. "Maybe...You can joke about it, and that's great in its own way, but...Maybe, if you finally say it..."

Cam's hand shook.

"I know it's hard, Cam," Vic whispered, "but saying it will help you own it. Help you accept it. It gives you control of it. Not him." Vic moved his hand up to Cam's shoulder, and felt his brother act out taking a deep breath, even though he didn't need it.

Slowly, Cam typed out, *He raped me. Then beat me into a coma, and threw my body in a garbage heap.*

Vic squeezed Cam's shoulder, holding his breath while he waited.

Gods, Cam continued after a moment. *It really happened, didn't it?*

Vic swallowed down the emotion clogging his throat. "Yeah, it did."

Cam was silent for a long while, then typed, *It feels like it's outside of me now. Like...I don't know. I can't explain it, but it's not so scary now.*

Vic smiled. "I'm so proud of you, kiddo–"

"Mr. Lucius?"

Vic looked up and saw another woman standing by the counter.

"Mr. Jarvis will see you now," she told him.

Vic nodded, then whispered, "You ready?"

Yeah. Yeah, I think I am.

Vic pocketed his phone, stood up, buttoned his jacket, straightened to his full height, and followed the woman down the hall.

They passed a series of offices, then stopped at a door. The woman knocked, opened the door, and walked in, gesturing for Vic to follow.

Vic paused for half a second before stepping into the room, bearing himself up for the first sight of the man who had stolen his little brother's innocence.

Cam seized Vic's arm in a desperate grip, then slowly relaxed.

"Is that him?" Vic asked, keeping his voice as low and quiet as he could make it.

Cam leaned against him and nodded.

"Mr. Jarvis," the personal assistant said, "this is Victor Lucius with Sturmwyn Insurance. He works in missing persons and says he's here about a personal matter."

Jarvis frowned with concern, and quickly stood from his chair to reach across his desk and offer his hand. "Mr. Lucius. How can I be of service?"

Vic glanced at the man's hand, but didn't move to accept it. Jarvis waited, then slowly drew his arm back and sat back down, rolling his chair forward and clasping his hands on the desktop, a stern look on his face.

"You may want to have her leave the room," Vic said, nodding at the woman. It was the only courtesy he was willing to extend the man. Until he saw how Jarvis reacted to the reason for Vic's presence, Vic wouldn't decide just how far to spread the news of the man's crimes.

Jarvis scowled. "Audrey is my personal assistant and handles all of my business and personal affairs. There's nothing you can say that she can't hear."

Vic's eyebrows went up. "As you wish." He took a step forward. "Fifteen years ago, you met a fourteen-year-old boy in a nightclub. You spiked his drink, then kidnapped him, raped him, beat him into a coma, and left him to die in a pile of garbage in an alleyway."

Jarvis's eyes got wider and wider as Vic went on, the man breaking out in a sweat and a vein standing out on his forehead. Audrey, who had started taking notes, suddenly stopped and looked up with a gasp, a look of horror crossing her face. Jarvis looked from her to Vic and back, his expression helpless and desperate.

"You...But I...There's..." Jarvis began, then burst out, "How could you possibly know all that?"

Audrey gasped again. "Mr. Jarvis?"

Jarvis glanced at her and paled, clearly realizing what he'd just admitted.

The sight made Vic smile. Fifteen years of unknowns finally came to an end. Finally, he and Cam could get some closure. Cam's attacker had been found, and now the man had inadvertently confessed to what he'd done.

Vic pulled a folded stack of papers out of his inside jacket pocket, smoothed them out, and tossed them on the desk, pointing at them as he explained, "Your semen was collected from the victim's body, but no DNA match was ever found. Until now." Vic paused, watching Jarvis turn the pages, the man barely touching them as he did so. "You recently opened a new life insurance policy with my company, and standard procedure at Sturmwyn is to demand a DNA sample to attach to the client file for identification purposes. Our computer system is programmed to automatically analyze all new DNA samples to compare to all other samples in the system, looking for blood relatives or exact matches, to see if there are any relevant cases. Your sample was a ninety-nine-point-nine percent match to the sample taken from the victim."

Jarvis gasped for breath, still staring at the pages, then looked up at Vic with wide eyes. He glanced helplessly at Audrey, then swallowed hard and looked at Vic again. "Wh-What now?"

Vic hesitated. Now, he was sorely tempted to throttle the man. To beat him half to death. To subject him to all the same tortures he'd made Cam suffer.

But Vic wasn't Jarvis's victim. Not directly, anyway. It wasn't his choice what happened to the man.

"That's entirely up to him," Vic said.

Cam jostled Vic's arm, so Vic pulled out his phone and opened the texting app, then held the phone behind his back so Cam could write him a message.

At the same time, Jarvis gave a shaky nod. "So he's your client, I take it." He swallowed hard again. "Alright, then–"

"Actually," Vic interrupted, and felt Cam tap his arm again, letting him know he was done typing, "he's my brother." He caught the sight of Jarvis going pale again, then read what was on his phone screen: *Tell him I'm here*. Vic smiled and looked up.

"And," Jarvis said, dragging out the word as he eyed Vic uncertainly, towering over the man's desk. "You want me to meet with him and make amends."

Vic paused, then said, "You're already meeting with him."

Jarvis frowned. "What?"

A stack of papers on the corner of the man's desk suddenly flew off the edge, a flurry of paper showering down on the floor. Audrey shrieked and jumped back, and Jarvis clutched the edge of his desk, staring with wide eyes.

"What the fuck?" the man yelled.

Vic just stopped himself from laughing. Fifteen years, he'd hoped for and dreaded this moment, and now that it was happening, and in this way, the relief was indescribable.

"Logan Jarvis," Vic said, "this is Cam Lucius, my little brother. And your victim."

A pen moved across Jarvis's desk, and the man jerked back in his chair, gasping as he stared.

"What in all seven hells is going on?" Jarvis demanded, shooting to his feet and glaring at Vic. "Surely, we can have a civilized discussion about this without you resorting to…" He waved his hand helplessly. "Magic or parlor tricks or whatever this is."

"It's not magic," Vic told him.

Before he could say more, the pen moved across Jarvis's desk again, then a piece of paper shifted over. Vic watched in silence, reading upside-down as Cam wrote a message to his attacker.

I'm dead, in no small part thanks to you.

Jarvis read the words, then shook his head. "I don't know how you're doing this, but–"

I woke up with a gag in my mouth and your cock in my ass, Cam continued.

Vic tensed. He knew all the details of Cam's assault already, but seeing his brother write them again still hurt.

Jarvis paled.

I tried to struggle, to get away, but you grabbed my arm and twisted it behind my back before you punched me in the head and yelled at me to stay quiet.

"Alright, enough!" Jarvis gasped, staring at the words in horror. "Gods, please..." He sank into his chair, and Cam set down the pen, but those awful words were still there, heavy with accusation. The man looked all around the room, then gave a start as he looked at his assistant. "Audrey, get out."

"Mr. Jarvis–"

"I said *get out*!" he shrieked.

Audrey fled the room.

"And don't–" Jarvis started to yell, but the door shut behind her. He sighed, and finished in a mumble, "Tell anyone."

Silence settled over the office, and Jarvis sat there for a moment, shaking his head.

Finally, he looked up at Vic. "What do you want?" he asked in a defeated tone. "What do you want me to do?"

Vic considered the question, but before he could answer, Cam took up the pen again.

I want you to know that I know, Cam told his attacker. *I want you to live with the knowledge that you didn't get away with it. That I know who you are, and so does Vic, as well as anyone else in his company who happens to come across your file. I want you to know that, being a ghost, I can follow you anywhere. I know where you work now, and I can find out where you live, where you go, who your friends are. I can make your life a living hell.*

Jarvis paled again, glancing at the mess of papers all over the floor, his eyes darting about as though he were imagining all sorts of other things Cam could do.

And he'd never see it coming.

I want you afraid that everyone who looks at you, works with you, or loves you will find out what you've done. Maybe we'll tell them. Maybe we won't. Maybe your girl there has already started the gossip and it's too late. Either way, I want you to live out the rest of your days in guilt and fear. Guilt, to make up for all the guilt my brother has suffered, and fear, to make up for mine.

The pen dropped, and a heavy silence filled the room once more, broken only by the sound of Jarvis's rapid breaths.

After a moment, Jarvis slowly looked up at Vic from under his eyelashes.

Vic held the man's gaze, then gave a sharp nod and turned to leave. It was enough. He'd gotten to finally meet the man, look him in the eye, and hear him admit what he'd done. And Cam had gotten to face his attacker. Maybe his brother would want more retribution someday, but at least Cam had gotten the satisfaction of telling Jarvis, more or less to his face, that he wasn't going to live the rest of his life with a presumption of innocence. Jarvis now knew that others knew what he'd done. If Cam was content with that much punishment for the man, even if only for now, then Vic was happy.

He got into his car, shut the door, and sat back with a sigh.

"Cam? Are you still there?"

In answer, his brother leaned against him, resting his head on Vic's shoulder.

The next moment, Cam burrowed in closer and shook as though he'd burst into tears. Vic wrapped his arms around the ghost and hugged him tight.

"I am so proud of you," Vic murmured, pressing a kiss to the top of Cam's head. "You won, Cam. You know that? Just the fact that you could face him, that you could survive it all, means you won."

Cam nodded against him.

Vic let his brother cry as long as he wanted, sitting there in silence until Cam was ready to let go. Eventually, Cam pulled slightly away, and dug out his notepad again.

Thank you so much. For everything.

"You're welcome, kiddo."

Was it enough? For you, I mean. Did you get what you came for?

"Yeah, I did. He knows we know, and that's enough for now."

It's such a relief. Gods, I was so scared before, but now that I've seen him again, and especially after you made me write it out...

Vic smiled. "I'm so glad, kiddo."

It feels weird to say I survived it, considering I'm dead, but...Yeah. You're right. I finally feel like I did survive it all.

"Good," Vic murmured, and gave Cam's shoulder a squeeze. He paused, then said, "I'm gonna go see Dad next."

Cam stiffened.

"Not today. I think we've had enough for one day. But maybe tomorrow?"

Cam's pen wavered, then wrote, *I don't want to see him, Vic. I'm not ready. Not for that. Not yet.*

"That's fine," Vic said, and felt Cam heave a sigh of relief. "Hey, I understand. You'll face him when you're ready. But, right now, I need to do this. For myself. For–"

For Colby? Cam asked when Vic didn't finish.

Vic blew out a breath. "Yeah." He paused. "I can't very well keep hiding from my own nightmares after he's been facing his."

And worse, Cam wrote. *I can't even imagine surviving what he's been through.*

"Don't discount what happened to you–"

No, I know. And I'm not. I'm just saying...he's a tough little guy, isn't he? In his own way.

"Yeah, he is," Vic murmured.

I'm glad you found him, Vic. I'm glad you can help

him. Cam paused, then added, *I'm glad we can all kinda heal together.*

Vic slowly nodded.

Alright, Cam went on after a moment. *Go see The Asshole, if that's what you need. Maybe, someday, I'll be able to do the same. I'm just sorry I can't be there for you.*

"Don't apologize for that," Vic said, squeezing his brother's shoulder again. "Don't even worry about it. I know you're there for me even if you won't physically be present. It's alright."

Thanks, Vic.

"Anytime."

Cam mimed taking a deep breath and letting it out as a heavy sigh, his shoulders lifting and dropping under Vic's hand. *Let's go home.*

Vic smiled and started the car.

Chapter 25

VIC SAT in the rocking chair with Colby in his lap, fast asleep. He'd come home from his encounter with Jarvis to find the boy all bundled up and hiding under his comforter in his bedroom, the shades pulled and the lights off.

All Colby would say about it was that he wasn't scared, and wasn't necessarily hiding, but that he'd needed the comfort of the dark. No matter how Vic tried, he couldn't get anything more out of the boy than that. Colby seemed determined about something, but he insisted he couldn't talk about it until he was done.

Done with what, Vic could only guess, but whatever it was, it had so thoroughly drained the poor boy that he'd started falling asleep in the middle of lunch, right there at the table. For the first time since he could remember, Vic left the dishes for later, and held the boy instead, rocking him as he slept.

Patches bounced around the living room, playing with Cam, while Sharma lay at Vic's feet, being the silent guard dog, glancing up at Colby every few seconds.

Vic smiled. Getting the dogs had definitely been a good decision. Even considering yesterday's panic, and knowing that Patches was going to need a bit more training when it came to obedience, Vic was glad for them. His boys were happy. That was all that mattered.

Sharma perked up a moment before Colby stirred. The dog sat, wagging his tail as he watched his boy, then shifted closer and rested his head on Colby's leg.

Colby gave a sleepy grunt and opened his eyes. He looked up at Vic, smiled, and snuggled in closer, scratching behind Sharma's ears as he closed his eyes again.

"Hey, sweetheart," Vic murmured.

"Hi," Colby whispered back.

"Still tired? You could go lie down if you want a proper nap," Vic suggested, though he was reluctant to let the boy go.

Colby shook his head and blinked his eyes open again. "No, I should be awake."

"You don't have to be."

Colby nodded. "I have more to do."

"Yeah?" Vic asked, hoping Colby would tell him.

Vic's phone rang, stopping Colby from responding. Colby lifted his head away from Vic's chest so Vic could reach his phone, though Vic hesitated before answering. He was tempted to let it go to voicemail and keep enjoying this quiet moment.

He pulled out his phone just to check the screen, then saw that it was his boss calling.

"Mace?" he answered. Maybe there was another case. He didn't relish the idea of leaving town again so soon, but he couldn't very well leave a lost kid out there, all alone in the world.

"*Hey, Vic.*" Mace's tone was all wrong. It wasn't serious enough to be about a case. If anything, the man sounded amused. "*The weirdest thing just happened.*"

Cam wandered over—rather, his notepad did—and wrote, *What's wrong?*

Vic shook his head, then asked Mace, "What's that?"

"*I just got a notification from the bank,*" Mace said. "*Seems someone just made a rather generous donation to your department's account.*" Mace paused, and Vic heard keys clicking. "*One Logan Jarvis, who appears to be a client of ours, but he's never used your services as far as I can tell.*"

Cam's pen jerked back before it wrote, *The hells?*

Vic scowled. "If he thinks throwing money at it is going to ease his guilt–"

"*So you do know something about this?*" Mace asked when Vic broke off. "*Not that I'm going to complain about money coming in, of course, but it's just such a sudden, large amount.*"

Vic sighed. "If you check his file for links to other cases…"

He immediately heard clicking, followed by a brief, heavy silence before Mace said, "*Oh.*"

"Yeah."

"*Did you…*"

"I didn't extort him," Vic rushed to assure his boss. "But, yes, I did meet with him this morning. I needed to finally face the man, now that we knew who he was."

"*I see. Well.*" Mace paused. "*Considering the severity of his crime against your brother…I suppose this is a start,*" he finished with a chuckle.

Vic blinked, then breathed a laugh. "Yeah. I was happy with him just knowing I knew, but…Yeah, I'm not gonna argue with him making amends in some way."

"*I'm sorry there's nothing he can really do for your brother now, but…*"

"But it'll help me find and take care of other kids, so that's something."

"*Indeed.*" Mace paused again. "*Are you alright?*"

Vic blew out a breath. "I am, sir. Thank you."

"*Good. Good. Well, that was all. And I'm sorry to hear about Hunter. I saw the preliminary case notes you sent in.*"

Vic nodded to himself. "He may still call."

"*Here's hoping he does*," Mace said, and Vic made a sound of agreement. "*Well, I won't keep you.*"

They said their goodbyes, and Vic set his phone aside.

Wow, Cam wrote.

"No kidding." Vic looked at Colby, and saw the boy frowning in thought. "What's wrong?"

"Is Hunter gonna be alright?"

"I sure hope so."

Colby nodded slowly, then frowned again. "Vic?"

"Yeah, sweetheart?"

Colby was silent for a moment, then asked, "Are there a lot of boys out there like me?"

Vic hesitated before answering. "Not a lot who go through what you did, but…Yeah, there are always kids out there who need help. Runaways, or kidnappings, or kicked out of their homes for various reasons. Boys and girls."

Colby nodded again. "Why can't we make all the bad men go away?" he whispered.

Vic held him close. "It's human nature, unfortunately. There will *always* be bad people. It's just a fact of life. No matter what you do, there will always be bad people. But there are so many more *good* people in the world. Lots and lots of good people."

Colby smiled. "Like you."

Vic's heart swelled. "Thank you, sweetheart."

Then Colby sighed. "I just wish I could help. I wish there was something I could do. But everything's still so big and scary."

"Well, you've got time. Let's get you a little further down the road to healing, and if something comes up, if you find something you want to do, we'll look into it. How does that sound?"

Colby looked at him carefully. "That sounds like a long time."

Vic shrugged. "So? What matters is that you're happy, and that you feel safe."

Colby started to smile softly, then ducked his head and snuggled in closer again. When Vic looked down, the boy was blushing and fighting a grin.

Vic wasn't sure what to make of that, but he wasn't going to press the boy. Besides, he still had another confrontation to mentally prepare for, one that would be even harder than what he'd experienced that morning.

Facing Cam's attacker had been one thing. Facing the

man who had taken Cam's life—stolen away Cam's chance at recovery—was an entirely different matter.

* * *

VIC PROCRASTINATED for a week before he finally got into his car and drove across town to confront his parents. First, he claimed he had too many contracts piling up in his inbox, in need of processing, and sat down to get them all done. Then, he found the household in need of groceries and dog food, just for a start, and took the time to run a few errands. Finally, he ran a search on his family's old address, only to discover his parents no longer lived there, so he had to spend a few hours tracking them down.

Once he knew where they lived, though, he no longer had any excuses. Besides, they'd all barely been on speaking terms since Cam's attack fifteen years ago, and it had been nearly three years since Cam had died. It was well past time they had it out.

Vic found the house, parked his car on the street, and spent several, long minutes just trying to convince himself to keep calm before he managed to get out and walk up to the front door.

He rang the doorbell, held fast to Cam's bracelet, and counted his breaths as he waited. If the latter worked for Ryley, maybe it would work for him, too.

The door opened, and Vic heard a gasp before he looked up to see his father standing there.

"Victor," his father spat, staring at him. "What in the gods' names are you doing here?"

Vic scowled. "We need to talk." He pushed past his father and entered the house.

"I didn't say you could– Just where do you think you're going?" his father called after him, slamming the door shut and hurrying to follow.

Vic headed for the kitchen. Sure enough, he found his mother there, and she dropped the dish she was drying at the sight of him.

"Victor! My gods, I–"

"How dare you just barge in like–" his father fumed.

"*Silence!*" Vic yelled.

His mother gasped, and his father clenched his jaw, turning red with fury.

"You've said more than enough over the years," Vic told them. "Telling me what an abomination I am. Telling me that what happened to Cam was all my fault. And then that *gods*-awful phone call, telling me you'd taken him off life-support yourself." He paused, fighting not to completely lose his temper. "Now it's *my* turn to talk, and *you're* going to listen."

Mother pressed a hand to her mouth, and Father stared him down, both of them blessedly silent.

Vic reached for Cam's bracelet again, clutching it in a tight fist as he took a deep breath. "Yes, what happened to Cam was my fault. If I'd just stayed home with him, or even taken him straight home when I realized he'd followed me to that club, the attack never would have happened. He would have grown up, and continued with school, and met a nice girl. Hells, he may have eventually even found some small way to finally make you proud," he spat at his father.

The man scowled, but didn't say anything.

"But I turned my back on him, because I wanted just one night to myself," Vic went on. "Just one night to be free while you were away. And Cam was taken because of it. I've been carrying the guilt of that every single moment for the past fifteen years. I've spent every day since then, trying to make up for it. Trying to help other kids in similar situations so that no one would ever have to suffer like he did ever again. I've made my life about trying to do the hard, painful work of finding lost kids or getting teenagers off the streets, all in an attempt to make up for my complete and utter failure with Cam."

His father muttered something under his breath, and Vic shot him a look.

"And while you only ever visited Cam in the hospital the one time," Vic went on, "when Dr. Garrison called you to tell you what had happened, and you came home early from your trip, and screamed at me in the middle of the hallway for letting Cam get hurt, *I* visited him every week. Sometimes more. I spent countless hours begging his forgiveness, begging him to wake up, promising him that I was going to do everything in my power to make sure he got to live his life again." Vic paused, shaking his head. "But you never came. Not once. And I *checked*. Believe me, I did, checking and double-checking the visitors log every time I came in. I kept hoping I'd get to go in one day and tell Cam that his loving parents had been there to see him while he was sleeping, but you never showed. So, instead, I kept telling him you were probably just busy, and that, surely, you'd be there next time. But the days and weeks and years passed, and you never came. You *abandoned* your son."

"Victor," his mother cried.

"Until the day you pulled the plug," Vic went on, ignoring her interruption. "Twelve *years*, he was in that hospital bed, all alone, and not once, in twelve years, did you go see him again, until the day you snuck in there like thieves in the night, knowing that I was out of town and couldn't stop you." He glared at his parents in turn. "You took your own son off life-support and let him *die*." Vic sucked in a breath, fury and grief clogging his throat. He swallowed hard, and said, "You let him die right when he was about to live again."

His mother gasped, and his father blinked dumbly for a moment before he demanded, "What?"

Vic slowly inhaled through his nose while he clenched his jaw, fighting the urge to scream, and said, "Cam was going to live again. I'd been working with a team of doctors for several years, looking for any sort of treatment that might repair the damage to his brain and bring him out of the coma."

His father scoffed. "Well, if any such treatment did exist, they would have done it—"

"That's just it," Vic interrupted. "It didn't exist, but it does now, thanks to the research they did on Cam. They were *weeks* away from performing the operation, and if you had only *talked* to someone—me, or one of his doctors—you would have *known* that before you went and *murdered* him."

"Don't be putting that on me," his father fumed. "You can't be sure that it would have worked–"

"Well, it would have!" Vic yelled. "Four weeks after Cam died, they performed the surgery on a patient with a similar condition, and it *worked*. The patient woke up and *lived*."

Father paled, and Mother choked out a sob. "Oh my gods…"

"But–" Father worked his mouth, failing to find a response.

"Cam would have lived if you'd only given him a chance!" Vic yelled at them, unable to contain his grief any longer. "We were so close! Twelve years of waiting and hoping, and we were so close, but you took that away from him. You took his life away. You took away his chance to live again, to walk and talk and breathe and learn and love. You took away everything. He couldn't even come with me today to face you because he still hates you so much for it."

His mother's sobs stuttered while his father blinked dumbly at him. "He what?"

Vic almost blushed when he realized what he'd just blurted out, but he couldn't take it back now. Besides, his parents deserved to know just how much Cam was suffering because of them.

"Cam's a ghost," he told them. "We've spent a lot of time over the past couple years, talking and healing. I've been helping him try to deal with it all, trying to give him therapy as best as I can. It's not enough, but it's something, and he's getting better every day. He's just not ready yet to face either of you."

"Bullshit," his father spat. "You've gone out of your mind." The man barked a laugh. "Ghosts. My gods. Has your guilt really made you that insane?"

Vic glared at the man. "*'Good riddance.'*"

His father frowned. "What?"

"*'Good riddance.'* That's what you said after his heart stopped. You muttered those words under your breath so that Mom wouldn't hear, then patted Cam on the leg and walked out of the room."

His father paled, then stumbled back and caught himself on the counter, chest heaving as he stared up at Vic. "How– When did– But how could you possibly know that?"

"Because Cam was there," Vic told him. "The moment he died and left his body, his ghost was there in the room with you. Saw you standing over him. Saw Mom crying, and heard you say those words."

"Oh my gods," his mother sobbed, covering her face with both hands, then whirled on his father. "You said that about our *son?*"

"I–"

Vic watched his parents stare at one another, wondering if he should tell them the rest. Would Cam want to say it all himself someday? Then again, Vic needed to get it off his chest now, while he had the chance. This would be the last time he ever planned to see these people, so he was going to make it count.

Still, the memory of Cam telling him this part still sent a chill through him, almost able to hear his brother's voice as he pictured Cam stuck in that hospital bed.

Swallowing down the grief yet again, Vic said, "And he heard you, before you did it." His voice was thick, so he cleared his throat, sniffed, and tried again. "Even in the coma, he heard you in the room, heard you talking about him. He was so relieved you'd finally come to see him, until he heard you talking about doing it quick before you got caught."

"Oh gods," his mother cried, hiding her face.

"And he screamed at you," Vic said, unable to stop a few tears from racing down his cheeks. "He screamed and begged you not to do it. He didn't want to die. He knew exactly what you were doing, and he was powerless to stop you. He knew there was a treatment just weeks away, that he was going to live again, and that you were taking that chance away from him. He screamed at you to stop all the while you were taking him off the machines."

His mother wailed, and his father sank to the floor, holding his head in his hands.

"And I wasn't there to stop you," Vic continued, dashing the tears away, only for more to show. "Once again, I failed to save my brother while he was lying there, helpless. And you killed him."

Silence fell over the room, made heavier somehow by the soft sounds of his mother's sobs and his father's panted breaths.

Vic scrubbed his tears away and squared his shoulders. "Cam might come to you one day." He sniffed, then continued, "And when he does, you're going to listen to every gods-damned word he has to say." Vic paused, looking down at them, then turned and started to leave the room.

"Oh, is that all?" his father scoffed, the bully making a reappearance through his grief. "No other hate to throw at us?"

"Isn't that enough?" his mother cried, glaring at her husband for a moment and then hiding her face again as she continued sobbing.

Vic turned and looked back at his father. "Do you really want more?" he growled. "Because I could go on. I could tell you how terrified I was, growing up, knowing that you'd never accept me if and when I came out. I could tell you how exhausting it was, trying to always be perfect for you so that you'd stop berating Cam for all his health issues. I could say how frightened I was, at sixteen years old, being kicked out of the house at a moment's notice with nothing more than a bag of clothes and no way to support myself…But you know what? None of that matters," he said, realizing their truth only at the moment the words came out of his mouth. "Not anymore. I've waited so many years to air my grievances with you, but my own don't matter. I only came here today for Cam's sake, so you could know just how much you hurt him, how you destroyed him by robbing him of another chance at life. Besides, all the things you did to me? I wouldn't change a thing. I have a good life, with work that I love, that makes a difference. And I have Cam's forgiveness."

With that, Vic walked away and let himself out of the house, more weight dropping off his shoulders with every step he took. He never slowed. Never looked back. The battle was won, even if it was all in his own mind.

He got into his car, and before he could reach for the button to switch it on, he felt an invisible weight grab his arm and lean against his side.

"Hey," Vic gasped, and reached out to hug Cam. "I thought you weren't coming. Are you alright?"

Cam nodded, then grabbed his notepad. *I was in the car with you when you came over here.*

"What? Why didn't you say anything?"

I knew this was gonna be hard for you. Didn't want to throw you off your game once you'd worked up the nerve to go in there. Cam paused. *I don't know how you did it, Vic. How you walked in there. I'm not sure I can ever face them.*

"That's fine, kiddo. That's completely up to you. You never have to see them again if you don't want to."

It's just…I feel like I should, *someday, you know? But I'm still not ready.*

"Nothing wrong with that. You just take your time."

Cam nodded against Vic's shoulder again. *It was hard not to go in there. You guys were all thinking of me so hard, it was difficult to resist the pull.*

"Shit." Vic kissed the top of his head. "I didn't even think about that. I'm so sorry."

It's alright. I managed to stay put. And I wanted to be here when you were done, to see how you were.

Vic blew out a breath. "It was rough," he admitted. "But good. I feel…lighter now. Freer."

Good. I'm so glad. Cam paused, tipping his head back for a moment, then wrote, *You look better. Not quite so haunted.* Cam paused again. *Is that ironic, considering you have a ghost sitting beside you?*

Vic barked a laugh, then threw his head back and let the laughter roll out of him. He felt Cam laughing along, and they let it all out together until Vic had a tear running down his cheek again. At least it was a tear of joy and relief that time. He wiped it away and shook his head.

"Alright, brat," he said, chuckling again as he kissed Cam's hair and reached to switch on the car. "Let's go home."

Cam drew a smiley face, then set his notepad aside and leaned against Vic the whole drive back.

Vic held his brother and smiled to himself, feeling even more weight leave him. Fifteen years of carrying the guilt for what had happened to Cam, and he was finally starting to feel like he could live with a little less of the burden. It would never be truly gone—he knew that—but he'd never be worthy of Colby if he didn't also face his demons.

His smile faded away as he realized there was one more thing he had to do.

Chapter 26

COLBY SCRAMBLED out of his nest when he heard the doorbell ring. He wasn't quite done with his task, but Treble were having another rehearsal that day, and there was no way he was going to miss it.

He rolled up the shades, the sudden daylight flooding in through the windows making him wince. Blinking rapidly, he waited for his eyes to adjust, then straightened the comforter back out, fussing with it until it was just right and the bed looked untouched, and left his room.

The sight of all those big men in the entryway made him pause and hold his breath for a second, until he remembered that they were all nice and safe and that being around them meant he'd get to hear their music again.

Vic had said it would take time for him to stop reacting with fear whenever he was around other people. A part of him wished it could just *happen*, wished it could all be over, but he knew that couldn't be. The more he talked to Vic—and Cam, for that matter—and learned just how long it could take to get over a trauma, the more he understood that the journey was unpredictable, but at least he was making progress. A few, tense moments were so much better than running away to hide in the dark.

Slowly but surely, things were getting better.

Colby even surprised himself by smiling as the others

greeted him. The sight of Zac's collar was still unsettling, but the more he watched Zac and Adrian interact, the more he saw just how connected they were. The same with Ryley and Asher. The depth of feeling in the couples was almost a tangible thing.

He envied that.

Colby glanced at Vic, seeing the smile on the man's face as he got settled on the couch with his cello. The sight made his heart beat faster. He loved seeing Vic so happy.

Curling up in the rocking chair with Sharma sitting on the floor beside him, Colby watched Treble play, eyes darting from one instrument to another. It was all so beautiful. Like the gardens in the backyard were beautiful. If those gardens could have been turned into music, it would have sounded just like what Treble played.

"Alright!" Zac said when one piece came to an end. He and Ryley had been playing off one another, almost seeming to playfully fight as they faced one another in the middle of the room. "I think we're ready."

Ryley grinned, and Vic gave a nod as he smiled.

Colby looked around, wondering what they meant.

"We're gonna be doing some shows," Vic explained to him, and nodded at Asher. "Asher's uncle got us a regular gig at one of his places, so we'll get to start playing in public again."

"Oh," Colby said, though he wasn't quite sure what all that meant.

"You could come watch," Ryley suggested with a beaming smile, then his expression slowly sobered. "Though, it'll be crowded..."

Colby tensed. Being out of the house and around a lot of strangers? Even to hear Treble play, he wasn't sure if he was ready for that. Watching them in the house, with just the six of them in the living room, was difficult enough. Getting easier, but still difficult. He couldn't imagine anything bigger.

But he was getting better.

"Maybe someday?" he asked, looking at Vic.

Vic smiled at him. "Yeah. Someday. When you're ready."

"We'd love to have you there," Zac said, and Ryley nodded along.

"And," Asher added, "Adrian and I would be right there with you, so you wouldn't be alone. We could all go together."

Adrian gave a shy nod of agreement.

Colby blushed and ducked his head, feeling all of them watching him. Sharma tried to crawl into his lap, clearly sensing that he needed the comfort, but the dog was too big and only managed to get his front legs draped across him. Colby sank his fingers into Sharma's fur and looked at Vic. The big man was smiling softly at him.

"Someday," he whispered, making it a promise to both Vic and himself.

Vic grinned, and the sight eased something in Colby's chest.

When practice was over, Colby saw a tense look come over Vic's face, and the man pulled Ryley aside while the others packed up their things.

"Is there some time this week that we could meet?" Vic asked quietly.

"Yeah, of course, babe," Ryley said. "What's going on?"

"I can't talk about it here," he said, nodding significantly at the others. "And it's not something I want to say over the phone."

Ryley frowned. "Now you've got me worried."

"No, no, it's not bad. Well, it is, but..." Vic huffed out a breath. "There's something I need to tell you, and you deserve to hear it in person."

Ryley's eyebrows went up. "Alright," he said, dragging out the word. "How about we meet for lunch tomorrow? Our old place?"

Vic gave a sharp nod. "Yeah. That works. Thanks, Ry."

"Of course, babe." He reached out and rubbed Vic's arm. "Whatever it is, it's gonna be alright."

"Gods, I hope so," Vic muttered.

Colby frowned, watching Vic as he said goodbye to his friends and shut the front door. Vic wandered back over to the living room and put his cello away.

"Vic?"

Vic looked up from fastening the last clasp on the cello case. "Yeah, sweetheart?"

Colby nudged Sharma aside and stood, fidgeting beside the rocking chair. Vic gave him a smile and sat in his place, drawing Colby onto his lap. Vic held him close, and Colby let out a sigh.

"Are you alright?" Colby asked.

"Yeah, of course," Vic said, looking down at him with a frown. "Why wouldn't I be?"

Colby reached up and rubbed the frown lines out of Vic's brow.

Vic chuckled.

"You looked sad when you were talking to Ryley," Colby told him.

"Oh." Vic's humor faded. "Don't you worry about that, sweetheart."

Colby touched the furrow in Vic's brow again, and Vic put on a smile, then grabbed Colby's hand and kissed his knuckles.

"It's just something I need to tell Ryley," Vic said. "I owe him an apology." He paused, then lowered his voice almost to a whisper as he added, "And then I need to tell Cam."

Colby snuggled up to Vic, resting his head on Vic's chest. It all sounded like something big that he probably wouldn't understand.

Vic sighed. "Once I tell Cam, I'll tell you, too, if you want." He paused. "I'm just afraid you'll hate me if I do."

Colby frowned. He couldn't imagine ever hating Vic, not after all the man had done for him.

Then again, considering what Colby was planning to do—and the fact that it might upset Cam—he started to wonder if Vic might hate him, too.

* * *

VIC WALKED into the restaurant and looked around. He spotted Ryley at a table near the back, the booths constructed in such a way that they could talk without being overheard even by the next closest table. It had quickly become their favorite place to go for lunch after they'd started working together, a place where they could discuss work and personal matters in relative privacy.

As Vic sat across from Ryley, he realized it was at that very table—in the midst of a debriefing on a rescue case that came to Vic too late and thus ended in recovering a body—that Vic had first asked Ryley out.

"Lots of memories for us in this place," Ryley said, clearly thinking along the same lines as Vic.

Vic nodded. "Yeah." He chuckled. "I'll never forget sitting here, listening to you talk about walking that scene, so much passion and excitement in your voice, and then blurting out an invitation to dinner."

Ryley laughed. "Seriously. I think my jaw hit the floor. I had no clue you were gay until you asked me out."

Vic chuckled again. "I was almost determined not to date," he admitted. "Especially knowing your history, knowing that you were a case I needed to follow up on. But...seeing how much you loved your work, seeing you light up just talking about it, even as dismal as it all was...I couldn't resist." He shook his head and held up a hand. "I'm not trying to get you back or anything—"

"No, of course not," Ryley said.

"I just didn't want you to think that's what this was—"

"No, not at all. You're not that type of guy. I know that." Ryley grinned. "But you can totally go on, if you want. I don't know a man alive who would turn down hearing how irresistible he is."

Vic barked a laugh, then quickly sobered. He could easily think of *one* man who would probably never want to hear how irresistible he was, and the thought made his heart ache.

But that wasn't why he was there. He had a confession to make—long overdue—and he was damned well going to do it, no matter the consequences.

Ryley managed to wait until both their drinks and meals were served before he shot Vic a look and asked, "So?"

"So?"

"So...what was it you wanted to tell me?"

Vic took a bite of his sandwich to buy himself a moment even though his appetite was suddenly gone. Guilt weighed heavily in his stomach. He was going to have to tell Ryley the truth. He swallowed the bite, set the sandwich down, and took a deep breath.

"I owe you an apology," he began.

"Oh?"

Vic gave a tight nod. "One of our longest-running arguments...about me denying you in the bedroom–"

"Vic, babe," Ryley interrupted, waving his hand. "Seriously, I'm over it. I understand, and it's all behind us–"

"Except it's not," Vic cut in. "Not really."

Ryley frowned. "I don't get it."

Vic reached for Cam's bracelet, then drew his hand away at the last moment. He couldn't be thinking of Cam just then. There was no way he could draw the ghost to him while he explained this, not wanting Cam to overhear. He'd have to say it all again to his brother later, but he wanted to do it when they were alone, as Cam deserved.

"Cam, if you're here," he whispered, "I need you to stay away."

He waited, but there was no sign of the ghost, so he clasped his hands on the edge of the table, took a deep breath, and looked up, forcing himself to meet Ryley's eyes.

"I wanted to," he admitted.

Ryley's frown deepened. "Wanted to what?"

Vic sighed. "Wanted to...be inside you."

Ryley's eyes went wide and his jaw dropped. "What?" he breathed.

Vic nodded and grimaced. "I'm so sorry. I know how much you wanted it, and I did, too. Hells, I've *been* wanting it ever since my first time, that night that Cam went missing. But after what happened to Cam, I just couldn't do it. After what Cam suffered, I didn't deserve it. I didn't deserve anything I wanted, but especially not that."

Ryley stopped eating halfway through Vic's explanation and just stared at him.

When Vic finished, he fell silent and held his breath, watching the emotions play out on Ryley's face as the man tried to process everything he'd said.

Finally, Ryley dropped his burger and scrubbed his hands over his face, shaking his head. "Wait. Hold on." He lowered his hands, revealing deep frown lines in his brow. "You're saying...the whole time we were together...you actually *wanted*–" He broke off and shook his head, staring at Vic with a mixture of shock, anger, and frustration. "Vic!"

"I know, I know," Vic pleaded. "I'm sorry, but–"

"I always assumed you really didn't want it, and that Cam was just one more reason for you not to," Ryley said, his tone and expression more serious than Vic was used to. "But you're saying you actually *wanted* it, and you never *told* me?" Ryley sat back, shaking his head. "The hells, Vic?"

Vic sighed. "Look, I'm sorry, alright? I didn't think it would matter since I was never going to be able to bring myself to do it anyway."

Ryley slowly shook his head. "Fuck, Vic, do you have any idea what a difference it would have made to at least know you wanted me that way?" He paused, then rolled his eyes at himself and said, "Yeah, it probably wouldn't have changed anything in the long run—I probably still would have ultimately cheated on you—but at least it wouldn't have felt like such a blatant rejection–" He broke off and looked away.

Vic pushed his barely-touched lunch aside. "Ryley, I really am sorry."

Ryley shook his head, staring at the wall. "Fuck," he breathed. He brought a fist down hard on the table, making the plates and utensils rattle, then waved an apology when a few other diners looked their way. Ryley blew out a breath and shot Vic a look. "Hey, at least I'm not burning out the light bulbs."

"I wasn't gonna say anything," Vic murmured, though it was strange to see Ryley have a mini-meltdown without causing the electricity to run haywire.

"I'm learning to actually express and release my anger rather than keeping it bottled up inside," Ryley told him, then huffed out one breath, took in another, and sighed, closing his eyes for a moment before looking at Vic again. "So you really did want me that way?" he asked in a whisper.

"So much," Vic admitted.

Ryley slowly nodded, then laughed and shook his head. "Gods. I know it's irrelevant now since we're no longer together, but..." He blew out another breath. "Thank you. I wish I'd known that a long time ago, but thank you for telling me at all."

Vic nodded back, the knot in his stomach easing when he saw Ryley smiling again.

Still, the guilt ate at him. "I'm sorry I let everything get in the way between us."

Ryley shrugged. "Hey, I'm pissed you never told me, but...Hells, we both know we're better off as friends. It's over and done with. I've moved on with Asher. It's time you did the same. Go out and find someone, love him and fuck him and *live*."

Vic shook his head. He could certainly love someone again—hells, he already *did* love someone—but as for the rest? There was just no way, no matter how much he wanted it.

"Vic?" Ryley asked, then got an exasperated look as he studied Vic's face. "Don't tell me, after all that, you're still gonna deny yourself–"

"I have to, Ry," Vic insisted. "I have to say all this to Cam next, and I'm afraid it'll destroy him. How can he ever accept a brother who wants that after it was forced on him?"

Ryley grimaced. "Yeah, alright. I get that."

"Besides," Vic blurted out, then stopped himself.

Could he admit this to Ryley? Then again, he already had, to a point, so what would it hurt to say the rest? "The only person I want is someone I can never have. At least, not that way."

"Who–" Ryley's eyebrows went up. "Oh. You mean the kiddo."

"Yeah."

Ryley started to nod, then laughed. "Not that he's exactly a kid, though, huh?"

"Well–" Vic began. He stopped, thinking it over, and slowly nodded. "He's gonna be twenty-two here pretty soon."

"There, see?" Ryley teased. "That makes it less creepy sounding."

Vic tossed an olive at him.

Ryley ducked aside and laughed, then said, "But seriously, what would he say about it all?"

"What do you think?" Vic sighed and sat back. "The poor boy has been used all his life. He'll never want that. Not ever."

Ryley shrugged. "You never know. I've seen the way he looks at you, after all. It might be possible." He paused, then said, "If nothing else, you could always tell him how you feel."

Vic gave a grim nod. "I know. That's the plan. He deserves the truth, even if he hates me for it." He took a deep breath. "But, first, I have to tell Cam."

Ryley reached across the table and gave his hand a squeeze.

* * *

VIC GOT home to find Colby tucked away in his room again. He still couldn't make sense of why the boy had suddenly taken to hiding out so much after getting so much better about being out of the room, but every time Vic asked, Colby said he wasn't ready to explain.

He quietly shut the bedroom door, and headed for the backyard, taking the dogs with him. They needed to go out anyway, and Vic needed the tranquility of the gardens to maintain a calm atmosphere for the conversation he was about to have.

Vic watched the dogs dart about for a few minutes, then wandered off to a bench that was tucked away under a tree. He sat down, taking a few moments to really enjoy the peace and beauty of the gardens, something he never truly appreciated beyond a simple aesthetic pleasure before Colby came along.

When he couldn't put it off any longer, Vic pulled out his phone, opened a texting app, and set the phone at his side, thinking of his brother.

"Cam?" he murmured, looking all around for any sign of the ghost.

Patches darted over, yipping at something, and stopped near the bench, bouncing excitedly in place. Vic saw his phone float up off the cushion, and realized the dog had followed Cam over there.

I get the feeling I'm not gonna like this conversation, Cam typed on the phone.

Vic nodded slowly. "No. No, I don't think so."

I stayed away like you asked me to when you were talking to Ryley, but...

Vic cringed. "I was worried you were there."

I was, at first. But then you told me to leave. So now you've got me worried.

Vic felt around and found Cam's arm, giving it a squeeze. "I don't want you to hate me, but you deserve to know the truth."

A heavy pause followed, then Cam typed, *Alright. Whatever it is, tell me.*

Vic gave a nod, then took a deep breath. "I want...so badly...to know what it's like to be inside someone." The phone jerked, and Vic held his breath as he waited for Cam to type a response. When nothing came, he said, "It's never gonna happen, of course, but...I just needed you to know..."

Another tense moment passed, then Cam finally wrote, *Go on.*

Vic blew out a breath. "It was hard enough dating while you were in the hospital, feeling guilty for everything I wanted while you were struggling just to live after what was done to you. But even when I gave in and became intimate with someone, it never went all the way. Never that far, no matter how much I wanted it. And, gods, Ryley begged for it, but I could never give it to him. The very idea felt like such an utter betrayal of you. Somehow, it felt like cheapening what had happened to you."

After a moment, Cam typed, *And now? You've never really dated again since I died.*

Vic nodded. "I wanted to. I tried to, but knowing that you could follow me anywhere, knowing that you could see…It would have felt like I was throwing my sexuality in your face, like what Jarvis did to you didn't matter."

Vic stared at the phone, waiting, but Cam remained silent.

"I'm so sorry, kiddo," Vic went on, wishing he could see Cam's face. "I promise, even if I ever seriously date again, I'm *never* gonna act on that particular desire, but you deserved to know the truth, even if you hate me for it–"

I could never hate you.

Vic sighed. "Cam–"

Alright, so maybe I hated you a little when I was first in the coma, but after you started visiting all the time and taking care of me and doing everything you could to give me my life back…

"I'm so sorry."

But I don't hate you, Cam went on after a moment. *Not even for this.*

Vic held his breath, staring at the words. "Are you sure? I mean, it's–"

An invisible hand smacked him upside the head.

"Hey–"

You used the 's' word again.

Vic blinked. "Oh." He breathed a laugh. "I'm sorry."

You should be, Cam wrote, then added a winking

smiley face before he continued: *Now, as for the not acting on it...*

"I promise, Cam," Vic rushed to assure him. "It won't ever happen."

The cursor on the screen was still for a moment before Cam wrote, *But it should.*

Vic stared at the words, trying to make sense of them. "What?"

The phone lifted and dropped slightly, almost as though Cam had sighed, then Cam started typing again. *The thought of you...you know...Yeah, it kinda freaks me out, and I* really *don't ever want to see it, but that doesn't mean you can't have it.*

"Cam–" Vic started to argue.

No, listen. The cursor paused, and once Vic shut his mouth, Cam continued: *All this stuff you've been doing lately—taking me to see Jarvis, facing The Asshole—it got me thinking. Ever since I got attacked, you've made your whole life about me–*

"I had to," Vic interrupted.

I get that, Cam went on. *In the beginning. But not now.* Cam paused, then went at it again: *It's been fifteen years. And after everything you've done...Not just for me, but saving all those other people, rescuing all those kids...Vic, you've put off your own life for so long.*

"Because I had to," Vic reiterated.

Vic. The cursor paused again, then Vic felt the weight of Cam's form moving to sit closer beside him before it went on: *You've done nothing but make up for it ever since it happened. You kept me sane, all that time in the hospital, and now you're helping me cope with the fact that I'm dead and I'll never get to experience certain things.* There was a slight pause, then Cam wrote, *So I need you to experience all those things for me.*

Vic frowned. "What?"

There are so many things I'll never get to do, Vic. I'll never graduate, or have a job, or drive a car. He paused. *Actually, that last one I might be able to do...*

Vic narrowed his eyes. "Not a chance."

Cam shook with laughter, then went still as he continued: *I'll never eat my favorite foods or feel the sun on my face ever again. I'll never know what it's like to fall in love or how it feels to make love to someone.* Cam paused, and Vic felt him chuckle. *That probably sounds weird coming from a fourteen-year-old kid, but it's true. I had way too much time in that hospital bed to think and imagine and...*

Vic waited, watching the cursor sit there, blinking, before Cam finally finished the sentence: *want.*

"Cam..." Vic swallowed hard, a fresh wave of guilt washing through him. Then he frowned. "Wait, fourteen? But you were twenty-six when you died."

Cam brought up a blushing smiley face on the screen. *I know, but in my head, I'm still fourteen.* He paused. *Can I even say that? 'In my head'? Since all I am is a mind now?*

"Cam—"

Cam added a laughing face, then went on: *I did see myself right after I died. It made the whole thing so much harder. I didn't recognize my body at all.*

The words came out slower toward the end, giving off a sense of melancholy.

Vic swallowed hard again. "I'm so sorry, kiddo."

But none of that is your fault, Cam quickly typed out. *It's Dad's fault. You were going to find a way for me to wake up, so that I could get to experience all that. Dad's the one who took all that away from me, not you.*

"Cam..." Vic whispered. It seemed to be the only thing he could get out while a mixture of heartbreak and fury threatened to overwhelm him. He'd finally had it out with his father, but he *still* wanted to kill the man for what he'd done.

Dad deserves all the bad karma he can get—and so does Mom, for not stopping him—but you've more than served your sentence, Vic. You've served it a dozen times over. It's time for you to live. You're allowed to have the things you want, even if I don't like them.

Vic slowly shook his head. "I've always known I

could never have that, Cam. Not without feeling like I was betraying you."

The only way you could betray me now would be to keep punishing yourself. I forgave you a long time ago. It's way past time that you finally forgive yourself and move on.

Vic kept shaking his head, staring at the words. He wanted to. Good gods, he wanted to give in to his desires so badly, but he wasn't sure he could ever let go of that last shred of guilt that was holding him back.

Besides, the only person he wanted—and far more than anyone else he'd ever wanted in his life—was someone he could never have.

Chapter 27

COLBY DARTED into his room the minute he saw Vic's car pull out of the garage. Vic was going somewhere to play music with Ryley and Zac, and said he'd be back in a couple hours. Colby was going to need every bit of that time to prepare.

He locked his bedroom door for the first time ever, and made up his nest in the middle of the bed, burrowing under the comforter and closing his eyes. There was only one scar left to get rid of. Once it was gone, he'd be ready for the next part of his plan.

Assuming he could follow through with it.

Hidden away in the dark, wrapped up in warmth and silence, Colby turned his focus inward and traveled down through his body until he found the last scar, the worst of them all. He went to work, ordering the damaged tissue to fall off, cell by cell, only to be replaced by new skin, slowly but surely knitting its way across the scarred area. When he was finished, he lay there for a long moment, trying to work up the nerve to go see the result.

Finally, he got up, tidied the bed, and went to the washroom. He switched on the light, dimming it down as much as he could, and stripped out of his clothes. Colby turned on the shower and stepped in under the hot water, skipping the mirror for now. He could do that part later.

Colby tilted his head back under the spray, letting the tension melt from his limbs as the heat soaked into his skin. He washed his hair, fingering the strands. It was getting long again. Part of him was tempted to have Vic cut it back, but the hair that Bad Man had touched had already been cut off, and Colby himself didn't like the way it looked when it was all chopped short, even if it did make him feel more comfortable. Besides, he got the feeling Vic had been sad to see it go, and anything he could do to make Vic happier would, with any luck, make his plan come about a little easier.

Once his hair was clean, Colby scrubbed all over his body, then did it again, paying special attention to certain areas. When he finally couldn't linger any longer, Colby got out and dried himself thoroughly, taking slow, deep breaths as he hung up the towel and walked over to the door.

A full-length mirror hung on the back of the washroom door. Colby had always avoided it as much as he could, but today was different. He stopped in front of it, eyes focused on his feet in the reflection. With another deep breath, he slowly looked up, scanning his body as he went.

The scars were gone. They were really and truly gone. Colby twisted to one side, then the other, checking all over, then slowly ran his hands all over his skin, feeling the smoothness of it all, no longer able to either see or feel the rough marks from Bad Man's cigarettes, knives, or hands. For all that Bad Man had been adamant about his party guests never permanently harming Colby, the man had never applied that rule to himself, punishing Colby in painful ways that marked out his ownership of the boy all over his skin.

But, now, the scars were no more. All those marks of ownership were gone.

Except for one, and it was one that couldn't be seen. It existed only in his mind.

Somewhere in the house, Colby heard a door close.

"Colby?"

Colby tensed even as he smiled nervously. This was it. His heart raced and his hands shook, but he knew what he had to do. What he *wanted* to do.

A knock sounded at his door. "*Sweetheart? Are you awake?*"

"Yes," Colby called back.

After a pause, Vic asked, "*Everything alright?*"

"Yeah."

"*Alright.*" Vic paused again. "*I'm gonna go shower, but I just wanted to let you know I'm home.*"

"Alright."

Vic was silent, then his footsteps moved away down the hall.

Colby stood by the door for a long moment, then darted over to his closet and grabbed his hoodie, pulling it on and zipping it all the way up.

Then he went back to the door, listening and waiting.

* * *

VIC GLANCED down the hall through his open bedroom doorway as he crossed from his washroom to the closet. Colby's door was shut, no light showing from underneath, and Sharma lay curled up on the floor, apparently standing guard. Vic frowned. Why the dog wasn't in the room with Colby, he couldn't begin to guess.

But Colby had been acting secretive for days now. It didn't have quite the element of fear that had once accompanied Colby's hiding away, but it didn't seem exactly carefree, either. Vic sighed and continued to his closet to grab his sleep clothes. He hoped Colby would tell him someday.

Unless Vic made his own confession to Colby first, and it sent the boy running as far away as he could get.

Vic yanked on a t-shirt and went to his bed, turning back the covers. He sat up against the pillows and picked up his phone, checking to make sure he hadn't missed any calls, though of course there was the usual barrage of emails, showing him all the new files that had come in for him to process. Looked like he'd have a busy day tomorrow.

He started to set his phone aside when Sharma suddenly stood, wagging his tail and panting as Colby's bedroom door opened.

Colby paused there, gave Sharma a quick scratch behind the ears, then murmured an instruction for the dog to stay put before he actually set foot outside his room.

Vic's eyebrows went up. The boy was wearing only his hoodie, just like he had the last time he'd come to Vic, offering himself in exchange for Vic letting him stay.

Surely, Colby wouldn't still be worried about Vic making him leave, would he?

Somehow, assuming this was the same thing all over again, Vic was going to have to keep his hands to himself, despite all the things he so desperately wanted to do. Of course, he could just tell Colby how much he wanted him. The boy would definitely run away then.

Colby stopped in the doorway when he glanced up and realized Vic was watching him.

"Hi," Colby whispered, fidgeting with the pulls on his hood and looking up at Vic from under his eyelashes.

"Hi, sweetheart." Vic paused. "Everything alright?"

Colby nodded, then slowly crossed the room.

Vic blindly set his phone on the nightstand and waited, wondering what in the gods' names Colby was up to.

Colby stopped by the bed, fidgeting with the zipper on his hoodie, then left it on and climbed up, straddling Vic's lap and resting his little hands on Vic's chest.

The boy took a deep breath, and looked up.

"I need you to make me yours," Colby whispered.

Vic's heart started galloping away in his chest. Colby couldn't seriously mean what Vic thought he meant, could he?

"Colby…"

"I n-need to be yours," Colby said. He looked down shyly, then seemed to have to force his gaze up again. "I need you t-to be inside me."

Vic stared at him, his mouth going dry as his pulse

sped up even more. All day, Vic had been worrying about how to admit to Colby that he wanted him exactly that way, and here was Colby offering that very thing.

Fuck. He wanted to say yes. He was desperate to say yes. To finally experience something he'd only dreamt about since he was twelve years old? To finally share that kind of exquisite intimacy with someone? Especially someone he loved? Vic pressed his hands down on the bed, both to hide their shaking and to stop him from seizing the boy. He wanted to say yes, but he couldn't. Not when Colby wasn't truly ready.

"Sweetheart," he began, then swallowed hard. "You don't have to do this. I'm not sending you away—"

Colby looked up and pressed the fingertips of both hands over Vic's mouth.

"No," Colby insisted. "Listen."

Vic's eyebrows went up. He'd never seen that kind of fierce determination in the boy, and it stunned him into silence far better than the presence of Colby's hands ever could.

Colby watched him intently, seeming to wait to make sure Vic actually wasn't going to speak, then sighed heavily through his nose. "I need this, Vic." He paused, looking all around as though trying to physically find the words. "When Patches got out that day, and Bad Man found me while I was trying to get home, he kept trying to grab me. He couldn't—his hands went right through me—but he kept trying anyway, and the whole time, he kept called me *boy* and telling me I belonged to him."

Vic's heart clenched. "Sweetheart..." he murmured behind Colby's fingers.

"And it made me think," Colby went on, "of all those years in the basements, with Bad Man telling me the same thing, over and over. That I was his. His slut. His whore." He paused, frowning. "I don't even know what those mean, but they sounded bad. And the others all did the same thing. Calling me their toy. Saying...they owned my ass. That they owned me."

Good gods. Vic squeezed his eyes shut for a moment,

too easily able to picture all those things, his sweet boy subjected to such cruelty.

"But then," Colby continued, his voice sounding a little brighter, "I thought of what you said to Ryley. That day you were talking to him, when I wasn't supposed to hear."

Vic cringed. It was that very conversation that had driven Colby to offer himself the last time.

But Colby didn't look upset. If anything, he looked more determined than ever.

"You said," Colby whispered, "that you wanted me to be yours." He paused, frowning in thought. "That…you wanted to make me yours in every sense of the word." Colby met Vic's eyes again. "And if you were inside me, I would be yours. I'd belong to you instead of them."

Vic gently grabbed Colby's wrists and pulled the boy's hands down. "Sweetheart," he began, shaking his head and trying with all his might not to throw Colby down and consume him then and there, "that's not–"

"Vic," Colby interrupted. He took a deep breath, and reached for the zipper on his hoodie, slowly pulling it down.

"Sweetheart–" Vic tried to grab his hands to stop him, but Colby batted his hands away.

"I need you to see," Colby insisted, and unzipped the hoodie the rest of the way, shaking with nerves as he shrugged it off, leaving him naked as he sat there on Vic's lap. "They're all gone, Vic. I made all the scars go away."

Vic tried not to look. He tried so hard not to, but temptation won out, and Colby's insistent, pleading stare didn't help matters. Holding his breath, Vic looked down. He'd seen the boy naked before, of course, but this time felt different. This time felt bigger, more important.

He blinked, then gasped as his eyes went wide at the sight of all that unblemished skin. Colby hadn't been joking. All the scars were gone.

Without thinking, Vic reached out and traced his fingertips along Colby's ribs, where what Vic had assumed was a whip scar had once been. Now, there was nothing there. Not so much as a hint that the skin had ever been broken.

The same was true of all the other scars. The cuts and cigarette burns had all simply vanished. Colby's body was no longer painted with the marks of his torment.

"I feel so free, Vic," Colby whispered. "I mean, I know it doesn't change what happened, but it's like part of him is gone. Like he owns me a little bit less, like I've taken my body back." He paused, his voice more firm as he continued: "But it's not enough. I can still feel him inside me. All of them. It's like they're all still with me, reminding me they own me, that my body isn't mine. That it's theirs. And I don't want to keep feeling them, Vic. I don't want to belong to them anymore."

Fuck. Vic took a deep breath. "Sweetheart, that'll come in time–"

"No," Colby insisted. "I want to belong to you. I need it *now.* I want to be yours. And I know you can make it beautiful, somehow, like you did the last time. Even if you send me away after, I need this, Vic. *Please.*" Colby rested his hands on Vic's chest again and leaned closer, pressing their foreheads together and whispering over Vic's lips, "Please."

Vic's whole body trembled, all his muscles straining as he fought the desperate urge to give in. Colby was offering everything he wanted, but he had to resist. There was no way Colby could truly be ready for this.

He cast about for an excuse, and blurted out the first thing that came to mind: "I don't have any condoms."

Colby's eyes brightened. "But that's good," he said. "Even better, because Bad Man always used condoms, so it'll be even more different than before."

"Colby." Vic shook his head. "Unless you're committed to someone, that's not safe–"

"Not safe?" Colby asked, tilting his head.

"No. I mean…Alright, technically, you and I would be fine, but…in any other instance, that would be a risky attitude. There are so many diseases that can be passed sexually…"

"Diseases?"

"Illnesses," Vic said. "Things that make you sick."

Colby paled.

"No, Colby, no," Vic blurted out. "You're fine. Sweetheart, you're fine."

"But–"

"They tested you in the hospital the day we found you. Everything was negative. The bad men didn't give you anything."

Colby let out a shuddering breath, then looked carefully at Vic, his eyes slowly going wide. "Are you sick?"

"No." Vic shook his head. "No, I'm clean, too. That's why I meant that technically we'd be fine without condoms, but–"

"Then that's good!" Colby brightened again. "If I can't make you sick, and it'll be different from when Bad Man had me…"

"I'm still not sure it's a good idea," Vic murmured, shaking his head again and gripping the sheets in both fists like his life depended on it.

"Why?" Colby whispered.

Vic struggled to find an answer, then asked, "What if you regret it? What if you resent me for it once it's all over? I don't want you to be afraid of me. I don't want you thinking of me like you think of him. Of all of them. I'd hate it if that happened. I don't want to lose you."

Some of Colby's nerves seemed to fade away, his brow smoothing a bit and his shoulders dropping slightly. "Please, Vic," he whispered. "Please? I need it to be you."

"But why me?" Vic asked. "Why now? Why not wait a few more years and see what happens? Maybe you'll meet someone and fall in love–" Vic broke off, hating to even imagine it. Colby in love with someone else? Just thinking of it broke his heart.

Colby looked down, then sighed and leaned close again, resting their foreheads together. "I have this feeling," he whispered, tapping on his chest, "and I don't know what to call it, but it's happy. It's beauty and smiles and laughter, and I feel it every time I see you." He pulled back just enough to look Vic in the eyes. "You've given me so much. And I'm not saying that's why I'm doing this," he rushed to add. "I'm not...looking to pay, or anything. But it's true. You've given me so much. You found me. Got me out of the basement. You gave me shelter, and food, and taught me things, and made me so feel warm and safe. You showed me so many beautiful things, so many happy things. The gardens. Music..." He smiled softly. "You saved my life, Vic. I was almost dead—in so many ways—and you saved me. You brought me back to life. You made me *want* to live. For the first time ever, I don't want it all to just end. I don't need to die or escape. I'm free, and now I know what happiness feels like. What friendship feels like. What safety and warmth and comfort feel like. And that's all thanks to you."

Vic stared at the boy, feeling at a complete loss for words.

"You saved me," Colby whispered. "You saved me from the bad men. You're so *good*, Vic. How could I *not* want to belong to you?"

Vic let out another shuddering breath. *Good gods*. It felt like Colby was reading years' worth of thoughts in his mind, saying everything Vic had ever wanted to hear. He'd failed to save Cam's life right when Cam was on the verge of being able to live again, but somehow—be it fate or chance or even the gods themselves—he'd gotten a chance to redeem himself, finding Colby just in time and rescuing him from the brink of death in more ways than one. Sure, he'd rescued plenty of other kids over the years, but none with so dark a past as Colby had suffered. Now, the boy lived, and was well on his way to thriving.

"Please, Vic," Colby whispered, trailing his fingertips all over Vic's face. "I want this." He paused, then added, "I need *you*."

Vic gasped out a breath and pulled his sweet boy in for a kiss.

Chapter 28

VIC SHIVERED at the first touch of Colby's lips. He sucked in a breath and wrapped his arms deliberately around the boy, planting his hands firmly on Colby's back as he struggled not to race forward. This had to be done right. Now that he was finally going to experience it—and with Colby, no less—it couldn't be rushed.

It couldn't be anything as crass as fucking. It couldn't even be just sex. The moment demanded that it mean something. That it matter. The only way for this experience to be right for both of them was to have it be making love, in every sense of the word. To make it beautiful, as Colby said.

Vic couldn't afford to fail in this. For both their sakes. He was going to have to remain absolutely focused and not lose himself in the heat of the moment, keeping himself in tune with Colby's every sound and expression so that he wouldn't go too far before he could step back and salvage the situation.

The kiss went on endlessly, so soft and achingly sweet. Tilting his head slightly, Vic tried to deepen the kiss, running the tip of his tongue along Colby's lips. The boy whimpered and opened for him.

Vic focused on breathing as they kissed, trying to run a pep talk through his head, hoping it would get his body to accept the idea that this whole thing was probably going to come to a screeching halt at some point, long before the finish line. Just because Colby said he wanted this didn't mean the reality of it wasn't going to send him into a panic. Vic would have to be ready.

Just at the moment he had himself convinced that Colby wasn't going to go any further than kissing him, the boy shifted closer and reached up to run his fingers through Vic's hair.

Vic moaned before he could stop it. Moving slowly, he slid one hand down to Colby's hip. The boy shivered, but didn't break the kiss, even managing to move closer and hold Vic a bit tighter.

Then Colby hissed, breaking the kiss, and glanced over his shoulder.

"It's alright, sweetheart," Vic quickly murmured. "It's just us here."

Colby whimpered and checked over his other shoulder.

"Colby?" Vic waited until the boy met his eyes. "We don't have to do this."

Colby nodded. "I want to."

Vic took a deep, unsteady breath. "Alright." He brushed his thumbs back and forth on Colby's skin, fighting the urge to move his hands any more than that. "How do you want to do it?" he asked, knowing he had to get that out of the way while he still had any use of his brain.

Colby frowned and tilted his head.

"Like this?" Vic asked, nodding with his chin. "Right here? Or something else?"

"Oh." Colby's frown deepened, then he started to look all around before glancing nervously over his shoulder again. He curled in closer to Vic, and looked around once more. "Um...On my back, with y-you on top of me."

Vic studied his eyes for a moment. "Are you sure? You won't feel...trapped?"

Colby shook his head. "I'll be able to see you," he whispered. "And..." He glanced over his shoulder again.

Vic gave a slow nod. "And there'll be no one behind you," he realized aloud.

Colby nodded.

"Alright, sweetheart. Here." He rested a hand on Colby's shoulder and gently pushed. Colby got the idea and shifted off Vic's lap, then slowly lay back. The boy looked startled at first as Vic loomed over him, but once he was fully settled on the bed, he breathed a sigh of relief. No chance of anyone behind him, sneaking up on him or touching him.

Vic shivered as a horrid image of someone doing just that—and of Colby crying out as a man grabbed him from behind, assaulting him while Colby couldn't see—flooded his mind. Forcing the gods-awful thought aside, he took a deep breath and looked down at his sweet boy. Vic studied his face. Colby still looked nervous, but he was there, and he was safe.

And Colby wanted to be his.

Vic smiled and leaned down. Colby met him eagerly, their kiss picking right back up where it had left off.

Colby clung to him as they kissed. The boy was still tense, his legs pressed tightly together, his hands shaking a little as they toyed with Vic's hair. Easing himself down onto his side, Vic slowly pressed their bodies alongside one another, then took a chance and shifted one leg so it draped over Colby's, effectively pinning him down as well as guarding him from the idea of anyone else getting to him.

It was a bit of a test. He wanted to see how Colby would react, to know if the boy truly wanted to go through with this or not.

Colby's tension increased for a moment as Vic's leg slid into place, then relaxed as he let out a sigh. He even shifted closer, essentially urging Vic to be more on top of him.

Vic kept kissing the boy as he began to let one hand explore, stroking lightly over Colby's face, his arms, his chest. He moved the hand down to Colby's legs, then stroked inward. His thumb brushed alongside Colby's cock, leaving Vic worried but not surprised that it was still completely soft.

Pausing the kiss, Vic rested his hand on Colby's hip. There was no way in all seven hells he was going to go through with this without Colby getting just as much pleasure out of it as he would. He wouldn't use the boy. He couldn't. He refused to be just another one of the monsters.

"May I touch you?" Vic whispered, nudging at the base of Colby's cock with his thumb.

Colby nodded.

Vic shifted his hand over and just let it rest there for a moment, watching Colby's face. He curled his fingers around the soft length and lightly stroked. It took a few minutes, but between that and kissing the boy, Colby slowly grew hard in his hand.

Colby gasped when Vic twisted his hand around the head. "Vic…"

Vic smiled and did it again, watching the boy's eyes glaze over as he finally started to let go and enjoy the sensations. After a few minutes, Colby trailed a hand down Vic's body, slipped it under the waistband of Vic's pajamas, and wrapped his little fingers around Vic's cock as well, matching his strokes to what Vic was giving him.

It was almost too much. Vic was already so damned hard that he wasn't sure how he was going to be able to last.

Then again, maybe this would be enough for now. They could start with just touching one another, and move on to more intimate things later when Colby was more ready.

But Colby had been insistent. And Vic wanted this so badly, he thought he might burst.

He grabbed Colby's hand and gently pulled it away.

"Vic?"

Vic smiled at him and shook his head. "I'm too close."

"Oh." Colby took a deep breath, and nodded. "I'm ready," he whispered.

"Not yet," Vic said. Colby frowned, puzzled, so Vic said, "We're taking this slow. If you really want to do this, I'm going to prep you first."

Colby tilted his head. Maybe he'd never been properly stretched and prepped before. Vic cringed at the thought, though it would explain the scarring that had shown up in his scans when they first rescued the boy.

Yes, he was definitely going to do this right. Colby deserved it.

Vic stretched out, reaching for the nightstand drawer, and dug around for the small bottle of lubricant he was pretty sure he still had there. He found it, checked to make sure it was still good, then squeezed some out onto his fingers. He took a moment to warm it up, making sure Colby was watching.

"Ready, sweetheart?"

Colby shivered a bit, then nodded.

Vic leaned down and brushed their lips together. "The moment you tell me to stop, I'll stop."

Colby stared into his eyes. "Promise?" he whispered.

"I promise."

Colby took a deep breath, and nodded again.

"Alright," Vic murmured. He shifted his leg out of the way but kept himself pressed as close as possible. "I'll need you to spread your legs for me when you're ready."

Colby glanced down, blushed, looked back up at Vic, and nodded as he slowly opened his legs.

Vic rested his wrist along the inside of Colby's thigh and slowly moved his hand closer. "It's just me, sweetheart. I'm right here."

Colby nodded, watching Vic's hand move.

Vic paused when his fingers brushed Colby's balls, then reached behind them and lightly stroked, inching back until he felt puckered skin.

Colby hissed, his whole body going rigid.

Vic went still. "Colby?"

Colby let out the breath he was holding. "I'm alr–" He broke off with a yelp.

Vic hadn't even heard Sharma come into the room,

but suddenly the dog was on the bed, his cold snout nosing against bare skin as he tried to investigate and push Vic away.

"It's alright, boy," Vic said, trying to calm the dog.

"Sharma, *down*," Colby ordered.

The dog immediately jumped off the bed and sat there, wagging his tail and watching them.

Vic stared at Colby, shocked at the firmness of his voice. Then he laughed.

"What?" Colby asked.

Vic shook his head, still chuckling. "Nothing, sweetheart." He kissed Colby and sat up. "Let me put him out."

Colby nodded, and Vic scrambled off the bed, urging Sharma out of the room. The dog looked like he wanted to play now that he knew Vic wasn't hurting Colby, but this was hardly the time. Vic shut the door, sighed, and turned back toward the bed.

"How are you doing?" Vic asked as he lay down beside Colby again.

"I'm alright."

"You ready to try again?"

Colby nodded.

Vic pulled off his t-shirt, moving slowly so as not to startle the boy, then checked Colby's reaction before he settled back into place. Colby looked slightly more nervous, but he held on to Vic and spread his legs again, watching as Vic resumed exploring behind his balls. When he found Colby's hole, Vic let his fingertip just rest there.

"We'll take this slow," he promised again. When Colby nodded, Vic leaned down and kissed the boy, then lightly massaged Colby's hole. The boy's cock had gone soft, but Vic was determined to change that. Of course, if Colby couldn't handle even having a finger inside of him, this wasn't going to go anywhere. "I'm gonna press inside, alright? I'll start with one."

Colby tensed, but nodded.

"Alright. Take a deep breath for me."

Colby did so, and held it.

"That's it. Now breathe out slowly and try to relax."

Colby parted his lips and blew out the breath, and Vic pressed the tip of his finger past that tight ring of muscle. The boy stopped exhaling as he tensed.

"Easy, sweetheart," Vic murmured. "It's just me."

Colby swallowed hard, nodded, and relaxed slightly as he let out the rest of the breath.

Vic kept his finger there, in up to the first knuckle.

"Take another breath for me."

Colby looked at him, took in another breath, and slowly let it out, relaxing his body by degrees as Vic began to lightly thrust, stroking in and out until he managed to get one finger in all the way.

"How are you doing, sweetheart?"

Colby shivered. "I'm alright."

"We can stop if you want," Vic suggested, halting the motion of his finger.

Colby shook his head. "I need this. I need *you*."

"Alright." Vic went back to gently stroking, trying to get Colby used to the sensation. Granted, Colby was *used* to it, but Vic wanted the boy to get comfortable with the idea of him being the one to do it. Vic kissed the boy to help him relax, then murmured, "Look at me."

Colby opened his eyes, and watched as Vic slowly shifted down Colby's body, trailing kisses all along the way. He nuzzled Colby's balls, and the boy blushed.

"I'm right here," Vic breathed over Colby's sensitive parts right before he ran his tongue along Colby's soft length. The boy whimpered and started to grow hard again.

Vic maintained eye contact the whole time as he continued stroking the one finger inside while he worked on Colby's cock with his mouth, groaning when he felt the length harden against his tongue. He bobbed his head and sucked hard a few times, then slowly backed off and flicked his tongue all over. Mouthing at Colby's balls, Vic kept his eyes on Colby's face as he curled his finger and slowly explored.

Colby shouted and almost bucked off the bed.

Vic grinned and did it again.

"*Oh*," Colby cried. Panting, he stared down at Vic and stammered, "Vic– What– *Oh*."

Vic moved back up so he could kiss the boy, keeping his finger trained on Colby's prostate the whole time. "That's how it's supposed to feel."

Colby moaned and threw his head back. "Vic…"

Vic's heart raced, and he started panting in time with the boy, watching him writhe on the bed to the point that he actually started riding Vic's finger, seeking out more sensation. Vic snatched up the lube, squeezed out some more, and eased a second finger inside. Colby winced at first, but the moment Vic's fingers found their target again, the boy moaned.

"*Vic–*"

"That's it, sweetheart."

"Oh gods. Vic…"

"I'm right here."

Colby grabbed him, his little hands clinging with far more strength than Vic ever imagined the boy could have. Vic watched Colby completely fall apart beneath him in the most beautiful way, throwing his head back with a cry as he came just from Vic's fingers, not so much as a whisper of pressure on his cock.

"Vic…"

Colby went boneless, head lolling and eyelids drooping as he slowly came down. Vic eased his fingers out and gathered the boy into his arms.

"Vic…" Colby whispered.

"Right here," Vic murmured back.

"What did you do to me?"

Vic chuckled.

Colby slowly blinked his eyes open and looked up at him, the dazed look slowly fading from his face. "You were supposed to be inside me."

Vic hesitated. His cock was still rock-hard and quickly getting painful. But he wanted this for Colby more than himself, and he'd just achieved that. Maybe that was enough for one night.

Before Vic could say anything, Colby scowled at him. "Vic."

"Only if you're sure," Vic asked.

Colby gave a sharp nod.

Vic blew out a breath. "Alright." He moved slowly, pushing off his pants and underwear, making sure Colby could see everything he did, then shifted over on top of the boy and eased himself down between his legs. Squeezing out some more lube, Vic stroked his cock and bit back a groan. He had no idea how he was going to last, but he had to. Suddenly, that one orgasm for Colby didn't seem to be enough. If Vic was going to be inside the boy, he was going to have to make Colby enjoy the experience.

Nudging Colby's legs farther apart, Vic lined up his cock.

Colby hissed.

"Look at me," Vic told the boy. Colby glanced up. "Just me, sweetheart."

Colby flicked his gaze down at where their bodies touched, then looked back up at Vic's face. He nodded.

"Deep breath," Vic reminded him.

Colby sucked in a breath, held it, then tightened his hands on Vic's arms as he slowly let it out, bracing himself for the intrusion.

But Vic couldn't move. He sat there, staring at the tiny point of contact between his cock and Colby's hole, and he couldn't move.

"Vic?"

Vic glanced up at Colby's face, then blew out a breath and shook his head. "Sorry, sweetheart."

"What's wrong?"

"I–" He exhaled heavily. This whole thing felt so much bigger than he'd imagined it might, his heart slamming away in his chest. "I've just never done this before."

Colby frowned, tilting his head. "You haven't?"

Vic shook his head. "I never could." He paused, then said, "Because of Cam."

Colby's frown slowly faded, and all the nervousness on his face disappeared along with it as his entire being seemed to brighten with a soft smile. The boy sat up, curled a hand into Vic's hair, and kissed him.

"Make me yours, Vic," Colby whispered.

Vic swallowed hard, gave a shaky nod, and kissed the boy back, easing him back down on the bed as he did so. Then he pressed forward until the head of his cock popped inside Colby's body.

Vic went still. *Fuck.* That tiny bit of sensation, and he already wanted to explode. Finally, he had a taste of how it felt to be inside someone. His whole body was screaming at him to just slam forward and wildly thrust away, chasing down that exquisite pleasure, but he couldn't. Taking a steadying breath, he watched and waited.

Slowly but surely, Colby relaxed around him. "I'm alright," he whispered.

Keeping his eyes on Colby's face so he could read the boy's expressions, Vic eased in another inch. He pulled back, and slowly pushed in again. Vic forced himself to stick to slow, shallow thrusts, back and forth, over and over, fighting with everything he had to keep from coming right then and there as he moved deeper and deeper.

Finally, he pushed in once more, and found himself all the way inside.

Vic gasped out a breath that was just short of a sob, and gathered Colby in his arms, nuzzling the boy's jaw. "*Mine.*"

When he pulled back just enough to see Colby's face, he found him smiling.

Holding his boy close, Vic slowly eased back until only the tip of his cock was inside Colby's body, then tilted his hips and thrust back in. He tried it again, changing the angle.

Colby gasped.

Vic went still for a moment, then repeated the motion. The boy gasped again, so Vic kept at it, pegging the boy's prostate with every stroke.

"Vic…"

Vic smiled. "I've got you, sweetheart."

Colby choked out a cry. "Oh my gods. *Vic…*"

Bracing himself on his left arm, Vic captured Colby's mouth in a kiss while he snaked his right hand between their bodies, wrapping his fingers around Colby's cock and stroking in time with his thrusts. If Colby wanted Vic inside him, Vic wasn't going to stop there. He was going to make Colby come while his cock was inside the boy, no matter what it took.

Colby gasped. "Vic…"

"I'm right here," Vic murmured.

"Vic…"

"You're safe. You're right here with me."

"Vic– *Oh*."

"Let go, sweetheart. I've got you."

Colby stared at him, panting and chanting Vic's name. He sucked in a breath, his whole body tensing up, then cried out, squeezing his eyes shut as his cock began to pulse in Vic's hand.

"*Vic!*" Colby screamed.

Fuck. Vic went still, holding the boy through his orgasm. That beautiful scream was almost enough to make him come on the spot. Fighting to hold off, Vic tried to steady himself and focus on the precious boy in his arms.

Colby's head dropped to one side, nuzzling Vic's arm as his eyes slipped closed.

"Vic," he whispered.

Vic's relief was so hard and sudden that it made his eyes sting with the threat of happy tears. He tilted Colby's head back up and brushed their lips together.

Colby sighed, kissing back slowly and lazily, making little hums of pleasure deep in his throat.

Vic beamed. He couldn't imagine anything more perfect.

While Colby lay there still looking slightly dazed, Vic started to pull out. They'd gotten so much further than he'd ever imagined they might, and even though his body was begging for its own release, he figured the boy could use a rest. He could worry about his own pleasure some other time. Just getting to experience being inside Colby was enough for now.

Before the head of his cock could slip out, though, Colby gasped and tensed up, his eyes going wide and his legs locking around Vic's waist.

"Wait," Colby panted.

Vic went still, watching him.

Colby blinked, still seeming to come out of his daze, then glanced down at where their bodies met before looking intently at Vic's face. "You're still hard."

Vic tried to shrug it off. "It's alri–"

"*No*," Colby insisted, squeezing his legs so that he effectively pulled Vic back in. "Vic, you have to come inside me."

"Colby." Vic grimaced. "I don't want to hurt you."

"You *have* to."

Vic shook his head. "I wanted this for you–"

"And this is what I need," Colby demanded. He held Vic's gaze. "Please, Vic. I need you to come inside me."

Vic groaned as his cock slid home again. "Fuck." He took a deep breath. "Are you sure?"

Colby nodded emphatically, holding on to Vic even tighter.

"Colby–"

"Please, Vic. Come inside me. Make me yours."

Vic's hips pulled back and slammed forward as temptation began to win over his better judgment. He went still, checking Colby's face for any sign of uncertainty, then thrust again. Gasping out a breath, Vic gave in, pounding into the boy and clutching that little body in his arms as he raced toward orgasm.

"Colby–"

Colby held on, even going so far as to tighten his muscles around Vic's cock, sending him over the edge.

"Oh gods…"

Vic stared into Colby's eyes, panting, heart racing, as his cock pulsed, shooting deep inside his beautiful boy's body. Through the haze of pleasure, Vic braced himself for the panic.

But it never came. Amazingly, as Vic stilled after the last pulse of his cock, Colby smiled.

Vic stared at the boy as he slowly caught his breath. He'd never seen Colby look quite so serene.

The sight made him smile back. "Now you're mine," he said, the words coming out as more growl than murmur as he leaned down to kiss the boy. "All mine."

Colby gave him a smile, though it trembled as tears started to form in his eyes.

"Sweetheart..." Vic carefully pulled out, gathered the boy in his arms, and dragged the comforter over them, wrapping Colby up as tight as he could manage.

"I'm alright," Colby choked out, snuggling in closer. "Just...overwhelmed."

"I've got you," Vic murmured, pressing a kiss to Colby's forehead.

Vic felt a few tears drip onto his chest and run over his shoulder.

"My sweet boy," he whispered.

Colby breathed a laugh.

"Although," Vic went on, chuckling to himself, "I really should stop calling you that."

Colby tipped his head back to look up at him.

"You're a man," Vic explained. "I have trouble remembering that sometimes."

"Vic." Colby trailed his fingertips down Vic's face. "I told you before. I like being your sweet boy."

Vic smiled. "Yeah?"

Colby nodded.

Vic chuckled and kissed his forehead again. "Good. Because I like you being my sweet boy, too."

Colby smiled and snuggled in closer.

They lay like that for a long while, warm and silent. Vic was determined to hold on to the moment as long as he could, just waiting for Colby to decide that he'd had enough of touching, of being naked, of being exposed. He wasn't going to let go until Colby decided.

Finally, Colby wriggled in his grasp. "Vic?"

Vic loosened his hold. "Sorry, sweetheart." He carefully brushed Colby's hair out of his eyes. "You wanna go take a shower and go to bed?"

Colby nodded slowly, then whispered, "Can I stay with you?"

"Yeah, of course, if you want."

Colby nodded again.

Vic pushed the comforter away and slid off the bed, Colby sticking close to his side as they headed for the washroom. He started the shower, and nudged the boy in under the hot water, holding him close as they took a few moments to just absorb the heat.

They washed themselves and each other, then stood under the spray again, neither one of them seemingly ready to leave that warm cocoon.

"Vic?"

"Yeah, sweetheart?"

Colby tensed in his arms. "What if I can't ever do that again?"

"Hey," Vic murmured, hooking a finger under Colby's chin and gently tilting his head back. "Don't you even worry about that."

"But–"

"Nothing like that ever has to happen again if you don't want it to."

Colby frowned. "But you want it."

"I do," Vic admitted, "but that doesn't matter if you don't want it, too."

"Oh." Colby's frown deepened. "You won't be mad?"

"Of course not, sweetheart. I won't be mad. Or disappointed. *Nothing* is as important as you feeling safe."

Colby started to smile, then put his arms around Vic's waist and hugged him close. "I feel safe with you."

Vic grinned. "I'm glad. Thank you."

Colby shook his head and pulled back, looking up at Vic's face. "No. Thank *you*. For everything. For saving me." He paused, glancing in the direction of the bedroom, and blushed. "For making it beautiful."

Vic bent down and kissed him. "You made it beautiful for me, too."

Colby smiled shyly and hid his face as he hugged Vic again.

Vic held the boy until he felt his cock twitch with interest, and knew he had to pull back before Colby felt it. They'd had enough for one night. If there was any chance of any sort of intimacy ever happening again, Vic would have to take it slowly and be patient.

"You stay here for a moment," he said, kissing the top of Colby's head. "I'll dry off and go get you some clothes for bed."

Colby nodded, then hugged himself when Vic drew away.

Vic quickly dried off, retrieved his discarded clothes from the bedroom, and hurried down the hall, gathering up all of Colby's layers, just in case the boy needed them, and took them back to the washroom, setting it all on the counter. He tidied the bed, turned down the sheets, and settled in to wait.

Colby came out just a few minutes later, wearing only a t-shirt and flannel pants.

"Hey, sweetheart." Vic eyed him carefully. "How are you feeling?"

Colby hid a yawn behind his hand. "Tired."

Vic smiled. "Come lie down."

Colby climbed up on the bed and snuggled down at Vic's side with his head on Vic's shoulder. Vic held him close, smiling to himself. He'd fully expected the boy to go hide out in the dark, but instead he was there.

Vic reached for the lamp on the nightstand, but before he could switch it off, his phone lit up with an incoming call.

Colby lifted his head. "Vic? What's wrong?"

Vic grabbed his phone. "It's Hunter."

Colby gasped. "Is he alright?"

"I don't know," Vic said, and answered the call. "Hunter?"

A sob and a sniff greeted him. "*Vic?*"

Vic sat up. "Yeah, kiddo. I'm here."

Hunter sniffed again. "*I...Um...I need help.*"

Vic looked at Colby. The boy's eyes were wide, and he nodded insistently. Putting the phone on speaker, Vic set it down and grabbed a tablet off the nightstand, pulling up the site for the local airport. "Where are you?"

"*The next town north of where you found me,*" Hunter said, his voice unsteady. "*I think. I don't know. I don't know what it's called. I–*"

"Hunter, shhh. It's alright. Take a breath for me, champ."

A shaky breath came over the line.

"Good," Vic murmured. "Now, look around you. Tell me what you see."

"*Um…*" Hunter paused. "*There's…a bakery. On the corner of Magnolia and Bennett.*"

"Magnolia and Bennett," Vic muttered to himself, typing that into a mapping app on his tablet. The image zoomed in on a bakery storefront. "Got it." He tapped an icon that found the nearest airport, and linked that address over to the site where he could buy a ticket, then covered the mouthpiece on his phone and looked at Colby. "There's a flight out tomorrow."

Colby nodded rapidly. "Go."

"Are you sure?"

"You have to save him, Vic."

Vic smiled as he sighed, then quickly kissed the boy and uncovered the phone. "Hunter?" He bought the plane ticket, then switched back to the map to do a quick search.

"*Yeah?*" Hunter sniffed again.

"There's a shelter four blocks from where you are. I want you to go there, tell them I sent you. They'll give you a bed and food for the night, and I'll find you there tomorrow. Can you do that for me, champ?"

"*I– I don't–*"

"You've got this, kiddo. Just head north on Bennett. I'll stay on the phone with you until you get there."

Hunter gasped out a cry, then sniffed again before he said, "*Alright.*"

Vic waited, and Colby grabbed his hand, giving it a reassuring squeeze.

"My sweet boy," he mouthed.

Colby smiled.

Vic smiled back, and held on to Colby's hand as they listened to Hunter's rapid breathing.

"Where are you, kiddo?" Vic asked.

"*Um...Bennett and Rosemary.*"

Vic checked the map. "Good. One more block, then turn right."

He directed the boy all the way to the shelter, then listened as Hunter spoke to the shelter's director and got settled in for the night.

"Hunter? I'll be there tomorrow, alright? You've just gotta sit tight and I'll be there, I promise."

Hunter let out a shaky breath. "*Thanks, Vic.*"

"Get some sleep, kiddo. It'll be better in the morning."

They said their goodbyes and rang off. Vic set his phone aside, then kissed Colby on the top of his head and got up to pack.

Colby followed him to the closet. "Can I help?"

Vic stopped, turned to look at him, and smiled. "If you want, thank you." He picked out a suit to wear the next day, then another for packing in case he needed to stay down south overnight.

"Vic?"

"Yeah, sweetheart?"

"Where is Hunter gonna go?"

Vic paused in going through his ties, and blew out a breath. "I have no idea. I might have to do some research on the plane."

"Oh."

Vic went back to packing.

"Vic?"

Vic chuckled. "Yeah, sweetheart?"

"What if you bring him here?"

Vic stopped again. "Here?"

Colby nodded, then took a step forward. "He could have my room. I can sleep in the basement and–"

"Whoa, slow down," Vic said, holding up a hand. Colby snapped his mouth shut. "Why would you sleep in the basement?"

Colby fidgeted, tucking his hands up under his chin. "Because I'm braver now, but Hunter is new and scared, so he should be up here where he's close to you, and–"

"That's very thoughtful of you, sweetheart, but...you are *not* sleeping in the basement."

Colby's expression fell. "Oh." He swallowed hard and gave a slow nod. "So you *are* gonna send me away," he whispered.

"What? No!" Vic threw down the pair of socks he was holding and stepped around to pull the boy into his arms. "No. You're not going anywhere."

"But...Vic...Hunter can't sleep in the basement! He'll be scared, and–"

"Neither one of you is sleeping in the basement," Vic told him, "not even if it *were* finished, which it isn't yet."

Colby frowned. "I don't understand."

Vic looked around, smiling to himself as an idea took shape. "Tell you what: How about, tomorrow morning, before I go, you help me rearrange all this," he said, gesturing at the walk-in closet, "to make some room, and we move your things in here?" Vic turned away, zipped up his bag, and took Colby's hand, pulling him back out to the bedroom. "That way," he went on, "Hunter can have your room...and this can be our room."

Colby's whole face lit up. "Really?"

Vic nodded, then looked over the room and pointed when another idea came to him. "And that odd corner over there? I was never really sure what to do with it, but...I'll build you a little nest there. We'll call it a reading nook, I suppose, but if you ever need to sleep alone—if there's ever a time when you can't even stand to let me hold your hand or kiss you—you can hide away there and I won't disturb you. And I'll get some blackout shades for the windows. How does that sound?"

Colby's lower lip trembled. "Does that mean I can stay?" he whispered.

"Of course, sweetheart. For as long as you want."

Colby glanced away for a moment, then looked up at Vic from under his eyelashes. "Forever?"

ILLUMINED SHADOWS

Vic smiled, and had to swallow down emotion before he could answer, "Forever."

As the boy surged up to kiss him, Vic saw Colby's eyes bright with happiness, and when they curled up together under the blankets, his boy safe in his arms, Vic felt all the weight of his past failures melt away.

Epilogue

Twelve months later…

VIC LUGGED his cello out to the car, then headed back inside, adjusting his tie as he went. Treble had been playing at Sapphire Lounge—owned by Asher's uncle, Gregor Arden—every other weekend for the past several months, slowly but surely regaining their old following. And then some. The administration at Denmer University found out Treble had made a comeback, and invited them to play at the Founder's Day celebration, an event that the whole city seemed to get involved in every year, held in honor of the man who'd made the university—and, thus, the entire, beautiful city—possible.

With so many other music acts out there, being invited to play was a huge honor. Treble couldn't pass it up. And when Vic had told Colby about the gig, the boy had insisted on coming to watch. He hadn't yet seen Treble play in public—he didn't often leave the house, and certainly never alone—but he wanted to support Vic as well as continue his work in facing strangers, so he was determined to go.

Especially since Hunter had just moved out on his own, so Colby no longer had his new friend to keep him occupied. Of course, Cam was always there, and they were expecting their first two foster kids tomorrow now that the basement was finished. The whole therapy-office plan was still a work-in-progress, but Colby was helping Vic set up the halfway house part of it in the meantime, rescuing abandoned kids and giving them a place to sleep while they worked toward living life on their own terms.

"Colby?" Vic called, heading down the hallway. "You ready, sweetheart?"

"*Um…*"

He found Colby by the closet, staring down at himself.

"What's wrong?" Vic asked. "Would you rather stay home?"

Colby slowly shook his head and pointed. Vic glanced down and saw that Colby's jeans stopped about an inch above his ankles.

"Did I do something wrong with the laundry?" Colby asked, tugging at the sleeves of his shirt. Even those were shorter than Vic remembered.

"Huh." Vic strode forward. "Come here."

Colby stepped closer, and Vic moved them right up against one another.

"Stand up straight for me."

Colby did, and Vic rested a hand on top of his head.

Vic chuckled. "Nope. You've actually grown."

Colby took a step back, looked down at himself, then back up at Vic. "I did?"

Vic nodded. "At least an inch, I'd guess. We'll have to get you some new clothes."

Colby's eyes went wide. "But–"

"No, hey. That's a good thing."

"It is?"

Vic nodded again. "It means you're healthy."

Colby smiled, then got a confused look on his face. "Am I gonna keep growing?"

"Hmmm, probably not much. You're twenty-three now, and men usually stop growing around then."

"Oh." Colby nodded. "Good."

"Good?"

Colby looked up at him from under his eyelashes. "I didn't wanna get too big. I like being your little guy."

Vic grinned, bent down to kiss him, then steered him into the closet. "Let's find something that still fits."

They went through Colby's clothes until they found pants and a shirt that were long enough. His shoes were also a bit snug, but they'd have to make do until they could go shopping. For now, he managed to get Colby dressed so they could head out to the university and set up in time for Treble's show.

"You sure you're up for this?" Vic asked as they climbed into the car.

Colby nodded. He looked slightly anxious, but he really had made tremendous headway over the past several months. He still had days when the memories threw him into a panic, and probably would for some time, but he was fighting back every step of the way, determined to live a normal life.

"If you need to leave, you just tell me," Vic insisted, reaching for his hand.

Colby squeezed back and nodded.

They got to the university, found a place to park, and headed across campus hand-in-hand. Vic carried his cello, and kept Colby close to his other side. The little guy glanced around nervously at the crowds, but he kept going, determination showing through his anxiety.

Vic found the stage where they'd be playing, and went around to the back of it, where they found Zac, Ryley, Adrian, and Asher. The latter two surrounded Colby and escorted him out to a place on the lawn while Treble ran through some warm-ups, Vic glancing up every few minutes for any sign that his sweet boy might need him.

The announcer called their name, and Treble took the stage to a roaring applause. Vic settled himself in a chair with his cello between his legs while Zac and Ryley worked the crowd, waving at people and leaning down to shake hands before tucking their violins into place and setting their bows at the ready.

As the first notes of a reworked Will Knightley classic filled the air, Vic glanced into the audience. On a blanket, right in front of the stage, Colby sat securely bracketed by the larger figures of Adrian and Asher. All of Treble's lost boys, right there in the light.

No more shadows. No more nightmares.

Vic watched Colby smile as Treble played.

For more information on the world in which the *Treble and the Lost Boys* series is set, check out grlyonsauthor.com

And see what becomes of Vic's rescue, Hunter, in a new m/m/m taboo trilogy, beginning with *Kacey*:

Hunter Fitz keeps running from his past, but the dark claws of memory follow him everywhere he goes. Taking another new job in another new city, Hunter hopes that maybe, just once, he can finally settle down.

Then he meets Kacey Reynolds, a free-spirited student who is as beautiful as he is exasperating, to say nothing of the unbearable arousal Hunter feels whenever the boy is around.

Hunter knows he can't give in to temptation. He's managed to stay celibate for two decades, and breaking that streak would make him just as bad as *them*.

But Kacey might prove more than he can resist.

And don't miss Cam's own story, *Surviving Death: A Treble and the Lost Boys Novella*

GLOSSARY

Agoran – an Isle, originally the southwestern region of the land before the **Breaking of the World**; an anarchist society (free market, property rights, no government)

Agori – a person who lives on or originates from **Agoran**

'Ax and fawn' – expression used often by **Falsiners**, referring to the god **Father Zhagos**, who is depicted carrying an ax and sheltering a small animal

Breaking of the World – an event that took place on the 5th of **Sulinel** in the year 2952; **Father Zhagos** struck the land three times with his mighty hammer and broke it into separate Isles, thus beginning the **shift cycle**

Ceynes – an Isle, the largest, originally the central region of the land before the **Breaking of the World**; under imperial rule

Ceynesian – a person who lives on or originates from **Ceynes**; of or pertaining to the Isle of **Ceynes**

Erostil – an Isle, originally to the south of the land, between **Jadu'n** and **Agoran**, before the **Breaking of the World**; an exotic, tropical paradise; a constitutional democracy

Falsin – an Isle, originally the northernmost reaches of the land before the **Breaking of the World**; a place of constant snow and ice and little sunshine; organized into clans and under the rule of a king

Falsiner – a person who lives on or originates from **Falsin**

Father Zhagos – one of the lesser gods

holoscanner – scanning device, usually found in **Agorani** hospitals or labs, used to scan a body and render a hologram that displays healthy and unhealthy tissues, organs, bones, etc. in blue and red, respectively

Jadu'n – an Isle, originally near the southern coast of the land before the **Breaking of the World**; also known as the Hole in the Ocean, as it is a valley almost entirely below sea level; home of the **magi**

kuryavsu – **Falsiner** word for 'wolf pup'

mage – man born with magical powers (plural: magi); one who studies magical craft on **Jadu'n**

Master – common title for a certified **mage**

sevgani – **Falsiner** term for 'lifemate'

shifting / shift cycle – a process similar to our plate tectonics; after the **Breaking of the World**, the land was no longer anchored as one mass, and instead became separate Isles that shift across the globe, sometimes grazing coastlines or directly colliding

Soldis – second month of the year; originally (and still, by tradition) part of the winter season before the **Breaking of the World**

Sulinel – third month of the year; originally (and still, by tradition) part of the spring season before the **Breaking of the World**

Tanasian – a person who lives on or originates from the Isle of Tanas; Tanasians are known for having insecure minds which allows them to engage in telepathy, telekinesis, and bioengineering/regeneration on a cellular level

ABOUT THE AUTHOR

G.R. Lyons stumbled into writing as a form of trauma recovery when traditional therapy wasn't working.

Then the story ideas just kept on coming.

Pulling from a vivid imagination as well as real-life experience as a trans man, a sexual assault survivor, and a person living with mental illness, Lyons has written multiple, interconnected series set within his fictional world of the Shifting Isles.

When not writing, Lyons can be found belly dancing around the house, studying anarcho-capitalist philosophy, buried in his never-ending TBR pile, or working out at the local CrossFit gym.

Connect with the author online and discover other forthcoming works!

Website: https://grlyonsauthor.com
Goodreads: https://www.goodreads.com/grlyonsauthor
Bookbub: https://www.bookbub.com/authors/g-r-lyons
Pinterest: https://www.pinterest.com/doumteksonata
Amazon.com: https://www.amazon.com/author/grlyons

Printed in Great Britain
by Amazon